Hassan Daoud, born in Beirut in 1950, h[...] Arabic literature and has taught creative writi[...] ican University. He is the editorial director o[...] and is on the editorial board of the quarterly magazine *Kalamon*. He is the author of three short story collections and ten novels.

No Road to Paradise was awarded the Naguib Mahfouz Medal for Literature in 2015.

Marilyn Booth has translated works by Hoda Barakat, Latifa al-Zayyat, Nawal El Saadawi, and many other Arab writers, and is the translator of Hassan Daoud's *The Penguin's Song*. She is Khalid bin Abdullah Al Saud Professor in the Study of the Contemporary Arab World in the Faculty of Oriental Studies at Oxford University.

No Road to Paradise

Hassan Daoud

Translated by
Marilyn Booth

hoopoe
AN IMPRINT OF AUC PRESS

First published in 2017 by
Hoopoe
113 Sharia Kasr el Aini, Cairo, Egypt
420 Fifth Avenue, New York, 10018
www.hoopoefiction.com

Hoopoe is an imprint of the American University in Cairo Press
www.aucpress.com

Exclusive distribution outside Egypt and North America by I.B.Tauris & Co Ltd., 6 Salem Road, London, W4 2BU

Dar el Kutub No. 14202/16
ISBN 978 977 416 817 8

Dar el Kutub Cataloging-in-Publication Data

Daoud, Hassan
         No Road to Paradise / Hassan Daoud.—Cairo: The American University in Cairo Press, 2017.
     p.   cm.
     ISBN 978 977 416 817 8
     1.   Arabic Fiction—Translation into English
     2.   Arabic Fiction
     I. Title
     892.73

1 2 3 4 5   21 20 19 18 17

Designed by Adam el-Sehemy
Printed in the United States of America

Chapter One

ON THE DAY MY DOCTOR told me I was ill, my first and strongest reaction was that once again I must not let on how frightened I was. When he appeared in the doorway to my room I knew instantly what he was here to tell me. Still in his operating-room attire, he stood there frowning and silent for a moment before instructing my nephew—who had stayed close by for the whole of my hospital visit—to leave us alone. As soon as my nephew went out of the room the doctor came in, closed his fist around the doorknob, and pulled the door firmly shut. Whatever words he was about to say, I knew I was going to be informed that yes, I did have the illness that had long filled me with such dread. He didn't call it by name. Not then. He told me, as I sat utterly still in the chair next to the bed, that the biopsy had revealed something in the tissue they'd removed from my body. I was instantly in terror. I began to sweat and felt a wave of fever mounting to my head, leaving me dizzy. I had kept my eyes lowered and I was still staring at the floor tiles when he added that what I had was not life-threatening. But that didn't lessen the panic I felt. I didn't look up from the floor. I didn't look him in the eye and ask him to tell me something more, something—anything—that might reassure me. All I wanted at that moment was for him to be gone. If he left me alone perhaps I could at least rid myself of the terrible anxiety I felt about revealing my fear in his presence. If he left me alone I could creep into the bathroom and wipe away my sweat on the massive bath towel hanging there. Then I could go out onto the narrow little balcony off my room to let the breeze swab my face, though I knew there would be little air in that cramped space and what there was would be unpleasantly acrid.

Before he had come in I was already working on myself, hardening myself to hear his words. It wasn't so much about preparing to hear him say that this illness of mine had indeed arrived but more about how to conceal, perhaps even suppress, my fear of having this disease. Months before this day—or if the truth be told, years before—I had sensed it coming. This disease precisely, and no other. I never experienced this kind of dreadful premonition about my heart, for instance, although I knew that heart disease was the second most-feared malady among people I knew. It was as though I had chosen it myself. Cancer. The first of the two. The lion rather than the tiger. Whenever anyone said that word in my presence, I broke out in a terrible sweat and began to shiver. Maybe, I thought, I had planted the seed myself. I had sown it somewhere inside of me. And then I had tended it as it grew month after month, maturing silently, and then choosing its moment to appear full-grown in my body.

He did not call it by name, this physician who didn't stay with me long in that room. Reaching again for the doorknob he said that I should get ready to leave now. I should come to see him in his clinic tomorrow, or the day after. A day or two for me to rest and relax, as he saw it. He wanted to reassure me; that was obvious. He wanted to leave me with the impression that this disease was not moving so fast that a day or two would make my condition any worse.

My brother's son Bilal, who was not slow to show up at the door to my room after the doctor left, seemed to know already what it was I had. A single swift glance that managed to combine scrutiny with alarm told me he knew. Then he dropped his eyes, seeking a refuge elsewhere by fixing his gaze on every object he could find. I forgot my need to go to the balcony although I was still holding the towel, fully open as though I were trying to dry it out now that it had absorbed my sweat and was still giving off the damp heat of it. Taking heart from Bilal's presence, feeling fortified by our relationship—a paternal uncle speaking to his beloved nephew—I said we would have to come back to visit the doctor in a day or so. But even as I tried to draw encouragement from our bond my voice betrayed me. It came out thin and weak like the voice of a little boy. Even in front of him—this lad of no more than thirteen, and my own nephew—I found myself trying desperately to conceal my fear. At the back of my mind already was the realization that when I got home I would have to face up to the same thing all over again with my wife. She would already know anyway, since there was no doubt that she would have found someone who would phone the doctor to ask. My children too, the two boys first of all. They might be deaf, but it wouldn't be long before they knew what I had. Then there were the people who, once they heard I was ill, would come to visit me, but only really to see how sick I was and how I conducted myself as an invalid. And then my father, who for once would extract himself from his usual stupor, his eyes no longer drowsy and absent. His stare would be strong enough to stop the movement of my hand bringing the next spoonful of food to his mouth.

Returning the towel to the bathroom, I asked Bilal to fetch my turban from the wardrobe. In the mirror my face looked different, as though the heavy sweat streaming down it had whittled new wrinkles and left the skin raw and reddened. When Bilal returned with my turban, carrying it bottom up with both hands, he reminded me that I couldn't leave the room before I had their permission. Anyway I needed some time before going out into the long corridor where all the doors to the rooms, on either side, were wide open. I needed time because those people out there would not simply watch

3

as I made my way down the corridor. They would greet me and I would have to respond. As-salaamu alaykum, greetings to our Shaykh. And as each of them turned to me and spoke I would have to respond, in a voice loud enough to be heard. Alaykum as-salaam, I would say, over and over. In a film I saw once, a doctor studied his own blackened lungs on the X-ray image and said to a colleague standing nearby, Here it is, my cancer. I don't have much time left. He said it just like that, in such an ordinary way, as though the image he had put up against the lit screen was just another one of the many pictures he had to examine in the course of a routine workday. As if it didn't make a difference—he was capable of examining his own lungs exactly as he would observe those of his patients. At the time when I watched that film, I believed that the older people get the more able they become to control their own reactions and the expressions on their faces, whatever it is they are thinking about at the time.

Although I have been putting on the abaya and turban of my shaykhly profession since I was a very young man, I still find myself reacting as though I always had to put them on in spite of myself. It wasn't that I didn't know how to manage walking properly in this garb; or how, wearing it, I ought to address people on the way home; or how, as a man of the cloth, I must conduct congregational prayers or give a sermon as I stood before the worshipers in one or another Hussainiya. I could handle all of that perfectly well. Lingering in their seats after the prayer service, the congregation would be moved enough by what they had heard from me to raise prayer after prayer for Muhammad and his sacred family. But what I felt inside, every time I reached for my turban before leaving the house, was that I was having to urge myself on, as if I was saying to myself, each time, Come on, you! Let's go to work now. In the photograph that hangs in the room where I receive guests and where I normally sit, the two of them—my father and my grandfather, Sayyid Murtada—look like they couldn't be happier together wearing the robes of the Shi'i ulema. My father is showing how completely comfortable he is, since he has neglected even to have his cloak pressed. The stitching shows clearly even in the photograph: the thread is heavy enough to be visible, wandering unevenly across the fabric as if he had sewed up the abaya with his own hands, using a pack needle rather than the thinner version a tailor would use. It's like what men wear into battle, I used to say to my brother Adnan, comparing my father's outfit to a soldier's uniform. Only when I had been out there in Najaf did I realize that my father's inattention to what he wore was a matter of principle. It stood for a particular kind of religious practice, or an outlook, that he had adopted along with some of his classmates there.

I want to study at the university and they've offered me a place. That's what I said to him. Once. And then I had to say it again. Whenever my father did not want to hear something, he simply acted as though he hadn't heard it. He would go on stroking his beard—if that is what he had been doing when the unwelcome words were said—or if he had been pacing as he pondered some issue or other, he went on pacing, without breaking the rhythm of his gait. He only had one thing to say to me about this, and he only said it once. I was the one who must go to Najaf for training as an imam, he told me, and not my brother, who loathed study of any kind. It looked to me like I was being offered up as a sacrifice. Even worse, like other sacrificial victims, I had no right to object or even to ask any questions. Tell him to talk to his brother, I demanded of my mother. Mama, tell him to talk to Sayyid Aqil about sending one of *his* sons. My mother was the only person my father ever listened to, even if he wasn't going to act on what she said. The sons of your Uncle Aqil will be just like their father, she would answer me, forcing me to reflect on how he—my Uncle Sayyid Aqil, that is—always planted himself among the women when he was at our house. He teased them and told jokes to make them laugh, oblivious to his enormous body and the fact that it was draped in the robes of a religious scholar.

When I started wearing the cloak and turban of the religious, I felt like I was living in someone else's clothes. The sensation was so strong that when I returned to my village for the summer breaks, I even felt surprised myself at who I seemed to be. I felt a stranger in my own skin every time someone stared at me on the street. That first quick glance, before he alters his course to come to me and say, As-salaamu alaykum. I can tell he is thinking I am too young to be dressed as an imam. After greeting me and going on his way he turns back to stare at me, perhaps dropping back to walk behind me as he tries to ascertain whether what he finds so disconcerting about me is really there. Surely he is studying the way I walk. I had never been confident that it was the appropriate gait for a man who stands before other men to lead them in worship. I pick my feet up when I walk, and swing my arms to match my stride. Anyone seeing my light, bouncy walk through the village must have thought I was feeling particularly happy about something.

Even my practice sessions in front of the mirror at home couldn't alter the way I walked, nor did the single comment my father once made about it. I walked, he remarked, as though I had dance steps in my head and they might move down to my feet at any moment. Sometimes I did think at least that surely something would happen to completely change the way my feet and body moved. The bones in my feet might start aching, and the pain would slow me down; or I might come down with an infection that would send contractions shooting through my spinal column. I tried out alternatives in front of the mirror: I tried taking steps with just the edge of my foot touching the floor instead of the whole foot coming down solidly all at once. I would start trembling in that room where I was alone—for even here in our house it wouldn't look good if someone saw me imagining my own movements in front of the mirror. I would practice walking toward the mirror, but it was such a small room and only a few steps separated the mirror from the facing wall. Hilw, ismallah alayk! my mother would have exclaimed if she had seen me standing there and staring into the mirror at my own body, or bringing my face closer to it so I could study every detail.

Cute, may God bless your little heart! . . . This word hilw, on my mother's tongue, was the equivalent of a curt dismissive nod of my father's head along with a sharp little gesture of his hand. He didn't like it, and it was his way of saying he was chasing away whatever it was he didn't want to see. My father believed mirrors were only for women. Every time I saw him talking to the people who used to come around to our house I would say to myself, He doesn't even know what his face looks like when he speaks. It's not just that he doesn't look in mirrors now, I would think, but that he never ever looked into them before. My father would lift his upper lip off his teeth and gums as he stared at the person he was speaking to, staring hard as though his narrow little eyes weren't big enough to allow him to see clearly. In the presence of his congregations at the Hussainiya, he would yank off his turban, unconcerned about exposing the pale ring of flesh on his head that was whiter than the rest because it had always been concealed beneath the folds. And if, at a certain moment, he straightened up to tug at what he had on beneath the jubba he wore under his abaya, rearranging what was down there, beneath his robe and cloak, full in front of the two hundred or so people who had come to hear him, I would tell myself that he must be doing this deliberately. He must have been confident that people would not whisper to each other, disapproving of his behavior, as they huddled there together where they sat. They wouldn't have to work at suppressing their laughter either, since in such circumstances it wouldn't even occur to them to laugh.

That is because they trusted him, and they believed in him. They obeyed him, too. He wasn't simply testing their loyalty when he accused them, for example, of being lazy, inactive people who were always sitting on their backsides, and so—he would go on to say—it wasn't surprising if they found their rights gobbled up. Once they had even jumped up from their tables, abandoning their packs of cards and the money they were gambling with, when they saw him coming to the square where their card tables were set out from one end to the other. I was with him. I was already a man of religion like he was. I stood watching as he overturned the tables with his own hands, first one and then the next. By then the men had gotten up and scattered to the edges of the square. Come on, he said to me as he started to walk away, leaving the men standing where they were, waiting for us to get out of sight so that they could retrieve their coins and their cards and the other belongings that were spilled across the square.

He knew that whatever he did, they would accept it. He didn't even give a thought to what might happen when he upended their card tables, telling them as he did so that only bastards do unlawful things. As we moved further away, not once turning back to look at them, I realized that for him there was only the tiniest gap between him and whatever he was doing or saying. He didn't go through a series of complicated mental jumps when he saw something that angered him. I watched him out of the corner of my eye as we strode quickly along that lane. Whatever might be going through his head now, it was happening only inside his head. It was no longer about the people he had left there, nor about those he would find wherever it was he was heading. It wasn't about me, as I cast furtive glances in his direction and hesitantly followed him.

The wave of fever that brought on the dizziness was accumulating in my head again, and it would soon build up and surge through me and drain my strength. As we made our way from the hospital, my nephew asked if it might be better for us to find a taxi. That would have given me some relief but I was already walking toward my car, parked in the lane above the street where the hospital's main entrance was. My nephew followed me at a half run, hopping now to one side of the pavement and now to the other, trying his best to stay even with me so that, being at my side, he could shield me. Coming in the other direction, crowds of people were pushing forwards toward the hospital as if they were in a race to the door. I had to be alert, both hands ready to push away anyone who might collide into me. It made me anxious and wore me out even more; and with every two or three steps, I was looking over my shoulder to see if my nephew was still close behind me. He knew how I was feeling. Over and over, he said, I'm right here, Uncle. I'm right behind you.

Three days sitting on this street had given my car a coat of sticky dust and grime. But at least there was a vacant space in front of it which meant I wouldn't have to inch it forward and backward again and again in order to edge it out into the street. Once I was settled inside, resting my hands on the steering wheel, my nephew—still standing at my driver's-side car door—asked if I had anything in the car that he could use to remove the filth smeared across the front windshield. The blotch looked oily: thick and impenetrable, like it was affixed permanently to the glass. I peered into the dark corners of the car looking for the box of tissues I thought would be there, but I found it hard to care whether or not I could locate it. When I stopped twisting around to look, dropping back against the headrest to relieve my aching head and neck, my nephew stuck his hand between me and the wheel, groping for the button that would spray water across the windshield. All that came out of the two needle-sized holes was that familiar dry sound, something between a rattle and a gurgle. Without looking at me or saying a word, my nephew turned on his heels and headed for the line of shops on the other side of the road. By the time he was back, the box of tissues in his hand was already open. He pulled out a handful and began rubbing at the oily stain, but it seemed immune to his efforts, having baked itself into the glass. He had to go back to the shop and fetch a bottle of water. Before he turned completely away to go there again, I waved at him to climb in, even though I knew that for the entire journey the blotch would be there, inescapable, disgusting me and straining my eyes as I tried to look beyond it.

The eighty kilometers that separated me from the house would not make my fatigue any worse. It might even restore me somewhat, at least if the road we had to take wasn't too choked with traffic. Anyway, it wasn't the kind of tiredness that would make me drowsy. That woman who had come from Venezuela to live with us used to always answer my father, whenever he asked her if she was feeling better, with just one word. Sleep . . . sleep. That is all she ever said, in the hoarse metallic voice that issued from the steel plate covering the holes in her throat. When we were there at home, it was clear that she didn't sleep, because the raspy panting sounds she made just trying to breathe never stopped and we constantly heard her opening her suitcases and then walking from her bedroom to the kitchen at the other end of the house. She didn't sleep last night either, my mother would say in the morning to whoever woke up next. She kept her voice low because she didn't want this woman—who might be anywhere in the house—to hear her. She might even be right behind my mother as she spoke, or near the open door to the bathroom as I washed my face and ears, or in the corridor between the rooms, standing there even though there was nothing in the corridor to keep anyone occupied. My mother didn't grumble or complain or say to my father, Who else but us would let a woman they don't know live in their house, a woman who came here from Venezuela because she didn't want to die there?

And she—that woman—accomplished what she had come here to do. In our home she managed it. One day my father went into the room where she was lying flat on her back, and said immediately to my mother who was standing just outside, She has died. Just like that he said it, without even pushing up her eyelid to check the pupil of her eye, or taking her hand to see whether she still had a pulse. She has died, he said. Then he turned to leave the room as if nothing further needed to be done about it.

Sleep. For myself, now, I could sense already how remote it was, and how hard it would be to capture and hold onto, even if I were so exhausted that I could not handle a dog darting out into the road in front of me. And then, I couldn't shake off my memory of that woman standing at the door-way into the kitchen, the rough sounds of her breathing and her croaky attempts at speech, gruff and hollow at the same time as they issued from the tube puncturing her body. I was nine or ten years old at the time. I was just learning about the illness and how to name it. How to think about the thing and its label, crammed together bewilderingly into that little patch of bare, open skin at the hollow just below her neck. The disease of cancer. That's what my mother called it as she spoke to her visitors in a near whisper. It has gotten her, my mother would tell her visitors. She whispered the words but she named the thing and its definition. The disease of cancer. The illness and the name it bore, as if to let them in on some-thing they weren't familiar with. The disease of cancer! they echoed back, at once frightened and pitying. They did know it, this word cancer, but only as something that had to do with someone very far away, someone who had died of it in one of those remote villages, only the news of it reaching them.

When we reached the autostrade I stopped the car. I told my nephew Bilal to get out and get rid of it—that splotch I knew I couldn't help staring at for as long as it sat there just waiting for my eyes to latch onto it. He couldn't find anything

11

to use on it except a key he fished out of his pocket. He began scratching at the glass, making a dry whine. He gave me a look, wanting to know if he should stop making that sound which might also scratch the glass and harm it. I didn't respond right away, mostly because I felt so listless. It won't come off, he said to me as he returned to his seat. Not unless we use gasoline. His words brought me out of my torpor momentarily. I asked myself how this nephew of mine—he was still such a young boy, after all—could be wise enough to know what drivers do to get rid of messes that stick to the windshields of their cars.

So, do you know how to drive the car? I asked him. I realized that, to my surprise, thinking about my nephew and his knowledge of gasoline could take me away, if only for that one brief moment, from my obsession with my sickness.

Bilal knew or at least sensed the condition I was in. He waited for me to ask my question again. When it didn't come, he simply turned to look at me and then shifted his gaze forward to look again at the autostrade stretching ahead of us.

Should I take you home? Or do you want to come with me to our place?

I had driven almost the whole way back without saying anything, and I could tell that my silence was upsetting him. It made him uneasy. And of course he would not want to be with me at that moment when my wife was standing there at the door wordless, surreptitiously trying to look into my face at the same time she was avoiding meeting my eyes.

My mother's alone in the house, he said. She's been alone for three days.

His mother in her home: the image of it came to me. She was standing three or four steps away from where I always sat, in that large armchair. As exhausted as I was, now I held onto that image of her as though I were testing myself. As though I wanted to see whether my memory of her would give me some comfort. On my visits—I made them once a month—we always sat far apart, me at one end of the long sofa and her at the other. I never allowed myself to sit comfortably or to look relaxed, by for instance turning my face and body slightly in her direction. This is from my father, I would say as I put out my hand toward hers. Without saying a word she would reach her hand nearer to mine in order to take the money which was tucked into a folded piece of paper so that the bills could not be seen. It never happened that her hand touched mine. That hand. I never more than glanced at that hand even when it was close enough to me. I will make coffee, Sayyid, she would say. And I, wanting to make it look like my every movement was subject to strict time constraints, and that was what determined whether I would go or stay, always looked at my watch, studying it as though I was counting the minutes in my head before I said, Why not, coffee. Yes, all right. But no sugar.

I wouldn't keep my eyes on her form and the way she walked for very long, as she turned to go into the kitchen. Not more than an instant, perhaps even less. Then I would turn my head forward again. Face and body composed and aligned, as I perched on the edge of my seat.

But she doesn't get home until late in the afternoon, I said. I wanted to remind him that she was not spending all of her time alone. But I also wanted to learn from him that she was still going to her work just as before.

To support my attempt to reassure him that she hadn't been all alone, he said, turning to look at me, The teachers sometimes come home with her when school is over.

Are there a lot of them? I asked. And, after a pause, These women are her colleagues? But as I spoke I gave my head a little toss, wanting to show him that I wasn't much concerned about the answers to my own questions.

Sometimes they all come.

He always seemed aware that when I was asking about her I was anticipating hearing back something more than my question was actually asking. He knows, I thought. Sometimes his answers gave me what I was looking for, going beyond the vague question I would ask in the details he gave. Sometimes I got the feeling that this inquisitiveness of mine toward his mother pleased him.

So I'll take you home.

No, no—I can get out at the service-taxi stop. I always find a car there to take me home.

Because I always wanted to prolong these little moments of tacit collusion, where we seemed to understand each other without needing the words for it, I would go quiet and he would follow my lead, neither of us saying whatever it was we had been about to say. That's what I would always do. But right now my fatigue was getting the better of my desire to keep up a conversation about her—that desire I had given myself every encouragement to pursue.

Do you have enough money for the car?

Yes, he said, stretching his body along the car seat so that he could reach his hand into his pocket. You gave me enough, and my mother did too, he said as he shoved his open palm in my direction to show me the wad of bills.

When I stopped the car there, three service-taxis were waiting for their complement of passengers. But he took his time. His hand still gripping the half-open door of my car, he seemed to be having second thoughts about whether he wanted to get out. It only lasted a moment. He turned back to me and asked if I wanted him to stay with me. It was his way of apologizing for getting out of the car and abandoning me. Once outside, having closed the car door, he flipped around again and poked his head through the open window to tell me to wait here so that he could get rid of the splotch that still clung insolently to the window directly in front of my eyes. I wanted to drive off but his insistence kept me there. I watched as he hurried over to the service drivers who were standing together next to one of their cars, talking.

The plastic bottle he was clutching when he returned was more than half full of water, and grubby from so much re-use and refilling. But when I saw the water pouring down against the windshield I suddenly realized how dry my throat was and how thirsty I felt. He had emptied the bottle completely when he motioned to me to activate the wipers. But the stain on the windshield defeated him this time too. I motioned back to tell him to forget about it, and that I would go now.

Illness doesn't arrive just like that, unbidden, without some prior summons. The rest of the way home, now that I was alone, the onrush of thoughts in my head clamored for my attention as they tried to crowd each other out. Perhaps it was my home that had made me ill. The air I had been breathing was poisonous because it hung stale and still in the closed rooms of that house and refused to leave. Or maybe it was my wife who had brought on the illness. Though she never seemed capable of putting on anything but those worn-out, shapeless gowns that always had a water stain down the front, she never stopped letting me know—merely by the looks she gave me—that this was not how people lived. This life she was living, not knowing how to live any other kind of life, did not please her. Every time I had to encounter her in the narrow corridor, pressing her body against one wall so that I could pass by, I tried to imagine her looking different—some other shape, some other expression on her face—but I never succeeded. I couldn't even manage to add a little color to her cheeks, not even a smidgen. That wan yellow coloring that she seemed to have sucked in from the recesses of this stale house gave her face a thin, drawn, bloodless look, as if a layer of skin had been stripped away.

She plasters her body to the wall, her entire body, from her backside to the top of her head, as if to make certain that not a centimeter of me will touch her as I go by. When she is coming toward the sitting room where I am sitting with whoever happens to be visiting me, but she is still on the other side of the doorway, she is already summoning me to take what is in her hands, speaking in a tone of voice that is an instant rebuke. The tea tray, she snarls. Or—again, from the other side of the doorway—she snaps, Your father! It is her way of telling me he needs some help from me.

Sometimes I have a recollection that she was pretty once. Just once, when she stood in the entryway to her house, there at the top of the stairs. Mashallah! my father exclaimed as he craned his neck to give his small eyes a closer look. He said the same thing to her father, Sayyid Jaafar, once we were inside their house. At the time, she was twelve or thirteen years old.

Yes, I accept. That is what I wrote back to my father when he wrote to say that now I must get married. She is the youngest daughter of Sayyid Jaafar, our relative in al-Kawthariyeh, he wrote. And that was all he ever said about her, since he did not think it would be proper—as my father—to describe her in any other way. To say, for instance, that she was pretty, or to go into any details about her appearance, commenting on her eyes or her mouth or her voice when she spoke. Yes, I accept, I wrote back, exactly as if I had been standing right there facing him as he conducted the small ceremony affirming the marriage contract. As though I were not, at the time, so far away—all the distance that separated our village in south Lebanon from the holy city of Najaf in Iraq.

I didn't find her particularly pretty when she arrived in Najaf with him. But she wasn't like she was now, feeble and colorless. Yet in the four or five years since I had seen her that one time, she had changed. She was no longer the girl she had been on that day. They were strange, those first looks she gave me, long and direct. She didn't avert her gaze as other girls did. She kept her eyes fixed on me even when I finished saying whatever it was I had to say to her. As though she were informing me, by letting her eyes linger for two or three seconds more on my face, that I had harmed her by allowing them to bring her to me. I began thinking that perhaps she was like me. She was a person who was waiting for another life, even expecting a different life to be granted to her. Or, perhaps like her schoolmates, she was dreaming of a life that would be something other than the life she had lived with her family or the life she would live with me.

That reproachful, even censorious look: she always had it ready for me. When she stood up after a meal to carry away the tray and our plates into the kitchen; when, already at the door, I told her that I was going out; when I opened the door to let myself in after being out. Likewise, when I came to her at night; and then when, after our union, she bent down to pick up her gown from the floor and take it into the bathroom.

In those days—through the entire ten years that passed without her getting pregnant—I used to tell myself that anyway, the kind of union we made wasn't one that would produce children. When she did begin to have children, I began telling myself that a woman like her would get pregnant only with the sort of children she did finally produce.

When I pushed open the solid iron door that fronts on the street, gating our house, my daughter Hiba was sitting behind it halfway up the steps to the door above that opened into our house, her doll in her lap. She looked up but when she saw it was me coming in, she went back to the doll who was now napping on the step beside her, covered up to her chin beneath a scrap of fabric. She didn't raise her head when I stopped in front of her or when I spoke, asking her if she had fed her doll. Come. Come inside with me, I said to her, putting out my hand to help her up. But she went on sitting there, occupied with the pair of tiny eyes that rolled open again as soon as she had shut the eyelids with her fingers.

Get up, I said. Come on, come and play with her in the house, she doesn't like sleeping on the stairs.

When those eyelids went on resisting her she pressed her entire palm down over them to keep them shut, as if to force the doll to go to sleep against its will.

I left her there and continued climbing the stairs slowly, my legs heavy and sluggish. My wife had heard the sound of my steps. I saw her standing behind the door, which was only a crack open, straightening her hijab hurriedly, tugging it into place across her forehead.

What did they say to you?

No one had told her anything, then. She hadn't found anyone she could ask to phone the hospital. Or perhaps she didn't make an effort to find anyone.

They said to come back in two days.

I could have postponed any further response, but as I opened the other door—the one leading into the room where I received my guests—I turned back and corrected myself.

In two or three days. That's what the doctor said.

She followed me in, silent, and stood facing me. She didn't move or speak, just gazed at me steadily as I lifted my turban off my head and took off my abaya. She was waiting for me to finish saying what I had to say. When I collapsed onto the armchair, my body feeling heavy and lifeless, the look on her face informed me that her thin store of patience, which she had been holding valiantly in reserve, had now run out.

Two or three days? What happens after two or three days?

I don't know. He said I am sick.

Gradually, one feature at a time, her face went from blank neutrality to curiosity and then to the expression I knew so well, her way of showing surprise and disbelief. I knew she had finally reached the point where she couldn't avoid knowing what my illness was, and acknowledging it, calling it by its name at least in her head.

Is the doctor going to put you in the hospital?

I don't know. He said I should come back in two or three days.

She knew, as well, that she must—right now, in this very moment—stop asking these questions of hers that left me craning my head from one side to the other, unsure of where to direct my eyes. I will make you tea, she said, turning to go into the kitchen.

Sitting in my usual armchair, my thoughts turned to the photograph on the opposite wall. Long ago I should have brought it lower, I reflected. Every time he had come to visit, my brother Adnan had teased me about it. Why had I hung the three of them so high up there, as if they were strung up on the gallows? That picture—their picture—hung at such an elevation that its frame nearly touched the ceiling. Adnan went on telling me that I must bring it far enough down that it would be at eye level for a normal man. He was right, I thought. After all, I could no longer make out their faces, whether or not I had my glasses on, though it was clear enough that there were three men in the picture and they were the men I knew. Whenever I glanced at it, as high overhead as it was, and as tiny as it looked way up there in its braided silver frame, memories of them as they were when that photograph was taken would fill my head.

From where I sat I mused about what it would be like to see that picture from close up. To see my father at the age of thirty, the figure he made then, his narrow eyes staring at the photographer as if urging him to hurry, as if he wanted this stranger to pick up his camera and go away. Trying to compensate for the smallness of his eyes, or perhaps just to explain why they were as narrow as they were, my mother always used to say that those eyes held enough terror to frighten anyone on whom they happened to fall. Even the two cats who had lived with us since they were tiny kittens used to back off, one leg raised slightly off the ground, before scurrying away as if they were little boys. That's the example my mother always gave, sketching the scene of him coming out of the house and going over to the paved area between the house and the garden to give his eyes some temporary relief from the darkness of his room, as if he needed to stand up and assure himself that his legs were still working after the fatigue of sitting in that gloomy room with its row of square cushions that imams sat cross-legged on.

Do we have a ladder in the house?

My wife gave me one of her usual looks. She was standing over the little side table that she had just lifted off the floor in order to bring it over to where I sat.

Ladder? Why the ladder?

I'm going to move the photograph lower down on the wall. It's so high, no one can see who is in it.

She swiveled her head to stare up at the picture even though she was still half bent over the table where she had set down the tea. Without straightening up she looked over at me again.

You are going to move it down? Now?

Not right now. But that's where it should go, down there.

She twisted around again, this time presumably to look where I was pointing. But she made it obvious that she was staring into empty space as if to let me know that she was thinking about something else and that I too ought to be thinking about other things.

Well. Anyway. He got sick while you were there in the hospital.

Got sick the same way he always does?

Got sick like he always does, her voice intimating that he had worn her out as he usually did, and she wanted me to know it. A thought forced itself on me. Maybe what had made him ill this time was my being away.

Did he sleep in his own bed?

In his bed one night and on his easy chair one night. Drink your tea first, she said as she saw me set my hands down, palms open and flat, bracing myself to get up.

It's not just my being away, though. It's that he sits there in his easy chair all the time and no one ever comes in to talk to him.

The boys . . . I was going to ask her if the boys had entertained him by playing with their sister somewhere near enough that he could see them, but it suddenly dawned on me that I had not even asked her about them.

Where are they?

Out. When your father was willing to eat, it was Ahmad who fed him from a spoon.

I pictured my son Ahmad standing in front of my father, a plate of food in his hands, waiting for his grandfather to swallow what he had in his mouth before bringing the spoon close again. The spoon would be heaped with food. My father would not know how to take only as much as he could chew and swallow at one time.

Did he eat?

Who?

My father. Did he have lunch?

Feed him now. That was what I must do. And doing it would surely make me feel a bit better. Good, I thought. Coming into the room carrying his food will make it seem as though I was never away from him after all.

It's as though I am silencing him by putting this in his mouth. His lips take what is on the spoon but his eyes keep returning to me, staring at my face. He knows I will manage to dampen whatever curiosity he has, to keep him silent with these words I repeat time and again. Eat, Father. In good health, Father. Here, take this one, too. This will give you strength. But with every word I say, he makes me sense how much I am tiring him out. He even makes me feel I'm causing him pain.

Eat, Father, I say, even if I am just waiting for the insistence in his eyes to grow sharper, until it is so intense that I think I can see him summoning all the strength he has left to speak, and I imagine that forceful voice of his that he has kept imprisoned inside his body all these months. He is about to say to me, Where were you? Tell me—where were you?

Still, the voice I will hear would not be that first voice of his, that angry bellow ripping through his listeners to give them a good scolding. You two, over there, quiet! he would roar at two men murmuring together in the back as he delivered a sermon at the Hussainiya. If they did not stop talking immediately he would say to them—just like that, in front of everyone sitting in there—Get out! They would make a show of looking around, to let everyone know how genuinely chagrined they were and how they felt the awkwardness of actually getting up and leaving. And they would stay like that until the other people in the Hussainiya made it clear that they had to leave. He would not resume his homily until he saw their backs vanish, going down the stairs. He who knows God and worships Him . . . , he would bark, going back to his explanation of the passages he had recited from Abu Dharr.

You did well . . . you did well. That's what he began saying to me as I gave my first sermon on one of my trips back from Najaf. I did not deserve his praise. My legs, concealed by the pulpit behind which I stood, were shaking and my voice came out hesitant, careening unpredictably between my own normal voice and the more forceful voice of a seasoned sermon-giver. Good, you did well, came his voice from somewhere to the right of the pulpit where he was sitting facing the congregation. It was clear that he wanted to make certain they heard what he was saying to me. That way they would remain quiet and still, staying in their seats, and they would listen attentively to what I was saying. I knew this was his intention; I knew what his words meant. But I accepted those words of his anyway; indeed, I anticipated hearing them. I waited for him to say these words again. You did well. Once, twice, many times, so that perhaps even I would believe the truth of what he said.

I knew he would not say anything more—anything about my hesitant delivery—after they had all filed out of the Hussainiya. He didn't respond at all when I remarked that I wasn't the way I should have been. He remained silent, seemingly occupied in studying the road in front of him. At that moment I really felt I had embarrassed him, not only because of my weak voice and my confusion and my evident and mortified inability to rise above the situation, but also because I had put him in the position of having to demonstrate his approval, out there in front of the congregation, in a situation where he was not particularly pleased and certainly wasn't ready to show any true admiration for what he saw and heard.

Eat, Father . . . this food will give you strength. I went on repeating it. And he went on obeying me, opening his mouth every time I brought the spoon close. Perhaps he was waiting for me to obey him as he was obeying me, in his case by eating even though he felt full. Waiting for me to tell him that I had been in the hospital, and that I would be going back there in two or three days.

He ate everything on his plate, I said to my wife, who was standing halfway down the corridor. She was slapping at the dust and dirt that covered Hiba's clothes, and she did not turn toward me to take the empty plate from my hands. As I headed toward the kitchen to set it down next to the sink I could tell that Hiba was on the point of breaking into sobs. Her mother's blows against her backside were getting stronger and stronger. They were beginning to hurt, and Hiba understood that it was no longer about getting rid of the dirt; it was a punishment. Seeing me coming out of the kitchen she ran toward me, her arms outstretched. I picked her up and carried her over to where her doll lay sprawled on the floor. As I bent down to pick up the doll I told her it was still asleep. Take her . . . here . . . hold her. Before she wakes up, I said. But Hiba made a show of refusing to take the limp form by shrugging her shoulders to shake me off and then giving her doll a hateful look.

On my way to the mosque I was thinking about what Sayyid Abd al-Hasan could have meant when he called me lazy. He hadn't meant simply the fact that my house was so close to the mosque, nor that I spent so little time there. It was more about my unvarying refusals every time he invited me to go with him to express condolences to a family in one of the villages, where we would likely have to sit for hours on end. Was it you who chose to have your home as close as this to the mosque? he used to ask me. I answered with my attempt at a light riposte, saying it was the people of Shqifiyeh who chose the home for me and it wasn't my doing. The mosque was no more than eighty paces from my front door, and I counted them every time I went there. It was so close that I could keep well informed about who had shown up there at any particular time just by looking out the window of the sitting room that was also my official reception room.

And those people, too, would know that I had arrived at the mosque just by looking out their windows, and so they could follow me in there promptly. I wasn't usually alone in the mosque for more than five or ten minutes. I would seat myself in the middle of the congregational prayer space, moving my prayer beads through my fingers. That's what I did, because there was nothing I had to do before they showed up. There was nothing around me that had to be arranged or set right or returned to its proper place. My grandfather Sayyid Murtada had accused the folk of Hassaniyeh of stinginess because they did nothing for their mosque. He even turned their parsimony into a proverb: A space that's empty is just like Hassaniyeh's mosque—nothing in it but the ablutions pitcher.

Praise be to God for your safe return. Welcome back. That's what the two men who were first to enter the mosque after me said. They had seen me come out of my house, of course. Beneath their greeting lay a question more than a desire to congratulate me or even wish me well. They wanted me to tell them what the doctor had found inside of me.

Of all the folk of Shqifiyeh these two were the most frequent visitors to the mosque. It wasn't for the sake of prayer, or because they wanted to listen to pious homilies, but simply because this was a way to spend some of the long hours they had to get through, day after day. I knew them and I knew their needs. I conversed with them at the mosque the same way I would have talked with them if we were sitting in my house.

When their allusions to my sound health didn't yield any worthwhile response from me, they had to make their intent more obvious.

You stayed two days in the hospital?

Two days, I answered, though only after pausing to make it appear that I couldn't quite remember and had to count how much time I'd spent there.

Were you alone?

Bilal was with me. My late brother's son.

They wanted to know. I knew that if they were persistent in this curiosity of theirs, I wouldn't be clever enough to keep evading their questions by responding only to what they specifically asked.

While you were away they brought a doctor to see Hajj Zaino.

Again?

As usual, he forgets he has diabetes and he devours half a platter of the sweet basmaa pastry his son always brings him from Nabatiyeh.

They wanted to entertain me, and to make me feel better. They were doing their best to lighten the burden of illness by turning it into one of their jokes.

And his son? Doesn't he know that basmaa is bad for him? I added that the only way you can be certain of keeping a diabetic from eating sweet things is to hide them away, or better yet, to not even let them into the house. I think they realized

25

that my remark was aimed at putting an end to their ongoing banter at Hajj Zaino's expense. I rounded off my attempt to silence them by remarking, after glancing at my watch, that the late-afternoon call to prayer would be upon us in two minutes.

But the electricity has been cut since yesterday! they both exclaimed at once. In all of the villages, one of them went on to say, they were now operating the call to prayer on batteries.

To reestablish my rapport with them and to get the conversation going again, I said I thought that instead we ought to restore the call to prayer to what it used to be, dependent neither on the electricity grid nor on batteries. It suddenly occurred to me to share with them how peaceful it made me feel—even now, and as though a soft breeze was suddenly cocooning me—to remember Sayyid Amin stepping up onto the stone platform at the mosque and singing out his call to prayer. Still, only the people in the two or three houses nearest to the mosque could enjoy the sound of it, even though his eyes would bulge out with the effort he made letting out every last breath of air in his chest.

Sayyid Amin . . . God be merciful to the late Sayyid Amin, one of them said, his voice thoughtful and sad.

People filled every seat in the clinic waiting room. A young man hesitated visibly and then got to his feet to give me a seat. I waited a few moments to allow the woman sitting in the next seat—or the man sitting next to her—to become aware of the young man's gesture. The man exchanged places with her so that she would not be sitting next to me. Once they were settled Bilal waved me to the seat. He looked like a child imitating what he has seen grownups do. I gave him a smile as I tugged the edges of my abaya together before sitting down. He knew I needed someone with me to do these things. He knew that before I could handle any of this—like, for instance, sitting down in a waiting room, or standing up and coming to everyone's notice—I needed the ritual of being invited, at least apparently, to do so.

26

My entrance caused some commotion. I saw heads swiveling, faces turned upward, eyes shifting in my direction. But once I had sat down it didn't last long. Moments later everyone had lapsed back into a silent and motionless state. Bilal was standing up, leaning against the doorjamb and looking at me as though he thought I was about to say something to him. More minutes passed and then from behind her desk the physician's receptionist turned to me to say that he had arrived now and was inside, and he had asked her about me. Her remark flustered me; I couldn't help thinking that her words would lead everyone seated in that waiting room to stare at me again, perhaps trying to make out what my particular malady was. But even in my acute sense of discomfort, I knew and appreciated that I wouldn't be sitting among these people for very long. When the doctor opened the door, I knew, I would be the first to go inside.

Ahlan, Shaykh, he said, his hand firmly gripping the door panel to keep it from swinging shut immediately.

As-salaamu alaykum, I said, but only after I was inside.

How are we? he asked, turning to wedge himself in behind his desk where, still standing, he began shuffling papers, looking for whatever there was that pertained to me. He sat down, all the while staring at his sheaf of papers and riffling among them busily.

We will have to operate.

I didn't say anything. I was afraid I might stammer or that my voice would come out weak and trembling.

Are you afraid?

I responded, of course, with a passage from the Holy Book. Say: We will not be afflicted but by what God has decreed for us. But as I said it, my voice was as weak and tremulous as I had feared.

You are not going to die, he said, looking at me. Looking into my eyes, a smile on his lips. I couldn't help thinking how devious that smile looked.

Without an operation, what—

You would die. Not today, not tomorrow, not even a month or two from now. But . . . .

His voice was neutral, as if he were waiting to find out from me which of the two possibilities I would choose.

I didn't have anything to say. Or maybe I was just taking my time, not because I didn't know what I wanted or what my choices were but because I felt uncomfortable, and even uneasy. I was stalling. I needed to give myself time. To leave a space between what I had heard and what I would say.

Will the operation change me?

It is a difficult operation, and a long one too, because we have to take out some organs and replace them with equivalent devices that perform the same functions.

And a dangerous one?

He moved his head in a way that suggested he hadn't understood, or perhaps that he didn't give answers to questions such as this.

What I mean is, while I'm in there being operated on, will . . . ?

In medicine nothing is completely certain or guaranteed, but in this hospital we have performed operations like this many times.

He did not go on but I understood that what he was implying—and wanting me to understand but without him having to say it—was that the patients who had undergone this surgery had not died. That when he came out of the operation room after performing one of these procedures, his patient would still be alive.

But when you go in you will sign a document clearing us of responsibility, he said. He repeated a sentence from the lesson he had dictated to me when he first informed me that I was ill. He had said then, and he said again now, that in this hospital doctors do not hide anything from their patients.

I repeated the question he had ignored. But will I still be like I am now?

It is a difficult procedure. There are things that will change in your body, I mean in the way your body functions.

Now I did not want him to go on. That was because his expression had changed and his serious-looking professional smile told me he was about to instruct me on all the changes I would experience and what I would lose with every alteration. As I saw and took in the look on his face, he realized that I had absorbed as much as I could handle for today. He said we would talk about all of these matters once I was in the hospital, and as he said it he gave me a wink to remind me of all those people waiting out there for his attention.

When do I come back?

We are not in a great hurry. Arrange your affairs and then get in touch with me.

When he opened the door for me he seemed already to be looking toward whichever person would come in next. When I crossed the threshold into the waiting room and was standing in their midst he said a quick word of farewell, and added, I'll be waiting for your call. As he spoke he gave me that particular doctor's look, which he almost immediately shifted elsewhere, already focusing his concern on his next patient.

Once outside his office I was immediately aware that my body was suddenly drenched in sweat. I had to resist a strong urge to lift my turban completely off my head so that I could wipe my hand over my skull to try to get rid of the perspiration that had collected thickly enough to seriously dampen the turban's edges. I turned to the receptionist, who said she didn't need anything from me right now. She gave me a card with a number so I could contact her or the doctor. Turning away I saw my nephew standing in exactly the same spot as when I'd gone inside, keeping his gaze steadily elsewhere so that he would not be looking at me in my state of awkwardness. I don't know why I stared down at the card she had given me, as if I needed to make out something written there, even though this little gesture slowed me down and exposed me for a few additional seconds to the stares of everyone in the room. There in front of them all I seemed to be moving in slow motion as I put the card in my pocket. As if I were putting off the uncomfortable moment of actually leaving the room, which was awkward for me because it meant readying myself to have to say as-salaamu alaykum as I walked slowly toward the door, where my nephew stood stiffly upright waiting for me.

It was better for me, his patient, not to hear in advance what would happen to me. And then, also, there was the tone of voice. It had fallen on my ears as a slightly threatening voice. I didn't find it at all a neutral voice, as he might call it or describe it. And he hadn't told me anything he didn't want to tell me. We will talk when we are in the hospital, he said. He sounded exactly like a schoolteacher I once had and remembered well. I recall that teacher saying to us, Now close your books, we'll finish our reading tomorrow. It's what he said, years ago, and it's what the doctor might as well have said to me today.

Fine. It would be better for me if I learned on my own, after awakening from my operation, what parts of my body I had lost. Or it would be better not to wake up at all. That seemed easier than trying to calculate in advance how I would feel then and what I would be missing.

Over here! This is the way to the car, Bilal was calling out to me, alerting me that we were on the wrong course in heading in this direction down the street. I obeyed him and changed direction to follow him. He had taken the lead, I knew, to spare me having to use my own head to remember where I had parked the car. And anyway, I had let him walk ahead of me so that he could clear a path for me through the crowd of pedestrians.

The car is close now, he said, pointing to the intersection where we would turn.

In the films I have seen in my life, people near death are always making decisions about what they will do in the time remaining to them. One character says he is going to live as he has always dreamed of living, while another declares he will try out things he has never experienced before, like traveling to other countries. Someone else decides to stop shouldering the responsibilities that have brought him to this state of exhaustion. He declares he will stop working immediately and will spend the rest of his time pondering all the years of his life that have somehow just gone by. In those films it was as if none of these characters could see anything in life except the passage of time itself. Anything to life but time, and they divided that time into perfectly equal segments, the first segment no different than the final one. The time that was left was all about the life that was left. They didn't set aside any time for the fear of death, specifically for that fear.

I would not die. That's what the doctor said to me, either evasively or as an outright lie. What they mean when they claim that they are telling the patient everything about his illness is that they are telling him half of what they know. They have to keep something back, something for themselves alone to know. Otherwise how could they ever reassure a patient under their care at one moment and banter with him at another, manipulating him so that he surrenders completely to them and to what they are doing to his body?

Over here, this way! Bilal repeated, every time he turned back to see whether I was still close behind him. When we reached especially congested spots he even put his hand out to me as though he thought I might need to hold it.

We're here—there's the car, right over there, he said, his gaze following his pointing finger. I saw the car. The two days since I had left the hospital had left it even dirtier. And then there was that splotch, which for an instant seemed to shimmer as though it were coming alive.

I'll wash it off, I'll get rid of it there, once we're at our house, he said to me. He sensed my repugnance and so he took the key from me and made me wait until he had opened my car door.

*

In that filth-covered car, through its open window came bursts of air that invigorated me and made me feel a bit stronger. The breeze even brought the surgeon's words back to me now sounding reasonable and true rather than evasive and suspect. It wasn't death that awaited me, it was loss: no longer being whole. Ever since the moment I had been told of my illness, my head had closed the latch, trying to block out any and every thought of it. But these cool gusts of air somehow opened up a passage-way. I even found myself, following this powerful little upsurge of wellbeing or at least reassurance, drumming my fingers against the wheel as though I was deliberately, and audibly, tapping out a tune that made me happy. At the sound, Bilal turned.

To your house or ours? I asked him.

Ours, he said. You can have lunch and relax a bit there.

What will your mother feed us?

Something that tastes really good. On the days when she doesn't go to work she cooks really nice meals.

I was imagining her silhouette, that strong firm form standing at the kitchen sink washing greens. In another scene in my mind she was taking a cooking pot down from the shelf overhead and then she turned to pick up something she had set down on the table behind her, her form always giving off a sense of energy and strength.

Her work colleagues won't have shown up?

She didn't say anything to me about it. She would have told me if they were coming.

I went back to drubbing the wheel with my finger, and he gave me another sidelong glance.

Yes, ours—we'll have lunch at home, he said, going along with my newfound serenity, clearly relieved and even a bit lighthearted. To show that I was playing along with him too, I said, But we don't know yet what your mother has made.

In my head I went back to imagining her, there in her kitchen. Now she was finishing up what I had already watched her doing in my mind, shaking her hands a few times to get rid of the drops of water clinging to them and then looking around the kitchen again as if she were searching for something and had simply forgotten where she had put it.

I sensed that Bilal was pushing me closer to her, although I didn't know exactly how, or what this meant. I mean, that kind of closeness that would go beyond where we were now, me and her. We who are both close to him, I thought, but are as far apart as can be when it comes to any communication between the two of us. Now and then I wondered about how I might help him along in this mission of his, if indeed that was what it was. For instance, I could ask him about his mother's colleagues at work and whether they were all women. Or I might say to him, without there being any particular occasion for the remark, You know, your mother might not be in the most sociable mood right now.

But what I said right then was: What will your mother say when she sees the car looking so filthy!

It doesn't matter, she saw it in the morning when you came to pick me up.

She was in the house?

We were waiting for you. She was waiting, and so was I. A couple of times she left me standing at the window while she went into another room to do something or other, but then she came back and stood there with me.

Bilal said all of this as though he were divulging a secret. He looked at me to see what impact his words might have.

I didn't have any wish to push him further, by objecting, for example, that she was just trying to hurry his departure so that she could go off to work. He would answer me by saying, No, that wasn't why she was standing at the window. Anyway, it was more than enough for me to go on picturing her standing there. In itself this revealed a different side of her. Or at least it began to dislodge that sense of neutrality, or of distance, which ever since my brother's death had kept us performing the same ritual over and over every time I visited her at home. Welcome to the Sayyid, she always said to me as soon as she opened the door. And then, Come in, Sayyid. She would wave her hand toward my accustomed seat. Next there would come the question, Coffee? And then I would be stealing the usual glances at her figure as she went out of the room to make the coffee. After this there would again be that very same distance, the remoteness that seemed to define these moments before she would say, her hand firm around the rolled-up bills inside the piece of paper that was there to conceal what was inside, Sharaft, Sayyid. You have honored us with your presence.

What do you think about washing the car at the station? It seemed to me that arriving there in a clean car—a glistening car—would make some kind of difference.

As you like, he said, though the look on his face made it clear he was in a hurry to get home.

Just a quarter of an hour, that's all it will take, I said, not ready to give in to his preference. I really did not want to arrive at her door with any detail awry in the picture I imagined.

This time, I thought. This time, surely, I could step just over that line I had never even dared to approach. Those strong, resolute footfalls of hers, always so steady and firm whether I was coming into the house or going out, had never left me even a tiny margin of space for maneuver, a pause or a hesitation that would allow me to swerve even slightly from the modest route I was accustomed to following and the phrases I invariably said. Her fulsome welcome didn't leave me any room to insert a single word that might get her to turn to me in surprise, or at least with a slight look of puzzlement in her eyes, in search of some further explanation. Some word that might get her to wonder, after I had gone, about why I had said that particular thing and what I had meant by it.

This time my illness would take on the mission of diluting that implacable force that I had never seen desert her. It

34

seemed to have already started happening, according to Bilal, who was intent on making me think he was giving me a clear signal when he had described, earlier in our conversation, how she had stood at the window waiting for me to arrive. I broke the silence.

Does she know what I have?

Who?

Your mother. Did you talk to her about me?

My words came as a surprise to him. He had thought that what we knew about that—what was between us, just me and him—wouldn't invade our conversation.

She knows.

He knew I would not want to embarrass him further by asking how she had learned of it. He waited a few seconds before getting up from where he was sitting across from me. I'll go and see if they've gotten the spot off the windshield, he said, walking out to the carwash that was located somewhere behind where I sat. He would linger there, I knew, watching them as they trained water on it, the jet of liquid I could hear gushing out, thick and fast, splashing onto the metal car body. He would stay out there and I would remain in here, sitting on this chair and to all appearances just waiting for him to come back.

It's like new! he said as he strode toward me.

You mean they've gotten all the way down to its original color? I asked. I wanted to tease him, to let him know we were back to where we'd been before I asked my question about whether his mother knew how sick I was.

It's like new, he just said. But hearing him say this for the second time got me to twist around and look at it.

It did look new. It was gleaming. It always surprised me to see how that bright paint could preserve its original intensity beneath the dust and dirt that covered it most of the time.

They cleaned the windshield too, he said, reminding me of that splotch which had been so stubborn with us.

35

When they brought it out into the sunshine I noticed how he circled around it to check whether there was anything they hadn't caught. His inspection completed, he looked at me and nodded, announcing that he was satisfied with their work. I stood up to put my hand in my pocket but he waved his hand briskly to let me know that he had already taken care of it with whatever money he had.

Even so, I put my hand into my pocket again. He shrugged elaborately and lifted both palms to make it clear to me that he wasn't going to take anything in exchange for what he had paid. I tried to push the money into his hand and then into his pocket but he objected all the while. I have money, I'm fine, he began repeating when I finally managed to shove some bills into his pocket. I gave him a smile and slapped his cheeks affectionately.

As we left the station he told me again that we were going to eat some good food. He said it as if he wanted a response from me. He wanted me to confirm that I would be there with him.

Good food, mmm, he repeated, when I was slow to second what he had said.

Are you hungry? I asked.

Yes, I'm hungry. You?

I'm hungry. But it's only half an hour until I eat some good food.

I didn't feel there was anything shameful or blameworthy in that desire that I had kept hidden inside all this time. Even the way I steal little glances at her when she turns to go into the kitchen is nothing to be ashamed of, I would think. It has been many years since my brother died, and surely what she has lived through since his death has cleansed her body and even purified it, ridding it of whatever remained there that belonged to him.

Yet I would find myself recalling my brother's face. He would be smiling at me exactly as he used to do, his expression fond but at the same time knowing. That smile that said to me, I know your intentions. I couldn't see any signs of anger or irritation in that smile, no blame or scolding. There was something else, though: he seemed to be deliberately assuming that artful, slightly sneering look, saying to me, I see you! Or perhaps even, Hey, I caught you in the act.

Despite what looked to me like indulgence on his part, I would find myself answering him back. You are dead, I tell him, and then I assure him that I'm not doing anything that could hurt him or give him pain. I'm only looking at what is already there to see. I respond to him as if I want him to stop showing up like this in front of me. I want him to stop smiling like this, and even more, I want him to promise me that his face won't suddenly loom up in front of me if it happens. If I go further with her than simply shifting my gaze to look at her lower legs or at her hands passing me a cup of coffee.

She was waiting for us to arrive. She expected us. She was probably standing at the same window where she had stood with Bilal in the morning. As soon as she caught sight of the car turning into the narrow lane leading to her home, she came out to receive us.

Welcome, welcome to the Sayyid, she said, standing not far away from the car and waiting for me to climb out.

Bilal had gotten out first and he stood next to her as if he too were receiving me, one of the two hosts for the day. When he saw me take a step or two forward he turned toward the open door.

Welcome to the Sayyid, she said again when I came up to where she was standing. Only the span of a single footstep separated us.

Did it tire you, getting here?

I don't get tired as long as Bilal is with me.

She smiled. She was about to say something about how attached Bilal was to me, but instead she simply turned aside to make way for me, and then she caught up with me and matched my pace step for step as we walked to the house.

At the door, when she stayed back to allow me to go in first, I sensed her giving me a rapid glance, quick but searching, as though the looks of welcome we had already exchanged had not told her anything worth knowing about how I was now.

Come in, Sayyid, she said, gesturing toward the interior and the familiar sofa. As I walked toward my usual spot I suddenly had the feeling that I ought to do something that would appear completely unexpected, something distinct from my behavior on all previous visits. Like taking off my abaya to show that I wasn't already thinking about leaving before even sitting down, or like circling the spacious sitting room and looking out the windows.

Or I could wait for her to initiate something, perhaps a question about whatever her furtive glances at me hadn't already told her about my condition.

If you'd like to rest a bit . . . .

She meant Bilal's room where, she was suggesting without saying so, I could take off my outdoors clothing and stretch out on his bed for the time she needed to get our lunch ready. I had given her the impression that I was expecting something of the sort. As I got up, glancing around the room, I told her that the journey had indeed worn me out. It gave me some kind of pleasure to know that she had thought about my resting, that she was suggesting I spend some time in a room in this house by myself, even if it was Bilal's room. I liked the idea that when I returned to the sitting room I would be coming from somewhere deeper inside the house.

It also pleased me that she walked those few steps with me, as if to guide me into the room that Bilal was vacating for me, and that she looked carefully around his room before declaring that she thought it was neat enough, and then saying mischievously that Bilal hadn't been home long enough yet to turn it into a mess. Her words delighted Bilal. Before leaving the room, he asked if I wanted to read. If so, he would find something for me among his books. Already in the doorway standing next to her, he asked if I wanted him to shut the door. I just smiled. Once I was alone, I sat on the edge of the bed and began to ponder what to do for the half hour, or perhaps the whole hour, I would spend in here behind the closed door.

So that I would look like someone taking a rest, I took off my cloak and turban and then my jubba as well. I came back to the bed and perched again on the edge. Perhaps I should have gone into the bathroom to perform my ablutions, I thought, and then have asked for a prayer rug. But if I were to do that, surely I would be taking myself many steps back. As though with my own hands I would be digging a trench where before only a line had separated us. Me and her, each on their own side of the line. But she must be asking herself how it could be that I was not praying. Or perhaps she was assuming that behind the closed door this was exactly what I was doing, allowing myself to make do with facing the qibla but without a rug or ablutions.

But it wasn't just whether to pray or not that was preoccupying me, I knew. It was my turban as well, and this beard of mine, and the abaya, and my gaze, which I had to try always to keep neutral or blank, because otherwise I might appear to be concealing something. Of course I knew well enough that men like me don't actually fortify themselves any more strongly by employing tactics like this. With women, men in my position flirt with their words and their gazes, and even with their hands, reaching for women's bodies in whatever way they can. In Najaf, through those evenings we all spent together, they used to talk dirty about what they were going to do and what they'd already done. It's nothing to get bothered about, Sayyid Mudar would say to me, adding that women had longings too, didn't they, and sometimes they too obeyed those longings.

By now, in that room I had sunk into a terrible state of indecision. I couldn't stop thinking about it: whether to initiate something myself or to wait for something from her that would push me somewhere further. In the midst of this I heard a light knock on the door.

It's time to eat, my mother says, Bilal called out from behind the closed door. For just a moment, as I got up from the bed, I wondered whether I would dare go out there as I was, dressed only in my thin white dishdasha.

Come in, Bilal, I called. It was as if I wanted to try this out, to see what reaction I would get looking like this, so contrary to my usual appearance.

Let's eat, my mother says, he replied, opening the door slightly, sticking his head around it and looking at me.

I'm coming. Tell her I'm coming. I wanted to hurry him out so that I could quickly put on my clothes. All of them.

They stood together at the door. She waited there until I got the car moving. Bilal was waving at me, first with one hand and then with both. I gave them a smile, turning my face to them before craning my head back to look at the road behind me so that I could back my car out of the drive. I was feeling slightly abashed about this visit, even though nothing at all had happened and I had not done anything wrong. I was embarrassed that, sitting with them at the dining table, I had launched into now one subject and now another, as though I were acting something out, and uncomfortable with the way I had spun out the time as I stood at the door, offering my effusive words of thanks and my goodbyes.

I needed to hear what Bilal would say about this. I wished he were sitting here with me in the car, next to me, giving me the words I wanted to hear. I needed him here, to tell me what she had said after she turned back from the door to go inside the house. To repeat to me the words she had said even if they likely didn't amount to more than a phrase or two. I wanted to hear this so badly that before I had even reached the main road, I was already thinking about reversing my car and sounding the horn, just once, so that Bilal would hear it and come out. What did your mother say? I would ask him, and he would know exactly what to say in response. And I would understand whatever he did say, since I didn't need anything more than those few words in order to send me off on my journey.

A single word, or even just a smile, on Bilal's face: that would be enough for me. After all, what I had felt embarrassed about might not really be so embarrassing. And what I saw as overdoing it, as I stood there at the door, might possibly have brought her closer to me. A single word or a smile that would tell me everything. It would tell me how my sitting there at the table had seemed, how my appearance had been, as I sat there with my back perfectly straight against the chair-back, conscious that my turbaned head rose much higher than their bare heads. How I was in the moments when I thought I might be having some success at bringing her nearer to me, although I had no indication of that at all other than my own slightly feverish speculations.

One of the things I felt embarrassed and pained about, as I drove down the road, was how I couldn't stop thinking about my illness. Surely my acute consciousness of it showed. It seemed to me that having this illness had added years to my age, and there in that house I had behaved and spoken in ways that weren't appropriate for me. Or maybe my sickness had added a new burden on top of the things that were already weighing heavily on me, leaving me—month after month after month—stuck where I was, unable to alter in the slightest any of what I had gotten so accustomed to saying in front of her. As I was driving, I closed my eyes, snapping my lids down over them suddenly and hard as if to put an end, once and for all, to this kind of thinking that wore me out. Think about something else, we always used to say in Najaf. That was what we advised each other to do even though at the same time we were joking about the stupidity of even giving such advice. Think about something else, Sayyid Mudar would say to me whenever he saw me looking pensive. I would toss his words back at him. You, Sayyid—you think about something else! Of course I was alluding to his everlasting preoccupation with women, which exhausted him and depleted the forces in his body.

Chapter Two

WHAT WOULD GO MISSING IN my body: the answer to this puzzle would require another trip to the clinic, another session standing there facing the doctor behind his desk. One body part, I knew, would not be enough for him. And I knew that all the while he was running through the list of the pieces he would extract from my body, I would be feeling this news like successive little lumps in my throat, to be swallowed not once but again and again. He would stare into my face, that wide-open gaze piercing me. He would pause after every word he said as if he were waiting for me to consent to what he was going to do. Or he would be studying me intently, trying (in a very obvious way) to gauge how bad my qualms were, listening to me stumble uncertainly from one word to the next even though in reality I would have little choice in this matter. I would not really be able to say *no* to anything he suggested. Choosing death over living with a loss of some kind is an event we see only in films or read in novels now and then. Meaning, choosing certain death. I figured that no one who lived before our era could ever be as certain about when and how death would happen as I was now. Those people in the past whom we read about, people who had every reason to expect or even hope to die before long, still knew that a space of time separated them from death. For death was hidden. It lay in their bodies but they didn't know exactly where it was. In the worst of circumstances they could believe that it might happen, or then again, it might not. It could come now or it could wait a year or even a few years. In those days they didn't have doctors who studied images and documents and marked out for their patients—in centimeters, no less—exactly how much distance still remained between them and their deaths. My grandfather Sayyid Murtada went on for many months tossing between life and death. One day those around him would be saying, He will certainly be dead by evening. And then on the next day they would say, Well, he opened his eyes and called out to my Aunt Hasiba to fetch him a glass of water.

Curses on this life, how it stretches out! my grandfather would moan. And then after he had been wakeful and alert for two hours, he would ask her to bring him some food, perhaps it would give his body a little strength. Eat, brother, eat, this will give you strength, she would say, bringing a carefully filled spoon to his mouth.

Eat, eat . . . it will give you strength. This is what I say to my father and he obeys me, for the sake of that slight lingering spark of life, though the amount he eats is never enough to give him the strength even to raise himself off the couch where he has slumped or to utter a word, which goes on rising from his belly up to his throat like a bubble of spume that he can't quite spit out. Eat, Father, this will make you well. Here, this bite will give you some strength. I say these things to him as I gaze into his face, which has gone so pale and wan, his skin as thin and dry and semi-transparent as parchment. I do no different when I start thinking about how this sickly paleness of his might go away, or at least stop getting worse, if only we would take him out every day into the sunshine for an hour or even half an hour. Staying inside alone like this will rot him, I say to my wife when I've finished feeding him and I come out of the room carrying his plate. She no longer even turns to me with that look that says: And so why don't you take him into the sunshine, he's your father, so go on now, take him out there.

Even when they lifted their rifles skyward, preparing to fire, my father strode forward toward them, his hand raised to slap whoever crossed his path first. Not even the sound of the bullets they began firing into the air diverted him. I stepped back, away from him—one step, and then another—as I tried to balance the fear that was sending me into retreat against my sense of shame at leaving him to go ahead on his own. When one of them put the megaphone to his mouth and started threatening us by saying that they were going to start shooting people, I leapt forward but only to grab him by the edges of his cloak to try yanking him back. But I couldn't. I was afraid that I might only agitate him further; that any action I took would just encourage him to surge forward even more quickly, determined to shake off the hand that was trying to hold him back. When they lowered their rifles just enough that the mouths were level with our heads, I don't know exactly how it happened but I let out a scream and began to retreat, now not just a step or two but enough strides that I separated myself completely from the group that still surrounded and followed him, those people who were not frightened by the thought that the soldiers were about to send their bullets roaring into real bodies and heads. I was afraid and ashamed of myself all at the same time. From back there—from where I was now, a distance apart from the last stragglers among those who were following him—that scream came out of me again but now it was addressed to all of them and not only to my father. They'll get you with their bullets! I was shouting. They're going to hit you! I don't know if he heard me, over there in the masses of dust that rose from the ground as soon as he and his companions reached them and began to engage them head on. I could still see him amid the swirls of dust, his tall thin body looming over the others unnaturally as though he were getting as much height as possible in order to bring his hand down sharply onto one of the soldiers. As far as I could make out, they seemed to be in retreat, but they weren't lowering their guns. In the instant when those few bullet shots resounded, producing general mayhem as more people pushed forward furiously toward the soldiers, I thought they had gotten him. Instead of heading directly over there, overcoming my fright, I began shouting again, calling on them to stop. They've killed him! They've killed him, I yelled over and over from where I stood, my fear now mingling with my anger at him and even a feeling of hatred. When the bullets stopped and the turmoil suddenly ceased, I saw him standing in between the two groups in an empty space. He stood alone, and motionless, shifting only those eyes of his as he stared at the ground in front of him. All the people around him were silent and still as well, as if they knew that only a short pause separated them from an encounter in which, they sensed, many of them would be killed.

This was not like shaking his cane in the faces of the card players or coming forward to slap a driver who had all but crushed a child to death. At times like that I would stand only slightly apart from him, waiting for him to finish his task. Indeed, as we walked away together after one of these incidents—companions, side by side—I would even have the feeling that together, the two of us, we had done what had to be done. But that time, in front of the soldiers with their rifles raised, it seemed to me that with every step forward he took, he was pushing me back, facing me with the prospect of plunging to that nadir I dreaded, the ultimate, lowest point of shame, fear, and ignominy.

That day I hated him. I hated the courage that had allowed him to transform his body—he was sixty years old at the time—into that of a young man, a body that could leap forward and jump high, oblivious to his turban and abaya and the prayer beads that never left his hand. At the same time, I was too abashed to go back and stand next to him in the moment when everything went still. It was the two men falling to the ground that had put a sudden halt to the clash between the two parties. He just stood there unmoving, staring at the two of them lying dead on the ground. Hovering there as if he wanted to prevent the men who crowded together a few steps away from coming any closer. He stood fixed in that pose for a long time. It made the soldiers nervous. They were already scared of what they had done. His silence kept everyone in a state of confusion and disarray, not knowing what to do with their anger, how to use it, or how to get rid of it.

I hated him and I hated that boldness of his that had caused the two men's deaths. My first glimpse of the two men's faces was in the newspaper a day or two later. They could not locate a photo for one of them anywhere in his family home. So the newspaper published a photo of him as a dead man. But the photographer snapped it only after they had lifted his head and chest off the ground to make it look as though he were sitting up, like his mate, who was there by his side but looking out from a different photograph.

The two of them had obeyed him so completely that they had left it to him to decide how far to go before stopping. And he went too far, stepping over the line that he should have kept them behind. But he—*he*—had saved himself by stopping at the last minute, the very edge beyond which any action would be reckless and foolhardy. He did not leave it to his anger or to his boldness to make that decision that would have led him to his own death. He knew he must stop here, at the limit beyond which the possibility that he would die became a certainty.

My son Ahmad grinned at me as he jabbed his finger at the white bandage wrapping his head. Then he pointed at my head and I realized that he was comparing his bandage to my wrapped turban, attempting to make a joke and suggesting that now he was just like me. As I gestured to ask him what was under the bandage, my wife said that one of the other lads had hit him with a rock and drawn blood. For his part, to show me his wound he raised both hands, wanting to slide the bandage off his head. No, no! I said, to stop him. I took his hand and steered him into my reception room so he could tell me how it had happened. My wife told me that the boys in the street were hostile and aggressive to him, and to his brother too. When I had him standing in front of my armchair, he used his hands and body to act out for me how the boys had kept him and his brother away because they didn't want to include the two of them in their games. When they—he and his brother—went over to them the boys stopped them by waving their hands around and turning their backs to walk away all together without them. I thought of Jawdat, deaf like them and, like them, unable to speak. I remembered how my playmates had screamed into Jawdat's ear, vying to see which one of them could get his voice into Jawdat's head. After trying this out several times they invariably turned their backs and resumed their playing, keeping him out of their midst. Sometimes they insisted he stay a certain distance away; they measured that distance out by seeing how far the rocks they pelted him with would go.

The one who had hit Ahmad with the rock was much bigger—a head taller than Ahmad was. My son compressed his lips and turned his palms upward when I asked him if he knew who the boy's father was. When I started pressing him to get answers to my questions, he answered with gestures that suggested the boy was very tall and liked to pick fights and always had a scowl on his face. My wife, who was standing near the door, inquired whether I was asking about the boy so that I could go and punish him. I turned to her as if to respond somehow, but then without saying anything—and she had paused there, waiting for me to speak—I turned back to my son Ahmad. I reached for the bandage on his head so that I could see the wound. It was hidden beneath his hair, and it hadn't occurred to my wife to shave the area. No doubt she hadn't made any effort to clean or disinfect it either.

He should have been taken to the doctor, I said, peering more closely at the wound.

I don't have a car, I couldn't take him.

And there's no one around here who has a car?

She didn't answer. I knew she would stare at my face for a few moments, from where she stood near the door, at an angle to me, and then would turn around to go into the kitchen.

Once again I asked him who the boy was and who his father was. And as he repeated the same gestures as before, interspersing them with repeated flourishes of his upturned palms to tell me he wasn't sure, my younger son Ayman came in and began immediately to act out what had happened. He was more energetic about it than his brother had been, and he scowled dramatically as he acted out the way the stone shot from the hand of that tall boy and flew through the air to careen into his brother's head.

Did you feel dizzy? Dizzy? I asked Ahmad, making motions as if to faint, moving as though I would drop to the floor.

He shook his head vehemently.

You, I said, pointing to Ayman, you know . . . . Then I completed my question about the boy's father by making the same gestures. I had to appear concerned, and to question them with a sense of urgency, since that is what families do to make their children feel that they are able to protect them.

When Ayman understood what I was asking, his face took on a pensive expression, like he was trying to remember. To help him out and to show how concerned I was, I lowered my hands to my middle and pressed them in against my waist, trying to ask if the boy was fat or thin. Then I reverted to raising my hands over my head as his brother had done. In response to my insistence, little Ayman raised his hand to his head. His gestures said he would recognize the fellow from his thick disheveled hair, which he pictured for me by blowing air from his mouth while his hands circled rapidly and chaotically around his head.

That didn't mean that I had really gotten Ayman to understand what I was asking. In fact, most often his movements were invented out of thin air because he wanted to convince us that he knew what question he was supposed to be answering. To make certain that I would believe him, he would give his gestures an extra volley of enthusiasm.

Looking in at us from the doorway, my wife said that most of the time the two of them played by themselves. I pictured them in my mind, standing together engrossed in their own silent play while several steps away, a group of boys made a racket with their shouts and their movements.

She stood there motionless next to the door, waiting for me to say something in response to her words. When I remained silent and kept my gaze on Ayman as if to tell him I was once again giving all my attention to what he was telling me, I heard her say, as she turned to go back to the kitchen, It's not your concern. You've got other things to occupy you, after all.

It had not taken her long to get used to the idea of my being an invalid. The last time I had come home she had given no appearance of waiting expectantly for my return in order to hear from me what the doctor had said. And even with my illness she did not stop complaining. She did not stop making those half-obscure insinuations loaded with indirect meaning from which I was supposed to understand that she was still and always carrying around her fatigue, burdened by this life of hers. She could barely endure them, her life and her exhaustion, and yet despite it all she would have to go on bearing up, in the circumstances.

There is no school for them. Neither here nor in Sidon, I said, raising my voice so that she would hear me, even if she was already standing in the kitchen.

I noticed that I was constantly watching myself. I was studying *me* just like a man who has to keep close watch over another man. Out on the street, holding onto my sons, one in each hand, I would have appeared—to someone who might see me from the window of our house, for example—as a timid man. My gait would have told them as much: I looked as though I were trying to conceal or erase every step I took with the step that followed it. I had to drag my sons forward with me, to urge them to go faster, in order to make it clear to them that my intention was to punish the tall boy or at least to face his father directly and speak to him in a commanding, even ominous, voice.

Where were you when he hit you with the rock, where? I asked, illustrating my intention with what I hoped was a suitably threatening expression to go along with my words. We were in the middle of the wide square, about where I figured Ahmad had been when he was struck. I thought he hadn't understood me, so I repeated my question and acted out the scene: the rock being thrown, sailing through the air to hit his head. But he just went on staring at me with that brooding, hooded gaze of his.

I started pressing for an answer, even though I was very aware that I wasn't the kind of man who would take the issue to its logical conclusion anyway. From above, from the balcony of our house, which sat high on its stilts and was now behind us, we would have been a strange sight, standing out there in the middle of the square. Me, my back stooped as my hands grasped both boys firmly, and them balking, both of them, trying to stand their ground and making no response to the flailings of my hands or my expression as I brought my face down and very close to Ahmad's. Here? From here? Is this where he threw it and hit you? I began asking, pointing across the square with a sweep of my arm. Here? Or there, was he over there? My finger now indicated the narrow lane at the end of the square. He made no answer, nor did his brother, who had been so full of zeal when we were still in the house. Ayman had understood his brother's reluctance. Perhaps he knew, with that sort of tacit accord that they shared, that it was better for them to remain reticent.

I tugged on their arms and then I let them go so I could show them my fists, closed and taut. They would sense the strength there and not be afraid. Their fear upset me so much that now I really wanted them to lead me to this lad. I started dragging them over to where the houses began, forgetting—or not caring—how we would appear to anyone who happened to be observing us, especially if they were able to study our faces. Now the two of them walked obediently, complying doggedly with the fierce tug of my hands. When we reached the head of the lane I pointed to one of the houses and asked, Here? Is this the one? Turning to the house facing it, I repeated my words. Dragging them, I walked the entire length of the little street. My anger was growing as I turned from one façade to the next and pointed, again and again. It did occur to me, as furious as I was, that I would not know what to say if anyone opened their door and saw me like this, propelling my two sons along in front of their home.

Did you find him?

She had left the door open so that she could ask her question the instant I appeared at the top of the outside steps. I didn't answer. My fury had tired me out because it had pulled me away from the person I was. Anyway, she didn't say another word. She meant her contempt to just hang there in the air, an oblique presence, fleeting enough that I would not really even be able to respond.

It wasn't that she was ignoring my illness or forgetting its presence. When I lingered in the doorway to the reception room she waved to the two boys to stay outside rather than going in with me. He wants to be alone, she muttered in a tight voice that they would not even have heard as she turned to shepherd them along in front of her to another room, away from me. No, it isn't that she overlooked or forgot my sickness. The way I saw it, she had demoted my illness from the position it ought to have gone on occupying, there at the front of her brain, and had left it to find its own little corner in that confused and complicated mass of thoughts at the very bottom of her head.

Your father didn't stop vomiting until mid-afternoon, she commented, this time not even coming near the doorway.

And now? Is he still vomiting?

Go and see for yourself.

The children, all three of them, were massed in that narrow space at the end of the corridor, leaving the door closed between him and them. I stopped there a moment to pinch Hiba's cheek.

She was sitting on her little chair, submitting to the slow advance of the large comb that Ayman was pulling through her hair.

I'm here, Father. I've come.

Everything around him looked clean. He sat slumped over, but his dishdasha wasn't soiled and there was nothing on the floor directly in front of him. But I did catch a whiff of vomit that soap and water hadn't succeeded in suppressing. When I bent over, wanting to get close to him, and brought my face near his, the residue of that odor got stronger.

We will change your dishdasha, Father, I said, keeping my eyes on his face as though I was waiting for him to agree.

He didn't answer. That is, he didn't make any of those usual responses of his that I understood and that told me what he wanted. He didn't raise his head, for instance, even that minimal movement that let me know he was awake and had heard me and understood what I had just said. He kept his eyes lowered, fixed somberly on the fabric of his dishdasha where it covered his legs.

We'll change the dishdasha . . . we'll do that now, we'll get you a clean dishdasha.

In his periods of alertness he would give his body an almost imperceptible shake, which meant that he was preparing himself for what I was about to do. This time, though, he remained exactly as he was, hands gripping the armrests, head bowed as though he were deep in thought or had fallen asleep sitting there.

This smell, we'll get rid of it, I said, which was my way of declaring that we would do that but at the same time of asking—as I did with everything I said to him—whether he agreed.

We'll bathe you right here, I said, twisting back to look at him as I was already turning to go out.

A few moments later I came back in, shutting the door behind me. The water is heating up, I said. Just a few more minutes and it will be hot. I didn't know if he could smell his own vomit, but with his head bent like this it would be hard to escape that smell, hovering there around the lowest part of his chest. I wondered whether keeping his head bent so low was his way of announcing that he had decided to shut down all his senses, or at least to bolt the door against the possibility that anything might reach him by means of his senses.

Here's the water. Hot water.

I set the little plastic tub down on the floor in front of him, as close as I could to where he sat. And we'll keep the door closed, I said as I retraced my steps to shut it. When I came back, ready to take off his dishdasha, he jerked his head upward—so suddenly that it seemed as if this movement was unexpected even to him—and he looked straight at me. But seconds later, his expression seemed to say he regretted this moment of alertness. He shut his eyes again after seeming to glance momentarily at the objects nearest to him.

I'm going to lift you now. Help me to raise you up.

He was so light that it only took one hand to keep him lifted slightly off his seat. After I had brought his dishdasha up above his waist I sat him down again, his legs exposed. The bare skin attracted his attention. He stared at his legs. Maybe he was surprised by how pale they were or how thin they had become.

I took him unawares, too, telling him to lift his arms so that I could pull the dishdasha off him entirely, tugging it from his chest and over his head. He had shifted his eyes from his legs to my face, as if he had just recalled something he wanted to ask me. It lasted only a second or two before he lowered his gaze. His eyes remained fixed on the floor as if he were deep in thought.

With the loofa, I'm just going to wash you with the loofa, I said, rubbing soap onto it. He sat there naked, so very thin that I had the feeling it could not be only his flesh and skin that had shrunk and thinned but his bones as well. He kept his gaze there, on whatever it was he was thinking about, and he remained utterly motionless.

We mustn't spill any water on your easy chair, I said as I rubbed his chest with the loofa. He was so gaunt that his chest looked hollowed out, giving his belly in contrast an even more pronounced roundness, like a little toy ball. As I moved the loofa to his arms and then down to his hands and fingers, I realized that before he had become ill and I had brought him to my home, I had never seen any part of his body, not his chest, not his back, not even his arms. Maybe they had always been like that, as sallow as the arms of a chronic, bedridden invalid.

The respite that separated what I was now from what I would be after the operation was not fixed. It wasn't a specific period of time set by the doctor. He did not tell me to come back in a week, for example, or in a month or in two months. He left that to me. He left it to me to measure the distance between who I still was and the moment when my illness would kill me. As for what I could rely on to form my own estimation, that came down to my sense of the words he had used with me and his manner of speaking; how he had said those things to me, all of this preserved in my memory, word for word. According to that language of his—and that little smile, from which he could not erase a touch of the cunning that was a mark of his profession—I could see that he was leaving it to me to subtract a little from, or add a little to, the period of time before returning to the hospital, which I had figured could be a month.

A month: and I could lengthen it a little, letting it eat into the next month. That way, I could reason that I was getting a little more benefit from the remaining time I had in which I could still think of myself as physically whole. What the doctor in effect told me was: Just take a month for yourself. That was so that I could compensate, in that one month, for what I would no longer be capable of doing afterwards. We use the days that remain to us profitably when we truly know that we have to use them fully. That was the doctor's thinking, I reckoned. From some film I had seen once, I remembered the doctor who told his patient he had six months left. So we will go to the Bahamas, the man responded, turning to his wife who was standing there next to him. He had already prepared himself for this, even before he fell ill, and certainly before he knew he would die. Maybe he smiled, there in front of the doctor, or his wife smiled. For they—she and her husband—would spend the time that remained to him in the best way possible.

As for me, I would spend this respite—this one month for me—wondering whether it would be better for me to go the next morning to the doctor and offer myself up to him then and there. Because I wouldn't be able to shake off the feeling that what would take place a month from now would be better taking place right now. I thought this way because I wanted to be rid of the worry and the fear of it all, but also because I couldn't help being curious. Those feelings pressed on me, insisting that what I wanted most was to find out what I would be like after it, were I to survive the operation. Were I not to die.

I knew I must guard against showing any hesitation or indecision in front of my wife: saying to her for instance that I would be going to the hospital the next day and then not going. Instead of telling her I'm going to the hospital and then she finds me back in the house only an hour later, I thought, I will put my hesitation to the test on my own. So here I am, turning the key in the ignition and backing away from our house. Here I am going all the way out of the village, leaving the last houses behind me as I reach the main road. But there my fear gets the better of me, putting an end to my indecision by telling me to stop the car. I turn it to head in the opposite direction and it carries me back to the house. There, my wife will not ask, Where were you? She is accustomed to my comings and goings, from one hamlet to the next.

My wavering over what decision to make was not the only thing sending me down to the car and out on those little trips from which I returned before they were completed. What pushed me even more was my restlessness and my sense of irritation with the house, an aversion to sitting there at home.

It got so bad that, with every return, the moment I arrived I felt instantly how much I loathed it. Even from the outside, not just when I was indoors. I despised the faded, badly leaning outside wall that hid the balcony and the high windows looking directly down onto the square and the passersby below. When I came back from Najaf, this house was already prepared. My father had said that it was the appropriate house for me. All I had to do was to respond that it would suit me, as though I had chosen it myself. What pleased him wasn't just the privacy of a house set high above the road and walled in, but also its proximity to the mosque. If people didn't find me there, they would find me here. He knew I would not be like him, always moving about, circling through the villages.

Just over there is the shop, it is very close by, he said, as the two porters lowered my belongings from the truck. He strode toward the shop certain that I would follow him. Here's where he is, he said as he waved his cane at the shop owner. He didn't complete this gesture for the man; he didn't announce to the shopkeeper that from today, I would be the imam of this little place. He came out and began walking me through the narrow lanes he knew.

As-salaamu alaykum, people murmured as we appeared, greeting us before we could greet them, as was proper; standing up as we drew near and remaining on their feet as we passed, while all he did was to raise his stick as if it was acting on his behalf, responding to their greetings. It was clear to me how, in all of his dealings with people, he didn't think ahead. He made these hazardous judgments of his about what to do. On the day of the confrontation with the soldiers, this was what had led to the deaths of the two men.

I wasn't capable of getting my voice to respond—Peace be upon you as well—on behalf of the two of us. I just lifted my hand to my chest and then to my head, once and then once more: the first time for myself, and then again for him. He wouldn't have seen me doing it, because he would have already stridden ahead. When we walked together he always stayed a step ahead of me.

Many years passed before I could explain to myself what he had meant when he said those words to me in one of those moments when he was giving me advice. A person's faith is not mature until he knows that people are no better than animals. He said this to me in the days when I was first standing behind the pulpit, my voice coming out weak and tentative as I faced the people seated in the Hussainiya. I couldn't feel satisfied interpreting that saying of his simply as an expression of scorn for human beings. I went on turning it over in my mind, reflecting on its various aspects, now linking it to Sufi sayings, now thinking it must have been pronounced by some orthodox jurisprudent, now deciding it had to do with the demands placed on anyone wholly immersed in his faith. On those days when he would emerge from his room—there in his house—crossing beyond the paved area before the garden to go out to the road where he stood—just stood—with his back to the door in the wall, his demeanor would make it clear that he was not a man to return the greetings of any man who might walk by. Those passing by understood this, and so all they did was to mutter their salaams without even raising their eyes to his face.

This is your house. This is your house and it is exactly the right house for you, he said to me back then. And he took me around to the people here as though he needed to show me to them but there was no need to do anything more than that.

I did not say to him that I would have preferred to choose my own house, or that I wanted to get to know people on my own, now that I had become the imam of their mosque.

Ahlan, ahlan. Welcome to the Sayyid, she said as usual. But she sounded surprised.

I didn't move. I stayed standing in the doorway as though I needed to ascertain for myself whether I ought to go in.

I've been wanting to see Bilal. So I thought I would come by and pick him up, and take him to our house.

Please, come in. Come in, Sayyid, she said, standing aside to make room for me to enter.

The instant I was inside I knew that she was alone. That made me hesitate but I kept walking, heading for my usual perch. She too sat down in her usual place, turning her face to me as she tugged her skirt down to cover her bare knees.

He went out with his schoolmates. If he had known you were coming . . . .

I didn't say anything.

Coffee, Sayyid?

This time I did not glance at my watch. I didn't make a point of looking as though I had to check on how much time I had.

But perhaps you were getting ready yourself to go out?

No . . . no . . . I'm here . . . I'm staying here, she said, getting up and straightening her skirt again.

She was on her way to the kitchen and I stole my usual glance, quickly at first, and then a second and slightly less fleeting look. Still, it was just a tiny glimpse. She wouldn't turn back and see me do it, I was certain, even if by chance it occurred to her suddenly that there was something she wanted to say. I was confident of this because I had an inkling that she sensed it, falling on her, that look, there, trained on the expanse of bare leg which she had left uncovered.

From in there, and before she lit the flame under the coffeepot, she said something to me about Bilal. When I didn't answer, she repeated it in a louder voice. He's been getting his things ready for the past two days. He's going to the camp with his mates.

Are they schoolmates?

She didn't answer right away. Then she said that they were all in his year.

I thought about going in to where she was. About going into the kitchen. This time I will get up, I told myself, willing

59

myself to pair the thought in my head with the movement of my body. To get up, exactly at the moment when it occurs to me to get up; to not stay as I am, only thinking about moving and instead staying absolutely still precisely where I am and waiting for her to return.

I got up. I had a strong urge to take these first few steps of mine, here, that she would hear. That she would hear as different, and then that she would see. She would see that I had really taken these steps. She would take her eyes off the coffeepot to see it. I did take those steps that, once they headed me in a certain direction, could not swerve or retreat. These steps of mine that resounded with all of the heaviness that was in me, mounting from my abaya and my turban and my beard, but not ending with this foolhardy venture of mine, an attempt to appear to her somehow differently, and as she had never known me.

To do something there, to employ my hands in some useful way, in whatever way they would help me out. But the cups were already there on the tray, and the coffeepot was on the burner. The sight of it stopped me at the doorway into the kitchen, a pause heavy with my own expectations, waiting for myself to say something, or to hear something.

Is anything upsetting you, Sayyid? She spoke without lifting her eyes from the coffeepot which she was monitoring closely.

This initiative on her part, which was meant to help me out, wasn't coming this time from her strength, I thought. It was a response to the discomfiture we both felt—she and I alike—at how close I was standing to her.

The coffee has boiled, she said, but more as if she were talking to herself. She set the coffeepot down on the tray next to the cups; but then she paused as if she had to think about what she should do next.

I'll carry it in, I said, taking a step forward.

No, no . . . , she said, her hands gripping the tray firmly as she turned toward me. Now I was the one who didn't know what to do. I didn't know whether it was better to step aside so that she could go by me, or to walk ahead into the sitting room to clear the way for her.

Ahlan wa-sahlan to the Sayyid, she said, striding forward and leaving me to follow her. She repeated her words of welcome as she bent to set the little tray down on the table between us. And I, who could understand that very ordinary welcome in any way I pleased, was thinking that my sitting here, this time, somehow must not be a copy of all my previous visits.

Are you upset about something, Sayyid? She had already sat down and was bringing the coffee tray closer.

For the second time she had substituted *upset* for *afraid*. What she should have repeated was that very first question of hers: Afraid . . . are you afraid? She looked at me, wanting to see, as well as to hear, how I would respond. What I would say about how upset and frustrated I was, and how it was my whole life that upset me, not just my feelings on this day that had driven me to her home so unexpectedly.

Upset . . .

I didn't know how to answer, even though by phrasing her question in this way she had steered the conversation to where I wanted it to be. Now it was up to me to confess my feelings of weariness and frustration. That was exactly what I wanted to do and what I meant to do. Perhaps like nothing else, such a confession, or complaint, like this one could be a means to carry us away from our usual cautious and circumspect exchanges, which kept us so very far apart from each other, each in our own solitary space.

Upset, yes, and other things, I said, not knowing quite how to launch my quest for something that could form the beginning of a real conversation. I was immediately conscious that I hadn't prepared anything to say to her. And, worse, that I was not capable of inventing anything. All a man like me could do was to try his best to come a little closer to her. To be less detached, only as far apart as the space that brings her hand close to his. That is, to begin from the place where I yearned to begin.

That's what she was waiting for. I knew it from the way we were silent together. It was a silence that held the two of us in suspension, as if we had already surrendered to a certainty that what we were doing was going to lead us to something other than speech. I knew also that when she got to her feet after that spell of silence, holding her cup of coffee between her hands, she would go out of the room but only to reappear a moment later. She would be giving me another chance to make my attempt.

What I must begin with is her hand . . . or her hair. I could just put my hand up and brush it lightly against her hair. I could run my palm across the top of her head and downward the whole length of those evenly cut locks of hair.

She came back and sat down a little closer to me. But not so close that I could be certain of anything. It was as though she was letting me know that this first step, which meant shouldering the responsibility for whatever might arise from the recklessness of it, had to be mine.

She wanted to preserve the weight of the silence between us. She didn't break it in order to say just anything. Only her hands moved, in synchrony, grasping the little coffee cup and raising it to her lips and then lowering it to sit motionless once again in her hands.

In that instant—the moment when caution collapses into risk—the pale skin of her hand and the bright red color she had painted her fingernails were what brought my hand closer. Desire, rather than a decision taken to go ahead. Desire. That was what pulled my hand to hers. I enclosed her hand in mine and our clasped hands dropped to hang halfway between us in that emptiness between us. I noticed how she turned her face to me, but I couldn't tell if her expression and the tilt of her head meant she was annoyed or simply quizzical. But she kept her hand in mine, motionless and inert as though the force I had seen in her lived only in my fancy.

It only lasted a few seconds. Her hand slipped out of mine and encircled her coffee cup, which must have been empty by now. Her face, which should have told me something, displayed only that confusing smile that didn't help me to understand anything, since it gave no explanations.

Had she wanted her hand in mine? Had she accepted this from me? Did she accept it but want to say that this was enough for one day? Had she left her hand to me out of pure embarrassment? Or was this just one of those signals women give that entice men at the same time they warn them off?

Even before she got up to look out the window, pausing before she opened it to let in some air, I already knew it would not be good for me to repeat what I had done just now. But at the heart of my confusion, spurring my questions, was the reality that she had let her hand rest quietly in mine for two seconds, or maybe three, or four or ten or more, it didn't matter how many if I could feel that it had gone on long enough.

As I drove slowly down the road her smile came back to me—now reassuring, now one of acceptance, now sly. What would I do the next time; from what point would I start? I had no idea. What I did know is that whatever I did, I would not lead up to it with words. Silently I would come in. She would be just as silent as she fell back from the door to let me enter. In silence we would sit down on that sofa and after a short interval we would shift position, so that we were slightly closer to each other. Pondering all of this in the car, I realized that I had nothing at all to say to her. Not even a single word. It wasn't a question of that sort of complimentary chitchat on her health, or about how Bilal was doing, but the other kind of speech, the kind of talk that lovers continuously prepare in their heads in anticipation that there will come a time when these words can be said.

I have nothing at all inside of me to say to her, I thought. Not one word. What I felt toward her as I sat there in my car was nothing more than my own desire for what I imagined the reaches of her body to be, those parts of it I had seen as well as those I hadn't. To look at each different region of it, my eyes close; and to stroke it as though to confirm for myself that I had achieved that closeness for which I so yearned.

That was it. I was not expecting her to say the kind of words that I should then respond to appropriately in an exchange that would leave me looking at her with some sort of bemused contentment afterwards. The kind of words that force the eyes closed momentarily as though they have to let this dream waft through the mind without anything troubling or corrupting it. The sort of talk that, after hearing it, would give me no choice but to take her in my arms.

I knew that if I could say something, whispering it into her ear so that only she could hear, and something I really meant, it would be: I love every square centimeter of your body. Just exactly like that and nothing more, falling back on vocabulary I had memorized in my schooldays.

My car journey halfway over, as I got farther away from her house I found myself resisting the idea of going anywhere that was a part of the life I knew. Not to the house—not to my home—and not to the mosque where I was also expected to be. Not even to drive through the streets and alleys that I often resorted to in my car when I needed to get away from things. I did not want this dream I had had—or this victory of mine, as I saw it—to be interrupted by anything that was familiar from my everyday life. Still heading toward the house, I swiveled my head in both directions at every intersection as if I was trying to choose the one that would best satisfy my needs. I would move the steering wheel slightly but then as the car swerved I would straighten it out and continue on my way down the main road. Here . . . or here . . . no, here, I muttered as I proceeded on to another intersection, farther on down the road, where I might park my car just off the main thoroughfare if the spot seemed pleasant enough. There, still in sight of the main road, I would just sit in my car, still enjoying the sound of the moving air that I would go on hearing after shutting the engine off.

It was not as if I could forget my illness just because something else was filling my head. It would still be there, crouching in the same location inside my body, a mass of matter whose size I could only approximate vaguely by opening my fist and stretching my fingers as wide as they would go. The mass sat there at the bottom of my stomach, quiet sometimes but then growing bolder as though those tiny huddled organisms that made up this density were stirring, and simmering, and then boiling over as some organisms rushed ahead of the rest and brought it all erupting to the surface. When that happened I had to get up. I had to walk, pacing slowly in one direction, and then taking the same number of steps back. Or, when that effervescent struggle inside of me flared up until it became too bad to ignore, I went down to my car and sat inside as the tug-of-war intensified. I would stick the key into the ignition and turn it quickly as though I meant to stay ahead of the turmoil that all of this movement inside of me was creating.

For the sake of keeping myself in the race, I would have to be very quick. As the mass feels like it is ascending all the way to my head, making me dizzy, I try to treat it with my own imaginings that are also fighting each other. Into the midst of it I introduce, among the objects I'm imagining, those shiny little medical instruments that treat you and are supposed to cure you, as well as pills that are tiny but so powerful that surely what they contain must have an otherworldly origin.

Even though I had some sort of premonition that this disease would find me, it was still a surprise. No one among my clan had died of a disease at this age. My grandfather Sayyid Murtada lived so long that he could be heard exclaiming how everyone he knew had died. My uncle Sayyid Aqil was killed by old age and its infirmities, while my aunt Hasiba didn't slow down at all even after she turned seventy. Every time he saw her approaching our home, my father would call out to her, Slow down! Slow down, Hasiba. You are seventy now! But the only thing that could kill her was one of those vehicles she used to climb into early in the morning to go out to one of the villages where she would spend several days in the homes of people she knew, doling out various fatwas she had memorized. Our venerable grandfather Sayyid Abd al-Husayn was the sage of his era, she would proclaim to her hosts. Or she would recite a fatwa handed down from some other ancestor of ours that went counter to what one of the senior religious authorities in Najaf had decreed—on the topic (for instance) of what was to be done in the case of a woman separating from her husband. They were all ancient, those people she invoked, but they went on living inside the stories she told about them and the things they had said that she passed on. I could not imagine them except as gray-haired figures stooped by the heaviness of their turbans. Alone among them all, I had been afflicted while still at this age. Surely it had happened to me because of my fear of illness. That fear, ever-present in my mind, made it seem as though I was beckoning the disease to come to me, or as though my unshakable foreboding that it lived in me kept it going until it really did become a real disease. Those who came before me, to the contrary, believed a man dies after he has aged. Their bodies believed them. And so their bodies obeyed them.

There are special schools for deaf children, she said.

One of the teachers here had told her so.

I know, I said, as I tossed my car keys down on the side table.

Have you known for a long time?

Everyone knows about them.

Why didn't you say anything, if you knew about them?

Because the boys are still young.

What do you mean, young? Boys their age started school more than two years ago.

Schools for the deaf don't take children that young, I told her. I was waiting until they got a bit older because I didn't want to send them off, and all the way to Beirut, when they were as young as this. Every time I imagined getting them out of the car and taking out their belongings, I would feel such sympathy and misery that I couldn't stand it. I could only imagine it as a scene of abandonment, with me leaving them alone and in the hands of someone who would not know how to treat them.

You just aren't interested. Because you never have to listen to them, that shrieking all day long.

I found it odd that she called the sounds they made shrieking. As if the only significant thing about the sounds she heard coming out of her sons was how annoying they were and how they gave her such bad headaches.

Today again they had a fight with the boys. Ahmad came home crying.

Which boys?

The boys, she repeated, as though she had to remind me of what she had just said a second ago.

I mean, which ones, what boys?

I don't know . . . all of the boys. She was standing in the doorway to the reception room, the threshold she never crossed except when she was bringing in the tray to set it down on the table, after which she always went out immediately.

The teacher said she would go with me, if I take them there, to the school for the deaf.

No, I will take them, I said, putting my hands down firmly on either side to lift myself up from the sofa. She knew this meant I was announcing that I was finished with the business at hand and that she must go out and leave me alone. But this time she did not go out. Not before saying—having raised her hand as if she were repeating an oath—that she was not going to leave the two of them like this any longer, in a state where they were not learning anything.

Out there in the kitchen she gave vent to her irritation and she made certain it was heard. The noises coming from there told me she was banging everything her hands picked up and slamming things around. The arrival of the two boys a few minutes later with their sister in tow just increased the loud fury of the show she was making.

Come! Come, now come, she began repeating as she pushed them all forward into the room where I sat. When she had made certain they were standing immediately in front of me, she clutched the doorknob and slammed the door shut.

The boys stood there staring at me. Their sister shifted her gaze from me to them as if she were waiting for something to happen, some action that must follow from the fact that they were all standing together in front of me like this. The two boys were also expecting something. Otherwise, why would their mother have pushed them so hard all the way in here, not letting go until they were standing directly in front of me? They looked afraid that I was going to call them to account. They seemed worried that their mother had denounced them to me for something they had done.

I didn't want to prolong their nervous wait. I put my hand out to Ahmad, expecting him to respond likewise by shaking my hand. He did so and then I tried to give him some additional reassurance by smiling at him, inviting him to grin back at me. Hiba was looking from me to them and from them to me, not understanding what was going on. Where's your doll? I asked her, as I reached out to clasp her empty hands. She didn't answer. Instead, she turned to her brother Ahmad and looked up at him. The missing doll came into my head, with its soiled hands, its straw-like hair and its vacant smile.

Still the two boys stood there solemnly, waiting and wondering. For a moment I panicked, thinking I didn't know how to chase away their wariness. I put out my hand to Ayman this time, aiming for his upper arm. I wanted to look like I was testing the strength of his muscles. He didn't tighten them immediately as he usually did. He was waiting to see if my little game with him was genuine. He needed me to shake his arm not once but twice before he tightened the muscles just slightly. His face remained unchanged, both questioning and watching.

Finally, when I saw that they were still standing there stiffly even after I had stood up, I began thinking their mother must have done something to frighten them. I left them as they were, standing and waiting, and went to ask her, there in the tiny vestibule outside the two bedrooms.

Yes I spanked them, she said. For stealing.

Who did you spank?

The two boys.

The boys, stealing? Both of them?

Maybe Ahmad was pulling the wool over his brother's eyes. But it was the two of them who took the household money.

And you spanked . . .?

I spanked both of them and locked them in their room, and I made them understand that you would discipline them when you got back.

What did they do with the money?

They didn't even try to hide the chocolate bars they bought at the shop. They even gave their sister her share so she could eat half of it and then smear the front of her dress all the way down, with the other half. They stole, and they lied too, said their mother. They had told her that the shopkeeper gave them the chocolate bars without taking any money from them.

When I went back into the reception room where they were still standing, she followed me. I went in but she stopped in the doorway. I stared back at her to make her understand that I wanted to be alone with them. I felt a lot of sympathy for the boys. I could imagine them cradling the chocolate bars, carrying them as they walked across the square from the shop to the house. I felt even more sympathy for the misery of their situation when it dawned on me that their joint participation in this theft just showed how alone the two of them were, with no one making any effort to even come near them.

I put an appropriately serious expression on my face. But, trying to give them some advice, I couldn't maintain my stern demeanor. The terror that Ahmad had tried to conceal was slowly revealing itself on his features. That reminded me of Jawdat, who always looked alarmed and scared. As boys, back then, we always used to say that when Jawdat laughed, it sounded like he was scared to death. It was that same look, terrified and silly all at once, that I was seeing on Ahmad's face: the lips stretched wide but with no suggestion of a smile or even a question. I couldn't make them understand what they needed to understand. That stealing was wrong. It was wrong and shameful and forbidden. It wasn't that this was hard to explain with the usual hand and body movements, but rather that I couldn't endure this scene any longer, seeing them holding themselves rigid like this, wary and frightened.

Their sister Hiba had tired of standing still, her only movement to look from one face to the other. She made a move to leave by scurrying toward the corridor but I asked her to come back. Run this way, not that! Because, I said, we were all going to go on a little errand in the car. When she came back in and was standing in front of me, she gave me a pointed look that I figured meant she was asking me if we could take the doll along. With a succession of gestures I got the boys to understand that we were not going to stay in here, frozen in place. We were going out. In the car. To get some fresh air.

The boys tussled over seats until Ayman gave in and allowed his brother to sit in the front. I picked up Hiba and put her in the seat directly behind me so that all three were sitting next to a window and could look out at whatever we passed on our way. The ball that Ayman had brought along, dented and half deflated, increased my feelings of sympathy. Suddenly it occurred to me—and I had never realized this before—that every time, in the past but in the future too, that he kicked this ball, he would never hear the quick whoosh that tells you how strong the kick is. He wouldn't even know the sound existed. He had no idea what it was like.

I had learned how to take myself away from such thoughts when they hit me unawares as they usually did. I put my hand out for the ball and tugged at it, trying to extract it from the arm that was wrapped so tightly around it. I raised it to eye level and began turning it over and over as I put on an expression of disgust and gloom. Then I made as if to throw it out my open window. Ayman responded to my playing by crouching in his seat ready to spring up to snatch the ball away from me. I moved it out of his reach, maneuvering it so he would think he couldn't take it from my hands. This delighted his brother too. Ahmad smiled, his eyes following the ball, and he tried to position himself to snatch it from my hands with a quick, darting movement. The game captured me as much as it did them. So much so that even after their outstretched hands were holding fast to one of mine, I did indeed throw the ball out my window. I drove the car on at normal speed for a few seconds as though I had no intention of going back to find it where it had fallen.

I managed to communicate to them that we were going to pick up Bilal at his place. Telling them this, I was conscious that I was claiming my share of our little jaunt. But I started telling myself that this would entertain them and make them feel better. If they simply went on sitting like this in the car, their interest would soon flag and they wouldn't even go on looking out at the passing scenes. Their enthusiasm had already peaked by the time I was able to get it across to them that now we were truly on the way to Bilal's house. Ahmad began almost standing up in his seat, and then collapsing down into it again, in a series of abrupt little lurches. His dramatic movements seemed aimed at telling his younger brother what Ayman had probably understood from the start. In the rearview mirror Ayman's face looked really grubby and his mop of hair was no better, looking stiff and ropy and dry. I was also conscious that, next to me, Ahmad's sandals didn't conceal any of the dust and filth that coated his feet. For a second I thought I had been too hasty promising them this stop. I began wondering about not taking them with me to Bilal's home, leaving them instead to play in a nearby plot of land while I went by myself to fetch him. But I decided against the idea, not so much out of a fear that she would figure out exactly what had pushed me to leave them behind and alone but because I worried that something might happen to them if I left them on their own in an unfamiliar place.

I don't know why it was that the ball, bearing so many scars of hard use, seemed to me the most scandalous thing of all, much more so than anything the children could show on their own bodies. The ball looked so scruffy. I reached again to take it from Ayman's hands but this time I stuffed it under my seat, having tried to get them to understand that I wanted to deflate it completely. With both hands I sketched the outlines of a fully inflated ball and then I nodded and flashed them a smile to show them I approved of my imaginary ball's clean and robust roundness. I wanted them to know that soon they would be playing with a brand-new ball. Still, at the back of my head the whole time was an awareness that coming here with them was simply a pretext for me. We had come here, I would announce—attempting to hide my discomfort with myself—because I knew they missed their cousin.

I stayed seated in the car when we arrived and I kept them in their seats as well. I waited a little after sounding the horn to see who would peer out around the door—Bilal or her, his mother. The door opened and Bilal flew out, already knowing we were there because he had seen us through the window. He came straight to the open windows of the car but hesitated as though he were uncertain which window he ought to pause in front of first. Then he began darting from one car door to another as if he intended to open them all. Bilal, Bilal! I said—to stop him, because I was suddenly realizing that I had to have a plan: what was I going to do with them? My mother is here, he said to me, reducing the number of choices that were whirling around in my head. Still, he stopped and waited for me to tell him what to do.

The Sayyid is welcome, she said from where she stood in the open doorway. She was wearing an off-white robe over her nightclothes. All that was visible of her pyjamas were the collar edges, which were open enough only to reveal a tiny sliver of skin high on her chest.

Help them get out, Bilal, she said from where she stood.

They were acting a bit embarrassed about getting out of the car. Ahmad stayed in his seat, not climbing down when Bilal opened his door and stood there holding it open. And Ayman was still in his seat when I opened the door on his sister's side and took her out, clutching her doll. From where *she* stood, there in front of the door, she started talking to Hiba. She would give her something sweet to eat, she said, and then she came closer to where we all were standing, none of us moving.

How are you, Sayyid? she asked as she approached me but with her eyes still on Hiba. I had been preparing myself for the possibility that she would come as close to me as she was now as she opened her arms to take Hiba from me. I wanted to be ready for a nearness that I could savor, silently but with full awareness of it as it was happening. I didn't want this nearness to occur so suddenly that it was gone before I could be ready to enjoy it. I did take in the sensation of it, the fragrance and the feel of it, even if this closeness was nothing more than the proximity of the clothes she was wearing to the abaya I wore.

She walked toward the house carrying my daughter and expecting us to follow. Bilal was exchanging gestures with the boys, carefully distributing his greetings between them and looking from one to the other. When he saw that they weren't budging, but were still plastered against the car, he asked me to sign to them that they could go with him into the house. They were waiting for my permission. Not to leave them in uncertainty, I went ahead of them, taking a few slow steps after having beckoned them to follow me.

Yallah, I said, with a light slap against the car door. The two boys were following me so closely that they couldn't take a step until I did so. Then as I went inside, they were lagging behind me by two or three steps while Bilal, smiling at their extreme shyness, was urging them to move forward by pressing his hand between their shoulder blades, first one boy and then the other.

She had sat down on the sofa in her usual place at one end, and with a damp washcloth she was wiping Hiba's face. I felt I must say something about why the boys were so dirty, too. But I changed my mind about what to say. I had been on the point of explaining that since early morning their mother had been busy with housework. But instead I just asked Bilal to take them into the bathroom and wash their faces. When I sat down in my usual corner of the sofa, she turned to me to show me how clean Hiba's face was now. And so pretty! she exclaimed, her words directed at Hiba. Then she announced that she was about to round out her task, telling Hiba that now the two of them would clean the doll's face.

They rubbed and scrubbed the doll's face repeatedly until the darkest smudges, the ones on her cheeks, had gotten lighter. But their efforts erased the pinkish tint of the doll's rubber face, leaving it a bleached-out, pockmarked white. When she turned the doll's face toward my daughter, Hiba looked confused and unhappy. She doesn't like it, she said, gazing intently at Hiba. She asked Hiba whether her doll looked pretty now but the only answer she got was silence, as Hiba stared into her doll's face. Turning again toward me, she said that she didn't have any girls' toys in her house. I delayed a little before getting to my feet and going over to take Hiba from her arms, which would mean regaining that momentary closeness to the pair of hands that had been embracing Hiba. As I did this, I tried to say that she must have found it tiring to carry my daughter around and to hold her like this.

As soon as I had picked up Hiba the two boys came into the room, trailing Bilal who was carrying all the parts for putting together a train and track. Hiba immediately started wriggling in my arms, wanting to be put down so that she could join them to inspect what Bilal's quick hands were creating. Once we were a bit apart from the children, she remarked that Bilal's intense attachment to this toy had made her feel so powerless that she had taken it all apart and hidden the pieces, back in the days when he was still so obsessed with it.

And now? Are you hoping to see that it's beyond repair?

With a laugh she got up from the couch and asked if I would like coffee.

Right now, nothing, I said. I stuck my hand out, trying to seize her by the hand in something that would look like a simple gesture to get her to sit down again. My action surprised her, even flustered her. Still on her feet, she said to me—leaving her hand in mine—that she would drink coffee along with me.

This was all that was needed, I thought. What I'd wanted out of my bid to take her hand was not precisely or specifically to test how receptive she would be but to make a tiny bit of progress beyond where I'd been when I reached for her hand on my previous visit.

We'll have coffee, she said, smiling as she freed her hand from mine.

I didn't want anything more than some indication of how receptive she was feeling. I knew I had to judge this for myself since I hadn't been lucky enough to stumble on a sure indication that I had succeeded in achieving what I thought I might have achieved.

Coffee, Sayyid, she said as she approached with the tray in her hands. I busied myself bringing the table close enough that the coffee would be within our reach and meanwhile she sat down, a little nearer to me than her usual position at the far end of the sofa. With the way I had positioned the table, and given where she was sitting, her hands as she lifted the pot and poured the coffee were closer to me than to her. I noticed that she was performing this task very slowly, as if to prolong the interval in which I could study her hands at such proximity.

There it is, she said, meaning the sound of the train. As soon as it began moving down the track it also began to whistle, a warning that anything standing too near had better move away.

As the toy train charged down its little track, my boys began hooting and clapping in delight. When I came over to where they were all squatting around the track, my hands still around my coffee cup, Ahmad immediately looked up at me as if he wanted to transfer the glee he felt at what he was seeing to me. Quickly he went back to following the moving train with his eyes as it sped up going around the sharp turns, giving the impression that it was about to jump right off the track. Also carrying her coffee cup, she joined us and we all watched the train avidly. She was standing next to me. She was getting ready to say something to me about the boys, I thought, since it would be odd for her not to say even a word or two about the state they were in.

My father knew I was ill. Those eyes appeared so oblivious to everything, as though whatever they saw just floated on the surface of his pupils and didn't penetrate to his mind. But his eyes were still capable, it seemed, of capturing images and then preserving them somewhere deep inside. That flash of light: even if I didn't actually witness it I would know it was there, just like a camera bulb that will produce a photo. And now he would be holding the image and he would have many hours to ponder it.

Every day, all day long, he would have nothing to occupy himself with except going back, again and again, to whatever thoughts and images had forced their way into his head. Whenever he tipped his face upward to stare at me, I knew that now he was affirming, and checking, and reaffirming, the information he already thought he knew.

Your father never did calm down today. He kept looking around, and was forever putting his hands on his armrests as if he meant to lift himself up. As if he thought he would get to his feet.

When I went in he was still jerking his head this way and that nervously. But once I got close enough to him that he could make out the shape of my body, he stopped twitching and began to look more like he was lying in wait, wary about whoever it was approaching him.

It's me, Father. Me.

I could see how tense he was. His anxiety made him more alert. So it was not hard for him to make me understand—by keeping his eyes fixed on me, indeed as if they were clinging to me—that he wanted me to sit down facing him. When I pulled the small chair up close to his larger chair and was on the point of sitting down he signaled with a nod of his head that he wanted me to come even closer. That nod looked like the gesture of a man in perfect health with all his wits about him, as though this one thing had managed to elude his illness. When I was so close that my knees almost touched his, he jabbed his finger at me, wiggling it as he pointed to my chest.

Me?

He didn't like my answer. He sensed it was my way of deflecting his questions or at least delaying giving any response. His finger came further, touching my chest and then even tapping against it, and then his hand made the movement that said, You—what's the matter with you?

I smiled at him: the sort of smile that disparagingly shrugs off an unwelcome question. That says incredulously, Me? What could possibly be the matter with me?

He shook his head as hard as he was capable of doing to tell me he didn't believe me. His narrow little eyes carried the remnants of the hard stare I had seen so often, and they announced that he was waiting for me to tell him what was wrong with me.

He wanted to know and he was determined to know. It wouldn't be any use for me to attempt a diversion, like suddenly rising from my chair as though I had been summoned because I had a visitor. If I tried that, it would just look like I was abandoning him, not only this one time but for every occasion in future when he might press me to stay with him. My evasive tactics were already suggesting that I was trying to wait out the time span in which he could keep himself awake and alert. It exhausted him to remain so attentive; the concentration tired out his body and in a moment or two he would be breathing heavily.

I am ill, Father. But it is not a sickness that will kill me.

He really had tired himself out completely. Suddenly his tense features collapsed, his body grew lax and he slumped over, not able to control himself even long enough to lean his back and shoulders against the seat back for support. It was as if what he had wanted was simply to know something—anything—even if what he learned would mean that an hour from now, or a day from now, he would find himself back in that same state of extreme anxiety.

Can I bring you anything, Father?

With the tiny sliver of strength left in him he jerked his hand upward to tell me that he didn't want anything. He just wanted to get some rest.

When he needed to put himself into that state of alertness, he could get there. This time he had been preparing for it ever since waking up in the morning. When he was on the threshold of this conscious wakefulness of his, he would start looking around, expecting me to come in or waiting for my wife to notice him and tell me that he wanted something. Using his eyes, and the way he manipulated his features—looking in pain every time he changed the expression on his face—he could make me understand what he had been getting ready to announce. He was so good at this that I could translate his movements into words that I would say out loud so that he could confirm my translation with a nod of his head.

You want me to go there, I say, pointing in the direction that his hand seems to be indicating. He gives me a final confirmation, of what he has already confirmed, by raising his hand slowly to lay it on his chest.

To go to your house?

Yes, to his house. He answered me with a flicker of his eyelashes. He didn't need to tire himself out much to make me understand that he wanted his books. All he had to do was to open his hands, showing his palms up as they would be when he was reciting the opening chapter of the Quran.

Do you want me to bring you a book?

Not one book. He turned over his hands, palms down, and lifted them to chest level, creating an imaginary stack of books.

All of them . . . all of your books?

There in his room, which he used never to leave except when he needed to give his body a break from those hours of sitting, they were all in plain view, lined up behind the glass doors of the cabinet. In the past, whenever I turned back to look at them as I left the room, I always had the thought that with those old-fashioned, ancient-looking black bindings, these must be the books of people from the past, which he had rebound with his own hands.

Are you afraid someone will steal them? I said this because it was very obvious to me that he would never go back to reading. Not now. His eyes wouldn't be of any assistance, nor was his mind capable any longer of turning whatever words he might be able to make out into meaning. I could imagine exactly how it would be: how he would stop halfway through a sentence and go back to the beginning, starting laboriously to read the whole passage again.

Should I bring the cabinet too?

He didn't respond. He left it to me to decide whether I would leave the bookcase there or bring it here. I pictured it lying on its back in a corner of the truckbed, completely empty, once all the books were gone.

He seemed to look around the room before arranging his hands in a way that said it did not matter to him whether I brought the cabinet along or left it behind. What he wanted was the books. The books, only the books. Those books which I had never seen him open, ready to read them. Not once.

Do you want to read, Father? I asked, holding on to my smile although I did not know whether he noticed it or drew any inference from it.

Do you have your glasses? Where have your glasses gotten to?

I started calling it his house after I came back from Najaf to live here in Shqifiyeh. He still kept his keys on his own person, taking them back from me every time I returned from that house after fetching whatever it was he had requested me to bring. This time though, as he neared them to my hand, dangling from the thick cord in which he had knotted them, he seemed to be delivering them to me for good. He clearly meant for me to understand this and to understand it now, because he drew his hand away and then repeated his action, the passage of his hand toward mine, clutching the keys, as he gave me that look which means: Take them. Take them, and don't bring them back to me.

On my way to his house I began thinking how it was that he saw himself in a race with me over winding up his final business, trying to stay ahead of me since he believed that this disease would be my death. Or perhaps he was attempting to conclude things for both of us at once, believing that if it were all left to me, the truly important matters were exactly the ones I was likely to neglect. The books, first. These books that I would not be given the opportunity to read as his successor, and nor would my sons, as my successors. It was not so much—or not just—that I had forsaken him. Or even that I

disappointed him with what he might have called my preference for inaction, or my lackluster pursuit of my profession.
It was more that I had not even been able to produce the sort
of offspring who would conclude what I had begun, would
fulfill my unused potential, would go on to become what we
had always been for hundreds of years, as he used to say. Our
grandfather Sayyid Ismail, or our great grandfather Sayyid
Abd al-Husayn, or our great-great grandfather Sayyid Ali
al-Amili, or even our very distant, far-in-the-past venerated
ancestor Sayyid Ali al-Rida: he would murmur those names,
recalling his grandfather, his father's grandfather, his grandfather's grandfather, indeed calling forth all the ancestral imams
in our clan, from the very earliest of those who lived just after
the Prophet's lifetime. Back when he was preparing me for
Najaf, he would repeat to me that we were a family that had
never been drawn away from our calling as men of religion.

I had disappointed and forsaken him, first of all because
I was so lazy, my lethargy giving me the appearance in his
eyes of a little boy who dawdles his way through life, postponing his schoolwork and avoiding his sacred obligations.
He saw me as thin in every sense, just a tall, raw, and scrawny
boy beneath the turban I wore. And he sensed how unsuited
I was to what I was doing, whenever I followed behind him
or walked beside him, remaining silent as he raised his voice
to whoever he was scolding at the time, or overturned the
tables where he observed men sitting at their card games.
And instead of my saying to him—as we left those men
behind us, already restoring the tables to their upright positions—that he had been too harsh, that he had insulted and
humiliated them, he would carry on with his insults, taking
them even further, completely unconcerned that they could
still hear him. He didn't leave any space for me to say even a
single word. I was expected to do no more than assume the
role of listener, and to wait until he had calmed down before
I was allowed to do the same.

Months had passed since my last visit to his house. Behind the outer door, made of solid iron, the soil in the front patch of garden was dust-dry and the plants that had looked thirsty the last time I had been there had now turned black. Not for the first time, as I climbed up to the wooden front door into the interior, I remembered thinking what a falsehood it was, those words that a certain poet had uttered about his longing for the first place he ever lived. Even on the day I went away, carting my belongings to Najaf, it never occurred to me that I might miss this house. And in Najaf, on some of those occasions when Sayyid Mudar and I were talking, he would start laughing whenever I said I had no feeling for the house anyway since it couldn't exactly be considered my *first* house: after all, we had never moved away from it to live in any other house.

I pushed hard on the wooden door panels, using both hands and giving it a kick as well. The panels stuck because the place had been closed up for so long. The familiar smell hit me; it always seemed to come from the direction of the kitchen. This time too I headed immediately for the task I had come here to accomplish, hurrying as fast as I could as if try-ing to ignore the shapes that had appeared and grown larger in the corners of each room once the house was empty. I went directly to my father's room. Not to simply pick up what I had come here to fetch and to leave with it, hurrying out as fast as I had hurried in, but to have a look at the cabinet in hopes that it would tell me what to do and where to begin. When I realized that first I would have to take out the books myself, before anything else could happen, I found myself going out to the corridor again as though to prepare myself for this job, and then entering the room a second time and striding imme-diately over to the cabinet.

The black leather bindings had all stuck together. In order to separate the books I had to pry each one carefully away from the next. Years had passed, I was certain, in which he sat facing his books without ever thinking about getting up and going over to open one of the glass cabinet doors. Perhaps he was so certain that he had already read them all and knew their contents so thoroughly that there was no need to read them again.

As I took out stack after stack, setting each one down on the floor, I realized I had not achieved anything by coming here today. The books would remain here, sitting on the floor and waiting for someone to come who could hoist them all—the books and their cabinet—and carry them out to his truck.

The doctor ought to have fixed a time for me to make my appearance. He should have said to me, for instance, You must come at three o'clock in the afternoon on such-and-such a day of the week, on such-and-such a date. By leaving it to me to choose when to come back—within a month or maybe just inside of two months—he instantly stopped me from going ahead with my usual activities. If Sayyid Mudar were here with me I would have put it to him like this: one of my hands is free and the other one is tangled up in chains. Something like that, for these were the sorts of things we used to say to each other, so proud of ourselves in our youth, as though we had invented such clever sayings on our own. Stacking the books on the floor, watching the piles grow, I told myself that even now I was occupying myself with a worthless task since I had piled half of the books from the cabinet on the floor but had left the other half still lined up on the shelves. Before turning my back to the cabinet to leave the room, I even asked myself why I had bothered to close those glass doors.

It took me several more minutes, as I pulled the street door shut and headed for the car, to come to the understanding that what was keeping me suspended somewhere outside of normal time was not that I was trying either to bring time forward or to hold it back. It was because the feeling dogged me that nothing I did in this interval before giving myself up to the hospital and its physicians could be of any value. Because I was conscious that this realization would be followed by thoughts that were likely to distress me and drain my energy, I tried right away—still walking toward the car, with the door to the house shut behind me—to change my line of thought. It didn't require much concentration to summon her form. My brother's wife, those firm legs striding toward the kitchen, bare and visible as far up as the knees, the sound of every footfall reminding me of their well-built shapeliness. As I turned my car onto the upward slope of road, I was recalling all the images I had of her and also conjuring up new ones, shifting my lens to reveal different parts of her body. There in the kitchen, putting my hand over hers as it holds the coffeepot. And in there as my hand touches her leg, which is both soft and firm, at the uppermost part of it that is visible, then moving all the way up to the top of her thigh. And then there in the bathroom, and finally on the bed where I did sit, one time, and removed my jubba and my abaya. Or perhaps on the sofa where we sit but only after I have made certain that there is no one outside and the curtains are completely drawn. That firmness I noticed especially in her legs would diminish, and then fade away altogether once she was no longer wearing the clothes that revealed only her lower limbs; once she was sitting, in her nakedness, on my thighs. And then, as I would start to pass my hands along her exposed lower body I would be able to see how she was yielding to me. If I so much as lifted her hand slightly, she would stand up, having understood that I wanted her to face me and offer her nakedness to me so that I could see it all, there in front of me.

She was obeying me in these scenes I imagined of the two of us together, responding to me, so much so that I found myself turning the car toward her house. It was because this readiness of hers—indeed, this submission to me that I saw in my imaginings—was really there in her. She will display it in the moment she begins to close her eyes, whether out of her shyness or because it marks the onset of her pleasure.

When I came out of the hills and reached the stretch of straight highway cutting across the level plain, I gunned the car to as high a speed as I dared, perhaps because this was a way of maintaining my state of nervous excitement at its peak, and likewise of keeping her exactly where she was in my imagination, sitting there and waiting for me. I couldn't let the distance that remained cool my feverish state of mind. I set about nourishing this state of pleasurable anxiety by returning again and again to these images I had made, getting myself to move beyond everything I might see or touch so that I could picture what would happen next.

The car was obeying me. On the incline that marked the end of the plain the engine was suddenly much louder as it tried to handle the ascent; my car did not slow down before reaching the top, where the road leveled out again. In any case, it would not be long now. No more to get through than these two villages. Nothing more than maneuvering between their houses before reaching the downward slope at the end of which sat her house. Ten minutes, or maybe even less if there was no traffic where the road came into the villages. Not much longer now. The first village was coming up and from here it looked empty. It would not delay me: surely I would get to the other side of it without finding anything to block my way or slow me down. And then, the short distance to the next tiny cluster of houses. A few minutes and I would be there. No more than a few minutes.

As I reach the trees marking the point where, as soon as I pass them, her house will become visible, I begin thinking about what it is I must do upon arriving. Shall I stay in the car until I see the door open and she appears from behind its half-open panels? Or should I sound the horn and leave the engine running so that she also hears the sound of it? And then, what ought I to do if she is slow to appear at the door? Should I get out of the car and wait for her, leaning slightly against the car door, which I will leave partway open? Or perhaps I should not even be thinking about any of this, and should just act in response to whatever might happen . . . ?

Bilal. The sound of the car brought him out of the house as I drove slowly toward the parking spot and the little walk beyond it. Probably he had looked out the window first and then, with the speed characteristic of a boy his age, was outside the house in a matter of seconds. He was already standing there and watching as my car approached. He ran toward me as if he wanted to compete with me over who would reach the midpoint of the walk first. The moment I stopped the car he hurried over to open the door for me, waiting as I extricated myself from the driver's seat and got out.

I gave him a little pat on his head and touched his cheek lightly. Only then did I tell him that I had been in the vicinity and was missing him and wanted to see him. So that my visit would not be simply a passing one he took my hand and tried to tug me away from the car door, his other hand going out to shut it.

Mama will be here soon, she won't be late getting back, he said, lifting my hand and turning it to look at my wrist, checking the time to see how soon she would be back. She won't be long, he said when he could show me that the watch confirmed it for him.

I won't be long either, I said to him but I went along with his insistence, walking with him toward the house.

She told me she wouldn't be late.

We can sit here, I said, glancing toward the slightly raised front entryway, akin to a tiny balcony just inches off the ground. I didn't want to be inside when she arrived because that might suggest I had been here for some time, waiting.

Or—no, let's not sit down, I said. I won't stay that long. But Bilal had already hurried inside to fetch two chairs.

And then, if I stayed here outside, it would look like I was on the point of leaving.

No, no, leave them there, I said to him as he was turning slightly so that he could squeeze through the door carrying both chairs out together. Unsure of what to do, he halted, still

86

holding the two chairs by their backs. He set one down, and then the other, and gave me an inquiring look.

Come on, let's walk, I said, putting out my hand to him and beginning to take the two steps from the entryway down to the ground. If I were there, near to the car, as soon as she arrived she would have to take the initiative, making an effort to convince me to stay. Bilal thought my refusal to sit down meant that I wouldn't stay long, or wouldn't wait. And I, who knew that I would stay, must continue getting him to believe that at any moment I could take that first step toward climbing back into my car and driving off.

Would you like me to bring the chairs over here? he asked, pointing to the space in front of the car.

No, no . . . better for us to walk.

He wants me to stay. Not just for his sake, but for the sake of my seeing her. He wants me to stay so that we—she and I—can be together. He likes that. I know he does. I know it; and I know that his desiring this does not make him a bad or immoral person. But I must go on ignoring, or appearing to ignore, this desire of his.

Do you have holidays right now? I asked him, meaning the vacation that schools grant their pupils.

There's one day left, he answered, smiling but with an expression of obvious regret washing over his face.

Anyway, you've been having a good time with your schoolmates?

Not all of them. There're only three of them I spend time with.

He began to tell me stories about them, beginning with their names. I had the feeling, listening to him, that he felt most comfortable speaking in a manner that boys younger than him would normally use. Perhaps it was the way I had asked him about his school and classmates. After noticing this I thought I had best keep quiet, or alter my manner of speaking. I must talk to him like a grownup.

I preferred to stay silent, turning to stare at the car windshield as though something inside had drawn my attention. I couldn't think of anything to say and he—who was likely feeling anxious about insisting on holding onto me when he had no control over how long this wait would be—was anticipating that I would find something to say.

I wasn't eager to exert myself in this way, and so I started walking, dragging my feet slowly down the short concrete path. I would come to the end of it with ten steps or not much more. He walked with me, following my movements exactly, pausing when I did and—like me—turning to the little rosebushes planted to either side.

It is best if I go now, I said, lifting my arm just high enough to see the time on my wristwatch.

I know how to make coffee. My mother says she loves my coffee.

Anyway, I've been able to see that you're fine, I said, putting my hand on his shoulder and giving him an affectionate smile.

You'll leave, and a minute later she'll arrive.

Slowly I walked toward the car, and slowly I opened the door, and just as slowly I lowered my body onto the seat, counting on her arrival in the space of that very short interval when I was making the motions of leaving.

Give her my greetings. Greetings to Mama, I said, as if to satisfy his wishes even if I could do that only by mentioning her.

He had committed to memory the books of his that he had read, and he would not need to ever read them again. In the Hussainiyas he could recite hadiths and pronouncements and fatwas word for word, and always correctly. Many of them would be ones I had never heard before, and had never read either. He gave his own rulings on matters that the men of religion who used to come to our house debated. Go on now, give us the rest of the passage, he would say to whoever was speaking, letting him know that *he* knew that what the speaker had uttered was only a beginning. For its rightness to be proven, the entire text must be recited. What is the second half of that line? Don't you know? He said that once to a university graduate who was declaiming grammatical riddles in verse to the men of religion gathered there. The young man with his education did not know how to finish the line, even though it was the second hemistich that gave the answer to the riddle. Say it, say it, demanded my father, shaking his stick at the lad. If you don't say it out loud, how are they supposed to know how the words are inflected? Even in the few words that the young man had memorized it was clear that there was an error, and my father corrected him. Then he explained the whole line to the puzzled men—and to the brash young fellow who did not know how to finish what he had begun.

He had preserved everything in his head and he no longer had any need for these books as reminders. He had left them there in the cabinet with his chair facing it, since all he needed was to look at them in their collective bulk, pressed together in their bookcase. It was as though, in the hours he spent sitting motionless in that room, he reviewed the contents of those books in his head, while they sat there closed and silent in front of him. Indeed at the distance between him and the glass doors it would not even have been clear which book was which, and where exactly the book was whose content he happened to be mulling over at that moment.

While the two men I had brought with me were removing the rest of the books from the cabinet, I began to open the volumes that caught my eye, either because they looked especially ancient, or because I happened to see a title on the binding that attracted my attention. It wasn't just that I had never seen my father reading from a book. Indeed, when in one book I saw his name written on the frontispiece, with words to the effect that this book was his possession, and his property, I suddenly realized that I also had never seen anything written in his hand. I had never seen his handwriting on a sermon, or in a letter or fatwa or marriage contract. These letters with their longer than normal stems on the lam and alif, I mused, suggested the handwriting of a young man. This must be his hand as a very young scholar, in a moment when he likely felt delighted about this book he had just purchased or received as a gift. It reminded me of the photograph of him at home, and it made me wonder how old he had been when it was taken.

We're finished, Maulana, said the older of the two men. His voice startled me and it took me a moment to get my bearings; I stared at the book that was still in my hands as though I were trying to fathom what I could possibly be doing with it.

The cabinet had been taken away too, leaving the wall behind it looking slightly damp, a different shade than the rest.

Shall we go ahead of you, Maulana?

I let them precede me out of the house so that I would be alone as I came out and shut the doors. As if I needed to consider, alone, whether I should shut in the square prayer cushions that still sat in the room, in the exact positions where I had always known them to be.

Outside, the cabinet had been trussed up but the men had left it standing upright, as it had been in his room, rather than laying it out on the ground. The pair of them were standing in the shade of their truck, waiting for me.

Shall we go, Maulana?

I nodded and turned to my car, the book still in my hand. Seated behind the wheel, I waved it at them to indicate that they should go ahead and I would follow. I didn't want their eyes fixed on me the whole journey back.

The books are here, Father.

An earnest, questioning look came over his face, as if he wanted to say, Here? In this room with me?

He really would like to see them, I thought. His expression did not change. Perhaps he wanted them put in front of him, piled up on the floor, and only then would we decide where exactly in the house they should go.

Shall I bring them in here?

The men had put them in the reception room that I usually inhabited. All of them, the books and their cabinet, like an order of merchandise stacked up and waiting. I brought him one stack. Five or six books. On top was the book in which he had written his name in ink on the first page.

This is the *Tabaqat al-Ja'fariya*, do you remember it? *The Lives of the Jaafari Shaykhs.*

He raised his eyes to me as his hands took the book that I held out. He stared at the cover, bowing his head close. He didn't ask about his glasses. What he saw as an opaque stretch of cloudy brown barely allowed him to make out the large script of the title. Even so, he opened the book, not to the first page but to a random page inside. I wanted to show him his name written in his own hand, and so I reached over to turn the pages back until we were on the title page.

Here's your name. You wrote it there.

He would not be able to see it, for the opacity of age had left the paper even darker here, as though a thick film coated it, leaving the writing even fainter beneath.

Glasses, where are your glasses, where did we put them?

He gave no sign of wanting them. He was satisfied enough, it seemed, to turn the book over in his hands and riffle through it as if he were acquainting himself with its shape and contents. I thought that perhaps his illness had destroyed his ability to read, or to even recognize the letters—that is, had he been able to see them. But I was wrong. Ready, apparently, to return the book to me, he closed it, shifted it round in his hands and turned it over so that the front cover was face-up. He handed it to me with the title on top, right-way up, exactly in the position it had been when his hands took it from mine, as I brought it close to him.

He did not want to see the other books I still had in my arms. He did not seem to be interested in doing anything more than this: opening the one book and turning a few pages. He had requested his books but it was enough for him to know that now they were here; in my house, with me. By the way he handed the book back to me, he seemed to be leaving it to me to do as I liked with these books. Or perhaps he was just doing what he thought he must do: to pass on to me the legacy he himself had inherited.

Back in my sitting room I told myself that I must not leave the books here, where the men had set them down. If I left them as they were today, I thought, then tomorrow I would be lazy about dealing with them, even though my wife would not cease reminding me that they were here, in this room, dumped on the floor. It would be easy enough for me to return them to their cabinet, stack by stack. But I felt an urge to page through them first and then to return them to the shelves but in a more suitable order, grouping together the books that belonged together.

Tomorrow I will start going through them, I said to myself. Right now I'll just look at one of them. That's enough for now. The one my father wrote his name in. It may have been the first book he ever owned.

Chapter Three

THE DISEASE ITSELF TOOK CONTROL of setting an end to my waiting period, during which I asked myself incessantly how long I would go on before deciding when this respite of mine must end. A lot of blood had pooled inside of me and it began forcing its way out in foul and smelly spurts. The sight of it plunged me back into my earlier state of terror, that dread that instantly made me break out in sweat, the feelings of panic that left me not even knowing where to turn my eyes. I could not wait out the few remaining hours of daylight that would soon turn into the shadows of evening. I'm going to the hospital, I told my wife.

Right now? She didn't move. She just looked at me, not knowing how exactly she ought to react. Are you going to the doctor or to the hospital?

The doctor won't be in his clinic by the time I get there. There in the hospital they know what they have to do.

Should I get something ready for you to take, something to eat, your clothes . . . ?

No, no. They can give me what I need there.

She thought she must do something. Erase that expression she always wore, perhaps, never seeming able to alter it. And then tell me for example that this hour of crisis brought on by my illness would return her to her true bearing. On my part, I ought to exchange something meaningful with her. To say to her, for example, Watch out for the children. Or to express, even indirectly, some kind of hopeful gratitude that she would take care of my father's needs in my absence. But I was completely occupied with the turmoil in my body and my brain, and consumed by the efforts I had to make to keep my fear hidden.

It's getting late, I said as if I were trying suddenly to justify to myself such an abrupt departure. I lifted my hand, dangling my keychain, to confirm my hasty exit. At the front door, I suddenly realized that I ought to say something to my father.

As I turned back and went into his room, I saw that he was peering in the direction of the corridor as if he sensed what was going on and had already prepared himself, anticipating that I would come in and speak to him before leaving.

I am going, Father, I said. Just like that, without any prevarication. As though he already knew that going meant going to the hospital, and that I was merely confirming it— the hunches he'd had about my illness must all be true. The expression in his eyes, which he kept fixed on me, did not change. He did not want to know anything more than what I had told him. When he felt he had given me a long enough stare, he lifted his thin, veiny hand to shake mine. It was soft in my grip and had no weight.

I will go now, I said, covering it with my other hand. I hurried out, not wanting night to fall while I was still on the road.

The car looked very dirty: it was coated with dust. Even amid my disorder and haste, I chided myself for being so slow to get it washed. That made me think of Bilal—of my brother's son, Bilal—and as I closed the car door I even considered for a moment going by his house and getting him to come with me. As I eased the car forward toward the turn that would bring me out onto the main road, it occurred to me that my wife was likely to be standing on the balcony, alone, to say goodbye, but not expecting me to raise my head and see her.

I drove slowly at first. I didn't want to look like I was in a hurry, speeding away because of my illness and the anxiety it was causing me. I even smiled at a man and a woman who were walking along the road and stuck my hand up in greeting. As I reached the more heavily trafficked road I was thinking about my sons. They were probably coming home about now, jostling and sweaty and paying no attention to the state of their clothes. I felt so much tenderness toward them that it brought a throbbing to my head—that sense of watery pressure behind the eyes just before a tear forms. Hurriedly I pressed the radio button hoping to find something I could listen to that would keep me occupied. At the loud sound of static I twirled down the volume and changed the station, and then tried another two or three before switching it off to be rid of the screeches that seemed to be the only sounds it could emit.

At the beginning of the stretch of straight highway where the traffic picked up speed I felt a little better, regaining the sense I always had at this point that I was about to start a race. I pressed hard on the gas pedal, knowing that the speed I could build up on the bit of flat road would give me added comfort. I forgot my notion of stopping at Bilal's; or maybe I was ignoring the idea deliberately despite having already pictured him standing in front of the door to his house, waiting for me to say, as soon as I drove up, Get in, Bilal. Quick! I had retrieved that scene of him standing there and I clung to it as though to keep away other images that I didn't want to see and that might well take its place if I weren't careful. But I knew that I would not be able to go on with this, keeping fixed in my head only what I wanted to keep there. In less than a minute the image of Bilal would be overtaken by other images, like that of my sons returning home not knowing where I had gone; or of my father, who really wanted to keep his hand there pressed in mine as if he were telling me something that was going to happen and would frighten me when it did; or of the hospital where they would start using their instruments on me, those sharp wounding tools, their metal so cold and bright and starkly clean. Still, I must hurry, I must go even faster than this, passing one car after another. I must get there before the flow of blood gets any faster or thicker—this blood amassing in my belly to form a ball the size of a large orange. Increasing my speed appeases my fear somewhat: my fright at this continued bleeding, even if it is only drop by drop. I am trying to shake off the grim insistence that the bleeding seems to communicate, as it tells me to stop by the side of the road, get out, go a little ways to hide myself behind a rise of ground or a tree where I can lift my dishdasha and stare at my urine to check on how much blood is mixed into it, unless, that is, the blood has taken its place altogether.

These ever-changing successions of images and thoughts that run through our brains help us get through our hours of peril. And we're helping ourselves when we repeat over and over, in our heads, that we must be getting there, we're almost there now, nothing will slow us down or get in our way. Not now. This time, if never before, the speed I've picked up will drive me there: the speed will do it and I will simply follow. This time I am not going to circle endlessly through the streets around the hospital looking for the right parking spot. I will just leave the car, and maybe I will even leave the door open, in the hospital driveway. It's true that anyone who sees me walking in—or more likely running in—will think the scene I'm making doesn't befit the person I seem to be. I'll say to the guard standing at the door, The car—I left the car over there—as I twist my head halfway back toward it. The blood—that's all I will say to the nurse who is already coming to me holding a metal basin in which she has put cotton and a needle. Surely what I say will startle her, and her eyes will search immediately for a spot where she can set down her basin, as soon as she hears what I have to say.

In the hospital they take over. These nurses and doctors and everyone else who works there, they just take over. They assume full responsibility for the body of the invalid. But I can walk, I said to the young man who lifted my body down from the X-ray machine. He would have none of it. He insisted on putting me in the wheelchair and pushing me to the room they had just gotten ready for me. There he would do it again, lifting me and putting me down, his arms around my body or his hands going to my armpits to lift me. I no longer say to him, I can get up by myself. I don't tell him I'm perfectly capable of standing up on my own. Next he will set me down on the bed they have already made ready for my night, folding down the edge of the sheet on one side because they want me to feel that everything is here and ready to receive me. They, and the bed they have prepared, are ready and waiting for me to lie down. He—the strong young man, and he's a big man too—will even cover me up, all the way to my chin. He will straighten the sheet over me, tightening and smoothing it across the top and down the sides so that my body looks—for the benefit of whoever might catch a glimpse of it through the narrow crack left by the almost-closed door—as arranged and organized as the sheet looks. My body is in good order beneath its covers, firmly in place, and the bed has exactly the look that the young man wants.

I'll put your clothes in there, he said, with a glance toward the tall narrow wardrobe. My abaya and dishdasha had been folded so many times that they made small square packages. He came back to pick up my turban from the little table. His hands encircled it with a gingerly caution that suggested he wasn't accustomed to this task. Just as carefully he carried it over to place it on top of the abaya and dishdasha. It sat there exactly as though it were sitting on my head.

Do you want me to do anything else for you? As he spoke, the robust young man was already turning away to attend to the wheelchair in which he'd wheeled me into the room.

No, no, I said, shifting my gaze to him but keeping my head motionless under the covers.

As he took a couple of steps toward the door I asked, still without daring to move my head, What showed up in the X-ray? I knew I should not be asking him that. He looked back at me and shook his head slightly, quizzically, letting me know he wanted me to repeat what I had said. Either he hadn't heard it or he hadn't understood my words because he wasn't expecting them.

When he did understand he said, The doctor will tell you.

I couldn't stay completely still for long. I pulled my hand from beneath the carefully smoothed-out sheet to set it down on top. Hoisting my body up to a halfway seated position where I would be able to reach the telephone hanging on the wall, I reflected on how I had just blighted, or undone, all the hard work of that strong young man. I wouldn't be able to refrain from doing more damage, either. As soon as I tried to get out of bed I would spoil the whole look of the room. I was alert enough, and I still had enough energy, that if I were to climb out of bed I would not go over immediately to sit on the chair on the other side of the bed but would move as much as I could around the room. I would walk through its sterile, compact emptiness, circling round the bed time and time again, occasionally glancing up at the TV where the young man had muted the sound.

It wasn't one doctor who came. A lot of them came. Doctors, all of them; they seemed to be very young new doctors. Last time we were here, my nephew Bilal told me that the doctors we'd seen were medical students doing their rounds of in-hospital training.

Are you comfortable? asked one.

Everything all right? Al-hamdu lillah? inquired another.

In a little while your doctor will be here, and he will give you the results of the X-rays and the examinations.

I would not attempt to compete with this by asking any questions of the doctors who were swarming around the room. I knew they would give me the same answer that the strong young man had given me.

Why don't you get some rest? urged the one who stood at the front of the group. He looked to me like the oldest of them, and he was the tallest, too.

I'm not tired.

Not hungry, either? Are you in any pain? he asked me, inviting me to sit on the edge of the bed or to lie down. I obeyed him by sitting, first, and then I stretched out, my arms away from my stomach, down at my side, as though to show him that I was offering up my body for examination.

Any pain here? he asked me, having lifted the short, loose hospital gown off my stomach. Here—is there any pain here?

No, I answered, after giving myself a moment to figure out whether I was hurting anywhere.

Here?

No . . .

He was running his hand over my belly, from the middle down to the sides and underneath almost to my back, without finding any indication of where the pain he was searching for was located. I slowed him down by pausing before I offered the information that I didn't feel any pain anywhere right now, and that I wanted to cover up my body where he had uncovered it.

Like those who stood behind him, none of whom were speaking or moving, he had come here to learn. I knew that from the way he suddenly went silent when the surgeon came in. Quickly he removed his hand from my body and stepped back to join the group. All of them seemed to recede in the doctor's presence, him most of all as he slipped to the back of the group.

Have we tired you out with the examinations? asked the doctor, who had come to stand at my bedside. He reached over to tug my hospital gown down over my middle. But neither that nor anything else reassured me. What the doctor's behavior, and this whole scene, reminded me of was the gesture people make as if to say, There's no point in going on with this. Almost as though he wanted to make me even more wary of what he was about to say, the doctor remained silent, giving himself a little time. Worse, he even gave the fellow who had been talking to me a long look and asked him something in the medical English that they used between themselves.

We are going to do the operation, he said to me as soon as he got a response, a very terse one, just one word or maybe two.

When?

As soon as possible.

Now? . . . Today?

Possibly tomorrow, or the day after. But you will stay here, now.

I wanted so much for them to go out, all of them, those other doctors who were gazing down at me. The senior doctor understood this when he saw my eyes shifting back and forth, from him to them. Whatever it was he said—and he said it in English, again—it got them to turn their backs and leave the room behind that classmate of theirs who had been at the head of their group.

Uhh . . . is it dangerous?

The operation?

I didn't say anything.

No, not in principle. Here in this hospital we've done many, many operations just like it. No, it isn't dangerous. In principle.

He'd gone back to that language of his. Clearly, he was oblivious to how his manner of speaking affected a patient listening to him. When I had visited his clinic after my first release from the hospital, I remember being acutely aware that he was rehearsing possible scenarios where death and danger were not at all remote, not even unlikely. In medicine, he said to me then, nothing is certain. The statistics varied from two to five in a hundred, a fluid number that could float upward, or could rocket upward like the mercury in those thermometers they stick into patients' mouths.

Here, in this hospital, our policy is to speak frankly to the patient, not to hide anything.

But if I do live . . .

You will live, you don't need to worry about that.

What I mean to say is, if I do live, will I be the same as I am now?

Some things will change, but you'll get used to them.

He made it obvious that he was preparing himself to launch into his ready-made speech about the changes I would face. He pulled the sheet tight at the end of the bed, his action announcing that he was about to sit down, to demonstrate how relaxed and comfortable and close to me he was, as he spoke about these difficult things.

It's hard for me to nap in the hospital bed. They encase the mattress in their sheets of thick plastic so that the patient's excretions don't soak in even around the edges. Whenever I try to turn over my body slides and my feet can't gain any traction to help me reposition my body every time the plastic sends me slipping down toward the end of the bed. In my earlier two-day hospital stay I had felt reluctant to ask my brother's son Bilal if he would exchange places with me: the chair for the bed. I wanted so badly to sleep on that reclining chair. I did think, though, about how strange it would look to them, opening the door to find him in the bed meant for their patient. So instead I would say to him, Come on, Bilal, let's walk a bit. Rubbing the drowsiness out of his eyes with the back of his hand, he always got up to accompany me. But now that I'm alone here, I feel too embarrassed, in this skimpy hospital gown, to walk out into the open space where the night nurses are always on duty. I can't see myself parading the length of the long counter those women sit behind.

I knew I would spend the night moving between the bed and the chair, and skipping between TV channels, none of which would keep me entertained. The only recourse I had now, as I faced the start of a long night, was to act as though I were embarking on an ordinary evening—that is, sitting up in bed and resting my back against the headboard to watch some TV. Here I was adopting the posture and the expression of an ordinary person on an ordinary evening, comfortable and relaxed, reclining in my clean bedlinens. Just someone entertaining himself before the sleep that he knows will come an hour or so from now.

I had put the finishing touches on this scenario when there was a rap on the door. A nurse appeared, pulling behind her a trolley carrying all the instruments for a proper examination.

The doctor who will be handling your anesthesia is coming in.

So—the operation?

Tomorrow. They'll take you in for the operation tomorrow.

She seemed pleased to see that my temperature was no higher than it should be: peering at the thermometer, she beamed at me as if she thought congratulations were in order. She concluded her business by checking my blood pressure. She asked if I needed a pill to help me sleep. The doctor had already prescribed it.

She came back with a pill and a glass of water. It would put me to sleep, she told me. She left it there in its little cup on the table next to me so that I could decide for myself when to take it, whenever I felt ready to go to sleep.

Tomorrow at six the barber will come, she said. She flashed me a little smile, trying to tell me something that it wasn't her job to tell me.

Your beard. That was all she said, insinuating a question about whether I was ready to allow the barber to shave it all off when he came.

I smiled back, although for a moment I suspected maybe she really did mean this as a question that she wanted me to answer. But she didn't wait for a response from me anyway. She just paused in the doorway to ask if I wanted her to turn out the light, but before I could answer she informed me that I could turn it out myself, pointing to the light switch at my side.

Once she had shut the door firmly I did start thinking seriously about my beard. Surely I would look very peculiar stretched out naked on that table in the operating room but still wearing this beard of mine. Not only peculiar but even laughable, maybe. My naked body in their hands and under their instruments while my face retained all the signs that people associate with a man of religion. In fact I myself still counted the view of it a bit odd and somehow just not quite right, when the bathroom mirror reflected back my face and half my body. And then, here in the hospital, lying on this bed, there was nothing about me to indicate to anyone that I was a man of religion except this beard, which was precisely the cut of a man of the cloth and nothing like the beards other types of men grow to make themselves look more handsome.

Good evening, Shaykh, I heard the doctor say. It was the anesthetist, coming in to ask me the same questions I'd had to respond to the last time I was here.

Do you have any allergies, to medications, food . . .

No.

Last time, did the anesthesia give you any trouble?

I think it was stronger than it needed to be.

Do you smoke?

I used to.

Do you drink? He was careful to frame this question with a broad smile, meant to suggest this was just a little joke. I answered him with a smile. Nothing more was needed.

Have they told you we're going to operate tomorrow?

I wanted him to tell me something about it but I hesitated to ask. If I did ask, I thought, surely my fear would be obvious to him.

Is there something you'd like to know?

No . . . no, nothing at all, I said, shaking my head slowly as though I was asking myself carefully whether there was anything I needed to know.

No, nothing at all, I repeated a bit insistently, like I wanted to encourage him to leave the room so I could take my pill and go to sleep.

As I raised it to my mouth I thought how tiny it was—too small, surely, to subdue my body as long as it remained in this alert, even restless, state. I thought about pressing the call button to ask for a second pill, but I didn't. A pill this size was capable of killing a live human being, I reminded myself, visions of what I'd seen time and again at the cinema mounting in my head. I took it with a little swallow of water, just as the nurse had instructed.

There seemed to be an overwhelming number of them around me as, lying in the narrow bed, I was wheeled down the corridor. Family members who were there for the night with their sick ones turned to peer at me as they came and went from their relatives' rooms. But I no longer felt any embarrassment at being transported like this in front of them all. I figured that the barber's work on my beard had changed my appearance completely. Or it had changed me. Anyone who saw this person now, flat on his back and clean shaven—the self I had been now concealed from them in this new guise—would not recognize who it was. As if I wasn't even the person I had been before. Meanwhile, I was staring at these faces among whom I was passing. Some seemed high above me and others closer to my level, but I felt as though I was seeing all of them through a screen that was like a low ceiling separating me down here from them somewhere up above. The barber had known that I was a man of religion, my beard that of a man of the cloth. Do you really want me to shave it off? he asked me. Twice, and then a third time as he was starting. He was already almost touching my face with his electric shaver. I nodded. I had made this decision the night before as I waited for the pill to put me to sleep. As long as there were going to be some changes in me, I had said to myself, as long as I wouldn't be as I had been anyway, as the doctor had told me, I would have to alter my appearance to suit the change about to come over my body. Anyway, I thought, there were many men of religion these days who no longer let their beards grow out. I began trying to recollect the faces of all the men of religion I'd ever encountered. I summoned up their images and as they marched through my head I tallied how many of them had kept their beards and which ones had decided that a mustache was enough. I told the barber to keep a light mustache on my face. Do you want to see what it looks like now? he asked me, swinging the mirror close to my face. But I didn't look; in fact, I shoved it away abruptly with the edge of my hand. I had already had to prepare myself. It was important that I not see my face looking so changed, as I knew it would look, until I had had sufficient time to imagine it from every angle; indeed, until I had pictured it to myself time and time again. He wasn't a physician but the barber undid my hospital gown, revealing my body, and he even tugged my underwear down below my buttocks. But I didn't feel embarrassed by any of it—not by his being there or by the state I was in. Likely that was due to the needle they had plunged into the little sac they had attached to the sac of serum. I was already beginning to doze, suddenly waking up and then immediately dropping off again. Opening my eyes I was instantly wide awake, as though I was trying to control my sleepiness and then my fierce alertness, moving between them as if I was determined to hang on to both of them. Probably the injection was already doing its work when the fellow who had been in the lead when those junior doctors came into my room asked me now whether any of my family were here with me. When I told him I was here alone, he said I must sign the papers myself in that case. I knew that these were the papers declaring that I accepted responsibility for the operation and that I was fully conscious as I did so. I signed it without feeling any new surges of fear. The needle in the little sac had certainly had its effect. I slept, woke up, slept and then didn't care what was happening around me in that cramped little area of corridor where they had parked my bed and were talking above and around me. They and a lot of others, it seemed—they all seemed to be there in the corridor. Their conversation wasn't limited to their work or the invalids, me and the others, all of us in these narrow beds lodged in this corridor. They were talking about what had happened to them yesterday, not here in the hospital but outside, wherever they had spent their evenings. I found it irritating because it felt like they had forgotten about me, lying here on this bed in the corridor. But soon enough I would be oblivious to them. I was forgetting them even as I was telling myself how I wasn't afraid now, since it was these very same people who would soon be taking me into the operating room. You won't feel a thing, the anesthetist had said to me before going down to get himself ready for the operation. Nothing, at all? I asked him. It will be just as if you're asleep, he said. And then, as if he were entertaining himself, he added that actually it would be just as if I were dead. Just like that he said it, probably thinking the injection had already taken me far enough away from the zone of consciousness that I wouldn't hear him. Are you certain no one is here with you? asked another man. No one at all? I hadn't seen this man before. He hadn't been around that morning or the night before. I'm by myself, I said. He wanted to know what to do with my belongings that they had put in the little cabinet, as long as I was going to be drugged and wouldn't be aware of anything that might happen nearby.

They were pushing me in. This time I could see the lamps overhead, in the ceiling or perhaps a little lower, lights so strong that they instantly forced me to look away. The beams were so powerful that I shut my eyes but then somehow I was catching partial glimpses of faces around me. A woman's face came close as she said—and it felt like she was almost whispering into my ear—that now they were going to move me, lying down, to another bed. She patted my bare shoulder and then my hand which was hanging down at my side. There were a lot of them, these people who lifted me, gripping the edges of the sheet I was lying on. They lifted me all at once and then I could hear them letting out their breaths with those loud sounds you hear in shops or on the street when people are lifting a heavy load together. Done . . . you can rest now, she said, the same woman who had patted my bare shoulder and my dangling hand, before she turned to say something to one of the others hovering nearby. Earlier, when I was still in my room, the nurse had taken my hand in both of hers. Although I was expecting to feel pain as she jabbed the needle into the back of my fisted hand, what I felt instead was a fresh touch, a light and soft stroke as she pressed her fingers against my skin at the point where she thought the needle could go in.

Yallah, let's start, said a voice, probably that of the surgeon. I hadn't seen him since waking up this morning. He came to stand over me. Marhaba, welcome to our Shaykh, he said, and then I began to have the sensation of falling. Tumbling somewhere deep, and then deeper and deeper, and I had to tell them, I had to let them know I was falling, before I reached the bottom of that pit . . .

Some amount of time must have passed, though I had no sense of how many hours it could have been. But time had gone by, surely: foreshortened time, the way hours can get pressed together into minutes sometimes. The voice that woke me said that my operation had been a success but I had made the task very difficult for the surgeon and his team. Another voice said, Hamdillah ala s-salaama, Praise God for your recovery. A woman's voice. She seemed to be sitting somewhere a bit away from me, in this place I imagined as a vast empty space that must contain only my bed and two chairs. One was over here, where I'd heard the voice of the

107

man who woke me up, and another was over there where I guessed the woman was sitting. I knew that they were here to stay with me in case anything went wrong. I knew that simply because here they were with me in this echo chamber where I was the only patient. I started making attempts to speak to them, saying things springing from my sense of something like relief, I suppose. Not because I had come through it safely: that didn't occur to me, exactly; or maybe I didn't want to think about it. But in some way I did feel reassured, and even happy. I spoke slowly, feeling at my ease. It felt good to be able to say something genuinely warm to them. I asked the man whether it was night or day right now, as if I earnestly wanted to be more awake, more attentive to my surroundings. But suddenly, in this state of calm contentment I felt dizzy and faint. Something inside me seemed to be dwindling away, and fast. My spirit, I thought—somehow, it had shrunk to the point where it was no longer strong enough to keep me in the alert state I'd tried to maintain. I'm dizzy, I'm very dizzy, I said. The man whose voice I had already heard said calmly that he would lower my head below the level of my body and feet. This relieved me enough that I was able to resume speaking quietly and calmly to him and the woman, whom I imagined changing position: perhaps right now her legs were sliding off that high stool in case she needed instantly to hurry over to me. Speaking from that far-off place where she sat, she said my dizziness was normal and I mustn't feel any anxiety about it. Her voice sailed across this vast room I imagined myself to be in as though she were directing her words not specifically to me but rather to no one in particular, or perhaps to the world at large. I wanted to see her; I wished she would come closer and show me her face, like the woman who had patted my shoulder and hand earlier in the day. But I couldn't lift my head to look at this woman, since I wasn't capable of moving anything at all in my body. The bedclothes draped over my body seemed very heavy. I couldn't lift them off and I couldn't raise my head by propping myself up on my elbows. The heaviness that was like a huge weight that had suddenly been dropped on top of me left me feeling immobilized. Even if I were able to raise my head I would still not see her, though. The light in the room seemed very faint, making me think of twilight, but more precisely the late dusk when people begin feeling their way forward as they walk. I would be able to see her if she were to come over here, if she were to bring her face close to mine. Do you see any blood on my clothes? I asked the man. In my mind's eye, the covers and sheets were heavily stained. No, no . . . everything is clean, he responded without even a glance toward the heavy wool blanket they had spread over me to keep me warm. I don't think he even looked at the hems of the bedlinens that showed beneath it. Did they clean me? I asked him. He answered immediately: Patients are never removed from the operating room before they are clean. Yet I couldn't shake the feeling that the blood that the operation would have released was still here, staining me and the blanket over me and the covers beneath it. I sensed blood, I felt its stain and its smell. At that moment I saw the man's hand move abruptly, lifting the covers slightly to tuck them in tightly around me. You're cold, he said to me. I was shivering. And my teeth were chattering, too. I'll turn the heater on, said the woman. I pictured her long legs slithering to the floor, ready to come to me. I was trembling so badly that my entire body was jerking back and forth beneath the covers. I asked the man—my voice trembling as hard as my body—to turn on the little heater and bring it over here. I was able at least to raise my eyes enough that I could see the disc facing me redden. I began to feel its warmth and its brightness, both so powerful that I had to close my eyes . . . .

I had dozed off. What woke me was the heaviness of the covers, which they hadn't lifted off although they probably could tell that I had warmed up so much that I was beginning to sweat. Some relatives were here and wanted to see me. That's what the man said. They were here, he said, waiting for me just outside the door, which was closed. The sleep into which I had suddenly been pitched had not erased the dizziness from my head. The heaviness of it probably made my sense of feverish sweatiness worse. I didn't know if what I was feeling was really there in my body. They had lowered my head so much that it felt like I was hanging from my feet. I asked the man if this was really so. Was I upside down? He told me that I had been talking in my sleep and I seemed to be having a hard time breathing. Now that I had woken up, he asked, was I was still finding it hard to breathe? When I said it was the dizziness that bothered me, I heard the woman's voice. This happens after operations, she said. They couldn't give me a medication that would relieve the dizziness.

Somehow I had forgotten, or perhaps I ignored, his announcement that relatives were here and they wanted to see me. When he said it again, I looked at him hard, as though he had just said something startling.

People from your family, he said again, thinking that the look I had given him meant he needed to explain what he had said. They were still here, he added, pointing toward where I figured the door must be.

Her face was suddenly there and seemed to be high above me. I almost thought that she must have been waiting here next to me and not behind the closed door. I didn't know if the lighting in that room was really so low that I could barely see, or whether my exhaustion and pain had weakened my vision, but the wan glow seemed to highlight the bones of her face; it looked even more drawn than usual. She had gotten thinner in the few hours since I left the house to come here, I thought. She did not know what to say, and I imagined her hands dropped awkwardly at her sides and probably pressed to her body. Trying to look at her I had the impression that she saw my eyes wandering, looking unfocused as the eyes of very sick people do. As dizzy and exhausted as I was, still I could predict that she would not know what to do or say. That was because she would not know how to shed that singular attitude she shows to the world, the demeanor she has clung to for so long that I no longer remember when it started.

I came with Abu Abd al-Karim the driver, she said. And he's waiting for me at the main entrance.

I just stared at her, images tumbling through my head: her tall thin form coming out of the house; yanking the car door open, and saying to him the instant she closed it that she needed to go to the hospital. In my mind's eye her movements were those of some other woman. One of those women who are accustomed to leaving the house and know exactly how to behave. For a moment I did actually consider bringing my hand out from under the blanket and reaching for hers; but I was too lethargic, or perhaps simply reluctant. After all, I wasn't any good either at overcoming my usual ways of behaving when she was around.

Are the children at home?

She gave a slight nod, her eyes still fixed on my face.

You're in pain, she said, or almost asked, when she saw the muscles in my face tighten as a sharp burning sensation heaved up from the region of my abdomen.

Dizzy . . . I'm just dizzy, that's all.

She turned as if she were looking for that man, who by this time had joined the woman and was talking to her. I could hear his voice.

He's dizzy, she said, directing her words toward where they stood. He says he's dizzy.

The anesthesia does that, it always happens after an operation, he said, coming over to see whether I was showing any new symptoms.

It's from the operation, she said to me, as if the man's words had not reached my ears. Still, she remained where she was, her arms at her sides and her hands stiffly pressed, I figured, into her thighs.

Are the children on their own there?

Don't worry, they're big now, old enough to take care of themselves.

She ought to have said something about my father. I didn't want to think about him and I thought it likely that the few words she had for me would not go as far as to include anything about him.

Your beard—

I suddenly remembered that my beard was gone. I thought about bringing my hand out from beneath the covers to feel my face in its present state but I didn't move.

They shaved it off . . . here in the hospital? She gave me a smile. It was a very slight and fleeting smile, but even that showed a playfulness on her features that I had never seen the slightest hint of, even after so many years. I didn't respond. Surely it was my dizziness that kept me reticent, or maybe I was so slow to respond because her reaction was a complete surprise to me.

I could not really see the outlines of her thin body as she slid away toward the exit. The man had told her that I must rest now, and she—with an easy seemliness that startled me as much as her smile had surprised me—said that it was almost time anyway for her to leave, and she didn't want to delay the driver's return home. Before she had stepped too far away from my bed I asked her if she had explained to the children that I was here in the hospital. Her terse answer increased my sense of dislocation. I will reassure them, she said.

The days that followed my operation were not a quiet period of steady improvement, as happens when we recover from a fall or a minor illness or a slight wound. The pain got worse as it traveled from place to place in my body. In one of his visits the doctor told me that the whole body can erupt when one body part is attacked, just as when a bullet hits an animal's body and buries itself inside. I was beginning to live my pain, as the doctor put it. When the pain got very bad, it was this expression of his that made me think of my body as a thing disconnected from me that somehow was unleashing these spells of insanity on its own, according to its own logic.

Waking up in that room I had imagined as a large chamber, I didn't particularly notice the many tubes coming out of my body. I wasn't even really aware of the one tube that could hardly be ignored since they had poked it into my nose and mouth as soon as I woke up. I was amazed that my wife, seeing me, hadn't reacted in a way that would have told me instantly that it wasn't just the loss of my beard that drew attention to my face. Her cold thin countenance didn't show anything apart from that startling smile. Almost a teasing smile, and a cold smile too. Even in my state of pain I could see that this unprecedented trip of hers—leaving the house to come here, just this one time—couldn't help but reveal things I hadn't known she had inside her.

I had to stay in bed even though my body was sore from rubbing against, even sticking to, the mattress. My skin was so dry and flaking that I could almost hear the rough sound of its raw tearing every time I turned over onto my side or moved an arm or leg. Still, I had to stay in bed; full bed rest was prescribed, said the nurse every time she came in, almost at a run, to check my blood pressure and body temperature.

I had been there for days before I decided that I must get myself out of this room. I was determined to get up and walk, pulling behind me the metal frame that held my medications. I waited for a male nurse to appear. I asked him to dress me, to cover the parts of me that the hospital gown left visible. He asked if I would like him to come along with me, adding that he would have to ask my doctor if I could walk on my own without anyone else along. In that first attempt to leave my room, I couldn't manage more than a few steps. Even that much left me immediately weaker and feeling that I had no strength at all. I collapsed back against the wall and asked him to carry me back to bed.

You're better today, the doctor said to me every time he passed his stethoscope over my belly and back and studied the sacs that held everything my body expelled. I hadn't imagined that even in the hospital one could still experience bouts of unendurable pain. We can give you an anesthetic to put you to sleep, the doctor said. But if you go to sleep your organs will go to sleep too, and we want them to start working again.

I must have dropped off. When I opened my eyes I had the feeling that Bilal had been here in my room for some time. He was standing at the foot of the bed, over my feet, looking at me. In fact, he was studying me closely so that he wouldn't miss the minute I opened my eyes. He didn't know whether he should give me a smile or just go on looking at me closely. Staring at me. Trying to extract himself from his hapless embarrassment, he pointed to the door and said his mother was here. He would go to fetch her. I was clean, and under clean bedclothes, which I quickly tried to straighten enough to cover my feet. I tried to imagine what my face must look like, putting my hand up to my chin, which they had shaved again when they had come in this morning to wash me and tidy the room.

As the two of them came into view I could see Bilal trying to keep up with her stride, as though he wanted to lead her to my room. Inside the room, he fell back to let her approach me first. Although she was never unmindful of what her features gave away, this time she did not seem to know exactly what expression she should put on her face. I could tell that as she came up to me.

Praise God for your recovery, she said when only a step away from me.

As I looked up at her I was trying to imagine how my eyes appeared. They must look unusually wide but they probably also seemed unfocused.

We didn't know until yesterday afternoon . . .

She didn't come any closer. I began looking around the room as though I wanted to invite her to change her location. I tried to wave her to the chair on the other side of the bed. I noticed that she had covered her head with a brightly colored small kerchief, the ends knotted under her chin.

Tell them to bring you a chair, I said to Bilal who had returned to the end of the bed and stood there, gripping the low bedrail with both hands.

No . . . no, I'm not tired, he said before turning to gaze at the television above him, which was on but with the sound muted.

Minutes passed—or at least it seemed like several minutes—before anyone said anything. Then Bilal asked us if we would like him to bring us coffee; somehow he intimated that he knew where to find it. His mother looked interested. He pointed at me and said, At the moment, coffee isn't the right thing for you.

After he left the room, she told me he couldn't bear staying at home once he learned that I was in the hospital. She lapsed into silence again but then asked, Why didn't you bring him with you?

This time I'm here for more than two or three days.

Standing like this, close to my bed, disconcerted her. She began looking around to see what she could do about it.

Here, I said, turning my face to the armchair. I could have gotten up but what kept me prone was that I wanted to maintain my status as an invalid.

Have they given you any trouble?

It's a major operation. That's what the doctor called it.

She came a little nearer the bed but not as far as a single long stride of hers would have brought her, right to its side.

She came nearer in order to relieve me of having to twist my head to look at her. In that instant I truly felt the difference between her strong full body and my weak one. But what I was imagining was these two bodies close together. These bodies pressed together, and how obvious this very great disparity between them would be.

Have I changed?

You seem weaker. And then, the beard. I could never have imagined you like this, without a beard.

I'll grow it back anyway, I said, wanting her to respond with something more about me and how I looked.

All these days here, and you've been completely alone?

She had learned of my wife's visit, of course, she must have. But because I did not want to say or do anything that would interrupt this closeness of ours—face to face, and alone, she and I, with no one else around—I just said that before coming I had prepared myself to be here alone.

Have we bothered you, then, by showing up? she asked, smiling and raising her hands to loosen the knot that kept her colorful kerchief tightly wrapped around her chin and upper neck. I was waiting for her to come even nearer, so close that I would be able to see her abdomen pressing against the bed. I wanted her to be the one who deliberately lessened the distance between us. Her, and not me, the invalid who simply because of his condition had to wait for others to take the initiative.

I wonder what is taking Bilal so long.

Perhaps, I thought, he was taking his time deliberately. I knew him and I knew that it was something he would do. But all I said was, He won't get lost. He knows where everything is in the hospital.

She had removed the bright red polish from her fingernails. Perhaps she thought it wasn't right for her to prettify herself when she was visiting a patient at the hospital, especially since that patient was me. A man who (as she would have pictured it) would still have his beard, with his turban sitting on the small bedside table.

I was expecting you to come, I said, making the leap across the gulf between us because I wanted to arrive somewhere beyond these hesitant words we were exchanging. I was also trying to keep ahead of Bilal's arrival, not knowing when he would decide to stop tarrying and return to my room.

What I was expecting in response to what I had said was an extended hand, her hand, strong but very soft, and fleshy to the touch. She would reach her hand out to place it over mine, which I had now brought out from beneath the covers and laid flat and inert alongside my body where it would be nearer to her. It would be easily within her reach.

I wouldn't have waited so long to come if I had known. No one told us that you were in the hospital.

Instead of waiting for her to take that step I wanted her to take, I turned my palm upward and lifted it slightly, meaning to go half the distance toward what I anticipated her response to be. I saw her hand come out, a bit hesitant but surely strong with desire when she took mine, her fingers feeling for it and then pressing on it, keeping her eyes steadily there as well, and gazing at our hands together, as if she were getting herself to understand—and telling me at the same time—that this little act of hers was a carefully considered one.

And so this time she had done it deliberately. Now she couldn't retreat to where she had been before. This couldn't be a momentary, passing incident, I thought, just a minor slip or a careless touch to be ignored and then forgotten as soon as the impress of her hand's touch was gone. Bilal's here, she said, turning to address him as he hurried over to the table where he set down two plastic coffee cups, making it dramatically clear that they were about to burn his fingers. Even in front of him, behaving as though nothing had happened, her eyes revealed what had taken place two minutes before. Moist and shining, they seemed to me to carry a breath of joy that showed they were already elsewhere, somewhere beyond the reach of anything she might say, as she began asking Bilal how he had carried those two cups when they were so steaming hot, and then why he had brought two, as long as it wasn't permitted to me, as an invalid, to drink coffee.

I joined in on joking with Bilal. He must have taken a long time, I remarked, because a pretty girl had delayed him there at the coffee machine. She echoed me, saying how much he liked the girls and how he would stand endlessly in front of the mirror for their sake. That pleasant funny intimate sense of connivance which Bilal loved—and I could tell that too—told me she was happy about what had happened in his absence. It told me she had been anticipating it. It was what she had wanted.

I was about to leave the hospital on my own, provided, or loaded down, with all the things they had left attached to my body. At least I could keep it all concealed beneath my clothes. As he instructed me on when to come back, and then on what I must do between now and then, the doctor let me know that now some of my bodily functions had changed. I must accept this and get used to it, he said. In my continuing state of pain, I somehow knew already that I would never again be exactly the person I was before. The spells of pain I was enduring were not going to end even when I was officially healed. It was hard to understand, let alone accept, as a man of religion who knew that those who are patient reap the rewards of their patience. But I felt sometimes as though I were in a permanent and losing struggle.

Is that woman well now? I asked the nurse when I saw one of the patients walking past my door in normal clothing accompanied by a man carrying her belongings. I meant: she won't be coming back to the hospital?

I had often had to wait for this nurse to finish making my bed so that I could get his attention and ask him about what they had taken from my body and then, what they had done with these body parts. Well, they examine them, he would say. But then? I would press him. I mean, after they do the examinations, what do they do with these organs then? He didn't know. He just muttered or put me off, trying to get me to understand that he hadn't studied anything beyond what he was doing for me now; that he was on the lowest rung of the professional nursing ladder. He knew less and did less than she knew and did, the female nurse who came in now and then.

I must get used to my new situation, the doctor said to me. My new condition. With these vague words he was suggesting that this 'condition' was nothing more than a few little alterations to my bodily functions. But when I went out into the daylight for the first time, I was suddenly and powerfully conscious—the awareness of it came like a sudden gust of wind—that in the company of others I would be hiding something. I would have a secret. This realization embarrassed me, and it scared me too, so badly that my face flushed a deep red as, for the first time since my operation, I had to step in among the crowds of people coming and going at the hospital entrance. Trying to skirt them, worried that they would bump into me, attempting to protect my body with both hands, I remembered how Bilal had walked in front of me to clear a path, turning back to check on me with every few steps. This time he wasn't here with me to push away the bodies that might collide into me. He wasn't here to step up to do things that would relieve me. But I smiled at the thought of him anyway, and I guess I smiled also as I thought about him coming to visit me at home.

My wife knew I would arrive at home about when I did. She had gotten herself ready for this event by putting on the same clothes she'd worn when she visited me in the hospital. She prepared the children to be waiting for me, their faces clean and their clothing well-arranged, though it had all been done hurriedly, I could tell. She must have been looking out the window from one instant to the next, for she saw me the moment

I arrived. She assembled the children around her, there in the entryway at the top of the long flight of stairs. They were all waiting for me, silently, as I walked up the steps slowly. They didn't move. They went on standing there without making a sound as I turned to face them. They were all staring at me from where they stood, there at the top of the outside steps. They didn't come down to meet me, and I didn't see any smiles on their faces, not on any of them. She must have somehow gotten the boys to understand what I had gone through, and they were waiting for some sign from me. Would I laugh, for example, or joke with them somehow, or wave to them as a signal that I had arrived? Only then would the two of them know, perhaps, how they ought to act. I halted partway up the steps because I needed to rest. I smiled and raised both hands fisted the way boxers do. The boys smiled but only cautiously. The gesture I'd made didn't conceal how exhausted I was. It must have made them even warier to see me without my beard. They seemed to be fixing their eyes on my smile as I resumed climbing the stairs, except that by then I was no longer smiling. Reaching the top I felt completely depleted. I was panting and I couldn't finish my words as I spoke to little Hiba, or rather to her doll, or indeed what was left of her doll. The doll is still so little, I said to Hiba. She hasn't grown at all while I've been away. I was barely able to move my arms, to brush my hands across the boys' faces and heads. I did make the usual gesture to ask how their playing had been.

I didn't try to fight off the dizzy spell that came over me as I stood there in their midst, expecting them all to go inside ahead of me. I told their mother that I was dizzy and I must sit down. She shoved them away to make way for me to walk to my room. Here, here, she said, pointing to the armchair near the door. When I had collapsed onto it, she told me to lower my head and lean it over the edge. I was crooked over, my eyes closed, when I felt her hand stroking my forehead, trying, I figured, to get the blood circulating there. It wasn't a real faint, just a few moments and then I opened my eyes to see her still there, standing in front of me. Better? she asked. I nodded, and asked where the children were.

I'll make you something to give you some strength, she said, turning and at the same time giving me that look, which I knew meant I must stay as I was, alert, and not go dizzy again. She wasn't long in the kitchen. She hurried back in, stirring the glass of lemonade vigorously as she brought it up to me, unsure of whether I could hold it in my own hands. I lifted my head from the seat back and tried to sit up straighter. Lots of sugar, to wake you up, she said once I had taken a sip. As I looked around, just trying to prepare myself for another sip, my eyes fell on my father's books, still on the floor exactly as they had been.

I left them. . . . I figured you would arrange them when you got back. . . . Anyway, no one has been in here.

How is my father?

You will go in to see him as soon as you've had a rest.

Anything happen to him?

No . . . no, you'll see him now.

I handed her the glass; I needed to try to stand up. She wanted me to stay there, resting and finishing the lemonade, but I felt I could not put off seeing my father since he knew I had come back.

They had moved his bed to where his chair had been. His bones were aching, my wife explained as she went out, carrying the glass of lemonade to the kitchen. As I studied the bed, which they had now placed immediately next to the door, I wondered why they had blocked the way, making it difficult for anyone who wanted to be inside the room. No one had made that little bit of extra effort to put it in the middle of the room, over there where it ought to be.

Are you asleep, Father?

The skin ringing his closed eyes seemed thinner and his eyelids just above the lashes had reddened.

Are you asleep, Father?

He opened his eyes suddenly. I sensed that he had heard me the first time but had held back, wanting to be certain that the voice coming to him was real; that it was coming from somewhere outside and was not merely a sound circling around in his head.

Do you have a fever? I asked, resting my hand on his forehead. Taking my hand off his brow I saw his eyes widen. He looked surprised. I did not know whether it was my thinness that astonished him or my clean-shaven state or simply my changed appearance overall. To reassure him, I said I was a bit weakened and that I looked like this because of the operation and because they hadn't allowed me to eat anything solid after it.

He made an effort—it clearly tired him out—to bring his hand out from under the sheet and raise it a little, just enough that he could point his finger at me, and then perhaps even make a series of circles in the air with it, as he did whenever he was trying to ask about something. I tried to come up with an answer; I had to assume that I knew what was concerning him, and what he wanted to know. The operation? I queried, wondering if this was his biggest question, and if so whether he would listen to me, whether he did really want to hear something about it. But when I paused after finishing my answer, which was sketchy in any case, he moved his hand again. Fifteen days, I said, thinking he wanted to know how long I had stayed there, in the hospital. Then I said, trying to deflect any further questioning, that I would be starting to read the books. Not right now, but as soon as I had gotten some rest.

He wanted to know if the operation had rid me of my illness. He wanted me to tell him how I was now, after the surgery. Not with a few easy words of reassurance but with the truth. I would have to show him the long wound running the length of my belly, if he really wanted the truth.

The operation wore me out, I said. But it did get rid of what was making me ill. That was all I said, and I just placed my hands flat against the location of the wound as though by doing so I was thanking God for giving me back my health.

His unfocused yet questioning eyes and his raised hand, supported by his elbow, showed me he meant to persist in seeking the information he wanted. It wasn't simply that he had to know about my illness and recovery; he wanted to push me. He was challenging me to speak to him as though his present state of oblivion had not affected his consciousness at all. I responded to this desire of his. I described to him how I had woken up from the operation to find tubes coming out here, from my mouth, and here, from my nose, and also from my stomach; and that they kept me from having any food or even water to give my body a chance to get accustomed to the alterations they had made. What I had to do from now on, I explained, was to go back to see the doctor every so often in order to make sure everything was going . . . . But now it looked as though I had said all of these things simply in order to put him to sleep.

That nap I needed so badly was interrupted as she came repeatedly just barely inside the doorway to see whether I had woken up. The minute I raised my head she came over to the little table in front of where I was reclining to pick up the tray of food. Looking at what remained on both plates she remarked that I hadn't eaten a thing. She was already setting the tray down again when I said I had eaten and my stomach was full. She returned from the kitchen almost instantly, this time sitting down at the end of the sofa closest to me. She didn't wait to ask me how I had found the children. Before I could even give her a puzzled look, she said she had learned where the school for the deaf and dumb was. That's exactly how she said it, repeating the school's name in her description of it.

In Beirut?

The teacher at their school gave the driver directions. He took me there, the day I came to visit you in the hospital.

The boys weren't with you?

I was by myself. But at the school they asked me a lot of questions about the two of them.

She knew I would not be able to keep up my side of the conversation and so she had prepared herself to fill up my silences by talking about what she had seen there. There are more than two hundred children at the school, she said. Boys and girls, and they can talk, to each other, with signs and sounds.

Have you said anything to the boys?

Maybe they've realized something. But I was waiting until you were here to hear from you what . . .

In passing, I couldn't help thinking that it seemed she was trying to hurry their departure; that she wanted to be rid of having them always here in the house. I couldn't help thinking that; because, as she spoke and as she seemed to be readying herself to hear what I would have to say, she was showing a level of keenness that I had never seen in her.

So, then, when would they go?

At the school, first they told me me that the two of them would have to wait until the start of the new year. The new school year I mean. Then they said, the end of this term, in April, so what do you think about that? Finally, they agreed with me, and said they would receive them whenever we are ready. That's exactly the words they used.

She was hurrying to get them into the school because she wanted to embark on whatever it is that women begin to do when they decide they must change their lives, now and not sometime in the future. Maybe she wanted something like the life of that schoolteacher who never stopped giving her advice on the boys' education.

Where are they right now?

She got to her feet instantly, assuming I wanted to summon them to tell them about this.

They were with their sister at the bottom of the outside stairs in that cramped space behind the door to the street.

They had left it half closed, making do with the dim light that seeped in through the opening in the solid metal gate. Hearing her mother's call, Hiba looked up and clapped her hands. And then my son Ahmad turned his gaze toward us quizzically. Come up here, she said. Come up here. As she spoke she beckoned them to climb up to where we were.

Like her, I did want them to go. If they were to really learn something, somewhere other than here, I thought, they would relieve me of my feeling of constant pity. And they would be among other children just like them. All of them, in the same condition—surely, there, they would have playmates who would not turn their backs or shove them or pelt them with stones to make certain they never came too close.

You two, I said, with my tongue and my mouth. With my fingers I said it too, raising two fingers directed at them. You must go to this school, I said, and accompanied my words by opening my palms flat and then pressing them together as if they were two pages in a book whose words I had just been reading with my own eyes. It is a school far away—my hands started creating this distance, repeating the same movement over and over so that they would realize that they were going to go there, and by themselves. Then it occurred to me that perhaps if they could recognize that I was moving my lips unusually slowly, they might think I was telling them that they would learn how to talk there. Beirut, I said, stretching my lips exaggeratedly wide to accommodate the long vowels. Be-e-e-ru-u-ut, I repeated. I could see that they were both trying to hide a laugh which was already playing on their lips.

It didn't take me very long to realize that my additions and flourishes were simply the pitiful equivalents of what garrulous people do when they add in extra words just for the sake of it, even though there is no need. The boys knew already where they were going to go and what they would do there. To get me to realize fully that they already knew these things that I had detained them here to inform them about, Ahmad threw his arm across his brother's shoulders and tugged him over: the two of them appeared to be going off somewhere together. Then my son Ahmad began to point, his fingers held tightly together, first at his body and then at his brother's body. It was his way of telling me that he approved of what they were going to go off and do.

Perhaps it was because when I was little, he was the only deaf person I knew. Or maybe, due to him dying early, before he reached thirty, it was because I was able to see the span of his entire life, from his childhood to his death. Unlike the other children, I approached him where he stood by himself. I nodded at him in greeting. He smiled at me, though it was an uncertain smile, as he probably suspected me of getting up to one of those tricks the boys played on him. He just stood there, unmoving, his hands in his pockets to warm them up, his gaze on some faraway object that he could make out on the horizon where the land rose high and craggy. So that I wouldn't just have to go on standing there awkwardly nearby while he occupied himself with whatever he was staring at, I touched him on the shoulder. When he turned to me I made a shivering movement with my whole body to suggest how cold it was. He smiled again. His cheeks looked very dry, the skin even peeling, probably from the staggering cold. Would you like to go for a walk? I asked him, making two of my fingers move like walking legs. He nodded, but only after giving me a long and intense stare.

That first time, as we set out, taking a few steps in silence, I couldn't help feeling weighed down by what I had just catapulted myself into. It didn't look to me like Jawdat would do anything more than walk. I didn't have any idea what more we could do, anyway; all I seemed capable of was shivering inside my coat. After taking about twenty steps, or perhaps thirty, I even began to wonder how soon it would be all right for me to stop and flip my hand at him to signal the question in my head: How about if we turn around and go back now?

As we returned he simply kept warming his hands in his pockets. He seemed absorbed in whatever was going through his mind. I started thinking, too. I was thinking about how—because of his deafness—he couldn't even know the boys by name in the way that they knew him by name. He didn't know any of them, or he knew them only by sight. As we arrived at the spot where we had begun our walk, I got the idea of running a little experiment. I wanted to test whether he would pick up anything if someone very close by were to say something. Not that he would hear it exactly, but would it somehow reach him, through his body perhaps? Jawdat, I started to say to him, without moving my lips or appearing in any way to be speaking. Then I started repeating it, in a louder voice, and then even louder: Jawdat . . . JAWDAT . . . JAWDAT. But nothing at all changed in his expression. In fact that set look on his face, unchanging as I spoke, gave him the appearance of someone who was finding it painful to have the thoughts, whatever they were, that were going through his head.

Perhaps because when I was young I didn't know any deaf person but him, I found myself comparing his appearance, and his way of conducting himself, to my son Ahmad's. I saw resemblances even where the two of them were completely unalike. For instance, I would picture my son Ahmad bending his neck, keeping his head low out of shyness, when in fact I had never seen him do that. Or I would imagine his eyes, smiling in the way they did to show how delighted he was with his own cleverness, reverting instantaneously to hold the somber look that Jawdat's face always had.

Where's Ahmad? And then: Where's Ayman? I seemed always to be asking her this question, in the days I spent entirely in the house. Even when people were coming to visit me I would go to her in the kitchen, or whatever room she was in, to ask her, Where is Ahmad? or, Where are the two boys? She must buy them clothes before their departure, I would say to her urgently. It grieved me to think of them—there among the children in that school—being in the same state they were in here. Take some money and buy them new clothes, I would press her, before going back to whoever it was I had left in the reception room.

Who will take them there? You or me?

Do you want to take them? Or do you want me to take them, with the driver?

Since she was the one who had spoken with the school authorities then let it be her, with the driver and with the teacher she knew.

But we'll see them here in the vacations?

In the vacations, and if we want, at the weekends. If we want, she repeated, looking at me to see what I might say.

I felt such sympathy for them but I also found myself feeling anxious for them to leave. Sometimes I would ponder how this feeling of urgency in such moments is so typical. We are eager to accomplish quickly something that we know has to happen anyway. It's a bit like clearing a canal only to find that there's already water in it, and it has been sitting there for some time.

She woke them up before there was any glimmer of daylight. Even so, she seemed in a hurry, as though she had overslept and was running late. She began tugging at their hands and feet to get them out of bed quickly. Then she drove them into the bathroom and stood at the door. When they came out shivering from the cold she seized their hands and dragged them in to where their new clothes lay. She had put them all out neatly and precisely arranged as they would sit on their bodies: the two shirts at the top with heavy sweaters laid over them and the trousers below, placed as exactly as possible where their waists would be, and likewise two pairs of shoes with socks, there on the floor exactly in position as they would put their feet into them.

Is the teacher going with you?

She is too busy right now. No, she won't be with me. But the driver is coming at six.

In her behavior and her words, she continued to defy everything I had grown accustomed to since first knowing her. In the remarkable efficiency of everything she seemed to put her hands to right now—one task after another—she was beginning to look to me like an entirely different woman. Even her thin face, which always looked as though the skin had been stretched beyond the breaking point, looked different, as though a subtle shade of color was spreading across it and giving more distinction to its features.

She was giving them her final scrutiny before they all went out. In a moment she would shepherd them quickly to the door. I stopped them, giving a cautious little wave toward the door we had closed on my father's room. They immediately turned and headed there. Ahmad gazed at him, asleep with his face turned to the other side, and looked back at me, clearly wanting to know from me whether he ought to wake up his grandfather. When I nodded, he went around to the other side of the bed followed by his brother, so that they were facing the sleeping man who had settled into the position he wanted to be in. Instead of trying to awaken him with a sound or shaking him gently by the shoulder, Ahmad just shifted his gaze from his grandfather to me, once, twice, again, asking me to back him up, to confirm that his grandfather was truly asleep and that he must leave him that way. His mother helped out. Hurry . . . hurry! She was whispering it; she knew he could not hear.

Under the black abaya that she always put on before leaving the house, she was wearing new clothes too, and in addition over her arm she had a shiny little black bag. Ushering the boys hurriedly out the door, she said I shouldn't tire myself out by coming down. She turned the two boys to face me so that they could say goodbye. They were confused by her actions and they moved slowly, waiting for a signal as to what they should do. I waved my fist mock-seriously in my son

Ahmad's face, inviting him to be as strong as my fist was. I gave my son Ayman a big smile and ruffled his hair.

As they went down the stairs, their mother in the lead, they didn't raise their eyes again to look at me. Once they were close behind her at the door giving onto the street, I hurried over into my sitting room so I could watch them from the window as they climbed into the car that was waiting for them.

There was no longer anything to distinguish his periods of sleep from his times of wakefulness. If no one woke him up— giving his shoulder a little shake or speaking quietly into his ear—he remained absent from this world, covered up to his beard in the bedclothes. When I saw that as he slept he kept himself for hours in the same prone position on the same side without the slightest movement, I recalled how my mother used to describe the deaths of people she knew: they were like candles in the moments just before the wax melted completely and the candle went quietly out.

My mother always accompanied these words with her own illustration, holding up her thumb and index finger and bringing them together slowly until there was no longer any space between them. The candle had gone out and the man near death had died. All that was left to my father now was that final moment when the two fingers come together and which is always a surprise—even though to all appearances he was moving slowly and steadily toward his death. It would come as a surprise even if I was present in that moment when the candle was snuffed out, which would be not so different than the moments when I told myself that he was probably not even aware that I was there, as I came in and lay my hand on his forehead to check his body temperature. I delayed doing what I ought to be doing for him at particular times, such as feeding him, as long as he had no idea, with his eyes seemingly permanently closed, what time it was anyway.

I told myself now that I would delay feeding him until my little Hiba woke up, even though I knew that there wasn't the remotest connection between these two events. In the room where I received guests, the books were piled up exactly where the two men had left them. The cabinet was open, its glass panels flung wide. I considered trying to distract myself by returning the books to their shelves. But my enthusiasm waned quickly. All I did was to sit down close enough that the books were within my reach.

By now I'd forgotten which books I had leafed through before my admission to the hospital. I forgot because my way of reading was to turn the pages in search of phrases my father might have scratched onto their margins. I was doing the same thing now, going through whole series of pages rapidly, searching for a sign of that handwriting, those elongated letters, the tall stems of the alif and the lam and the taa, the sweeping tail of the miim at the end of a word. Maybe he had meant to shape his handwriting into something resembling his oratorical style, loud, high-toned and drawn out, attuned to holding the attention of his listeners. Perhaps he had assumed that anyone finding these inscriptions would be awed into silent reverence as were the people who came to listen to him in the Hussainiyas.

I had to know, now, whether he had written anything himself. If he had written things, people would have known about them, and he would have been known for them. They might even have memorized the words he had written. My grandfather Sayyid Murtada's fatwa on how a husband could return to his wife after divorcing her was still known and talked about, as was his ode to the Imam Ali in which he had refuted the Azhari Sunni shaykh who tried to deny the Imam Ali his right to be the first Caliph after the death of the Prophet. I had heard villagers, even those who likely didn't know how to read or write, repeating lines from my grandfather's ode.

On your way, pause in honorable Najaf
    And pass my greetings to the Imam most pure
Whose tireless efforts were spent on the noblest cares
    And whose nobility places him higher than the
        firmament's Jupiter
For I am the son of the lady of virgins, I am the son
    of Fatima
    And I am the progeny of Abu Turab Haydar

But my father did not write anything. He did not utter anything that became part of a public legacy. All that remained were the stories people told. How he would rush forward with his cane lifted high, ready to pounce on the men sitting at the tables, and how they were clueless whether to brandish their own sticks in response. Or how he stalked down from the pulpit to cuff the officer in military uniform who sat down in the front row, his chest a mass of stars and medals. Get him out! Get him out of here, he said, and the men to whom he addressed this challenge were so emboldened by his audacity that without any instructions from him they ganged up to start a fight with the soldiers outside who were merely waiting for their officer to emerge.

My father never had any of that inner stillness that might have allowed him to sit back and think as a writer would, pen in hand as he muses over the next sentence. He was never like those wise and learned scholars who spoke carefully and judiciously to those who came seeking counsel. I always sensed that his anger was stronger than whatever the source of it merited. I saw this most forcefully when he confronted the villagers, just men seated around their tables playing cards. He made it appear as though these men he was lambasting had done something as awful as repudiating the faith. But whatever they were doing, it was never as bad as that.

Sometimes I convinced myself that he had inherited this anger that fueled him from a legacy of oppression, a wrong that pursued those who lived hundreds of years before we did, or the residue of the terrible struggles they suffered, emerging broken, their heads bowed low. I speculated that maybe somehow he still felt the blood of the Prophet's family flowing through him, hot with the wars of those times. Maybe that feverish blood still rose within him, and no conceivable stretch of time could drive the possibility of it away. The centuries elapsing since the battle that felled those ancestors of ours did not make enough of a difference. Perhaps he chose—it must have been a matter of choice—to read narratives in these books of his that stirred up his anger beyond a point that would merely push someone to regret or weep over what had happened to the family of the Prophet, as people used to do during the solemn days of our Ashura commemoration, as they listened to Sayyid Amin reciting the story of how so many in that family had been slain.

In this sense he was not at all like his father or his grandfather, nor the ancestors before them. Among the books he read, those he clung to were the ones that answered to his sense of rebellion and fed his anger. Whenever I listened to one of his sermons or heard him speaking to others I always anticipated that his words would come laced with incendiary quotations, things that had been said by men like him to incite others. The train is stoked with flame not smoke—Hellfire is surely on its way, he would say as he cited the legendary Abu Dharr attacking the ruling class for plundering other people's property, while a member of that very class sat before him in the front row, unable to get up and leave lest my father sing out from behind his pulpit, Where to? Where do you think you can flee?

It would take me a very long time to locate what it was he had searched for in his books. It would be easier for me to rest satisfied with what I already knew about him. Likewise, if I really wanted to rearrange the books on those shelves according to their relative ages or the topics they covered and their area of expertise, it would require so many hours that for a long time to come many of them would remain in these piles, stacked up on the floor next to their bookcase. Instead, I must go and look in on him; I must not wait any longer to feed him even if the hunger he ought to be feeling has not yet pulled him from his sleep.

Still, I was slow to get to my feet. It was more comfortable to remain where I was, sunk into my armchair and completely inactive. I had even begun to doze off when I became aware that my daughter Hiba was standing in front of me, her little hands rubbing the effects of sleep from her eyes. She looked desolate. No doubt she was unhappy that her mother and brothers were not at home. After giving her a hug and clasping her hands in mine I told her that this morning it would be me who would wash her face and feed her. I asked her what she would like to eat. Then I repeated my question, following it with a list of the dishes I could prepare without much trouble, foods I figured she knew. I waited for the after-effects of sleep to wear off, waited to hear her say her first words of the day.

I knew I would be spending whole days at a time sitting in the house as I waited for my strength to return. But that day in particular, forced to stay in the house, I felt imprisoned. Several times I almost acted on my craving to get out. Only to go into the square below our house, where I would pace a few steps in either direction but not go so far that I would be unable to hear any sounds coming from the house. It was a very long day. I didn't do anything beyond concerning myself now and then with Hiba, and feeding my father twice, although the second time he fell asleep almost immediately and I left the plate and spoon on the little table next to the bed. The rest of the time I spent sitting near the piles of books, readying myself to reach for whatever book might present itself first. But I couldn't overcome my sense of lethargy every time I so much as thought about reading.

As the hour approached when according to my calculations my wife was likely to return at any moment, sitting in that room began to feel truly oppressive and deeply irritating. From time to time I got up and went to the window to see whether the sound I could hear of a car somewhere outside was the car that would stop at the street gate to let her out. I had never been in this situation, waiting at home for my wife to return from an excursion. Indeed, it occurred to me—but without causing me any irritation, and without leading me to actually believe it was true—that today we had exchanged the roles we were each accustomed to playing. Every time I confirmed that the car I heard and then saw at the window was not the car that would disgorge her, that sense of having exchanged places grew stronger, and the new image I was developing of her became more real—this demeanor that made her seem so at odds with the person she had been for so long.

I remained seated there near the pile of books. I was still there when I heard the tap-tap of her feet coming up the outside steps. I had already heard the gate clanging shut and her brief exchange of words with Hiba, who was squatting out there just behind the outer door. As soon as she came in she looked into the sitting room, just in time to see me shift position. I turned toward her exactly in the moment when she appeared. I wasn't pleased about the coincidence. I didn't like being caught in this position, as the person who was so obviously waiting for someone else with the sort of look in his eyes that must be in mine now. She was fanning her hand in front of her face, trying to stir up some fresh air, and she remarked that it had become very hot outside and that two of the car windows had been stuck shut. She turned around to face the corridor, but before taking a step she asked if I had fed Hiba. I just gave her a slight nod. I didn't like her asking me if I had fed Hiba, putting me in the position of having to answer that I had. My curt response stopped her from going on to ask me how I had looked after my father.

She stayed a long time in the room where she had gone to change her clothes. Waiting for her to come back to where I was sitting, I figured she was deliberately taking her time; it was her way of punishing me for the indifference I had shown by giving her no response beyond that unconcerned little nod. And then when she left the room she went directly into the kitchen, from where the sounds of pots and plates prolonged my wait even more. Perhaps she was expecting my patience to run out, expecting I would get up and go to her. To stand there supporting myself with my hands planted on the door frame as I asked her—and she would not stop busying herself with the dirty dishes in the sink—how the boys had been, and how they seemed when she left them there.

But I didn't do it. I stayed where I was. Five minutes or perhaps a little longer. Then I got up, went over to my abaya and turban and put them on, and walked to the outside steps. Before I started down, I swung the door harder than usual so that it would let out a particularly loud screech. In the dark little area between the steps and the high, solid iron gate I paused, but only for a few seconds to speak to Hiba. She had set out a few empty cans and spread rags over them to make a house for her doll. I asked her if she would like to go outside with me. When it seemed clear that the only response I was going to get was the stare she was giving me now, I opened the door to the street and went out. But I wasn't going any farther than the very short distance I had imagined myself pacing as I sat inside feeling imprisoned.

No more than a short distance, twenty steps perhaps, pacing back and forth, willing the time to pass.

As-salaamu alaykum, Maulana, said Abu Atif, one of the two men in the neighborhood who seemed to enjoy keeping me entertained. He and his friend had already come once to visit me since my return from the hospital.

Praise be to God, you look much better, Maulana, your face looks better. And the beard as well, he added as he studied me, smiling as he noticed that the hair sprouting on my chin was somewhat longer now.

Are you going to the mosque? he asked me. His words reminded me that the time had probably come for me to wind up my period of home rest and return to the mosque. I hadn't gone in there since my operation.

Come, we'll go together, I said. I found it pleasing, the idea of going there with him. Doing that would use up twice the time I would spend otherwise, and time would pass before I was even aware of it and without my having to do something to hasten its passage.

Chapter Four

MANY THINGS HAD CHANGED IN my body, and I was the one who had to figure out what those things were; or rather, to acquaint myself with them gradually, one by one, in the days after I left the hospital. The doctor had told me I must get used to these changes inside of me. I must form a new memory of my body. For example, he said, you must find another way to do what you do with your wife. He was studying my face closely as he said this to me, trying to make out the impact his words would have on me. For my part, I was waiting to hear what he would say next. I expected him to explain something to me, to guide me along by telling me what he knew. What he must know, which was certainly much more than I knew. You will see for yourself, he added before busying himself fishing his pen from his coat pocket to write something down on the piece of paper that would be my permission, once the nurses had it, to leave the hospital and go home.

By now I was tired of sitting at home but I was also weary of going around to the mosque, where I had begun to spend the interval from the late afternoon prayers until evening prayers were over. Those who came to the mosque were very few, four or five men who came for the prayers but didn't stay long afterwards. After they had left Abu Atif and his companion would show up to keep me diverted, or simply to help me get through the long stretch of time late in the day that, like me, they did not know how to spend, or where. It pleased them to see how attentive I was to the village news they spun for me, and they seemed just as delighted to be able to say things in front of me that are not normally said in the presence of men of religion.

Hajj Khalil brought his wife a box of lokum sweets so she would kiss him in bed, one of them would say, the other one chiming in to add that the box of lokum was a waste of money anyway since Khalil's thing had shrunk and now it was even smaller than it had been before. I laughed at what they said, but my laugh had a note of reluctance in it. I knew I ought not to humor this tendency of theirs. Instead, as they were getting up to leave, I ought to instruct them to stay on for the evening prayers. It would be tantamount to reminding them, once again, that they must not assume I would play along with their little jokes any more than I already had.

The house annoyed me as much as the mosque left me feeling restless and dissatisfied. Sometimes when I left the mosque I considered continuing on, walking on my own two feet like a normal person setting out on a leisurely stroll. But I found myself always turning immediately toward the high solid iron door that marked the entry to our house. I was conscious that a person like me really should not walk just for the sake of walking. I wasn't someone who should be seen out on the street, walking along the edge of the road alone with my cloak flapping open and shut. So that no one who saw me would think I was simply out taking a walk by myself, I must appear to be heading somewhere, to a particular house or some other destination, and giving the impression that I did not particularly like walking for its own sake. I had to look as though I was going to a particular address at someone's request because they needed something from me. But if that had been what I was doing—or what I was trying to look like I was doing—then the walking would no longer alleviate my feelings of boredom and weariness. So I would simply return to the house where, established in my usual seat, I would start

140

thinking about what it was I would have been thinking about if I were walking down the road.

I would remember scenes at her home, like the entryway as I was taking off my turban and looking around for a place to set it down. Or I would picture her emerging from the doorway, a little hesitant as she lingered there, waiting for me to pull up, or taking one tentative step and then going on, walking down the narrow paved path toward me. At other moments my imaginings would begin with the sight of Bilal scurrying over to grasp the door handle in time to open the car door for me. As they were wheeling me out, lying on the hospital bed, his voice and his face came to me. The image and the sound of him comforted me, beginning to bring me back into the life that the anesthetic and the dizziness I felt after they administered it had chased from my memory. He had a smile on his face; he looked clean and fresh and his hair was combed carefully into place as—in my head—I gazed down at him, waiting for him to precede me into their home. Come in, welcome, Uncle! I heard his voice rising from the pale gleam of his smiling face. There were times when my mind took me far enough away from my surroundings that I could concentrate on searching out some sort of resemblance between him and her. It wasn't the sort of likeness that people agree on eagerly when they are describing other people—yes, that's it, their faces look alike, or they have the same manner of walking. It was a kind of congruence that left me seeing traces of her in his face and gestures. I didn't know what that something of hers was. I couldn't see it with my own eyes but I felt it.

Get up, come, right now! Your father is choking . . .

My wife's voice jolted me out of my reverie. I stood up quickly and hurried after her. She had lifted him enough to elevate his head above his body and bring him out of his prone position. He was opening and shutting his eyes with every raspy breath he drew, as if he had to call on every morsel of strength that remained in him just to bring air into his lungs.

Lift him up. Lift him!

I hesitated, afraid that I might constrict his breathing even more if I pressed my hands into his chest and back. Seeing my indecision she went over to him and was about to tug him further up but I pushed her away. I must take a chance, I must gamble on being able to make his body do what it was not strong enough to do on its own. I put my hands under his armpits and pulled with a burst of strength that I discovered immediately I did not need. His body was very light because there was so little of it left and as it jerked upwards in my hands, he turned his eyes to me as if now he wanted to truly see me, and not simply to know that I was trying to help him get his next gulp of air.

I'll open the window, she said. I was still hanging on to him, keeping him lifted, uncertain whether he was capable of sitting up with his back supported against the headboard. His breathing seemed to be getting rougher and louder and that suggested to me that the sitting position I had dragged him into was causing him pain and restricting his breathing. His head had dropped as if it were too heavy for the bones in his neck to carry.

Put him back the way he was before, she said as she walked quickly to stand at the other side of the bed.

He turned his eyes to me again, startlingly bright and alert-looking as though they had reverted to being the eyes he used to have before the cloudiness spread across them. He kept them glued on me even as he was summoning all his energy to expel the tiny gasps of air he had taken in with his laborious panting.

You will be all right, Father . . . . You'll get better, I said, responding to this sudden appearance of mental alertness. But I didn't know what to do. I turned to her to ask whether she thought it would help him if we took him out onto the balcony.

We didn't know what to do. I should have summoned a doctor as soon as his illness became apparent. They would have told me what to do when faced with a spell like this. But I hadn't done that. I had thought that his weakness and absence of mind were not the kind of symptoms that required a doctor. In fact, I assumed that doctors would be of no use because his condition was not an illness that might vanish with medication. Old age is not an illness: no one can return the elderly to who they were before.

It was a spell and eventually it was over. His breathing became quieter with every intake of air, although a thin grating sound still accompanied each breath. His sweating had sucked most of the moisture from his body. Leave the window open, I said to my wife as I pulled the sheet up over the lower half of his body. I jerked my head to tell her we were going to leave him now to get some sleep.

Standing in the reception room at the window that overlooked the square I began to mull over the certainty that there would be more seizures like this one. We could know that they would occur but we would be powerless to do anything except wait for them to end. I knew they could treat breathing problems with oxygen tanks that they could even put in people's homes. Yet, even though I knew we must watch out for more and no doubt stronger spells, I figured it was simply a matter of his age. Perhaps what convinced me and left me feeling resigned to it was the mental picture I had of an oxygen tank parked at his side that was as big as the gas cylinders that sit in people's kitchens, with tubes coming from it that we would be hapless about inserting into him correctly.

His eyes had widened as he stared at me, and they remained fixed on me. This was his way of trying to tell me something, I thought. Maybe he suspected that those loud, difficult breaths had been the beginnings of the death rattle. Or perhaps—precisely because he suspected this—he was determined to give me a final look that would get me to understand, only now, that although he had seemed so remote, in fact he had been awake all along. It was just that he had made a deliberate choice to absent himself from us.

We have to get him a doctor, right now, she said, startling me. Quickly she added that she could not manage another spell like this. What if it comes over him when I'm not at home? Or—take him to the hospital now, she said, putting on an expression that was meant to tell me that she had just now had this sudden insight: the hospital! That it occurred to her only in the instant when she began saying it.

He likes being here, where his son is. In his son's house, I said.

She didn't respond to my anger. She simply gave me one last glance and reached for the doorknob to shut the door loudly on me. A look of contempt, even threat; a look she had acquired in the course of her transformation, her progress toward becoming another woman.

The doctor I got to come to the house from Nabatiyeh said there was no point in taking my father to the hospital to be examined. After moving his stethoscope from one spot to another across my father's back and abdomen, he took hold of his jaws and opened them to peer inside. My father remained asleep throughout, or rather—I suspected—kept himself as somnolent as he could. Turning him over in the way we did surely would have awoken him had he been truly asleep. Back in my sitting room the doctor asked me whether he had been in pain. I don't know, I answered, and added that he didn't like showing how he was feeling, at least not in front of me.

That was true in the days when he was strong, the doctor said, flashing a light smile at me. I thought he would give me that same smile again when I asked how many more days my father had. I was not trying to hurry his death, I just wanted badly to know. That is God's command, he answered as though he felt he had to remind me, as delicately and indirectly as he could, that as a man of religion, I more than anyone ought not to ask about this.

144

And you—do you think he's in pain? I asked the doctor. He pressed his lips together as though he were asking himself the very same question.

Of course he is in pain. Perhaps not heavy pain, though—otherwise, everyone in this house would know about it.

Is he feeling pain, maybe, when he refuses to eat?

It's very rare for there to be no pain at the end of life.

Perhaps my father had prepared himself for the afflictions of old age. He knew what would happen to him and so he had readied himself for it by saving up the remnants of nerve he still had left over from his youth. It is when life is being pulled out by the roots, he declared once to some other men of religion who were gathered in our home talking about the final death-struggle and the days that attend it. It is when life is being pulled out by the roots, he said. Listening to him then, the picture I formed in my imagination was of a powerful hand, the veins bulging as it fastened itself onto what must be the roots that mark death's coming, proliferating in every direction and penetrating the chest of the man marked for death. That phrase, life being pulled out by the roots, which he used to describe the throes of death, seemed to resemble him—or rather, it seemed to echo the hard words he directed to his listeners in the Hussainiyas, as it also seemed to mimic the characteristic movements of his body and the workings of his mind: that brain that always went directly, instanta-neously, and forcefully to wherever it was headed, refusing to be deflected by any amount of verbiage.

But when it came to him, the death struggle was not as he had described it. Death approached him slowly. Death was taking its time: one small step every day. A step so minute, in fact, that it could not even be seen and so was not noticed. I reflected on how his way of dying didn't seem at all like him. And he knew it. Not now, in the very final stages, but earlier, when he had been able to wrap himself inside his meditations. We've brought you some food, Father, I would announce to him back then when he could still sit up. He would not turn to me or look at what I held in my hands. There was only that slight flicker in his eyes to tell me he was redirecting his attention from wherever he had been in his head.

My mind is like a little child's, I told myself, every time I had the feeling that my brother was looking down at me from somewhere up above. This didn't occur only in those moments when I was heading toward her house—like right now, my hands on the wheel, the car moving slowly along the road. It also happened as I sat at home, remembering or rather imagining certain places on her body, whether regions I had seen with my own eyes or places I imagined I was touching with my own hands. In that silent dialogue I conducted between me and myself, or perhaps it was between me and my brother who was somewhere far above, I would say to him, But you have died. Then I would find ways to justify the desire I felt, such as telling myself that the long period of time that had passed since his death had erased all traces of his hands from her body. Day by day they had vanished, year after year after year.

I knew that what these mental exercises of mine meant was that I had a need to erase the imprint of his fingers from her body. I was trying to remove those touches from her, every last one of them. In the car, driving slowly, every time I imagined her bringing those parts of her body close to me, I had to chase away my brother's face, sometimes even with a real wave of my hand as though I were brushing away a fly buzzing around me, warning me that it was about to land on my nose.

But you have died, I say to him, in an audible voice that I can't keep from slipping out through the space between my lips, even if it is so soft that it is almost a whisper. As for her—his wife—she goes on revealing her body to me. Not only to my sight but also through the heat I can feel on my hand. Or on both hands as the fantasy mounts of my hands moving as quickly as my eyes can move across the spaces of her naked body.

That I lacked certain things now because of my operation didn't attenuate the vividness of my imagination or the strength of my sensations that turned my imaginings into flesh, real and raw in its nakedness. As if it—her naked body in front of me—could not keep its effervescence from spilling ever closer to me, even if at the same time it preserved its unvarying distance.

As I drove, I couldn't avoid the thought that what was going through my head might actually take place. At that, I pressed my foot down hard on the accelerator to shorten the time it would take me to get there. To get to her. Her house wasn't very far away by now in any case. Ten minutes or even less. The car was eating up the distance and it wouldn't force me to wait much longer. I had to keep myself pulsing with those images filling me. If I could keep them there, they might be capable of pushing me to do what, before now, I had held back from doing.

I am only two turns in the road away from her now. There's the first turn. Now the first turn is behind me. Only two more minutes, or maybe one. Here it is, her house. I will not do anything. I will not gun the engine so that it's more easily heard. I will not press the horn announcing my arrival. I will leave her to hear the sound of the car, just the sound it ordinarily makes. When she opens the door, she will see me sitting here, where I am, behind the wheel.

Behind the wheel I sit, waiting for the door to open, waiting for her to appear there behind it. I think about possibly beginning the process of getting out, slowly; but then I don't move. It is better for me if she sees me looking as though I think she must be out of the house and so I am on the point of turning the car around and heading back.

The closed door, which in my imaginings was supposed to open a few seconds after I brought the car to a stop, remains as it was, both panels firmly shut. Only a few more seconds and I begin to slide from my heightened state of mind into a state of disappointment. I try first to extricate myself from the image I have chosen for myself: to be sitting here behind the wheel as she emerges from the doorway and comes hurrying toward me.

But she will come out, she must come, I say to myself. And when she does, I will still be waiting here. I could turn around, I could head the car toward the main road, but without actually going anywhere. I can circle back here every ten minutes, or maybe a little less, so that every arrival looks like it's the first one. And that way she will be able to say to me, as I inch the car forward, that she herself has just arrived. Or it might be an even better idea to drive up to that little rise covered in trees. From there I can see the house. From there, sitting in my car, I will see her when she reaches home. And then I won't go down immediately. I will wait long enough so that she can catch her breath. And then I will move slowly, and when I arrive it will be as though I was just now driving down the main road and decided to stop off because, as it happened, I had a little extra time.

Now I am there, on the hill above the house. I stop the car between two trees that don't cover the windshield completely, so that I can still see the house and the lane leading to it. I know I must not stay here long, only the fraction of time in which a man passing by won't see me still here on his return journey. If he has to greet me a second time he will get suspicious, of course. In fact, he will come up to me and lower his face to the open window to ask me if I need anything. I really must not stay here too long—ten minutes, for instance, or just a few seconds more, and then I will move my car. I will drive some distance and then I will return here.

Still, I did prolong my stay there longer than I should have. I turned on the engine several times but then I shut it off again. Nothing passed but a few cars that gave the impression of heading for distant destinations. But her house below, and the road to it, looked as empty as ever. Nothing moved. There was nothing there except the still silent image of it, which went blurry and seemed to shimmer every time I stared for too long. When I began to think that the scene in front of me, in its heavy stillness, had taken on a permanence—nothing was going to change now—I switched on the engine and began descending the winding lane that would lead me to her house. Something must happen, I thought, if only I alter my position, where I have been waiting for so long. Maybe after the few minutes it takes me to descend, taking as much time as I can, once I can see the house again I will also see that she has just arrived. I will see her opening the door, and then she will turn around to observe the car she has heard now coming up the lane.

But the five or six minutes of my descent were not sufficient to change anything. The door and window remain closed. And I was tired. I would not make another circuit around the house or the neighborhood. I must go now, and I must go quickly, not even glancing at the sides of the road. Only gazing at the road ahead of me. The way ahead and nothing else, which stretches between here and there and which I will try to shorten by covering it as rapidly as I can, having no thought for anything else but that length of road.

Your brother's wife was here.

Those were the words my wife said to me after turning aside from the door she had opened for me, and taking several steps toward the kitchen.

By herself?

She did not hear me. I hadn't raised my voice, wanting to keep it sounding unconcerned. But I did ask again, a little louder this time. Was she here by herself?

With her son, came her voice from somewhere in the kitchen. I wanted to know more but she—my wife—was not going to add anything unless she was asked specifically. Because I did not want to appear any more interested than would be proper, I decided that I must wait. I must find an opportunity to ask at a moment when my question would seem to arise inadvertently, perhaps out of my own absentmindedness. I found my chance before long. Going to my father's bedside ostensibly to check on his condition, I remained in there for a few moments inspecting him and pulling the coverlet over him up to his chin. On the way back to the reception room I looked in on her to ask, Did my father know who she was?

He was asleep. He didn't open his eyes once.

It was no use, standing here in the doorway. She was not going to say anything more. Any further explanation would amount to some kind of intimacy, a coming-closer that she didn't want and would never make an effort to achieve. But it wouldn't raise any suspicions if I asked her a different question. Her son—did he come, too? This time she dragged herself away from the kitchen to ask me to repeat my words.

Her son. Did he come with her to see his grandfather? Somehow, that reference to his grandfather came out sounding a bit artificial.

He came too, she answered. She said it in a manner meant to inform me that this exchange wasn't worth her having to stop doing whatever it was she had been busy with in the kitchen. Whatever else I wanted to know I would have to find out for myself. I wasn't interested in how long she had stayed here with her son, nor where she had sat, nor where exactly in the house she went. I wasn't even interested in what she was wearing . . . . What I had to know—and I had next to nothing to go by—was whether she had come to see me. Whether she came so that she could tell me that she had come for my sake, and that it wasn't so important whether or not I was there, as long as my wife would inform me of her visit. It's a long trip, I must start back now, I imagined her saying as she rose. And then she would have said, Give my best wishes to the Sayyid.

150

I can see her turning, propelling her son before her, and walk-ing through the doorway, for the door is already open. Give my best wishes to the Sayyid. What that really means is: Give him the news that I came.

She would not have taken her time going down the steps, her high heels tapping against them. She would not have waited to see whether I might by chance show up as she was descending those steps, or so that she could surprise me as she emerged from the door to the street. She would leave that for the next day, when she would be waiting for me. Surely there was no doubt of that. Waiting for me there, in her home.

Hiba isn't here?

She didn't answer.

Hiba isn't here?

She's asleep, she said coming out of the kitchen. When I figured that by now she would be in the children's room, I went into the kitchen to make myself a cup of tea, putting off the moment when I would go in to stand at my father's bed if only for a moment.

This time, and for the first time, I will not allow myself to be satisfied with simply attempting to test whether she wants something, or doesn't. This time I won't be satisfied by seeing only whether the one or two additional moments that I keep my hand lingering over hers, as I watch closely to see what will happen next, are enough to make any difference on their own. I will not conceal what I desire behind our usual words: like when she asks me about coffee and then I have to respond politely that I don't want her to go to the trouble of making it. I no longer want this to be a scene where I limit myself to a few furtive eyefuls of leg, whatever is visible from where I sit perched as always on the same end of the sofa. This is not going to require anything more of me than saying the first word. The first true or real words. I have missed you. Just like that, clear and honest, and not wrapped up in other words

151

that would leave me some latitude to take something back. Or putting my hand over hers for enough time that she, or I, will move after that to something beyond one hand placed over another. To give myself some courage for what I was envisioning, as I drove there I told myself repeatedly that if I didn't do it today, I never would.

All it would require of me was that first word, or that first act. I might stammer and stutter, and my face might betray total confusion. But I would do it. I would see it through, even if my embarrassment halted me momentarily or threatened to send me into retreat. What was important was the first step, after which everything else becomes easy. You have to get away from your cloak and turban, Shaykh Abd al-Hassan, who so adored women, always used to say in Najaf all those years ago. His advice was always that one must not be satisfied with any step that was less than perfect, one that it was easy to pull back from. If that's the way you feel then tell her so with your whole gaze, he counseled. Don't let it look like your eyes fell on her by mistake.

Soon I would be there. The distance from here to there wouldn't take long now to cover. I had preserved this determination inside myself; I was not going to let it dribble away in this very short interval before I reached the endpoint. Only a few minutes. Seconds, no more.

There it was, her home, there in front of me.

She was waiting for me.

She gave the impression, as she peered out from the narrow aperture made by the slightly open door, that she already knew it was me who was arriving. This time though, she did not come outside to welcome me and to say, with the smile of a courteous hostess, Welcome, welcome to the Sayyid. She stayed where she was, her hand on the door which she had only opened partway. With deliberate slowness I got out of the car; just as slowly I closed the door and turned the key in the lock. As I began walking toward the house, having surmised that she would likely remain standing there behind the half-opened door, I saw her turning back to the interior of the house. I saw her lean her body forward slightly as though her ears were trying to catch a voice coming to her from inside. In seconds she had disappeared but she had left the door open for me.

I would have stood waiting at the partially open door, having decided that was best. But she returned quickly, almost at a run. Ahlan, ahlan wa-sahlan to the Sayyid, she said, her greeting submerged in what seemed like traces of mirth creasing her face. She made way for me to come in. Since I was already looking out for what I might encounter, I wasn't surprised to see the three women. They also seemed unsurprised; they seemed almost to have been expecting me. They didn't say anything and they didn't move. Two of them were sitting on the sofa at the center of the suite of matching furniture and the third was standing, a coffee cup and saucer in her hand.

The Sayyid—he is the brother of the dear departed, she explained. These words fell on my ears as odd or even distorted, despite my awareness of how uncertain was my relationship with her, or hers with me. It sounded strange because it didn't sound like her. These words sounded like something that would be said by somebody else. What worried me, though, was that the three women would hear in it exactly what I heard, and that this would send them back into the laughter which had apparently run its course before I came in.

Welcome, come in, she said, her arms sweeping across the room to invite me to sit down, somewhere, anywhere, she didn't specify where. I didn't know either where I ought to sit or whether I should even sit down at all.

I was just passing by . . . I said. The situation lent itself to the excuse I had used so often before as a guest here, which served also as a kind of greeting. Spontaneously, it seemed, and exactly at the same moment, the two women on the sofa got to their feet, making a point of vacating it for me. I refused the offer, signaling them to sit down.

Here . . . over here, Sayyid, she said, pointing to the armchair. But even this would not leave me sitting as far apart from the two women as was appropriate, nor from the woman who stood, though at this moment she was bending over the table to set down her cup.

It's just a coincidence, my being here, I said, bringing my wrist up close and making a show of consulting my watch. I would have to go. But before I could finish saying those words of apology as a prelude to leaving, the woman who had put her cup down on the table spoke. You don't want to sit with us?

I hesitated for a moment, uncertain of what to do. My confusion led me to sit down. Sinking into the armchair and planting both hands on the armrests, I had the sensation of falling into a trap. All they wanted—these three women here in this room—was some cause for more laughter. They wanted to go on laughing and enjoying themselves as they had been doing before I showed up. But this was something I wasn't very good at, and I did not know how to handle it.

I'll make you coffee, Sayyid. She was speaking in a near-whisper, her face close to mine as though to inoculate me against their presence around me.

I won't stay long, I said, my voice also nearly at a whisper.

If that's because we are here, we can leave, said the woman who stood upright again, having been on the point of sitting down in the armchair across from me.

No, no, it's not because of you. I'll go now, I really don't have much time. I began to go through the motions of readying myself to stand up: I straightened my back and drew my feet closer to the chair. They didn't go back to giving each other those meaningful glances and they weren't showing those smiles that had played on their lips as they made a show of trying to conceal them. In the sudden stillness I heard the tap-tap of her high heels as she turned from where she stood behind me and made her way toward the kitchen.

Then I heard the same footsteps returning. She set down the chair she had carried in close to mine.

Now I'll make the coffee, she said, leaving the chair empty. The three women and I remained silent. I was waiting for them to speak. I hoped one of them would say something since the silence was becoming heavy enough to feel embarrassing. From in there she sensed what I was feeling and tried to paper it over by calling out to her friends that they had had enough coffee and she was making just one cup, for me. She doesn't want us here, murmured the woman sitting at the end of the sofa closest to my chair. I smiled but she probably couldn't see that. My head was bowed and I was staring at my hands in my lap.

We should have covered our heads, she added after a few more seconds of silence. I didn't say anything in response but I did raise my eyes to look at her. I thought about trying to say something lighthearted, but I didn't. I just looked down again at my hands. I knew that in my silence and the very, very limited gestures I made, I was creating a great deal of conversation for them. Once they were on their own, the words would come fast.

Coffee, Sayyid, she said. I had heard her footsteps returning. She was holding the cup and saucer: this time, she had not set them down on a tray. Taking the cup and saucer from her, I was very careful to make certain that my hand did not touch hers.

She sat down on the chair next to me. It was a little higher than mine.

We should have covered our heads, the woman said again, her words directed this time to my brother's wife. But she got no response, except perhaps a look calculated to cut short her speech.

I didn't find you at home yesterday, she said to me in a whisper, which in itself brought her closer to me. It was a gesture that seemed to suggest we were by ourselves here, the two of us far apart from the three of them. I could have brought us even closer together, had I responded by saying I had been here yesterday, here at the front door of her home. But I held back, wanting to leave that for a time when I was with her and no one else was there. Even so, I could not overcome my desire to hear more from her, something more that she would say about her visit, something to help me understand whether it was a visit specifically to see me, and not to see my invalid father and my house. That it wasn't a visit based on what remained of our family ties.

Did you stay long there?

An hour, maybe. I couldn't wait there any longer.

The waiting there that she could not do . . . the waiting that she could not go on doing, perhaps because she felt uncomfortable in the house, or maybe because by waiting she had made herself late for something else she had to do. Whatever it was, I picked up only the part of it that responded to what interested me. She could not go on waiting there any longer.

I probably got home very soon after you left . . . . In any case, my wife didn't tell me anything. Except that you came.

Did she tell you that Bilal came with me?

All she told me was that you came, and brought Bilal with you, nothing more. I didn't like to ask her, even though all day long I kept on hoping to hear something more from her.

I lowered my voice as I said this last sentence, and that meant I had to bring myself even closer to her than we already were, only that small space still between us. At this—as close as this, now—her face lit up with that smile that meant she understood what I wanted to say.

No one here wants to talk to *us*, said the woman sitting on the end of the sofa closest to me. She had had enough of talking to her two companions in voices they had kept as low as ours. So we had to stop speaking to each other. We had to sit up straighter and turn our faces to them, showing our readiness to speak, or to listen to whatever it was they had to say.

We were starting to feel like we were alone in the room here, added the woman. The only response her little jibe provoked was a stony stare from my brother's wife. These three would go on amusing themselves by sharing these insinuations of theirs privately, I thought. I couldn't go on sitting there waiting for them to leave. I was still holding my empty coffee cup. When she reached out her hand to take it from me, it was as though she was putting a period at the end of a sentence. She ended the paragraph by carrying the cup into the kitchen instead of simply putting it down on the little table that was within reach.

Something had to change now. Either they had to leave or we all had to leave at the same time.

When she returned from the kitchen, her stride suggested she expected something to happen. I stood up. Looking at my watch, I said I was late. As I began to walk toward the door, I said goodbye to the three women. Not more than a word or two.

Had they bothered me? she asked as she opened the door. Standing in the little entryway, no longer visible to them, she added that anyway, they did not come over every day of the week.

In that diminutive space that shrank even more every time I came nearer to saying something or she leaned toward me to speak, I sensed how very close she was to my touch. It was a true and genuine feeling, the sense a man has when a woman's hand is this close to his touch, or even to his gaze. Being this close when we were together meant to me that we were not just close to arriving somewhere but that we had actually already partly arrived. We had gotten partway there.

Feeling that way, as close as this to her, I felt I knew somehow what she would be like when she finally uncovered herself for me, when all of her was there and accessible, offered to my hands. Driving home, I felt contented. And then, I thought, when we were there at the door together, she had as much as summoned me into a time when we would be alone, her and me. They don't come here every day, she had said with that

157

elusive smile of hers. She was inviting me to come back at the soonest possible moment. That was what she wanted me to do. She wanted me to be here tomorrow or the day after, and no later than that. She would be exactly as I had left her now; the passage of time would not have made her forget where we were, she and I, when we abandoned the three women, when we acted as though we were detached from them, as though we had nothing at all to do with them.

She and I—with them, or between them, yet completely apart from them. We had never been as closely together as we had been on this visit. It was as though their presence—those three women, who were right there with us in the same room— had allowed us to do what we had not done before, when we had been alone. It seemed we had needed to be among them in order to isolate ourselves from them, or from everything around us. To have that proximity where it would have been possible for my shoulder to brush against hers, if I wanted it to do so, with- out it seeming deliberate. My feelings at that moment amounted to more than a simple desire for her. My desire, its limits well known to me, seemed to have gotten mixed up with sentiments that were more mysterious, less clear—affection, intimacy, a tender yearning for things long past. I began sensing that if I were to slip my hand under there, beneath her clothes, I would not be searching only for the desire my body was demanding me to pursue. The desire that was only in my body, that is.

For I knew well that this was not a love of the kind that singers and poets celebrate. I knew it because every time I thought of her, the only form she appeared to me in was standing in front of me: her whole body standing in front of me. That strong body of hers which possessed something that pursues and provokes a man more than it makes him love.

The moment I turned into the square that our house overlooks I knew my father was dead. The Quran reader's voice blared distorted from the pair of microphones attached to the top of the minaret. In the area just in front of the door to the street, which was now standing open, stood a little crowd of men. When they saw my car they all stepped back as if to clear the way for my arrival. Then they surged forward toward me as I was still bringing the car to a stop and then opening the car door. Their faces were grave and silent, some even frowning, and none of them said a word. They must have assumed that I already knew about my father's death and there was no need for them to say anything. And I, who did not know exactly what expression I ought to put on or what words I should say, simply nodded, swallowing. I walked to the iron door, passing through their midst, and they fell into step behind me as I mounted the steps.

In the house, the spaces between the kitchen and the inner rooms were packed with women who had come from their homes clustered around the mosque and the alleys that branched out to its left. My wife was moving among them and she looked more angry than harried. When I went over toward her I thought about asking how much time had elapsed since his death, that is, really asking how long I had left her alone with my dead father. The door to his room was shut although the throng of women seemed to press into the doorway. Like the men, the women stepped back so that I could pass them; they were all staring at me. Inside, once I had shut the door behind me, I heard the sound of a fly buzzing as it circled around the room. It was one of those big flies that always appear singly, always hovering alone wherever they enter. He—my father—lay there beneath the circles the fly was making, his head uncovered. He looked the way he had looked throughout his final days, submerged in that sleep where he never changed position. I even began to wonder how my wife had known he was dead, when seeing him asleep did not look any different than seeing him now, dead. Then it occurred to me that perhaps a lot of time had indeed gone by before my wife realized he was dead.

It would be some time before I could comprehend what his death meant, or even begin feeling what I ought to feel. Standing next to the bed, staring at his body lying motionless with the sheet pulled up over his chin, I found myself unable to react because I couldn't see that anything had changed around me. Just as I had done so often for others when they died, I recited the opening lines of the Quran for the peace of his soul. I recited only the first, short chapter. I did not even have to turn his face toward Mecca, in the direction of prayer. He had already done that for himself, many days ago. That was how he had prepared himself to die, suppressing any wish he might have had to give his side and shoulder a rest by turning onto his other side.

I did not stay long in his room. A few moments sufficed to have a good long look at him. Those few minutes were also enough to deepen my confusion about whether I should go out of the room or stay in there with him. When I opened the door I saw that the women had moved away, some to the far end of the corridor where they mingled with the men. They turned their heads to look at me—women and men alike—and again they made way for me so that I could go into the reception room. As I approached my usual seat and its occupant rose to allow me to sit down, someone spoke up in a powerful, almost thunderous, voice. He thrives who raises his voice in prayer for Muhammad and his folk. They all responded in unison and I felt tears in my eyes. I couldn't keep the sob in my throat, and someone holding a box of tissues came over to hand me one.

Then I was able to keep back my tears. I ought not to cry in front of them—me, who knew that death is the eternal truth, who was so familiar with death from the many, many occasions on which I had said prayers over the newly deceased. To occupy myself and avoid anything that would make me cry, I asked one of the two men who always sat with me in the mosque and was now moving among these seated men as if he were in charge of welcoming them, What time did he die?

He said he did not know. When he came up to the house, with two men who had been standing in the square, my father's body was already cold. He couldn't find a trace of warmth.

He turned toward the corridor, responding to something that one of the women out there had just said. God have mercy upon him, he said as he came back in, bearing a tray crowded with glasses of tea. God have mercy on him . . . There was no one like him, he said in a voice loud enough for everyone to hear. Some of them had turned to look at the photograph hanging on the wall, as high up near the ceiling as it had been for so long. I looked up there too after one of the men standing beneath it said we ought to make copies of it to hand around.

I knew they would take care of whatever needed to be done. They made that known immediately by taking down the photograph. Before they removed it from the frame they passed it from hand to hand, staring at it. It had not yet gotten all the way around when someone took it and began removing it from the frame, saying that he was going to go to Nabatiyeh right now. They would do everything themselves, and beyond that they would show how concerned they were for me by taking care of me—bringing me tea, giving me a tissue when I needed it, bending over me and telling me to stay seated, to stay here, and that if I wanted anything they would bring it to me.

The women's voices rose intermingling from the corridor and through the open doors around it. More people were coming up the steps between the iron door and the house while others were descending, as though the house had opened itself to all the people of Shqifiyeh. They were coming in and going out without necessarily speaking to anyone. Once inside the house, new arrivals joined one of the little clusters of people moving about and making the necessary preparations. The two men who were my companions at the mosque detached themselves from their knot of people and came to ask me whether I would deliver the homily on the day of formal mourning and then in front of me they began debating this and proposing that it should be left to the Jaafari Mufti, who ought to come anyway from Beirut where he was based. And then I could speak after him. The mufti, they said, must come. In any case, of course he would come, of his own accord.

Through the days of his protracted death struggle everything had gotten smaller, even his head. Even his skull. Wrapped in a shroud and lying in the bier in which they carried him to the mosque, he was so light that he did not require the combined effort that the men were preparing to make in order to bear him to where the rituals would take place. What a short trip it was that we were making, I thought, carrying his body. Likewise, the distance from the mosque to the cemetery would be very short. That was why there were very few people behind the coffin, I decided. They were mostly from the surrounding villages. Others—the shaykhs who likely knew of him and had been supporters of what he had once done long ago—were coming from farther away and would arrive too late for the burial. As they were lifting his coffin to carry it to the cemetery, I recalled the image of the crowd surrounding him, men as angry as he was, on that day when he led them, surging forward into the ranks of the soldiers who had already raised their rifles and were pointing the barrels at them. But most people had forgotten all of that. Or, those who had been with him, who had lived through those days, were now very old or even dead. After all, his own folk, whatever family members had remained in the vicinity, had all died too. No one was left but me. And if his funeral was to be worthy of the person he had been, I should have been something or someone other than the person I was now. People come together at such moments to honor those who are living, not those who have died. I should have been who he was, so that the scene of his death would be a true and fitting completion of his life.

It was a short path between the mosque and the burial site. Before his death he had said nothing about his burial. He did not instruct us to bury him in Najaf as his father and grandfather had been. He did not even say that he would like to return to his own village, where he had spent most of his years. Maybe he told himself that all places were alike as long as we—generations of men of religion—were liable to serve anywhere, so that a place that had previously not been ours would become our place. It was hard for me to ask him about this shortly before his death; and it would have been difficult to ask him when he was still in the early stages of his illness. Where do you want to be buried, Father? No, he had left that to me. He had left to me the decision of what to do and where to bury him. And then I had left others to do it in my stead. They were the people who took care of things quickly, leaving me throughout to sit back and merely agree to what they said; whenever someone came to me to say, for instance, We are going to send out this announcement of the burial to the villages, glancing at what was written on the piece of paper, I simply nodded my head and returned it to the person who had brought it over to where I was sitting.

They carried his bier only a short way, and then a short way more. This very short journey absolved me from sending him after his father and grandfather, there where they had wanted to be, in Najaf. If I had attempted it, the long journey and the heat would have destroyed me alive and destroyed him dead. Anyway, I was conscious that the turmoil and furor in which he had lived his entire life had made him different than his father and his grandfather. They had both been calm, sage men, whom others saw only as still figures seated on their mats and moving only their prayer beads. As a matter of course men like them had to be buried out there, so that their deaths came as natural continuations of their lives. Theirs had been an existence in which they always knew what the next day would bring, and the day after as well. They had had many

163

hours in which to think about things. They could ponder all of it before having to say to a son or to a family: When I die, I charge you to bury me in Najaf.

After they lowered his corpse into the earth they began inviting the mourners who had come from the outer villages to one of their homes here. They turned to me, too. Please come, Sayyid, please come with us, they repeated, adding that they had agreed on this plan the day before. I accepted immediately, and walked to the designated house surrounded by mourners and the men of religion who were our guests.

I ought to have told them—the people who had taken care that all of the funeral arrangements were made—to send someone to my brother's house to inform his wife and son. Even this task I neglected. Not because I forgot about it but because I was allowing myself to remain passive, to merely obey whatever they decided on. She learned of it anyway, although probably later than was right. But perhaps that was better for me since on that day—the day of the funeral—I could not be anywhere except among the men, and I had to remain with them as long as they were present. She would have had to stay in the house with my wife and the women who had come to mourn. It was likely that she did not know any of them personally.

I knew her delay in coming to us was not because she didn't care. She might have postponed her visit deliberately. It was still early morning when, on the next day, she arrived with Bilal. He acted as though he were an adult among adults, bending down to embrace me as I was sitting, before I even had a chance to rise to my feet, and wishing me a long life. Then he kept holding me, leaning his head against my shoulder. His mother, in black mourning garb, stood motionless behind him, waiting. Clasping him, I stood up to exchange condolences with his mother, shaking her outstretched hand. I pressed her hand as though through my skin I was transmitting

164

to her my yearning for solace, a longing that I felt came to me from her in the first place, from her very presence and the way she stood before me like this.

It was a soft, beautiful morning. The light coming through the window warmed the upholstery and spilled onto a stretch of the tile flooring, making a rectangle of sunshine there in the middle of the room. As was her habit, my wife did not step across the threshold into the room where guests were received. Stopping in the doorway, she asked her if she would like coffee or tea. When I spoke up to say I would also like tea, my wife turned to go to the kitchen but not without giving me that withering stare which meant I was showing more gusto than was appropriate.

She asked me about the boys. Had anyone told them of their grandfather's death? she wondered. Still displaying his adult expression, Bilal asked me whether they liked the school where they now were. Then he asked me about Hiba. She's here, I replied, looking around as though I were trying to locate her or wanted to ask someone where she was. Yesterday, I said, she was swallowed up in the crowds of women and men, there were so many people here in the house. I sounded as though I was seeking an excuse for why she was not here with us.

Such a great loss, said my brother's wife, feeling a need to mention my father or to commemorate his memory somehow. My role was to react by appearing to be deeply affected, my thoughts wrapped up in him for at least a few minutes. But I also said, to show how sincere my feelings were, and so that I would not simply be uttering clichés or flattery, that with every passing day he had been coming a little nearer to his death; and that I did not know whether the actual moment of dying itself had been difficult for him.

While my wife was still busy in the kitchen, I declared that the two of them—she and Bilal—must remain here until after the noon meal. I said it very quickly, not merely to get it out before my wife came back but also because I wanted my words to sound decisive and final, as though they were simply confirming something that had already been arranged. The words came out sounding more like a command; they reached to include Bilal in what was between us, me and her. All she did was to smile—that smile that included a passing glance toward the corridor between us and where my wife had gone. I had a strong desire to repeat what I had just said—perhaps to hear my own boldness—but she silenced me by biting her lip as a warning and making certain I saw the alarm in her eyes. I shifted my attention to Bilal. I thought he would understand what was going on between us. You will stay with us today, Bilal. We will receive the visitors together, you and I. He looked at his mother, waiting for her to accede to my request before he could agree.

My wife was taking more time than was needed to boil water and make tea. When Bilal looked over at the books lined up on the shelves, I flicked my hand at them and said they were his grandfather's books. I invited him to go over and look at them more closely. Once he had his back turned to us, I didn't try to say anything or make any kind of sign. Anything I could say or do would simply make me look like a foolishly insistent little boy. When I finally spoke it was to ask her how the traffic had been and at what time she and Bilal had left the house.

My wife hadn't been occupying herself only with making tea. When she returned carrying the tray, she was wearing different clothes and had patted into place what could be seen of her hair beneath her head covering. In fact, I thought, she might even have rubbed a bit of rouge onto her cheeks. In any case, her appearance had undergone some slight alteration since the moment shortly before when she had turned to go into the kitchen. As she brought the tray over to her guest she gave the impression of wanting to study this guest up close, as though she was searching for something. When she moved over to Bilal with the tray—for he had sat down again—I saw her do the same thing. After I took my cup she lowered the empty tray and let it hang at her side, the way she would have held onto an empty plate or a loaf of bread. This time, she had decided, she would sit down, here in the reception room. After all, this time the guest was a woman and indeed a member of the family.

But her sitting here with us was temporary, and muddled from the start by the presence of the empty tray. She laid it across her knees where it balanced awkwardly. She asked my brother's wife how the drive here had been, and then she looked at Bilal and said, Mashallah! He's almost a young man. Bilal responded by asking about Ahmad and Ayman and Hiba—exactly like that, each one by name. I was certain, as she kept her gaze fixed on him, that she was recalling exactly what her sons looked like and how they behaved. No doubt in her head she was comparing them to him.

I remarked that she would be more comfortable if she was not holding the tray. She should set it down on the table, I said, as though I wanted to bring her back to her evident hesitation about whether she should leave us or stay here with us. She did put the tray down on the little table beside her. She wants to stay, I said to myself. To stay, exposing herself to the possibility that she will see what crosses my mind as I shift my gaze from her to the woman sitting next to her. To force her to think about the way I might compare them, just as *she* had done by reminding my wife of her own absent sons.

You will stay for lunch, she said, directing her words to Bilal and his mother. That emboldened me to repeat what I had said earlier: Have lunch with us, you and Bilal. He has been missing his uncle.

She did not say yes outright, nothing more than a little murmur accompanied by a smile.

Bilal would like to stay, I said. Anyway, he wants to look through the books in his grandfather's library.

The morning was still fresh and invigorating, the clear soft sunshine lighting up a square, or by now a rectangle, of floor tiles and reaching almost to our toes. In only a few minutes the sunshine would creep as far as her, covering first her legs, pressed together and bare all the way up to her knees.

Here is Hiba, she said, looking toward the corridor.

Hiba was still half asleep, both hands rubbing her eyes as she came straight to me and stood in the space between my feet, only then turning her face to everyone in the room. My brother's wife had gotten up, either to hug her or to pick her up. Coming close to Hiba meant she was very near to me: as she stooped to the little girl's level, her chest was very close.

Hiba tried to ward off this attention by lifting her shoulders and then lowering them, shrugging again and again as she turned to me, swiveling her face and body fully as if she wanted to hide herself in me. I have a chocolate, my brother's wife said, turning to fish the little packet from her small purse. Here it is, she said, holding the wrapper between two fingers and jiggling it as if she thought it was a child's rattle that would make an inviting sound. Hiba hesitated for two or three seconds and then suddenly stuck out her hand to snatch away the candy in its shiny silver wrap.

Give her a kiss, Hiba. Give her a kiss and say merci.

My wife had never uttered this word before. Of course she must have known it, not only from her friend the schoolteacher but also from hearing many other people say it. But for her to pronounce this word—for her to dare to say this word—signaled a startling readiness to compete in a match I knew she could never win.

Before he had finished drinking his coffee Bilal went back to the book cabinet, in obedience to what I had said so insistently. Teasing his mother, I told her that likely he wanted to be like his grandfather and his uncle. She smiled and flicked her hands in a playful gesture of dismissal to protest that he certainly did not want that. He spent most of his time in front of the mirror staring at his face and his clothes and arranging his hair, she said to explain her gesture.

We will eat in here, said my wife, seeming to waver between continuing to sit there and getting to her feet.

No . . . No. We told the driver to come and pick us up before noon.

What I had been waiting for was not her agreeing to stay but my wife going out to the kitchen to set to work on lunch because of the likelihood that she might stay. She—my wife—turned to me, wanting to know what I thought she ought to do. I didn't respond. Rather than occupying myself with her and my brother's wife, I turned to Bilal as though the question of whether she stayed no longer concerned me.

In any case, I will get things started, said my wife.

What do you think of the books, Bilal? I asked him.

He twisted around to face me. They're difficult, he answered.

More than difficult, I said with a smile, in fact with a chuckle as I recalled their titles. Even those must be giving him a headache.

You've read all of them?

No one reads every book.

Even my grandfather?

Your grandfather—I don't know. Maybe.

He faced the bookcase again but the way he stood there, I could tell he was doing it only because he thought it would please me.

We must go to recite the Fatiha over him, I said to him, and then I turned to her to look like I was including her in the invitation. As though we were going on an ordinary outing together. Not to recite verses from the Holy Book over the grave.

Let's go right now, she said, and began immediately to get to her feet, straightening and tugging at her clothes to adjust whatever had gone awry as she sat.

The men who had taken charge of the burial had erected a small tent alongside the patch of dirt where no gravestone had yet been erected. When we were almost there I heard the voice of the Quran reader coming from inside the tent, sounding weak and exhausted as though he had been reciting without a break since the evening before. She tottered unevenly down the narrow zigzagging cemetery paths, pausing every two or three steps as if she already had to steady herself again, her high heels constantly threatening to disrupt her progress. I wondered about giving her a helping hand but I hesitated because I knew that we would be visible to anyone who happened to be walking down the road that ran alongside the cemetery. And anyway, Bilal was walking close behind her, his hands as ready as mine to grab hold of her if she stumbled.

When we were close to the tent she asked me if the man had spent the entire night here. Inside, he raised his eyes from the Quran to glance at me through the open tent flap but only for a second and without any interruption in his recitation. The lamp next to him was lit and as I pulled my head back from the opening I reminded him that outside there was plenty of daylight by now. She had the suggestion of a smile on her face but she seemed anxious to conceal it as she stared at the moist reddish dirt raked across the patch of land. I bent over and then squatted down to scoop up a small heap of soil. I scattered it, letting it dribble through my fingers as I recited the opening verse of the Quran. Bilal followed me, and did as I did, opening his hand to let the soil fall and keeping it outstretched over the dirt as he began to intone the Fatiha. When we had gotten to our feet I asked him if he had loved his grandfather. He did not know what to say, how to answer my question. It didn't appear that reciting the verse over his grandfather's grave had had much impact on him. I too had performed my sequence of actions without really thinking about my father or imagining him actually lying there beneath us. I was too preoccupied and enticed by her presence here, standing so near to me, as I brought back to mind the way she had teetered and almost stumbled as we wound our way among the graves. It was almost as though she wanted to display her need for me, I thought, coaxing me into reaching for her and giving her the support she needed to keep from falling. It almost made me dizzy to think that she was showing her fragility to me—right here in front of me, deliberately like this—as if her actions were meant to show me how a woman needs the protection of a man.

But she didn't behave like other women do when they are standing in front of a fresh grave. She did not shed a single tear and she said nothing about my father. To the contrary, I thought, she seemed to want to show that she was hanging onto the remnants of that little smile that hadn't left her face throughout her slightly off-balance walk through the cemetery. I didn't want to keep her there for too long, moving her eyes from the fresh soil directly in front of her to the graves that surrounded his. I jerked my head slightly as a way of asking her whether she would like for us to go back now and she assented with a similar little nod.

We had gone only three or four steps away from the grave when she spoke for the first time. I should not have worn high heels, she said. She crowned her declaration by inclining slightly toward me but without allowing herself to touch me. Then she asked Bilal to give her his hand, and he turned around and rejoined us, having gone ahead. Even he—even Bilal—knew, or at least he had an inkling, that there was something here that went beyond an ordinary walk. Even Bilal sensed that we were not exactly as we really ought to be. Take your mother's hand, Bilal, I said at the same time he put his hand out to take hers.

Once we were in the car he kept himself apart from us, immediately turning his face to the window and seemingly absorbing himself in what was going on out there. Moments later, his face still glued to the scenes outside, he told me he thought Shqifiyeh was pretty. He added, but more as if her were talking to himself, that it was pretty because there were a lot of trees.

I answered him right away, so that we—the two of us— would not remain somehow apart from him. So that he would not seem to be speaking only to himself. The trees on the road going to their house, I replied, were pretty too. As she sat beside me in the car, her features seemed to grow more serious. She looked as though she was going somewhere she didn't like to be, I thought. She wasn't slow to express it in words. I don't want to stay. It's better if we go.

I knew what she was thinking. My wife's face was already in my mind's eye: angular, desiccated, the skin stretched thinly over the bones, wearing that fixed and meaningless smile. As soon as she could tell from the nod I gave her that I understood her lack of enthusiasm for staying, she said in a voice she tried hard to keep Bilal from hearing, It's better if we meet at our house. I nodded lightly again and she put out her hand, inviting me to take it in mine. Our hands stayed clasped, pressing against each other. In the same whispered voice she said she would come back with me to the house, but only to say goodbye to my wife.

On condition that I take you home in my car, I said.

No, no. Today there will be a lot of people coming to see you. We will manage getting back on our own.

He should have died in those years when he was still vigorous and full of action, indeed full of noise and rage. Now people had forgotten how he used to walk at their head, exposing himself before anyone else to the guns that were trained on all of them. They had forgotten what it was like to have him standing up there at the pulpit in a Hussainiya. They had forgotten how he paid no heed to those he called the big guns of the state. Those things he had done required strength: not the force of anger alone, but the power of strong nerves. He was approaching seventy when he began telling me that the people of al-Babiliyeh had been trying to get him to come and speak at their wakes and their burial rites but he was tired out and he wanted me to go in his place. I went, and it was as though I was standing at their pulpit as both myself and him. That is, when they received me they treated me much more elaborately and formally than they would have if I had come simply as myself; if I had not been sent by him. I was myself there, but I was also him. I always did my best to adopt that manner he had, to speak in that way that could alarm and disconcert people or fill them with silent awe, but my voice never had the full force of his. My voice was his, and it was mine; I tried to make it a blend of the two. Ever since the very first times I had heard people saying to me, You are doing well . . . you are doing a good job now . . . , I had known that they approved of me only to the extent that I was able to imitate every modulation of his voice.

His dotage, and then his illness after his dotage, had left them all forgetting who he really was. I might as well say it, too—that I was one of the factors in that loss of memory. When people turn out in throngs for funerals, they do so for the sake of the one who remains and not for the sake of the one who has gone. I would have had to be the man he was; or I would have had to act as he had done, in order to preserve him as he had been, there among them, to keep him in their memories as someone who stood out; even to keep him recognized through his progeny, a man who was continued in me, as the books would say. But I had not had the energy or the enthusiasm to measure up to it. I had satisfied myself with limiting my energies to the immediate needs of Shqifiyeh and its people. I hadn't even served them as well as I should have done. This one single hamlet: I had not even fully met its needs. When people said that I was the imam of Shqifiyeh— giving a formal name to my position here—I sensed that even they were aware of how extravagant, how grandiose, the title sounded. The imam of Shqifiyeh: just as my uncle, the Sayyid Aqil, was the imam of Abbaniyeh, where the tiny population did not need him for anything beyond a few funerals and a wedding now and then.

At my father's funeral I saw that there had been no good reason to print those copies of his photograph. Only over a very few heads was that image lifted high. Someone at the ceremony must have been asking whether this really was the fellow who used to frighten the entire government? Was this truly *that man's* funeral?

It's because you're the only son now. That's what Abu Atif al-Shami said to me. He was one of the two men who had been keeping me company in the mosque. In the big funerals we hear about, he said, there are usually seven or eight brothers involved. Abu Atif was referring to families where the brothers had scattered to different locales and each of them had his own family, his own place, and his own circle of acquaintances. But you are on your own, he said. Probably he just stopped short of adding that not only was I was on my own and alone but that this place, Shqifiyeh, was not even my own village.

Every time a woman hovered outside the half-closed door carrying a tray of coffee cups, Abu Atif repeated, Sit down and try to relax, Maulana. This also—this Maulana—I found too much. It was too grand for me, especially when uttered in this small gathering of village people, the most people I ever had around me. But I sat down again anyway, and I let him take the tray from the woman's hands to offer it one by one to all the men seated in the room. I should have done that myself. I should be doing everything myself, I thought. Taking my father—or rather, my father's corpse—to Najaf, even though he did not charge me with this task. Surely that was what he had wanted, but he knew it would be too much for me, just as I knew that if I had taken him there it would have worn me out as it would have depleted him—even if he was already dead. The mere thought of such an undertaking exhausted me. Earlier in my life I would have taken days and days to prepare myself as well as I could for what would be at best a difficult trip. How could I have done it now? Having to take him, in his coffin, with me?

Perhaps I would have taken him there if I weren't on my own. If my brother Adnan were still alive, if he had not died, we would have gone together. He could have helped me and I could have helped him. I would have said to him, Take hold of it there. And he would have lifted the coffin with those strong arms and hands of his, the result of his many years of working with automobiles. We would have stood, the two of us, on either side of the coffin. And there would have been many men to accompany us in their cars, men who would have left us only at the border. That's the way it would have happened if we had been two and not just one. Two people together are not just one and another one, one plus one. They are something more, especially because more men will come along to join in, and to broaden the partnership they have formed between them.

But I was alone. I was his only son, as Abu Atif said to me. I couldn't do anything more than this, because I was alone. That was what I would say in response to my brother when his face appeared to me—always smiling—to remark to me how few people there had been at the funeral, even fewer than had been at *his* funeral. But that was because when my brother died, my father was still alive and those who came to the rites showed up mostly for his sake. But you did not do anything, he would say to me. You didn't even put your own shoulder in among all the other shoulders ready to hoist the coffin. As he spoke, I knew, he would keep that smile on his face. That smile, which would not change at all even when he told me that—even as all of this was going on—I had been thinking about his wife. Even in the very moments when the men were gathering around me and I was walking behind my father's bier, in his funeral procession.

There were even fewer mourners present at the prescribed rites on the fourth day after his death. A few men from the village dropped in so they could be there with me in the reception room to meet the needs of guests. The rest were mostly a few men of religion who had learned of his death belatedly and so had come here from their villages. I went out every day to recite the Fatiha and to see the man who sat reciting in the tent that was barely big enough to hold his body. Every time I came back from the grave I would find two or three more men waiting for my return. My wife commented that it would have been better if I had invited people to attend the memorial service a week after his death. That way, all of these people would have come at the same time. Abu Atif al-Shami began saying something like this to me as well. Because that is what people usually do, he would add.

Only one day had passed since the funeral when my wife remarked that I must treat the boys as if they were older. As if they were adults. I must not neglect to inform them of their grandfather's death.

You must tell them. They are older now and they understand things. She pointed vaguely at the top of her head. When she saw my reaction—which was nothing more than bowing my head, like someone pondering what he ought to do—she sent for the driver. She told him to fetch the boys from their school.

Tomorrow morning they will be here, she said to me as I was turning back from the front door where I had been standing to see off the mourners. Her face close to mine, she seemed to be waiting for me to respond to what I would undoubtedly see as a challenge to my authority, coming as it did from her. But all I did was to avert my face from her, leaving her standing there.

I missed them. I hadn't seen them once since they had been taken off to that school. Perhaps their absence seemed longer than it actually was, which allowed me to imagine that when I did see them I would find them truly changed after all of the learning they had accomplished there. When they were delivered home the next day, I noticed immediately how much they had grown, especially Ahmad. It wasn't just his body that looked bigger but his facial features. He looked older than he was.

The two of them already knew about their grandfather's death. The driver had told them. Their heads were bowed as they came in; they stared at the floor, avoiding looking anyone in the face. Mashallah . . . mashallah! those who knew them from Shqifiyeh were exclaiming. Still hanging his head, my son Ahmad bent over my hands to kiss them, and then so did Ayman in imitation of his older brother. When the two of them went on standing in front of me motionless, I kissed Ahmad on his forehead and then on the top of his head. As I lifted my head from his I noticed the way he was looking at me. Even his gaze had changed. Indeed, maybe his eyes themselves had changed. They seemed cloudier, and a deeper black than they had been before. Living with other people has changed him, I said to myself, patting his shoulder before I moved on to his brother.

In the presence of the three or four men who were sitting there, I did not want to try communicating with them in the way I would have to do in order to find out whether the school had done anything for them. All I did was to take a few moments to look at them fully as they stood before me and then, not to prolong their discomfort, I put my arms around their shoulders and ushered them outside my sitting room. In the corridor I pinched Ayman's cheek playfully and he looked up at me, trying to put on a smile. When we reached the kitchen door where their mother was standing, I made them stop, my arms still around them, and I turned their faces so that she could see them, could see that they were truly here in the house. She smiled, but to them and not to me. Or perhaps it was more that she knew how to keep her smile reserved only for them, how to keep it within the space made by their gaze, not letting it travel beyond them to reach me. We went toward the room that had been my father's. I turned to them and shook my fingers toward my mouth, my way of asking them whether they were hungry. I knew I was also testing them. I wanted to find out how they would answer.

All they did was to shake their heads to say no. Ahmad even rubbed his palm across his stomach to signal that it was aching and he did not want to eat at that moment.

Ahmad has a stomachache, I said to my wife from just outside the door to the kitchen.

That's from the trip, she replied, after giving him a quick look.

Patting each one on the shoulder I left them there, at the doorway into the kitchen, and went back to my guests. I left what I wanted so badly to know about the boys to another moment.

This was not speech. It wasn't even the beginnings of speech, not even the preliminaries that come before speech. These were the same sounds that I already knew, ones that issue from low in the throat, from the deepest and most buried regions of the throat, and come out as they are, elemental and raw. Neither he nor his brother could soften these sounds. They couldn't refine them. I used to ask myself whether they were even aware that they were making sounds; or, if they did know, did they also realize that anyone nearby could hear the sounds they made? In that school, I thought, they ought to be teaching them first of all how to stop making those sounds. How to leave those grunts where they came from, there at the bottom of the throat. They ought to begin teaching them how to have real voices, how to make the kinds of sounds that ordinary people learn to make. They ought to do this before they start teaching them speech. The words they have been taught to say—and they are very few in any case—come out accompanied by that rough-edged growl. My father, said Ayman, pointing at me, each letter sounding strange as he pronounced it, the vowels too elongated and the consonants too heavy. He had to close his mouth completely, even press his lips together, to bring that heavy sound he couldn't help making to a halt. They were still at the beginning of their training, their mother said to me. With time they would be able to say complete sentences and to write, too.

You are Ayman, I say to him as I point to him in turn, exaggerating my pronunciation and moving my lips and my whole chin as if I am imitating someone I don't know. And he answers me with the same words he said before— my father—pronounced again in that strangely distended, rotund way. I smile at him, but I'm thinking how much time their education will consume if it takes this kind of effort to introduce one phrase into their heads. It tires me out just to see how arduous this is.

Their mother said it wasn't necessary to take them to their grandfather's grave: that was the sort of obligation we could spare them. But when I asked them, they appeared willing to go and indeed they seemed to welcome the idea. As soon as I was able to get them to understand my question, they began nodding their heads vigorously. As we left the iron door behind I was watching Ahmad. It seemed to me that he was too big now—or too old—for the short pants he was wearing. His legs looked too thick to be a boy's legs. As he went around to the other side of the car, I was thinking that probably he didn't know how to decide for himself whether the time had come to stop wearing shorts. He went right to the front seat and as he sat down next to me, it was clear that he expected no objections from his brother. Apparently Ayman had conceded at least this to his brother's older age; or perhaps it was just that their natural shyness had reasserted itself, because of how long they had been away, and they did not want to make a fuss in front of me.

They sat completely still all the way to the graveyard. When I stopped the car at the entrance they were slow to get out, seeming to find every reason to dawdle. I took a few steps forward and they caught up with me, walking one on either side of me. When we reached the narrow path which curled around the graves impinging on it from both sides, we walked single file, like three attached train cars.

Here, I said as I pointed to the damp reddish patch of earth. The Quran reader was still inside his tiny tent but now he was silent. When he sensed our approach he poked his head out of the opening, looked at me and then at the two boys, and drew his head inside again. Pressing his open palms together Ahmad began to follow me as I recited the Holy Book's opening chapter. His brother seemed to be following him, imitating his every action, or that was the way it looked. But Ahmad didn't make any of the sounds that would indicate that he really had memorized the words of the short chapter. It was only his two open palms and his steady gaze at them which suggested he was performing the ritual. Like me, he passed his hands across his face at the end of the recitation.

They didn't show any signs of being sad or puzzled or unsettled, standing there at the edge of the patch of soil under which their grandfather lay. I knew that whatever they were feeling toward him, they wouldn't show it here in the grave-yard. But I did not have the slightest clue to what they were thinking, or whether the death of their grandfather really did grieve them to any extent. When I turned to the tent to ask the Quran reciter how far they had come with constructing the tomb marker itself, they also turned promptly to gaze in the same direction. He told me he had heard them saying they were waiting for the engraver to finish his work. I thought about asking him whether he would be here until they had completed all the work and the tombstone was in place. But I changed my mind because he might understand me to mean that he should prolong his stay here, and that would bump up his fee.

As I made to leave, turning toward the red dirt patch for a last look, they copied my movements precisely and then followed me back to the car. They climbed in, just as before, without any argument about where each boy would sit. As I switched on the engine I contemplated the ways they seemed to have changed. The few months they had spent there had distanced them from me. Now neither one of them came up to me to grab my hand, and neither one tried to ask me anything. Before I had the car turned around and ready to head for home, I attempted something that I hoped would bring them closer to me. I reached my hand toward the back seat and let it hang there, my open palm inviting Ayman to give it a slap. He hesitated, and when he did respond, the impact of his hand was very light and tentative. It didn't hold a trace of that love of play I had always known in him. It doesn't matter, I said to myself. I will try to make up for it. Maybe I can fix it in the remaining day and a half that they have here.

My wife told me it would be better, for me and for her as well, if I received any remaining well-wishers at the mosque. That way, you'll be receiving your condolences but you will also be doing your work at the same time, she said. She couldn't have given a clearer hint than this that she did not think I was doing what I ought to be doing. But what she said suited me. Staying in the house all day long, every day, during this interval since my operation, was making me restless and bored.

As usual the mosque was empty. So that people would know I was inside I left both door panels open wide. But anyone coming here of their own accord, because they wanted specifically to be in the mosque, wasn't likely to show up before prayer time. I had to wait. I sat facing the open doors which, even when open to their widest, brought in only a little bit of light. Those who wanted to pay their respects to me on the death of my father would come eventually and among them would be the men who dropped by to see me every day, although no doubt they would go to the house first. He is at the mosque, my wife would tell them from behind the door which she would open only enough to leave a narrow crack between her and them. Another half hour and they would be here. Or an hour, perhaps. I would stay here, just waiting, for there was nothing inside the mosque that could distract or occupy me.

Just like the mosque of a poverty-stricken village. That's what we used to say of empty mosques, those with nothing inside except a pitcher to hold ablution water. Maybe that was the way it ought always to be: empty mosques, with nothing inside to distract prayer-goers from their worship, for otherwise pious worshipers might not accomplish what they had come to do. But for the mats spread across the floor and the hollow of the dome, there was nothing at all in here. Every time I craned my neck to look up at the inside of the dome, I asked myself how they—the people of Shqifiyeh—had been capable of raising it so high. How had they been able to erect it in such a way that it didn't collapse onto the mosque floor? Here, sitting just beneath the dome, I found myself trying to think only about this hollow and the way it looked. Sometimes I would tell myself that I acted the way I did—giving my thoughts such free rein—because I was too familiar with mosques to be overawed by them. Their power could not take me away from whatever thoughts had occupied my mind when I was elsewhere than the mosque. Abu Atif al-Shami and his friend probably didn't feel any differently than I did, when they were here and chatting away about the people of the village, gossiping about them to give themselves something to laugh about and to make me laugh along with them. Even those elderly men who came only for prayers and then to sit quietly for a spell afterward were hardly different characters in the mosque than they were when they were sitting in the square waiting for someone to walk across it so that they could stare at him and share in low tones what they knew about him.

Like those people, the images that invaded my mind when I was alone in the house were the same ones that came to me when I was in here. Such as entering her home and closing the door behind me, using my back to do so and not my hand so that I am already facing her as she walks toward me, walking quickly so there will be no delay in embracing me. Or I imagine that I am already there with her, inside the house. As if I can see myself there, already on the scene, there inside, without anything having led up to it. Sitting on the edge of the bed as she lies there naked, giving me that look that is a true beginning for what we will do. Or it could also be the look that says we have just now finished doing what we set out to do. Or I might find myself somewhere in the middle of such a scene, halfway through it; or I catch fragments of scenes as they overlap and interrupt each other in my mind, my head moving through this succession of scenes at a feverish speed. These images vanish only when I can force myself to concentrate on the thought that somebody might be coming into the mosque at any moment.

When that occurs to me, my gaze is already shifting to the dome and I am reflecting on how the original, intense blue they painted it has faded now to the point that it looks lifeless. I start imagining a man high up there, on scaffolding, wielding a broad brush coated in paint that he is beginning to sweep across the remains of that ancient color.

That I had lost what I had lost in the operation didn't lessen my desire for her. No longer having it didn't stop those images of her body from pursuing me. The physical longings were just as strong as before. But although the desire itself had not been extracted, now it could only be satisfied in my imagination and when I was alone. I knew that what had been taken away from me would also be subtracted from the longing I might feel when I was with her alone in a closed room. There in that room, with her naked, lying on the bed while I sit on the edge. If that scene ever really did come to pass, her gaze would have to take on a different meaning. Her look would start to ask why I was hesitating, why I was still fully clothed, still wearing my dishdasha. Or perhaps her look would tell me she was already expecting to be disappointed, and she knew we would have failed before we even began. It would be a questioning look, in any case: the kind of look where the eyes always widen because they have to be large enough to hold emotions running all the way from bewilderment to a disappointed resignation. Then she would get out of bed and snatch her clothes from the floor, balling them up in her arms to cover her belly and what is just above and below. I would be standing up already, waiting for her to move away. I would only see her again when she was sitting on the sofa in the living room, fully dressed.

Because of what I was missing now, since my surgery, I knew I would have to keep myself on that threshold, pausing forever in the moment before we are together in that room behind the closed door. I knew I must behave as though nothing were wrong with me, nothing missing. I knew I would have to halt things immediately before the door to the room could be closed. Indeed I would have to bring everything to a stop even before the embrace that is a prelude to all else. Before the hands and arms that wrap themselves around the shoulders of another could move beyond them, going elsewhere.

But in all of the stretches of time there will be before that moment arrives, I am as good as whole. In all of those times I am a man who is whole and complete, because the same desire that takes over a man who is whole is there in me. It is there and it drives me forward. Only, as it reaches its ultimate moment it will find no door through which to escape.

The rim of things, where I knew I must stop: it is the final step, the pause just before one is there. I knew I must not think too much about that endpoint right now. What I could think about was what my desire was pushing me on to do. To get into my car and go to her house; to put no obstacle in the way of the fantasies of passion that would come to me on the road. When the longing intensified I would pick up my speed—as if, arriving there, I really would begin doing everything that had played out in my head. As if all I had to do was to imitate the inventions of my brain.

I told myself, for instance, that the next day, when the two boys had gone, I would go to her immediately. This time, I told myself, I would find her waiting, having already prepared everything for my arrival.

I decided to take the boys to Beirut myself. That way, I told myself, I would be able to stay away from the house all day long. I wouldn't have to see my wife or the belated mourners to whom my wife would say, He has taken the boys to their school in Beirut.

I waited for them below, warming up the engine and brushing off a coat of dust with a feather duster. They were slow. Up there, I thought, their mother must be filling them with instructions so that later on she could demand to know whether they had followed her guidance. When I felt I had waited a long time I tooted the horn, just a short blast, but I would have followed it with a longer one if my son Ahmad had not appeared. He came through the doorway with a small sack in his hand, food for the journey in case he got hungry. His brother came out after him also carrying a little bag.

This time as well they climbed in without making any fuss over where they would sit. Ayman appeared to have given in completely to the expectation that his brother would sit in the front seat next to me. As soon as he got in he rolled down the window directly behind me so that he could poke his head out and stare at the road. Next to me, Ahmad was wearing his shorts again. They only went halfway down his thigh and were so tight that he did appear to be wearing clothes he had outgrown. For a moment I thought about getting out of the car and going up to the house to ask his mother if he had any other trousers he could wear, ones long enough to reach all the way to his feet. His thighs were too thick: these were not the legs of a boy young enough to wear short pants. The expression on his face was not a child's, either.

I wished I knew whether they were feeling any distress about returning to the school. I had not asked them anything like this in the course of the two days they had spent at home, perhaps because I knew it would take a long time simply to get my question across, and at the end of it I probably would not have reached any firm conclusions anyway about whether they were happy and comfortable at the school. Here in the car I would not be able to learn anything either, at least not as long as I was keeping my eyes on the road in front of me. If there was anything to glean from them, it would be in the stories they might tell about what had happened to them there, with their teachers or their classmates. But telling stories was something they seemed to have decided to no longer do. In the two days they had spent with us, they never seemed to be in the frame of mind that storytelling requires.

When it seemed evident that they were going to remain like this, silent and still, as long as we were in the car, I started wondering whether what was keeping them quiet was a feeling that now—right now—they really were going back, to a place they did not like. But they had been silent and withdrawn in the house as well. Wanting to bring them out of whatever they were absorbed in, I again reached my hand back, palm open, hoping that Ayman would give it a slap. My gesture didn't seem to please him. In the rearview mirror I saw his eyes shift to look at the point where my hand must be; after some hesitation, he put out his hand to rest it over mine. I gripped his hand and began shaking it, trying to encourage him into a little play. He smiled, but just a little. He did almost laugh when I began to move his hand up and down the way small children move their hands when they are asked to wave someone goodbye like grownups do. Since Ahmad did not seem to be paying any attention to us, I turned my attention to him. I pressed my hand down on his thigh, once just where his shorts ended and then once further down, nearer to where the long pants he ought to be wearing would reach.

They didn't respond with anything like the playfulness that used to distract them when they were riding in the car. As far as it went was that now and then Ayman slapped his

186

brother's shoulder to get him to turn his face back so that the younger boy could communicate something to his older brother in the sign language they used together. They had added new signs that they'd learned at school. My frequent glances in the mirror told me Ayman was using his fingers now instead of only his hands, but his gestures reminded me of a toddler who is just beginning to learn how to talk, the words coming in stops and starts and stutters. I saw him placing one figure across another, making a cross. I made a sign to say I wanted to know what this meant. It stopped him. He seemed at a complete loss as to how he could explain it to me. Ahmad couldn't figure out how to tell me either, even though he had jumped in, apparently volunteering to help.

I felt pleased and a little bit awed that they were learning things there that helped them to understand each other. What they were getting out of it was something more that they could share, something they could use to put up a united front when facing the people around them. But my sense of delight was cut short as it suddenly dawned on me that if they were to make the most of what they were learning, they would always have to live with others who were just like them. The thought did not please me at all. I preferred to think that they would always remain with people who knew them, living in the village they knew. Jawdat's face came to me, smiling this time, a faint smile, happy enough because he had stayed here, in the village where he had been born. And his life hadn't been divided into two parts, changing sharply when he was still small and forcing him to change, to adapt to living with new people. With strangers.

I will ask about this at the school. Today. I will ask them about it.

Except for a few voices I could make out, raspy and grating as if they issued from sore throats, the hubbub seemed mostly the result of a lot of movement. The children seemed to be in a state of high excitement, running around agitatedly in the school playground. I could see how a child here dashed from one spot to another, explaining something to a classmate with the use of wildly gesticulating hands and fingers, having just been doing the same thing a few seconds before in front of another schoolmate at the other end of the yard. Watching their constant movement, it occurred to me that maybe each of them was searching for somebody who might understand what he was trying to say.

I could not even imagine my sons going in there among those boys, to move about as frenetically as they were doing, jumping from one classmate to another. I had the impression somehow that these children had all come to the school long before my boys had arrived. The boys here had built their lives together with their friends in this school. My boys were standing near me, waiting for me to figure out where we would go first. If the teacher had not come over to greet me, smiling at them, I would have just left them there, on the sidewalk that ran alongside the playground, and would have returned immediately to my car. But the teacher knew what she needed to do. Using both hands, she invited them into the thick of the play area. Then she turned to me and asked me to follow her to the school office.

A man who was sitting at his desk and studying some papers in front of him sprang to his feet when he saw me coming in. Welcome, welcome to the Shaykh, he said, extending his hand and at the same time slipping around his desk to come closer to where I stood. As I was sitting down I told him I was the father of Ahmad and Ayman. Clearly he hadn't known that their father was a man of religion: he looked astonished and I thought he must be startled that there could be any child here at this school who had a father like me. The teacher who had brought me to his office was soon back with us. She sat down on the remaining empty chair and expressed her condolences for my father's death. Reassured and more comfortable, now that they had welcomed me and shown some concern, I began to question them on the matters that I had decided I needed to know from them.

At home and also in the car, on the way here, they have been so quiet—

But before I could finish my sentence the teacher spoke up. She had been waiting for someone to come, she said, either me or my wife, so that she could speak to us. She knew things that the man in the office—who was clearly the school director—did not know. Even so, he asked her to bring in their files. When she returned with them he began to read without lifting his eyes from the page once, or showing any particular expression that would indicate what he was reading. When he closed the two files, she returned to what she had been about to say.

She asked me whether, before we had brought them to the school, they had been comfortable at home, and whether we had accepted them as they were. Was there anyone else in our family—in my family, in my wife's family—who was deaf the way my two boys were? Did they have any friends before coming to the school? If so, how did they behave with their companions? And did they have any brothers or sisters? Did their sister have any problems? Did . . .

We want to know all of these things so that we can determine why they are the way they are, broke in the director, seeming to feel he had to explain the questions she was asking me, and then turning again to the teacher to signal that she should go on with her questions.

As I listened and responded, I was readying myself to get up and leave this place and take the boys with me. Not out of any particular fear of mine but because I had the feeling that these people were being hard on my boys. They were being unfair.

But what's the problem with them?

They're not comfortable here.

I knew that these were the polite, considerate words that official people use to offer judgments that are in reality more serious than they sound. But I went on listening. I wanted to hear what she would say next. I didn't have to ask her what she meant by saying that they weren't comfortable there. They're rough, she said. They're showing violent tendencies.

Since I was continuing to listen and did not say anything, she added that they were antisocial. They were aggressive with the other boys.

The two of them? Both?

Especially the older one. Especially Ahmad.

And the other boys—they aren't rough as well?

They argue and fight sometimes, like all children do . . . But Ahmad and Ayman—especially Ahmad, as I said—are not at their ease here. They always stick together, they don't mix at all with the other boys. We told ourselves that separating them and putting each one in a different class might help them change. But they're no different. They are always sulking and they seem to be just waiting until they can go out to the playground and be together.

But how are they rough and aggressive?

They attack the other boys, pushing and shoving them. Sometimes they even look like they're about to really hurt whoever it is they are quarreling with. Ahmad even hit a boy on the face, and so hard that he got a nosebleed.

So the boys had gone from being the ones who were always hit, as had happened in the village, to being the ones who did the hitting. The boys they were attacking must have made them angry somehow.

But how can they possibly be acting rough or violent, as you call it, unless the other boys are ganging up against them?

Every new pupil finds that the others gang up, but after two or three days things always change. The child suddenly has playmates.

The director, who had stopped perusing the few papers he had in front of him, spoke up now, though what he said took us back to an earlier point in the conversation. The family of the boy who got the nosebleed protested, he said. They insisted on taking their son out of the school.

If this had happened to one of them, I thought—to Ahmad or to Ayman—we would never even have known about it.

But what should we do, then? I asked. I had already sensed that they were trying to push me to a point that they had already agreed on before I even arrived.

We, of course, would have liked very much to see them get used to . . .

Hearing these words I knew they had decided that they would not keep the boys here.

Maybe they just need more time to settle down.

More time to settle down—because Ahmad punched a boy in the face?

And he might repeat it. He might do such a thing more than once.

They did not want the two of them here. I was not going to try convincing these two people that they ought to show some patience with the boys or allow them a bit more time.

Now? You want me to take them away now?

Neither of them said a word. The only response they gave—both of them—was a sorrowful shake of the head. I was supposed to believe that they despaired of knowing what to do. And that they were leaving this decision to me.

I stood up. My eyes on the teacher, I said that I would take them with me. And then I added, in a voice that I tried to make even more peremptory, that she must get their things ready.

I did not know where I should go while waiting for the boys to return to me with their belongings. But I left the office anyway. I went to stand at the gate leading onto the playground. When the same teacher showed up there, I told her that I would be waiting in my car.

But there are some matters we must take care of. The administrative office.

School fees?

No, just signing some papers.

I will sign them here, I said, changing my position slightly to give the impression that I was now waiting for the papers they would bring to me.

The boys did not take long. They came right over to my car carrying one bag each, enough to hold their few belongings. They didn't look at me as they climbed back in to their seats, Ahmad next to me and Ayman directly behind me. Maybe they were feeling happier now, I couldn't help thinking, even though their faces looked as closed and remote as they had seemed earlier. Maybe they were waiting for me to make some gesture: for my face to give them an indication of how they must act. I didn't delay. I seized Ahmad's chin and turned his face toward me, wanting to dispel any worry he might feel as quickly as I could. I bent my head to his and butted his forehead lightly against mine, and then I smiled at him. He gave me a cautious smile in return. In the rearview mirror I could see Ayman, looking just as wary. To undo their guarded silence I struck my hand against Ahmad's full thigh and then reached it behind me, twisting it so that Ayman could slap his palm against mine. Then I started the engine, feeling a little easier. I was trying to keep my anxieties at bay. I could deal with them another time.

On our return journey, though, as we all sat still and silent in the car, I had to admit to myself that I was bringing them back in exactly the same state they'd been in on the journey there. This caused me some chagrin. The entire trip home, they made no effort to communicate anything, and I didn't make any further attempts to play with them. I simply let myself believe that they were contented as they were now; that they were even happy, because they had gotten away from this school that surely they hated. When I started to reflect on what it was about them that kept them estranged from other boys, suddenly many things crowded into my mind. There was something in their makeup, their character, that some-how made other boys keep their distance. Yet those boys at the school were just like them. These were boys who would have been just as likely to be driven away, if they tried to mix with boys who didn't have to deal with being deaf. That led me to suspect that perhaps there was something more in the two of them—some defect, some flaw—in addition to their deafness. The abrupt anxiety of it gave me the feeling of hav-ing a weight bearing down on my head. Wanting to lighten the sudden weariness I was feeling, I began recalling Bilal, the son of my brother, whose gentle expression, delicate face, and always well-combed hair made me feel so comfortable. His image, coming into my head, relaxed me.

When I stopped my car they hesitated for a few minutes before getting out. They were embarrassed about returning; or perhaps they felt that the house to which they were return-ing was not the same for them as it had been before. Perhaps they even felt that it was no longer their house. I felt a rush of sympathy for them. I didn't urge them to get out. I just waited quietly. I didn't put my hand out to either of them, since that would have said they ought to get out now. As we went through the iron door and headed for the front door they saw their sister Hiba. They both gazed at her but without any change of expression. At the top of the steps stood my wife. She waited until we were only a few steps away before she spoke. She asked me, in the tone of voice that said she was seeing more or less what she expected to see, So why did you bring them back?

I didn't answer. I just mounted the remaining steps and went inside, doing my best to avoid her. She had stopped the boys there at the top of the steps to ask them why I had brought them back. They must not have given her any response, because she came back to me in a state of exasperation. She asked whether I had even taken them to the school in the first place.

They don't want them there.

Who doesn't want them there?

When I was slow to respond, she said again, clearly suppressing her anger, Who are *they*—the people who run the school?

The people who run the school . . . . And the other boys there, too.

She went quiet. It seemed to dawn on her what I was really saying just as she was on the point of pressing her questions further. She stood there at the door for a few more moments and then turned to go inside. Maybe she was going to speak to the boys, or more likely, she would go back to whatever she had been doing when we arrived, as if nothing had happened at all.

Abu Atif al-Shami looked uneasy, as if he wanted to warn me about something. I must start going to the mosque more often, he told me. I got the feeling that his words were almost an accusation. I had been neglecting the mosque. Recently, I hadn't even been showing up for the noontime prayers. Every time I heard the call to prayer blast from the microphone, or looked at my watch already knowing it was only ten minutes or a quarter of an hour before prayer time and that the azan would soon sound, I could almost hear someone making that accusation. But then I would feel too lacking in energy to go out.

I know . . . I know, Abu Atif, but . . .

He cut me off. He knew that what was keeping me immobile was nothing more than sloth. Because, he said, they are going to take over the mosque. They will occupy it . . .

Who?

I guess it really has been a while since we stopped going, he said, including himself (I knew) in order to make it look like it wasn't just me who was falling short. It's occupied these days by men we don't know. They come every day—in the afternoon—and they stay in the mosque until after the evening prayers.

Men from here? From Shqifiyeh?

No, they're not from here. Not from al-Sharqi either, he said, naming the tiny hamlet closest to our village. In fact they weren't from anywhere nearby, he told me. There were three of them, or perhaps four, and they were living in a house just outside of Shqifiyeh, halfway between our town and the other village. They were all bearded, he said, even if they did not wear the abaya or wrap their heads in the turbans of shaykhs.

There are three or four of them?

Sometimes three and sometimes four, occasionally five.

Should we be afraid of them, Abu Atif? I asked with a broad smile. I wanted to show him that I did not share the fears he seemed to be expressing.

Shqifiyeh people are feeling very uneasy about them. They're saying these men have come to destroy our neighborhoods.

But what can I say to them? They're in the house of God. If I ask them why they're there, that's what they will say.

Those three men show up—or four of them, or five—carrying their own Qurans. They stay for long periods in the mosque where no one goes except one or two old men from our town. When they meet someone on the road they don't even look at him. They don't greet him. They act as if there's no one else there but them, said Abu Atif. And then, he went on, when someone does call out a greeting, maybe just to find out how they will respond, all they do is to mutter a word or two. And then they shrink their necks back into their shoulders, trying to make themselves look as if they are in terror of falling into some grievous error. They are always showing their fear of God.

As Abu Atif recounted the few real anecdotes he had about how apprehensive the people of our town were and why, I sensed that with every word he said he was trying to get me to understand that I was the very last person to be aware of what was going on here. He told me that the schoolteachers had come in to their school one morning to find the pupils' chairs overturned and nasty curses and insults scrawled across the blackboards. Whoever had done it had put the final touch on their work by peeing on the tables where the teachers kept their belongings and teaching materials. Who would ever do something like that except them? exclaimed Abu Atif, adding that nothing like this had ever happened—never, in the whole history of this little place.

I didn't need to do anything more than establish some regular times when I would be in the mosque, said Abu Atif, his advice quickly followed by a playful smile. He and Hajj Talib would be with me, he said. I wouldn't get bored. I wouldn't be sitting there all alone.

Let's go over there now, Sayyid, he said, starting to get up but only rising halfway from his seat because he didn't yet know whether we were going to go right now or whether we would stay here.

As usual the mosque was empty. Those three or four men had not changed anything. They hadn't added anything to it and there was nothing in there which they could have taken away.

If people know you are here, they will come.

No one will come, Abu Atif. People have abandoned the mosques. Not only here in Shqifiyeh but everywhere, in all of the villages. I used to come here but I was sitting here alone—well, alone with the two of you. Nothing can stir up enthusiasm in people any more. A lot of folks here in Shqifiyeh even say that the sound of the azan coming out of the microphone irritates them. I've heard them say that, I've heard it with my own ears. They say, If only we could go back to the call to prayer the way it was in the days of Sayyid Amin. What they're asking for is to go back to hearing an ordinary voice, but that's only because then they wouldn't even hear the call to prayer.

Those people had abandoned the mosques. In my position, and in their midst, I had become a useless appendage. I could be summoned to say prayers over their recently departed, and to perform marriage ceremonies for anyone who requested them. Those who sought me out for advice, coming to my home, were people who had done things they had to do or couldn't help doing, and what they wanted from me was a fatwa saying that whatever they had done was permissible according to the holy law and would not be held against them. But people no longer had any need for religion, nor for the men of religion. Even I found myself thinking sometimes how odd-looking I was in my turban and cloak, even if I had worn nothing else since my earliest days of adulthood. The things I said didn't sit comfortably in their conversations. My words seemed to me to be sending them back to somewhere they no longer wanted to be.

We stayed in the mosque for two hours, Abu Atif al-Shami and I. By ourselves. It was Abu Atif who said, finally, that no one was going to show up now. It would be a better idea, he said, for us to come back in time for the late afternoon prayers. They would be here then, he told me. Those men would be here, and when they saw me they would know that the mosque had its imam and that they must defer to me. And that when the time for prayers came, I must be sure to stand in front of them. I must take my proper place.

Fine, we will come back for the late afternoon prayers, I told him. Come by, and we will go together. As we started to go our separate ways I turned back to him. Bring Hajj Talib with you, I said.

When I came home in the evening, my wife informed me that Abu Atif al-Shami had come by in my absence. Tell him I came, and that I brought Hajj Talib with me, he said to her. He was letting me know that I had gone back on my word to him. That now I had truly abandoned my duty to face those who, in his words, were occupying the mosque. It was true. I had been unwilling that afternoon to expose myself to anything that might wrench me out of my good mood. I didn't want to stand in front of those people asking them questions, or listening to them say that they were here in the house of God. I wasn't likely to be able to match their obstinacy anyway, by saying to them at the end of our exchange of words, You may be here in the house of God but do not disturb the people of Shqifiyeh who are already feeling upset at your presence.

I hadn't taken my car out for any particular reason; I just wanted to get away from the house so that Abu Atif would not find me there. I had prepared a response that I could recite to him the next time I encountered him. Someone from al-Babiliyeh had come looking for me, saying they needed me there. I knew that Abu Atif would not grill me on what the folks there had wanted; he would not want to look as though he were testing my sincerity. I hadn't forgotten about those men, I would add. I would be in the mosque when they came, tomorrow or the day after. All I had wanted from going out was to get away, to not be in the house. And since I would have to meet those men sometime, then let me meet them by myself, without the presence of Abu Atif and his companion as witnesses to whatever happened between me and them. Maybe tomorrow, perhaps a day or two later, I would meet them, without Abu Atif around, and then I could say to him, whenever we next saw each other in the square here, or in the mosque just over there, that I had seen them and spoken with them; and then I could go on and tell him what he would want to hear.

I left it for the next day, or the day after that. Today—or what was left of it—I gave up to my own peace of mind. To driving around in the car and thinking, as I drove down one street after another, that the only thing remaining for us—for me and her—was to find ourselves alone in her home, whenever that might happen. But I would not go to her now. That wasn't because I could not bring my desire to that heightened

198

state that would send me immediately to my car ready to race there headlong, but because I wanted to leave a space of time—this space of time—when she would have to ask herself, Why has he not come today? Will he appear sometime before sunset? That was the way I was thinking. It is how people think when they are pursuing love, and how people think when they are at the receiving end of love. Even if, in the troughs between one intense moment of contemplation and another, I did feel an inclination to press the accelerator pedal to the floor, going against what I had decided, increasing my speed, so that I would be there before the day was too far gone.

But then it would not be long before that image of her, standing there and opening the door for me, would be superseded by another image: also one of her, upright as well, but walking slowly ahead of me into the room where, once I was inside, she would close the door. And then the two of us would be truly alone and truly together, inside. And then, once there, nothing more than one single act. Only her fingers beginning to undo the buttons of her blouse. The first button, the uppermost one, which she will have already undone when a realization suddenly comes to me that clouds the scene and puts a distance between her and me. It isn't always my brother's face that holds me back and stops me for good. Rather, it's that suddenly I see her in a different kind of way. As if that tumultuous and insistent craving inside of me can no longer endure itself, and so it flags, or perhaps it just softens. And then all I want is to imagine her face smiling at me. That's all, smiling and inviting me to want nothing more than the admiring look that her face and her smile offer me, bringing me closer to her, but only that: close, and hoping above all that she will accept me like this.

Perhaps she was no longer seeing her friend the schoolteacher. That's what occurred to me when she began asking me, every time I came home, Have you asked about a school for the boys? The school's rejection of them had frustrated her and thwarted her plans. She had reverted to that customary look of resentment that told me of her unrelenting anger toward me and how much she hated her life. The slight glow of color I had begun to notice on her face had disappeared: I never did figure out whether it was the result of cosmetics or simply the outcome of her attempt, this late in her life, to change herself and transform the way she lived. She must have thought that the death of my father would give her some relief and make the house feel less constricted. But the boys' return kept her from having that even more restful life, which she had been expecting and looking forward to.

You didn't ask about the school for the boys? This time her question came out as an accusation. She knew that my only response would be to turn my face away and go over to where I always sat.

But I was irritated as well by my indolence, even if I had found an excuse for myself. Schools. I didn't even know anyone I could ask. I was uncomfortably aware that I should have tried harder to restrain my anger on the day I took the boys back to the school in Beirut. I should have asked the teacher or the director to recommend which school they would advise me to try now. Here in Shqifiyeh and likewise in all of the surrounding villages, I would not find anyone who would know anything about such a school. But I just kept telling myself that I was only postponing this matter temporarily. I would deal with it soon. At another time, but soon. Let me just see them feeling more at ease here, first, I would tell myself. Let me see them forgetting what they went through at that school. But I knew perfectly well that these were excuses I was simply using, a way to avoid doing anything, putting the matter off with one artificial delay after another. I was especially conscious of this as I watched the two of them returning home where there was clearly nothing for them to do in the house, although they would not have found anything to do outside either. Ahmad was too old now for the games they used to play, or for pestering the other boys to accept him as one of them. And his brother Ayman had grown older with him, because he was always there, always close by his brother's side, and he imitated everything the older boy did.

Seeing them going out of the house or coming in, or sitting still and staring into the empty silence of the room where they sat, I couldn't help feeling that they were simply going to go on like this forever. The tableau they made didn't inspire me to imagine any possibility of change, any different sort of scene. What I did find myself predicting was that their silent stares would turn to gloom and their faces would take on permanent frowns. What I saw was the morose expression that Jawdat's face had assumed in the end, lips pressed together firmly in a straight line and a look of wary anger in his eyes. Many times I caught myself implanting that expression on Ahmad's face, if only in my own mind. On his face that had begun to look so adult. I would press his lips together and make his face hard, his expression angry. Ahmad and not Ayman, because I had gotten into the habit of comparing Ahmad to Jawdat, or because on account of his age, he would be the one who would become another Jawdat that much sooner.

Chapter Five

THERE WAS NO ONE—not in Shqifiyeh and nowhere else either—to whom I could talk as I so badly wanted to talk. I was alone among them—these people here—and the most they expected from me was a response when they requested something. Whenever I encountered any of them on the street, all they said was as-salaamu alaykum, pressing the palms of their hands to their chests in order to show what devout, obedient, respectful believers they were. Then they would go on their way and as soon as they had put a bit of distance between themselves and me, I knew they would resume chatting about whatever it was they had been discussing before. They thought I didn't need anyone to talk to. That I would just go on talking to myself, having dialogues with myself in my head about matters I knew and they didn't. Abu Atif al-Shami was not Sayyid Mudar, my companion in Najaf. The only way Abu Atif knew to speak to me was to throw me his little nuggets of advice on issues that—as minor and trifling as they might be—he thought I ought not to find out about on my own. Or he would pass on the jokes that were being told about various men in the village, trying to entertain me and make me laugh.

I wouldn't claim that it was my jubba and turban alone that so isolated me from these people. After all, I was like this before I started to wear them. I could remember how, when the boys seemed to go too far in their playing, I would stand apart watching them rather than trying to remain in their midst. Instead, I would go over to Jawdat, to communicate with him and stroll with him, as they were making fun of his deafness and pelting him with stones. I could remember how I felt when I went over to him: it wasn't that I wanted to placate him or make him happy, but rather that, inside myself, I felt some kind of closeness to him. I would try to prod him into saying something; that is, into expressing something. But the most he would do was to keep on walking at my side after giving me a smile that absolved him from making further efforts, the kind of exertions we both had to make if he wanted me to understand how he was going to respond to me or what he was trying to say. My brother, who was born the year after me, was every bit as boisterous as the other boys. In fact, he was the sort of boy who couldn't rush forward to snatch the ball from somebody else without shrieking at the top of his voice. He would give as good as he got out there in the square where they played ball, while I waited on the sidelines until he was close enough that I could remind him, in a voice that was not much more than a whisper in his ear, that we were not supposed to act like this. We weren't like the other boys.

He would slip away from me, scampering off to join their games again and add to the din they were making. Usually I would go home, leaving him to these games that were so inappropriate to us, the children of the Sayyid, as my mother always said. Go and say to him: your mother is going to complain about you to your father. That's what she would say to me. I knew I wouldn't do anything more than return to my usual spot, where I would stand there and wait for him—for them—to finish their games and scatter to their homes.

As we were heading back to the house he would be covered in sweat and still panting, his clothes dirty. He would begin kicking up the pebbles in the lane as we walked, because even the boys' games hadn't consumed all of his naughty energy. He didn't change once we were older. He told my father that he did not want to study in Najaf. When my father asked him why he was refusing, he answered that he did not want to become a man of religion. He didn't say that he could not be a man of religion; he said that he didn't want to be one, just like that, without trying to sugarcoat his words or make them sound less drastic than they were. In any case he had already made great strides toward becoming the person he would be. There was nothing about him that suggested he had been raised in his father's house. He began buying things to sell off to other people: sets of glassware, men's footwear, wallets, doodads or accessories people added to their cars to make them look fancier, dolls and toys and other things. He brought them to the house for storage. Only two days, he would say to my mother as he smiled and raised two fingers in front of her, wanting to underline the confident assurance in his voice that within a couple of days he would certainly have sold them.

His merchandising put him in the company of many men, and occasionally one of them came around asking for him. My mother didn't like the way they looked. She would snap at him that one of those peddlers of his who sold fancy trifles to women had come asking for him. Her choice of words displayed her scorn for the kind of work he was doing. He must have gotten to know a good many men through this itinerant work of his. He had to be as nimble and sharp as these types were. Whenever his image appeared to me in a flash of memory, what I saw was a shoulder and the turn of his back as he was leaving a man he had been talking to in order to hurry off to see someone else, since he was already late for their appointment.

He might as well have been born to another family and grown up in a house other than ours. I could remember walking with him—when I hadn't been in Najaf for more than two years, and I was home for the summer holidays—and he would say, wanting to embarrass me, that he was going to wink at that girl coming down the street. And then, to make it even worse, when the girl was almost passing us, he would say,

Look! Just look at those dimples! He was trying to make the pair of us uncomfortable; he wanted to humiliate the girl as much he wanted to mortify me. Once she had moved out of the range of our voices, I would chide him for behaving like this when I was with him. And also when I was not with him.

He was not like me and I was never the way he was. It wasn't going to Najaf that made me like that. It wasn't that I was obeying the prohibitions they recited to us so often that we memorized them. Do not do what the people around you do. Do not be like them. If you laugh, laugh as though you are ashamed of your own laughter. Do not look directly or closely at the person who is speaking to you. If a woman greets you, respond to the greeting but make your words hard to hear, as if you are just murmuring something under your breath or saying something to yourself silently. If you have to walk through a group of women, draw one edge of your abaya over the other edge as if you are trying to make yourself vanish, and quicken your pace as if you believe that spending any amount of time among them will corrupt something in you.

But these were things I would have done even if I had never put on an abaya. Even if I had not become a man of religion.

Welcome to the Sayyid.

She was alone in the house. I knew that from the way she went on standing with her back leaning against the door after she had closed it. She had been waiting for me to come, there was no doubt about that. This was why she had changed her hairstyle, piling her hair on top of her head and revealing her neck and the sides of her face fully. She wanted to show that this was her usual style when she was at home on her own, I thought. As she took a step forward toward where I stood waiting, she said that Bilal had gone to see one of his friends and wouldn't come back before evening. She went ahead of me to an armchair that was placed very close to the sofa on which

206

I was accustomed to sitting. I asked her how he was, as a way to slow down what I sensed we were heading for. She didn't answer, or if she did say something I didn't hear it. When she sat down, before I could do so, she sank back into her chair as though she were very tired. She looked around as if she was trying to locate something she hadn't properly put in place or check on something that still needed straightening. She was quite close to me, closer than the former arrangement of the armchair and matching sofa would have had allowed, much closer than she had been when we each sat at one end of the long sofa. Looking at her at such close range I noticed how the whiteness around her ear seemed to glow, lighting the soft little hairs high on her neck.

What I should have done was to put my hand out to touch those soft little hairs. That would have been a real beginning, and one that would spare me having to invent words that I knew would come out as meaningless stutters when I tried to actually say them out loud. But I missed my chance by not doing it in the moment when it would have been exactly the right move, that is, in the instant it occurred to me to do it. When several more minutes of silence had passed she got up to go to the kitchen, even though she would not do anything there, or so it seemed to me. But from in there she asked me if I wanted coffee. So that she would not stay in there, I told her that I only wanted a glass of water.

Her hand was trembling as she put the glass of water down on the table in front of me. That calm strength of hers seemed to have been thrown into confusion. She returned to her seat, again sinking into it as she handed over the lead to me, waiting for me to say something, or to initiate something, somehow. Just as reluctant to make the first move, I stood up and went over to the window. I peered through the narrow slit of light down to where my car was parked and then I turned as if to go to the kitchen. From where I stood, deliberately placing myself outside her line of vision, I walked back until

I was standing directly behind and above her. I put my hands there on the two sides of her face where her upswept hair had revealed the pale skin.

This time I was acting with deliberation, choosing what I would do, no longer hesitant or defensive. She remained silent, her gaze straight ahead. I began to stroke those soft tiny hairs and then I moved my hands over her cheeks and to the vicinity of her lips. She accepted it all silently, even submissively. But when it appeared to her that I was keeping my hands there, as though I hesitated to move them anywhere beyond what I had already touched, she brought her hands up to take mine and pressed them down against her upper chest as though she wanted to hold them captive there.

I changed position, to stand in front of her; this way I could raise her face to mine. She was blushing with confusion and her eyes, when she lifted them to look at me, seemed unfocused. Still, she gave me a long look. When I gripped her hands as if to signal that I wanted to pull her to her feet so she would be standing and facing me, and then when she was actually standing up and so close that she was all but touching me, she let her hands go slack. Then she placed them on my shoulders, the firm pressure of their touch signaling that I should wait. From that same narrow window opening where I had stared out, she glanced outside and swung the shutter inward to close it. Standing in the center of the reception room she looked carefully around to make certain that everything was closed. Then she came toward me, careful to ensure that her steps were soundless as she walked across the room.

That step that I had been picturing in my mind for so long: I feared it was about to happen. I worried now that she would take me by the hand, lead me into the room with the double bed, and close the door. Once we were in that room—really there inside—we would not be able to halt what we were doing until we reached the end. I will stay here, I told myself.

I will keep her here, in the living room where something could happen. For instance, we might hear a voice coming from outside, or imagine that we're hearing it. That would create an instant excuse for me to immediately stop whatever we were in the process of doing.

Here—we were in her house, after all—it would not take her long to regain her forcefulness, I knew; and then, with that strength of hers she would finish what I would have begun. With that strength of hers, which had drawn me in so inexorably at the same time that it scared me off, her hands had already begun to undo the buttons on my shirt, gradually uncovering my neck and upper chest. She brought her hands—unhurried, deliberate—up again to my neck to lift my abaya from my shoulders. It's gotten hot, she said, her words accompanied by a teasing little smile.

She touched my chest there where she had exposed it, and moved her hand to regions that my clothes still hid. Quickly I began to copy her movements. I undid the uppermost button on her blouse, revealing her cleavage and reaching my fingers to follow its downward course. As I cupped one of her breasts, filling my open palm, she moaned and closed her eyes, and her body went limp as though her strong legs had suddenly collapsed, and I had to support her, my arm encircling her middle.

If I moaned as well, it was because now I had reached that point that I had so often imagined attaining, all the while thinking it was forbidden to me. Her breast filled my hand; it overflowed from my hold. This is all going too quickly, I thought as, in response, she pressed her face into my chest and began to kiss and rub against it. Her breathing seemed strangely loud and fast as she moved her hands around my sides to press against my back. But then her urgent longings seemed to have tired her out and she fell back, still holding onto me, toward the sofa. There, sitting on the edge, I started undoing the rest of her buttons until her breasts were completely visible, spilling to the sides, and beneath them her soft and pale belly, fresh, almost moist, to the touch. Everything that met my eyes or that my hands touched I had already imagined so many times, altogether or separately. I wasn't trying to make any comparison between what I had imagined and what I saw now. I was completely absorbed in every part of her as it was revealed to me. Her breasts and her belly, and her navel that so tempted me: I wanted to put my finger into it, as if I was searching for an opening that would take me into the depths beneath it.

All there was left to do was to untie the knot that closed her skirt. It slipped down to show the soft froth that would give way to her still-hidden pubic hair. She was lying back on the sofa now; it supported her body but left her legs slipping down, apart. Here—I needed to keep my hand here, with her thighs, at the top of her thighs and at the verges of those tiny hairs. I must not go as far as where those tiny hairs would become thicker. She has to keep her last undergarments on. If she takes them off, or if I remove them, I will have to do the same so that I will be as naked as she is. Here is where I must stop, I said to myself. Stop or pull back, perhaps leaving my hands a little longer there at the hems of her underwear, keeping them there until she senses on her own that for now I will not go any further.

She did not remain prone for very long. A moment came when she suddenly, quickly, became alert to the fact that what we were doing had ended. She pressed her legs together and did up her skirt, bringing it down to cover her knees. She raised her hands to her open blouse and began to do up the buttons—but that was likely in front of the mirror, there in the room where she'd gone. I too began to do up my few buttons and to straighten and adjust my clothing wherever it was awry. When she came back her face was still a warm red and glistening with the sweat that had broken over it. She asked me whether I would like a coffee now. I replied that I would not prolong my stay, but I extended my hand toward her, where she was sitting, so that we could be together a little longer. It wasn't very long, in any case. Just a few moments when we remained silent, since it would have seemed artificial to talk about anything except what we had been doing. Then I said I would go now and I got up, picking up my abaya and asking her, when I had draped it over my shoulders, whether I looked suitably proper now. I smiled before making for the door, aware that I must be watchful as I opened it and went out.

A messy blend of rapture and dis-ease pitched me in every direction, as I drove home. The smell of her body was still in me and around me, and the roundness of her breast still filled my hand. It was a lot, all of this that had happened in this single visit, I began telling myself. Too much, perhaps. The weight of it felt severe. For a brief moment I was glad to be feeling the way I was feeling. It relieved me of fretting about what her thoughts or suspicions might be about my having stopped what we were doing, just like that, so suddenly and without any apparent reason. I was amazed at how my brother had not even entered my mind—neither his voice nor his face—in all the time that his wife was reclining there in front of me, her face flushed and her breathing rapid, allowing me to go wherever I wanted. No, my brother did not appear there between us. But in realizing he had not been there, I was as good as inviting him to join me here in my car, now that the scene was over and done. You will not go any further than you have gone . . . . That's all of it, his face said to me—that face that was never without a teasing little smile. A mocking smile. He stayed close by me for the rest of my journey. Even when I managed to force my mind elsewhere, on to other and random thoughts that put him at a distance, he was always quick to reappear. You will not go any further than that, he began saying to me again. He was rebuking me for something I could not even do.

Every time he reappeared, his smile was slightly altered. It was no longer a smile of amusement, or a teasing smile, though its shape was unchanged. That is, it turned more cunning, more sinister: a show of wickedness that his characteristic smile, as wide as ever, could not conceal from me.

I started to answer him back by saying that he had died. You are dead, I said to him in a tone of voice that matched the changes coming over his words and his face. But I could not go as far as making my whispered words into a real rebuke, lest the scene come to me of him wrapped in the thick shroud and borne on their shoulders. Quiet . . . quiet! Shut your mouth and be quiet, my father had beseeched my Aunt Hasiba, who was howling in a voice like a screech owl's. All she could wail in response was, But he has died . . . he is dead . . . Adnan . . . Adnan is *dead*! She spoke as though she had to get my father to realize that he didn't yet know what it meant for his son Adnan to have died.

But you were already giving her those looks before I died.

That had only happened a very few times, and when it did, I was immediately on my guard and I sought God's forgiveness. I told myself I was a man whose eyes had fallen by mistake on the slivers of thigh she left exposed. Lord be merciful, forgive me and I will show my repentance, I would murmur as I turned my face away, to block out what had been revealed. But the sight itself had attached itself to my eyes and refused to be erased. Remembering it, I would not lie. I would not say that my eyes fell on her just like that without any intention on my part. I would only be lying to myself and not to my brother, who preserved the behavior he had seen from me in his memory. He knew of my furtive glances at what was his property. He knew I was stealing something from him.

It wore me out and upset me, this memory of my brother and the way it—he—clung stubbornly to me. For months, for years, I had waited for this to happen with her, and now I had to stop myself from summoning the image of it in my head. I must not remember what had taken place. But I would not push myself to forget it entirely. I would return to it, once, again, many times over, in the house as I sat alone in the room where I received visitors, no one with me. When it wasn't enough for me to think about it, all alone, I could try to find someone to talk to about what happens between men and women who are not their wives. To bring that up casually as though I were reporting on a conversation I had had, something I had been told was going on between a particular man and a particular woman in one of the villages near us. I could even elaborate on it, describing at some length what took place between that man and that woman. I would have to find somebody to talk to. I might even encourage him a little to suspect that this man could possibly be me, and that was why I seemed so eager to go on talking to him, recounting it, telling him all about it, and then he would be just as keen to listen to me. He would ask himself, of course, why I was talking about it yet again, why I brought it up time after time, if the subject had nothing to do with me. The problem, Abu Atif, is that he has such a close relationship to her already, I say to him. To Abu Atif, since I never find myself talking to anyone but him. The issue, Abu Atif, is that she does already have a tie to him; you see, she's almost from the same family. So then Abu Atif asks me whether she's such a close relation by blood or marriage that he can be alone in the same room with her or accompany her on a trip. No . . . no, Abu Atif, she isn't. So he says to me, Then why doesn't he take her as a wife. Because he doesn't want her as a wife, Abu Atif. He wants to be her lover, the way men love women, and he wants her to love him back.

Abu Atif. He will wear me out, I thought. I knew I would not be able to keep up the fiction that this was about some other man and woman. It would be much more of a relief if I could say to him something like, Look, Abu Atif. I'm a man of the cloth, I'm the imam of this village's mosque, and secretly

I am seeing a woman who is the wife of my brother . . . . My dead brother, I would add, and I knew he would say to me, repeating himself, So marry her. Marry her and take care of her. It would be good for her to be under a man's protection. But that is not what I want. I want to be with her as lovers are together. I want to be the kind of person who aspires to what they have no right to have. I want to look at her as she is taking off her underclothes, and to tell myself that I have no right to see what I am looking at. To test every time whether she still wants me to do what I came to her to do. And to feel, every time I touch some part of her, that this is happening, right now, and that perhaps it will never happen again.

Where are they, the boys? I asked, having just picked up Hiba, who was crying as she followed her mother around through the corridor and into the bedrooms. Her mother hadn't responded to the sound of her crying. Hiba's bawling got louder by the minute, in protest at being ignored. After I picked her up and she was pressing her arms into my shoulders, her sobs began to subside but she did not stop looking toward wherever her mother was going in or coming out.

She didn't answer my question about the boys. I raised my voice and asked her again. Where are the boys? Where have they gone?

She came up to me, clutching her broom and staring into my face. At the mosque. They went to the mosque.

Her fury is what says this. What she wants to tell me is: They are at the mosque which is where you should be.

What are they doing in the mosque? I asked. I didn't expect a response.

They've found somebody who is teaching them something, she snapped at me, her anger and exasperation with me getting the last word.

I ought to have gone there immediately. I should have put Hiba down on the floor and hurried to the mosque. I didn't like the scene I envisioned though. Going there to be received by those men, as though I were visiting them in their own home.

Since when have they been going to the mosque?

She didn't answer. Maybe she didn't hear me. She was already at the other end of the corridor.

I kept holding Hiba but I dangled her as if I were about to put her down. Abu Atif would know what they were doing there in the mosque. Surely he was hurrying over here, at this very moment, to tell me. He would have seen my car and would know I was here. Still holding my daughter I even went over to stare out at the street below, thinking I would likely see him hurrying toward me. Then I considered going to his house, knocking on his door and saying to whoever opened it, Is Abu Atif here?

Hiba, who had remained quiet, began to get restless, wriggling out of my grasp. I put her down. Without even a glance at me she hurried off at a run toward where her mother must be, and where she would burst into a new fit of crying.

This time when Abu Atif shows up, he will seem half-absent and half here, I thought. He has given up on waiting for me to do something, anything at all. He will tell me, keeping his eyes on the ground and not looking at me, that they have occupied the mosque now and no one can get them to leave. He must come, I started saying to myself. Now he must come. I got up and went over to the window to scrutinize the road. There was no one at all anywhere beneath the window. But as I was turning away I saw the first boys come out of the mosque, followed by a few more, and then my son Ahmad appeared. After coming out of the door he turned to see whether his brother was following him. Ayman emerged, alone, and stood for a moment next to his brother before the two of them began their short walk home.

Other boys followed them out, three or four of them, but my attention had been diverted from them by the sight of my boys coming toward the house, and then because I turned

215

away from the window, heading to open the front door before they arrived. They would know I was here because they would see my car. When they came in they headed immediately to find me in my sitting room. As they were accustomed to doing, they stood in front of me as though they were ready for an interrogation. They waited silently for me to start asking them questions.

Sometimes there are seven or eight boys, Ahmad told me, holding up fingers but staring at them as though he needed to count them first. But today there were nine boys, the pair of hands told me after some confusion. And then, after an interruption from his brother, he said that the man who was teaching them was a man of religion like me. But he didn't wear a turban, just a skullcap that didn't cover more than a small circle on his head. He was fat, apparently. Ayman conveyed this by puffing out his cheeks and moving his hands out sideways from his body. Does he read to you? I asked them, by opening my hands palms up. They nodded. I didn't feel like asking them what they were gaining from it—the two of them, specifically, since they couldn't hear what he was saying.

No doubt this man had found some means of keeping the two of them there with the other boys. Perhaps he lifted his hand to the heavens when he was mentioning God, or made gestures of piety and devotion when mentioning the Messenger's name. He wouldn't have had to start from the beginning with them, anyway. These two boys knew things, just like Jawdat had. Even though Jawdat had had no one at home who could help him understand things, he knew what religion was about. It wasn't just a question of fasting through the month of Ramadan, which was one of the things he had learned by imitating his brothers and his whole family. It was that he knew right from wrong, what was permitted and what was not, and he showed he knew what was prohibited by turning his head to the right or to the left with an appropriate expression on his face. He knew that a frown marked out the realm of the forbidden. Sometimes he pointed a finger skyward to say that God sees us, and God watches what we do.

My boys would not need to read in order to know what Jawdat knew. They would have gotten that knowledge somewhere, though I didn't know where. But what would they get from the man who was reciting the Quran, and who must be focusing on those he knew could hear him? Maybe they were just enjoying themselves there, finding themselves sitting among boys who, in these circumstances, wouldn't be able to push them away or send them hateful looks from across the room.

But who are those people, Abu Atif? Where did they come from and who sent them?

They're not just here in Shqifiyeh, he said. They've shown up in all of the villages around Nabatiyeh. And there are a lot of them. It's their group that sends them. It's one of those factions, and they give them money for rent and food.

I didn't know any of these things that Abu Atif knew. Likely I didn't even know what everyone else in our own village knew. When Abu Atif began listing the names of these factions, I felt embarrassed. It was obvious that I was completely ignorant about all of them.

At first, Abu Atif said to me, I told myself that they decided to stay on here because they saw that the mosque was empty most of the time. Shqifiyeh people aren't very keen on religion, he added, as if he wanted to get me to believe that what had allowed them to stay here couldn't be explained only by my neglect. They weren't here simply because I had more or less abandoned the mosque.

Is it the same in the other villages? I asked. I mean, are they doing the same things in the mosques there as they are doing here?

Who?

These men who belong to different groups.

217

Well, in al-Amiriyeh the people kicked them out by force. They said the men were bothering the schoolgirls and going into the school and smashing up the chairs and tables. They said those men were peeing on the teachers' desks.

So should we do what the people of al-Amiriyeh did?

As fast as we can, especially since these fellows know how to operate here. In al-Amiriyeh the way they did things gave the impression that they were attacking the village. They brought in a shaykh named Husayn al-Kawari, who began preaching to everyone through the village mosque microphone two hours before dawn. He went after them for staying up all night and allowing men and women to mix at weddings, and he said that their daughters had no shame. But the ones who have come here know how to do their work without alienating people.

So they left al-Amiriyeh, did they? They took their things and went?

Maybe it was their faction who took them out. Because they created a scandal there, as people would say.

You mean their factions remove these men if it's clear the villagers despise them?

But see, the ones who are here, here with us in Shqifiyeh, they know how to operate. They always keep their eyes to the ground. If a woman crosses their path they make it very obvious that they are twisting their necks as far around as they can, to show that they haven't glimpsed a blessed inch of her.

So, me . . . what should I do?

I don't know, maybe you need to spend more time in the mosque . . .

With them, Abu Atif, in the mosque with them?

That is something I cannot do, I almost blurted out to Abu Atif, who was gazing at me intently. I cannot sit there with them. I cannot divide the mosque in two and share it with them. Just imagine it, we are sitting there, me in one corner and them in another, competing to attract every new

218

person who comes in. That is what I cannot do, I don't have the strength for it. Not now. Or in fact, I don't have the passion for it.

I had been neglecting the mosque for a long time. I didn't really care whether people showed up. In Najaf they would have explained this as a lack of faith, an absence of belief. As if they knew exactly what faith is and what would make it perfect and whole, as though faith were something they could see with their own eyes in just the same way they could gaze at their faces in a mirror. As if they could see it—faith—squatting there somewhere inside of themselves, in some specific part of their bodies. As if they could see it by uncovering their chests or their bellies. As though it was just a question of clothing and what it covered.

When you are in the mosque, said Abu Atif, lagging behind where my thoughts had gone, you'll be the imam of Shqifiyeh and they won't.

Strength, power, fervor. Not faith. My father wouldn't have let them get away with behaving like this in any mosque where he was the imam. Get out—get out of here! he would have said to them, addressing them as fiercely as he had addressed the two men who were talking, or exchanging whispered rumors, as he gave a sermon in the Hussainiya. You two, just get out of here right now! he said to them, and they were already getting out because they knew he would follow up his words with something more if they did not. They could imagine him charging at them, even if it meant leaping down from his pulpit ready to shove them out with his hands and kick them out with his feet.

Chapter Six

IT'S NOT AS IF I didn't do what I had to do. In those first days when I had to face it somehow, Abu Atif went with me, and his friend went too. The strangers, who went to the mosque early, before we did, made a point of greeting us before we could greet them, with deep bows as though to affirm that they were here with my approval and my permission. Ordinary people who came to the mosque followed their example, coming up to me as they entered and some of them even kissing my hand, before turning to those men as if to say, Look, we've done what we agreed on doing. It would not have been appropriate for me to try to make up for lost time—to throw myself into what had happened here in my absence, things I had been too slow or too neglectful to attend to. Like inserting myself into an issue that they seemed perplexed about. I waited to be asked, to find someone turning to me and asking, What is your opinion on this matter, Sayyid? Sometimes they did ask, and I responded with a flood of words, making myself appear as though I knew everything there was to be said on the topic they had raised. How well you have spoken, Maulana, Abu Atif would say every time I concluded an elaborate explanation of something I didn't think he understood. His companion would murmur some corroborating words of praise—God bless you and give you all good—even as his eyes were roving among the men seated there to see what impact my words had had on them.

I spoke at length with anyone who came asking me for advice. I went on insistently as though I was trying to hold onto the questioner, keeping him there because I wanted these men to see that I had someone with me who had come expressly to seek my counsel. Other times, when I was alone—many times—I would picture myself, what I must look like and sound like in these moments, and then I would feel ashamed. I would tell myself that I was offering myself up to people, and that I might as well be a shopkeeper waiting eagerly for a customer.

Sit down, Abu Atif! Stay a while longer! I said it every time he seemed on the point of leaving.

I won't be gone long, he said, with a little twist of his hand signaling a quick return. When he did come back an hour or two later, he found me itching to leave. When they saw me on my feet, they stood up promptly as well, but that was only to usher me out.

I am not doing anything here, Abu Atif, I said the moment we were outside. When the two of us arrived at my house he asked if I planned to return to the mosque in the late afternoon for the prayers? Come by and we'll see then, I said, pushing at the iron door. Mounting the steps I headed immediately for my chair, giving myself a little respite before asking about lunch, which my wife would bring in. First I wanted to study the photograph that brought together the three of them. But this time I wanted to bring my uncle out from this tableau that they made. Not because of his massive, soft body or his smile that gave him a bewildered, uncomfortable look in the presence of his father and his brother: he seemed not to comprehend why they were standing there like that to have this picture taken. He looked as if, standing there a little apart, leaving a space between his father's shoulder and his own, he was recalling a joke he had heard from some folks who were entertaining him. What did come to my mind as I gazed at the photograph was his apparent lack of effort, as long as I had known him, to acquire anything more than whatever he had scraped together, from the small sum of knowledge he had acquired in Najaf and then, after that, during his years as imam of Abbaniyeh. On his visits to us he never seemed to feel a moment's concern about teasing the women who were in our house visiting my mother, even though my father—his younger brother—was invariably sitting alone in his room not wanting to risk mixing with anyone. My mother used to say that my uncle had the heart of a child; it didn't suit him, she would say, and it wasn't good for him, to be a man of religion. It never upset him to hear such remarks, not even when they were made in front of the women as well. They would be giving him their full attention, not wanting to miss hearing something that would make them laugh. He would reply to my mother that, on the contrary, the job (as he put it) of a man of religion was what suited him best of all. The way he said it hinted that he was very comfortable indeed with having so little work to do.

His laziness didn't embarrass him. The people in Abbaniyeh who knew him told us on the day he was buried that his smile—that distinctive smile with the deep curve in his lower lip—was still there on his face even after he was dead. His laziness didn't shame or trouble him. He didn't feel any guilt about enjoying a languid existence, as he made it clear when he showed how lax his muscles were as he stretched his arms upward or heaved his body out of his chair. He would stretch and yawn and luxuriate in his own lethargy in front of people, and he even ended this performance with a deliberately loud and prolonged yawning sound.

Abu Atif arrived. I heard the reverberation of his knocks against the metal below and then the sound of his voice through the crack when he had pushed the door partway open.

Come on up, Abu Atif. Welcome, come on up.

When he appeared in the doorway to the reception room, I said to him, Let's take a breather today. I was making the most of my uncle's jovial mood, which now seemed to pervade my whole body.

223

Since we've already done what we needed to do, he said in response, looking around the room as though he were trying to decide where to sit down.

I'm even thinking of taking a vacation, I said. Like government workers and schoolteachers do.

We'll have to get their permission, he said, extending my joke. He meant the men sitting over there in the mosque.

I really do need a vacation, Abu Atif. I'm doing nothing here and nothing in the mosque, and doing all this nothing has tired me out. I have even been thinking about moving away from here, going to Abbaniyeh . . . . Do you know if anyone replaced my uncle there?

I don't know, but I can ask. . . . I'll find out today or maybe tomorrow.

Find out for me whether the place is still as small as it was, whether there are as few people living there now as there were then.

So you would leave Shqifiyeh? You would leave it to them?

I don't care. From the beginning I didn't care.

And your home?

You mean the house . . . this house, I said, pointing at the floor directly beneath me.

The house and . . . , he answered, spreading his arms to suggest that he meant the whole area, including the square and the houses around it.

There, in Abbaniyeh . . . it's just like here. The villages are all alike. The important thing is that, as in my uncle's day, there aren't many people there.

Not many people, and those few who were there had stayed as they used to be, not changing at all, because there were so few of them. That was what mattered. In Abbaniyeh, no one came in from outside and mixed with them. My mother used to ask my uncle, What's out there beyond Abbaniyeh, Sayyid? She wanted to know, because she enjoyed being able to rattle off the names of all the villages around us. Nothing, he would answer. There is nothing beyond Abbaniyeh. . . . It is at the end of the road and there is nothing beyond it.

When I was little and I heard him saying, There is nothing beyond it, I believed that the earth ended there, at the edge of the village. If we went there and stared out over that edge, we would see only empty space. Nothing.

The children, too—Abbaniyeh would suit them, I said. I was responding to a question that I knew was in Abu Atif's mind even though he did not ask it. I knew he figured that if I wanted to talk about it I would respond of my own accord.

There in Abbaniyeh, I thought, the boys would not have to exert themselves beyond their limits, just in order to learn something that they would never be successful at mastering anyway. Over there, life would not grow more difficult for them the older they got, year after year. In Abbaniyeh, people grew up without thinking about what they would have to do in the days to come.

For her, too. For my wife. Abbaniyeh would be the right place for her. There she wouldn't tire out her brain with constant thoughts about how a life was waiting for her that was better than the life she had. She wouldn't spend whatever was left of her life blaming me for the existence we had.

There, I would feel as though I were in a place where I had the only key. Driving my car across the edge where Abbaniyeh ends—or the edge where it begins—I could be confident that when I returned I would find everything just as I had left it. That was because I could easily believe that no one but me had gone out of the village or come back in during my absence. All of them would have stayed there, in their homes or very nearby. And that would be just as true of my children and my wife. Abbaniyeh would suit me—as it had him—because people would be satisfied with even the minimal effort I would make. And I would be at ease in that place. That is, I wouldn't find myself standing at the window expecting someone to show up with news I would not like.

We are going to go and live in Abbaniyeh.

We?

Us, me and you and the children.

Abbaniyeh—your uncle's village?

Yes, that's the one.

She took her time lifting the platter of food from the table in front of me. When she did pick it up and walk out, she moved slowly as though she needed to give herself time to react to what she had just heard. She seemed to stay longer than necessary in the kitchen. Maybe, I thought, she was just standing in there still holding the platter in her hands.

I was waiting for her to come back. I was preparing for that by turning my face toward the doorway where, when she came back, she would stop.

And the children, what will we do with the children there?

Her voice was calm and even, as though she had been thinking, and it didn't hold any of the anger I had anticipated.

We will see. We will find something for them there.

She didn't show any irritation at this, either. Her voice remained as even as before. She appeared to be still thinking it over in the few moments she stood there before returning to the kitchen. From in there, she asked me whether I had gone there recently.

She wasn't sending me into that unspoken struggle I had expected. Indeed, it seemed from what she said after hearing what she had heard from me, that she even wanted to know something about the village to which I had announced we were moving.

Tomorrow—I will go tomorrow, I said in a voice that I was careful to suit to this apparent acceptance on her part.

By yourself?

By myself. That is what I said, but then I thought that since she seemed to be very curious, perhaps she was hinting that she wanted to come with me. I added that Abu Atif al-Shami might be with me.

So she was tired and fed up, too. I didn't know what associations the name Abbaniyeh might form in her head or even if she was truly interested in knowing more about the place where we were going. She had gotten tired, just like me. And like me, she yearned for the feeling that something new might possibly happen to her.

You and Abu Atif al-Shami, by yourselves? she asked, as she dried her hands on a small towel.

I don't know, his friend might come with us.

She will not say it directly, I thought. She won't say that she would like to come with me. She has left that to me, who— she must think—has doubtless understood what she wants. For a fleeting second I felt some sympathy toward her, as she turned to go back to the kitchen carrying her towel. That must have been because I thought she was probably making some effort to imagine how it would be. How we would be, together, there in our new place.

Would you like to come with us? I asked, raising my voice.

No . . . no, she answered, from in there. But then she added, There will be men with you in the car.

I could not harmonize what was beginning to emerge in front of me with what I remembered. Perhaps these two houses had gone up here more recently, on the narrow lane leading into the village. They looked like very poor and slapdash houses at any rate, constructed out of building materials that didn't go together well. I will not let this change my thinking, I told myself, holding firmly to what my imagination had given me. I continued on my way toward the cluster of houses and the mosque.

Here among those houses, separated by empty patches of ground and a few scattered trees, everything did seem just as it had been then. I didn't have to circle around all the houses to sense this. It was enough to make my way down the first winding alley I came to, from which there rose the odor of cow dung and straw stored for the animals. It struck me as an old smell, the sort you would think was so old that it would have faded from memory, or would have been banished, long gone beneath the thick accumulation of time. This was the smell of that first house whose crumbled walls so many poets had described. Not just the ruins of them but the way the memory of that first house is supposed to dominate the way we live in every house that comes after it. I did not stop the car; I just slowed down enough to say as-salaamu alaykum to the two men I encountered. Their hands went up in response to my greeting, in what looked like a synchronized movement. They went on staring at me sitting there in my car, craning their heads and leaning their bodies closer to get a better look as I went by. It was likely that no man of religion had come along this alley, indeed that they had not seen any man of religion here in this village, since my uncle's death. When I had gone past them, still going very slowly—no faster than a man could walk—they raised their hands again, this time in what looked like a hesitant wave, uncertain whether the eyes of the man in the car would pay any attention or even see their gesture.

I passed other men, and every time I repeated my greeting and put my hand to my chest to show my sincere respect. Before my sudden appearance stopped them, they had been walking along the lane, but not together; several paces separated each one from the next. I didn't want to speak to anyone; I didn't want anyone to have an opportunity to really examine me so that he could say, if I were to come here to live, that he had seen me here, in my car. As I was repeating this sequence of actions—nothing more than greeting them and then turning my face away—I wondered whether I was acting this way because I didn't want to promise them anything, to create any expectations, at this point. I knew that village folk are quick to interpret everything that happens in front of them according to what suits them best and answers to their needs.

The mosque was easy to get to because I could see its minaret, which rose just slightly above the roofs of the houses. Passing alongside its high outer wall I could see that they had made the corner even higher by adding two additional blocks of stone. I was thinking that this must have been where the muezzin would stand, without having to go all the way up into the minaret—as short and squat as it was—to call the prayer. His azan wouldn't be audible anyway to more than the few houses that were immediately adjacent to it. Inside, the mosque was empty: nothing there but the mats covering its floor, just like the mosque in Shqifiyeh had looked before those people had shown up and placed two small, low tables inside. That was so that they could set their Qurans down and then sit to read them as well as other tomes that were the work of other men of religion but undoubtedly from their same faction. The blue tones in which the inside of the dome had once been painted had faded, leaving only faint patches of color here and there. At the apex of the dome, the thick plaster covering the stone was cracked. In one place it looked like the coating had been completely stripped off and the whole thing was peeling so badly that surely the plaster was liable to fall at any time onto the worshipers who might be praying just beneath it. With the same surreptitious haste with which I had passed the houses, I stayed no more than a few minutes beneath the dome and then I made a quick inspection of the old door panels. The wood was eaten away at the bottom.

As I went out, leaving the doors wide open behind me, I speculated how it was that my uncle had been able to wear clothing so different than what everyone else wore, in this village where he had spent most of his life. I pictured him in my mind, the massive body and distended belly, wearing his well-pressed and light-colored jubba, walking among them as though he were simply on a visit and would not stay even long enough for a single midday meal. I pictured him looking as though his long residence there had not brought him even remotely close to the walls he walked among and had not made him resemble the people among whom he lived. Yet they had come to love him, as he would tell us when he was at our house, perhaps because he knew (this man whose intuitions seemed so poor, as my mother and her close friends used to say, shaking their heads) that what he should have been doing was to set himself apart, aloof, so that they would respect him and leave him comfortably alone.

It would have been more fitting for my father to have made his home here. Living here would have been perfectly attuned to his yearning for the life of the era when faqihs wrote out whole thick volumes of legal rulings by hand while the world around them existed in barren poverty. Yet it would not have pleased him to think of me moving here to live. If he were here with me now, standing beside me and resting his hands and his chin on his cane, shifting his small eyes around to take in the scene, he would say to me, You will bury yourself alive here. In these plans of mine he would have seen the final stage of my lackluster ways, the culmination of my lack of ambition and energy, which I knew he had never stopped observing closely, even if he remained forever silent about it.

It was the forcefulness of his mind and emotions—it was his strong heart—that had carried him so far away from the reassurance he would have felt if he could have experienced at closer hand the places that yielded the memories of where our long-ago people lived. No, it would not have pleased him at all for me to live in Abbaniyeh, even if to me this village seemed the closest of places to that ancient era that, in what he wore and what he said, he seemed always to bear with him. That was the time in which all the utterances his brain had ever held were composed. It was the age of those pronouncements, and the people who had made them, on which he invariably drew as he delivered his sermons in the Hussainiyas. It was that elemental place, the one that reached him, and me, through the life histories of the First Family, the House of the Prophet.

Those histories that went on to tell how our people had moved from place to place. How they were besieged and their women were taken prisoner, out on that vast plain, in those lands of dust and dry sand and tents and houses that were like tents, and the scattered palms, thin across the dusty expanse. That first land, the scenes of it fixed forever in our minds. These were the scenes I could remember being acted out powerfully on the stage they used to erect for commemorating the Day of Ashura in Karbala, and near us here too, in Nabatiyeh: the slaying of Husayn and his companions and the family members who were killed with him. It was the first place that I truly found; that I encountered in a way that I could not ignore. No doubt that was my father's experience too, in Najaf and those villages in Iraq, and in the shadows of whatever other places we had happened to pass through. Bonded as he was to those olden days that seemed to have been sent forward prophetically to our own time through the live echoes of our people, the ones who lived then, surely my father should have found his footsteps guided by all of that history to Abbaniyeh. With its poverty and the austere appearance it gave to the world, it seemed the nearest of villages to that elemental time that has continued to inhabit our heads. Those earliest times, rooted in our memories, in the memories of those of us who were duty-bound to remain as close as could be to the faith. That was the era, those were the centuries, that made us who we are, in whatever era we might live, as though we have had no recourse but to live in a borrowed time, which is the time in which we do actually exist; or to come consciously as refugees into this time of ours.

My father's sturdy, impervious heart distanced him from that place of origin, but it didn't take him far enough away that he actively wanted to live somewhere else. That's why it didn't matter to him where he was, or where he lived. That's why, before his impending death, he didn't tell anyone that he must be carried to Najaf to be buried there and only there, next to those of his ancestors who had been interred there long before.

He was indifferent to place: to where he happened to be standing, or to where he lived. He was too uninterested to care where he would be buried. On many occasions when I saw him standing on the stone patio outside our home, giving himself some relief from his solitary confinement inside, I would ask myself where his gaze was directed, and if it truly softened his heart to see those little flower bushes my mother had planted at the end of the shallow depression separating the concrete walk from the gate. Indeed, did he ever regret leaving his home and coming to live with me, leaving behind everything he had had there, the doors locked on all of it? Only the books: Go and get the books and bring them here, he had said to me, since between their covers they held everything he remembered, everything he had learned by heart and debated with himself as he sat alone in my house, eyes closed, oblivious to his surroundings.

In the car on the way back to Shqifiyeh, I began imagining him sitting next to me, even now, and saying (but only to himself this time): What we witness when we are young—the words that are said and the stories that are told in those sad commemorations, and the scenes that are acted out in Nabatiyeh and Najaf—are memories that we must try not to preserve unchanged in our heads as we grow older. Those sounds and scenes ought to linger on only for children and for other adults, ordinary people, those whose minds have not been altered by the passage of time.

I was in Abbaniyeh, I told my wife.

By yourself?

By myself.

Abu Atif and his friend—they weren't with you?

I went by myself.

She did not remind me how she had shown her desire to go with me, beyond repeating her question as she mentioned the two men. She didn't move or look at me. I thought she was protesting my keeping to myself something that concerned others too. But she didn't want to be the one to shut down conversation. She was hoping to hear from me what Abbaniyeh was like.

How did it seem to you?

We'll go visit it together.

No doubt she figured I was saying that to spare myself from having to say anything more. From having to get through any exchange of more than a few words, in which it might look like I was the one being interrogated.

She didn't turn her back or vacate her position in the doorway immediately. She waited a few moments so that when she did leave, it would look like she was just slipping out when she needed to, not quitting out of irritation, even though she would have every right to be angry at me.

It's small . . . I said to placate her, as I saw her take a step toward the interior of the house. She stopped and waited, as though to test whether I would say any more. From where I sat, I imagined her form standing outside the doorway, poised to take another step, either forward or back.

Small and poor, I said, but this time in a voice that suggested I was merely talking to myself. She didn't take that step back out of the room. After waiting two or three seconds, I sat up straighter and she went off to her chores.

She is tired out, I thought. Like I am tired out. What she has begun wanting is to leave this house. That's all, without demanding anything or putting down any conditions. Just to leave, since she thinks that she will begin a new life wherever it is we move to. Maybe she has even begun thinking about how to rearrange the furniture, even though she knows nothing yet about the layout of the rooms or how many there will be. Or she is allowing herself to think about the lace tablecloths she will drape over the tables to add a little décor. Perhaps she has kept a few of these things in drawers somewhere, as women do when they are waiting for the house they imagine they will finally have, sometime in the future. What she wants now is to move. She wants to know the opportunity is there: that she

233

can take that step that she thinks will change her, now that her earlier attempts to remake herself by spending time with the schoolteacher have dwindled to nothing.

I'm here, said Abu Atif, his voice coming from the direction of the open door downstairs. I got to my feet before he could call out again, thinking I hadn't heard his voice.

Come on up, Abu Atif.

He wanted us to go to the mosque to begin our stint there. But reaching the top of the stairs, he grinned at me, and I knew he understood that today I wanted to take a holiday from that chore.

I was in Abbaniyeh, I said as we sank into our seats.

By yourself?

He must have also felt I had slighted him, since clearly I hadn't wanted him to accompany me.

By myself, I said, my voice faltering as though I didn't want my words to be audible. You'll help me to find a house there, I added.

You are bent on leaving us, then, Sayyid?

I'm certain now, though no one said anything to me, that Abbaniyeh still doesn't have an imam. They haven't had one since my uncle died. The mosque door was open, but the dust has been piling up for a long time. It completely covers the floor.

You didn't ask anyone about who is in charge of taking care of the mosque?

I didn't ask anyone, I didn't speak to anyone, I just drove around through the streets, and looked at the houses.

Did any of the houses appeal to you? So that we could go and speak to the owners? Abu Atif made no attempt to conceal the characteristic tone of light mockery in his voice, but then he quickly assumed the more serious expression of a keen listener. He didn't want me to clam up, since that would mean he would have to go silent as well.

Abu Atif, I know I won't find a house right now, a house waiting for me. I'm not going to load up my belongings tomorrow morning and cart them straight off to Abbaniyeh. We have to ask around . . .

We'll ask together. You and I. Abu Atif was announcing that he would not take on this mission on his own.

We'll see what happens. We won't start by inspecting houses, anyway. We'll get someone who is from there to do that for us.

We'll see what happens, he echoed. Then he asked me whether I was intending to drop in at the mosque. Just to take a look, he added. To greet whoever is there. As-salaamu alaykum.

We were on our way when he began to wonder out loud whether Abbaniyeh was able to support a man of religion. He made it sound as though he were just asking himself, but he looked at me, clearly anticipating a response. It was up to me to explain to him how I obtained my living. I figured that this was what he was thinking to himself.

Do you really believe that the people here, the people of Shqifiyeh, have been so scrupulous? Do you think they've given the zakat they're supposed to give from their earnings? A whole fifth?

Now it was up to him to ask where the money came from to allow me a decent living—that is, if he wanted to appear as though his curiosity and his concern were genuine. He knew, as did many others here, that I spent far more than I ever got from them.

And anyway, how was my Uncle Aqil able to live in Abbaniyeh? True, he didn't have a family to support but he always wore new clothes and always got them cleaned and pressed. And he spent most of his day going from one village to the next.

I left him in this state of confusion about things he thought he knew, like that I must be spending money from my inheritance and that presumably I was still getting something of the income from the funds my father's longtime acquaintances and supporters had pledged.

When we reached the mosque but before we stepped inside, he manufactured enough noise that those inside would know I had arrived. His action brought this uneasy conversation of ours to an end and returned our relationship to what it had been before the note of discomfort crept into it. The two men inside were alone now and were already on their feet, about to leave. But they made all the motions of a proper welcome—one fitting for a man of religion like me—by standing straight and offering me a greeting before I could say a word of greeting to them.

Suddenly the two boys seemed years older. Now the short pants that boys wore so much of the time were truly no longer suitable for Ahmad. His thighs had filled out so much—and shockingly, I thought—that they looked like those of a grown man. I couldn't help reacting by thinking them a bit shameful, those expanses of flesh that really ought to be covered up. Like other boys his age, his voice had roughened, though in his case this was only discernible in the intermittent growls and groans he let out, as though he couldn't keep them inside any longer, sounds of such girth that he must have brought them all the way up from the bottom of his rib cage.

Ayman had grown too, but unlike his brother he didn't give the impression that he was entering a new stage of his life. Despite these changes, the two of them were always together. They needed each other, after all. Or each one relied on the other's protection, even though both of them (and especially Ahmad, as the older one) were still at an age where other boys harassed them, brutally keeping them at a distance as they always had, by throwing stones at them. I knew this from the way they acted when they separated themselves from the knot of boys leaving the mosque: the two of them would exchange quick sidelong glances with the other boys, but these moments always ended in vigorous headshakes before my sons walked away from the rest of them and came home.

The eagerness they'd shown about going to the mosque seemed to flag. What they had learned there was as much as they would ever get. Twice I observed them in there, sitting among the other boys, their faces grave but their minds seemingly elsewhere. Once in a while Ayman would turn to look at me as though he wanted to know what I thought about the two of them, him and his brother, sitting there, and how they looked to me. Or, their behavior was more about the fact that the man who was teaching them was no longer giving them anything they could use, when he tried, by means of elaborate gestures and mouthing his words very deliberately and exaggeratedly, to explain whatever he could of what he had told the other boys with his voice. At these moments too, Ayman would turn to me, and occasionally Ahmad would as well, because they wanted to check whether I noticed and understood their lack of response to these explanations which they surely did not understand. But I would avert my gaze even before they tried to meet it. Mostly, I kept my eyes glued to the prayer beads in my hands or—if Abu Atif happened to be there at that moment—I fixed my gaze on him.

It relieved me somewhat to know that I would be taking them away from a situation that wasn't useful to them. These men weren't giving them anything of benefit, and in any case they were men of whom I couldn't help feeling suspicious even now. I was convinced that if my sons continued here among these boys, they would end up spent and upset because just being here among them would force the two of them to acknowledge at every moment how they were failing at what they were trying to understand. It won't be of any use to them, this, my wife insisted. They won't learn anything unless they're with special teachers, she added, putting the blame on me—because of my neglect as she saw it—for their remaining the way they were.

Anyway, they would have soon stopped going to the mosque of their own accord, and it wouldn't have been more than a matter of a few days. Maybe, I thought, it would truly make them happy too, to leave Shqifiyeh, which I couldn't imagine had given them any happy childhood memories whatsoever. I was putting off announcing our move to them, but I fancied they would see it as a gift.

After my shocked recognition that they had grown up, I didn't immediately become accustomed to this new state of affairs. I felt surprised every time I saw them, even if only a few hours had passed. When they came to stand in front of me in the room where I received guests, I exerted myself to get them to understand that they were older now and the short pants that revealed half of their thighs were no longer appropriate to their age. Ahmad stared at his legs, receptive to what I had said, indeed acknowledging the truth of it, and he hurried to press his legs together as if he could hide one leg with the other. But I didn't want his abashed reaction to become a source of worry or confusion either, and so I brought my finger up to trace it over his upper lip, trying to alert him to the fact that he was approaching the age where his mustache would start growing. And you too, I said, and signaled, to Ayman, who looked uncomfortable, not knowing whether he should smile.

I should have said something else, or made some other gesture, to reassure them and to relieve them of standing stiffly in front of me. It did seem to me that they had put more distance between me and them. I had been preoccupied with other matters for the past days—or weeks—and probably I didn't seem to care very much about what they were doing. Or perhaps it was because those men who were teaching them had passed on something they had heard about me. Or maybe it was the doing of the other boys, their classmates at the mosque.

I pointed vaguely at Ayman, at his middle but gesturing toward the space between his thighs, moving my hand like I was asking what the state of things was, and had it grown at all? All I got was that brief little smile. I was expecting to make him laugh and to see him put both hands over it as a precaution against my further teasing and to protect himself from my hands. But they just went on standing stiffly in front of me, keeping a distance that they seemed to have calculated between where I sat and where they stood. Maybe those men had gotten the idea across to them that I had let other things get in the way of my duty to the mosque, where of course I was supposed to spend my time. Or they had picked up the idea that I was neglecting the two of them, since I wasn't spending time with them and wasn't trying to find special-needs teachers for them, the accusation that my wife constantly made. I really must not go on basing my relationship with them on teasing, I thought. I would put off for another time any attempt to change the ideas about me that they evidently carried in their heads. What was best now, what I should do, was to tell them the news—to surprise them with it—that we were going to move away from Shqifiyeh.

I had hardly even put on an appropriately serious look before I realized that they already knew what I was about to say. They kept staring at me with no change of expression as I began my series of hand movements. Here we were in this house, I was trying to say, and then, here in Shqifiyeh, describing a large circle with my hand. Do you know about it, then? I asked them, pointing to the two of them. They did know. Perhaps from their mother, though I would not ask her whether she was the one who had told them. Or perhaps from the other boys, though I had no idea how knowledge of it could have reached them, either. Or from the men there. It was as if everyone here already knew everything. Abu Atif's face loomed before me, with its conspiratorial glint that could convey to others the words that had passed between me and him. But I erased this image from my mind because I didn't want to think of him this way. Everyone knew, not just the two boys.

Now that I knew this, I had to get rid of all traces of hesitation; of that slight possibility I had felt of changing my mind about leaving our town.

And you? I asked. What do you think?

They didn't respond to my question. That is, they could find nothing to say.

They had never seen Abbaniyeh and so they couldn't make any comparison between living there and living here. Anyway, I thought, they would not particularly care about the differences since they did not demand much of the place where they lived. They would continue over there just as they had done here, as long as they were not being separated from anyone to whom they felt an attachment. They would not answer if I put that question to them again. They wouldn't know how to answer. I would not ask them again. There was no need for it, and I didn't need to alter any of my plans, as long as the two of them remained with me. I wouldn't change my mind, whether they loved the idea of moving or hated it.

These villages that can be reached only by one road and are otherwise inaccessible to the outside world, these tiny hamlets from which the only exit is along that same narrow road: in a place like that, nothing will happen while I am away. When I drive away from a place like that I might as well be locking the gate to the village with a key that I will use to open it when I return. I will have the reassurance of knowing that the house in that tiny place will remain exactly as it was when I left, and the children will remain exactly the same, too, and so will the mosque, which will not require much effort from me, either in managing it or when presiding over it for those who go there to worship. And no one will wait for me there if I am away. One man, or maybe two, might poke their heads inside the door, one remarking to the other that I am not there, going back to wherever they came from or going in to pray on their own.

Find us a house there, Abu Atif. I had stopped the car and rolled down the window so he could hear me. When he saw me making no attempt to get out he gave me a sarcastic little grin as he stepped back from the car to give me room to get out. He would do it, though; he would search for a house for me. And he would find it, I said to myself as I motioned to him that I would come back and he should wait for me.

It doesn't matter, I thought, whether she—my brother's wife—learns that I'm going to move from Shqifiyeh to Abbani-yeh. It won't make any difference to her whether I am here or there. It won't mean a thing to her if I'm now in a tiny, out-of-the-way, forgotten village, which in itself means I have lowered my standards. That's something she wouldn't think about. The most she would ask would be those conventional questions that show one's concern, like whether the new place suits my wife and my children. And I would simply nod and give a dismissive wave of my hand to say that there weren't any issues and the difference between one village and the next is hardly notice-able. But I would need to make some allusion to doing it for her sake, or rather for our sake, mine and hers, because I believed that living there I would feel myself liberated from the moment my car reached the end of the narrow road out. Every time I left I would feel like the wide world was opening up to me and I was no longer bound to the place I was leaving as if a long rope extending from it was knotted firmly at my back.

Coming out onto the main road I pressed my foot on the gas in response to that sense I had of making an escape that would leave everything far behind. I felt such a surge of joy inside of me that I began to sing, my voice loud and my head swaying to the tune. Bitluumuunii layh . . . mmm-mm-mm . . . Why do you blame me . . . mmm-mm-mm . . . If you could see those eyes . . . How lovely they are . . . I knew I was taking a risk that someone might see me through his car window as he sped by, but I couldn't stop bobbing my head to the song. Sleepless nights . . . How can I help it . . . Why do you blame me . . . mmm-mm-mmm . . .

So that I could go on singing but avoid the risk of being noticed, I removed my turban and set it down on the passenger seat. I went back to the same song. Why do you blame me . . . . If you could see those eyes . . . as though it were the only song that had stayed in my head. Sayyid Mudar, my friend in Najaf, used to tip his head to either side along with the tune, although his singing voice was barely audible. He thought his voice was ugly. I would remind him that we were alone on the road and no one would hear us singing. When I started raising my voice, louder and louder, he would say, Your voice is ugly too! We would both go quiet, having maybe heard footsteps somewhere nearby but not knowing how close by they were. It's a woman, he would say to me in his usual loud whisper. I would answer by saying that women didn't go out on their own at night. Not by day either, he would say, in the usual way we corrected each other. As-salaamu alaykum, the voice that belonged to the footsteps would say from close by and we would return the greeting and wait until the figure had passed so that we could go back to our singing. Louder! I would say. I'm singing all alone. He would tell me that he was accompanying me musically, meaning he was moving his head in the sort of ecstatic response that music was supposed to bring on. Just in making those excursions of ours, we thought we stood out from the ordinary run of people with whom we spent most of every day. Why do you blame me . . . I would still often hum the tune to myself, without moving my lips. I would even entertain myself with it when I was in the mosque, as well as at home, getting ready to pour tea into my glass, or in front of the mirror, draping my abaya over my shoulders to cover my body evenly and setting my turban on my head. But without letting my voice be heard. Without making a sound, ever.

Bilal had grown too. When I appeared in the doorway he quickly changed expression, replacing the laugh he had brought with him from inside with a surprised smile. Welcome, Uncle, he said to me, but he seemed to hesitate a little before opening the door wide enough so that I could go in. I hesitated too, seeing that there were a lot of people inside. Teenaged boys and girls scattered through the rooms in little clusters exploding with chatter and laughter. They were his classmates, he told me. With another glance inside, he added that he had invited them today to celebrate his birthday. I thought about asking how old he was today but I held back. This was a piece of information I ought to know on my own. No doubt he would think so, too.

Come in . . . Come in . . . Welcome, he said again, stepping back from the door to allow me to pass. When he could see that I was still hesitating he told me that his mother was in the house and he would go and let her know that I was here. She did not take long. I heard the sound of her steady footsteps coming closer and then she came into view, her face reddened with exertion and a colorful kerchief around her head that I interpreted as the style mothers are supposed to adopt when hosting a party for their children.

I will come back another time, I said to her as I stared at that crowd of people inside.

But come in now—they are Bilal's classmates.

I know, it's his birthday.

They won't stay much longer. They've been here for hours.

I'll come back . . . I will come back another time. Anyway, you're busy with them.

She'd done everything she needed to do for them, she said. She could leave them alone in the house now. And she made the first move to do so, by reaching up to pull off the cloth tying back her hair. She signaled that I should wait just a minute and she disappeared inside the house. When she returned I was sitting in the car. She had put a white head covering over her hair. The redness that had tinged her cheeks as she immersed herself in the work of the party was muted now by a layer of makeup; I found myself imagining her applying it as quickly as she must have, in her room. Before she opened the car door to slip inside next to me, she glanced back at the door she had just shut.

Naturally, they would prefer to be on their own in there, she said to me after settling into her seat. As she tugged the hem of her dress down over her knees she added that she would not be staying away long anyway. And I, who had not known until this moment whether she intended truly to go off with me in the car, found myself turning on the engine and backing out, having no idea what the next step would be.

When the car reached the road she did not tell me which way to go, and so I had to decide. All she did was to shift her position, deciding to cross her legs and taking a couple of minutes to adjust herself. By doing so she was letting me know that she was leaving it to me to decide on our route, since all I had to occupy myself with was driving and watching the road ahead.

Bilal has changed, I said. He surprised me when he opened the door.

He's changed for me too. And every day he comes up with something new.

Because he's no longer a little boy . . .

He loves parties, he and his pals. They want to stay up late every evening.

Is he giving you trouble?

I'm afraid that soon I'll no longer understand him. Perhaps even just a year or two from now.

This was enough about Bilal, I reflected. If I were to answer her by saying that all children change at this age it would be too late: we wouldn't be able to find our way out of this topic of conversation. But I couldn't find anything else to say, either. It was as though I had suddenly, and once again, become very conscious that there was nothing between us to talk about— nothing, that is, outside of those dry little conversations where the sentences consist of no more than two or three words. We needed a conversation that would lead somewhere else, some- where beyond where we were. An exchange that would take me a step further toward reaching what I wanted. One step more, to get me to another stage, the next . . .

Even our being together like this, exposed to the gaze of any- one going by on the public road, would—she was thinking—move me a step forward. The step forward she wanted: that I would say, in actual words, what I felt toward her. A step forward toward my spelling out, for instance, why I desired her. Describing my emotions, like people do when the bonds of love attach them to each other. I ought to have insisted that she stay there at home with her son and his guests, and I should have left. By myself. I should have said I would come back in an hour, and then gone up to that spot I know, where I could wait for the young people to leave and for Bilal to go with them. And then I would have come down once she was alone in the house. I could have started again—with that meager conversation of ours, or without any words at all— but I could have started with her from where we had left off on my previous visit.

Her hand was resting at her side, close enough to almost touch my seat. Perhaps she let it sit there deliberately, displaying the delicate paleness of her skin, the subtle fullness of the flesh beneath, the bright red color she had painted onto her fingernails. Poised there, her hand looked as if it were offered to me; I would not need to find an excuse to take that hand in mine. But I wouldn't do it. Not because of the passing cars, which no doubt held the sorts of people eager to see who might be sitting next to a man of religion. But because, if I did so, I would not be able to go any further, like letting my hand move over to her leg which was again bare just above the knee.

I had been keeping the car at a steady speed, neither slowing down nor speeding up. The two of us remained silent and we both stared straight ahead at the stretch of road that we would soon leave behind us. For some reason, and I didn't know why, I seemed incapable of deciding on my own when it was time to turn around, even though I knew I was the one who must say something first to break that silence, which was becoming heavier with every meter of road we covered. And I was the one who must do something. Who must reach for her hand as it waited there motionless.

Not quite half an hour had passed when she said that this outing of ours was a fiasco. She said it after sitting up straighter and adjusting her head covering with both hands. A fiasco, she said, leaving me thinking for an instant of the heavy impact of that word and how different it sounded, in its stiff formality, to her usual way of speaking. Even though I thought it likely that she had borrowed this heavy word from the vocabulary of her son and his classmates, her use of it also felt to me like she had been recharged with that strength I used to sense in the days when all I did was to steal furtive glances at her as she moved around her house.

It's best if we go back, she said, after a quick look at her wristwatch.

I responded immediately. There was a turn-off just ahead where I could easily turn the car around. When we were heading back I told her, as though I were offering some kind of an excuse for my earlier silence, that I was moving to another village.

She maintained her stance of deliberate silence for a little while before speaking.

You—and your family, of course? She said this to correct me. To correct the way I had put my announcement.

It's called Abbaniyeh.

Again, she gave herself a little time before pressing her lips together and shaking her head to indicate she didn't know it and hadn't even heard the name.

It's the village where my uncle, Sayyid Aqil, used to live.

Likely that would mean something to her. Her expression changed just enough to suggest that her memory might be getting her somewhere.

I was waiting, thinking that her curiosity would push her to ask when we would move, me and my family. Or even just to ask lightly, perhaps jokingly, whether I was really going to take the place of my uncle, Sayyid Aqil, there?

But then we were silent again. To let me know that silence was the course she had decided on, she began intently studying

246

her brightly polished fingernails, raising her hands to her line of vision and then turning them over to scrutinize her palms as well. This meant she was removing them from the proximity she had granted to me; now, with every movement and every glance at them, she was inviting me to study them at a greater distance. She seemed to want not so much to entice me as to annoy me by flourishing them in front of me like this; I might glance over at them but she would make it clear that she was keeping me at a distance. When she lowered them again—but this time to place them open flat on her thighs—I sensed that she was testing me. She would lift them again, placing them out of my reach, if I so much as moved my hand an inch in their direction. I didn't. We were still far enough away from her house that I was alert to the possibility that something might happen to alter the predicament we were in. But if that were to be so, it could not wait. Or rather, I could not wait; not, that is, if I meant to take any action that could make any sort of difference. Inside myself I began to sense the heat of her hands, the softness of their flesh. I began to feel what it would be like to touch the sheen of that bright red gloss painted onto her nails. She would succeed if I were to give in to my desire to close my hands over hers, or over one of them, the one I could reach if I wanted to, with one quick move. But then she would surely jerk it away, her movement elaborately swift and sudden. Or I could wait, expecting and hoping for something to change, something that would come from her once she realized how much shorter the way ahead of us was by now. Her hands were still resting on her legs, offered to me. Gambling with the little time we had left, she turned her face to the window. I won't do it. I will keep my hands on the wheel and my eyes on the road. This is what I told myself. That's what I must do, biding my time until we arrive there, where the car will come to a stop at the edge of the walkway going up to the front door.

We arrived as they were coming out, clustering in front of the open door, talking and waiting for the rest of the group to make their way out. She opened her door before the car was even completely stopped. She went over to them almost at a run. Bilal was the last to come out and he waved to me before turning to look at his mother and then going to meet her. She didn't say much to him, nothing more than a few words, and then she gave them all a smile. When they started to move away from the house again, she went inside without turning back to look at me, still sitting behind the wheel. Bilal came over to me to say that he was going off with his friends, who were murmuring hellos to me as they walked by the car on either side. I asked him if they wanted me to drive them to wherever it was they were going, and he smiled and swept his arm in their direction to indicate that there were a lot of them. Then he slapped his palm lightly against the car to say goodbye in the way a fully grown man would do. I watched him in the mirror as he joined them at the end of the path. He began talking immediately, oblivious to what he had left behind. I couldn't help feeling embarrassed suddenly at the fact that I was still there, left behind and alone as they took their leave but still facing the door. It confused me that the door had stayed open. I couldn't but feel slightly humiliated at being there when no one had invited me to do anything. Had she left the door open deliberately? Was she still testing me and, when she saw me getting out of the car, would she close that door? Did she really want me to come in? And me—what would it look like if I did that?

I turned the engine on and slowly backed the car out. Slowly too I turned the car toward the road. When I revved up the sound of the engine as though to announce my departure, she appeared in the doorway, one hand on each door panel, looking at me.

Inside, they had left their mess untouched. Dirty plates and the remains of their meal covered the two tables that had been pushed together. Drink stains were splashed across the long white tablecloth, fruit peels were scattered on the floor, and little pools of liquid here and there were half-covered by napkins flung down to keep the liquid from spreading further. She stood there staring at the chaos, not looking at me as I also took in the chaotic scene. I almost thought she had summoned me in here just so that she could show me what the youngsters had left for her. She must have known that this was exactly what would be waiting for her when they had finished their partying. She spread her hands apart in a gesture of hopelessness: what was she supposed to do and where should she begin? More purposefully she beckoned me over to the armchair, which had been moved from its usual place.

Five minutes . . . I'll just pick up the plates and napkins.

I'll help you . . . . Do you want me to help you?

No, no . . . five minutes, that's all, she said pointing again at the armchair, which sat at a distance from the two tables and the mess around them.

I hesitated, not knowing what to do. The armchair had been pulled away from all the other furniture. There was no little table in front of it and nothing on either side. If I sat down there, I thought, I would just seem to be a spectator, watching scenes as they were performed only for the audience of one.

She didn't wait for me to show I'd made a decision by taking a step toward the sofa. She left me standing where I was and headed into the kitchen, her body charged anew with that sudden and powerful energy of hers, a different side of which she was about to show me.

Settled into that spectator-sofa, I would be in the optimum position to watch how she moved and composed herself; how she moved when no one was with her. This alone was tantamount to a kind of surreptitious thievery. When she returned from the kitchen she raised her hand, fingers spread apart, and said, Five minutes. She was carrying a large tray and some folded towels. I got ready to watch the presentation.

My eyes followed her figure as she went over to the two conjoined tables. She set down the tray at one end. She had changed out of her high-heeled sandals and now wore house slippers, which better displayed the soft fullness of her calves. She knew she had my full attention: that my gaze was wholly on her. And she knew it would not disconcert me if she were to surprise me with a sudden look that caught me in the act of spying. It was as though we had come to some agreement that I would get to see what I so wanted to see. But she would act as though she was trying her hardest to conceal from me the parts that would show if she stooped over or bent her knees, before standing up and tugging her skirt downward.

I lowered my eyes, following her as she—still bent nearly to the floor—picked up the napkins scattered there. She stood up and stretched, reaching around to put her hand against her back, sore from bending over, and I followed her with my eyes. She gave me a look, smiling as though she wanted to convey in confidence that she knew a thing or two about how older people get tired out and sore. When she turned and took a couple of steps toward the tray at the end of the table, in the space she vacated my eyes fell on a photograph of my brother that I hadn't seen hanging here on the wall before. The glass in which it was encased seemed lit up from the center, reflecting a bright light coming from somewhere but I couldn't tell where. I had never seen this picture hanging here; in fact, I had never seen it at all among all the photographs I knew. She was between us—she occupied a space between me and my brother in the photograph, as she bent over to pick up more napkins. With that look of his, at once mocking and pleasantly amused, it was as though my brother had been observing us ever since she had come in the house, and then ever since I had followed her in, so that we were in this house alone and together.

That's one of the photographs from the album, she said. Bilal wanted us to enlarge it and hang it here.

It might have been the very last photograph taken of him. There was nothing about his appearance to suggest that it couldn't have been snapped sometime in the final months—even in the final weeks—before his death.

He took it, Bilal took it, to the photography shop, and he came back with it all enlarged and in a frame, she added. She paused. She seemed to be waiting for something.

What I found startling about this photograph was the vitality of it. My brother looked as though at any moment he would change the expression on his face or bring his hand up to shade his brow so that he could better see what was in front of him.

He has become attached to the memory of his father, she said, turning her back as she spoke and busying herself with pulling off the tablecloth. She was keen to show her disavowal of her husband's return, or of his reclamation, so many years after his death. Perhaps she thought that this would mean once again having him in the house. Or that his presence, even if only in that one photograph on the wall, would signal that she had decided to make changes in the very different life she lived now.

I was also feeling very confused. I didn't know how I ought to feel.

This might be the very best picture of him to have hanging on the wall, I said, praising the selection Bilal had made, even if I did think that my brother's sarcastic look and the sense his demeanor gave that he was ready to spring on some unsuspecting victim weren't the most appropriate ways to commemorate the memory of a deceased man. But it was very important that we get over this uncomfortable moment and forget about that photograph hanging there on the wall. If I were to make too much of it I would be like those types who go on and on elaborately and insistently about how sensitive they are. Still, I couldn't quite rid myself of that gaze: that pair of eyes over which the eyelids would never again close.

Do you want me to take it down, for now? I could put it in the other room for as long as you are here. She said this a bit teasingly as she passed close in front of me to take what she was carrying into the kitchen. From there, with the sound of water spurting from the tap, she commented that these days Bilal seemed to be taking pride in his father. Today he had started telling his classmates about when he was three years old and his father used to pick him up and hold him high overhead, all the way up to the ceiling, it seemed! And just on the palm of one very strong hand.

It would be best for us to move somewhere else, not to move the photograph.

Do you mean, into the bedroom? she responded, crossing in front of me, her eyes on me but at the same time seeming to wander.

The bedroom—that seems a reasonable idea, I said, my gaze as indirect as hers.

But there's Bilal—he didn't say what time he would come back.

All that means is that we might be a little slow opening the door.

The possible danger of it, as well as the lingering effects there were sure to be from our unease about my brother's photograph, were convenient for me. This situation would help me to avoid going further than I must; to stop at the edge of what I knew I could manage. I could say, for example, that I had just heard a knock on the door. Or I could simply get up suddenly, as though I had just been startled, leaving her to say that she hadn't heard anything. What suited me best was that our togetherness remain fragile, or insecure—or that I had cause to consider it insecure, so that I could leave at any time, as she lay on the bed, minutes away from reaching the summit of her desire.

Today, no . . . not today, she said, with what I thought was a seductive glance in my direction. She didn't take long to finish this process of walking in front of me, going to the kitchen and returning from it. She picked up one of the chairs scattered around the two tables and brought it close to where I sat. So . . . where were we? she asked, beginning what she thought was the conversation that would transform my presence there into an ordinary visit.

252

Chapter Seven

JUST AS I HAD KNOWN that my disease was there inside of me long before it arrived, my fear alone enough to generate that intuition in me, I was so certain now that the illness would return to me that I had gone back to feeling very scared about anyone bringing up its name in my presence. I didn't see any visible signs of it on my body. Nevertheless, the sensation that it was coming was powerful. This time it would be more resistant to treatment. And anyway, I didn't think I would be capable of going through another hospital experience like the last one. I couldn't even picture myself there again, lying flat on that narrow bed with all of them around me, all of those doctors and nurses talking to each other before giving me the anesthetic that would send me plunging downward, colliding against the hard bottom of that abyss in no more than a minute or two. What I found most debilitating was having to keep my fear inside, not letting anyone learn of it. If I did say anything it would simply reveal my suspicions and anxieties; it wouldn't say anything about my sickness. My listeners would smile sympathetically and remark that yes, I had seemed especially on edge recently. They would smile the way the doctor would smile if I were to say to him that I felt my illness returning, when no signs of it had even appeared. He would smile even more broadly if I were to tell him that in the very beginning I had known, inside of me I had known, that it would come—and then it did come. With his smile beginning to vanish he would say, Stay here, stay at the hospital, any-way. And I would not be able to imagine any course of events other than, beginning with the first examination in the hospi-tal, having to set out on that same road, the one I would have to follow to the very end.

There wasn't a single sign of it anywhere on my body, and I wasn't in any pain. I didn't sense any hemorrhaging. But, I thought, what I cannot see now will show itself soon. That's what I would be saying to the doctor as I finished get-ting dressed. Sometimes I had the feeling that it wasn't just a matter of my sensing its presence. That I was actually speed-ing up its arrival. I knew I could distract myself from thinking about it by doing things that helped me to forget about it. Like accompanying Abu Atif to Abbaniyeh, where we would make the rounds together asking about a house. Or spending more time in the mosque: but there, I would not be able to avoid the sight of those men who used their time in there so well. The place had acquired a new coat of paint and some of the old mats had been replaced with new ones. They had brought in a microphone, which allowed them to address all of Shqifiyeh at once, in a clear and easily heard voice, while they remained seated where they were.

Get up and let's go, Abu Atif, I say to him, standing up and beginning to get myself ready to go outside. He gets up but only after he has given a good look around, as though he wants to see whether any of these people at the mosque have noticed how he obeys me by getting up when I say, Get up. On our way, sitting in my car, I notice how he is silent for longer than usual, looking out the window at the passing scene. When he is ready to break his silence, he starts by reminding me, again, that no one leaves Shqifiyeh in order to go and live in Abbani-yeh. What he's getting at is the difference between being imam of the mosque here and imam of the mosque there. I answer by reminding him that, having just left the Shqifiyeh mosque, he could see—and he even commented on it—what it is like for the two us to sit there among those people who have occupied it. But that won't go on for long, he protests. And then he adds that it's not natural for these types to be sitting in our mosques. Their game, as he calls it, won't last.

They are not real men of religion! he says, his expression a blend of puzzlement and mild hostility. Where did they study the religion? What he means is that they didn't walk out of Najaf wearing abayas and turbans; and furthermore, they don't have the bearing of sayyids or shaykhs. I respond only by telling him that I'm worn out. That I'm no longer young enough to be able to expel them from the mosque on my own and keep them away, and then on top of it to go back and work there, to do as much in the mosque itself as they are doing.

He said at one point that I was a man of religion and not a government employee who could stop working when he reached the age of retirement. The older a man of religion gets, he added, the more important he is and the more status he has. No doubt he was remembering those elderly men whose beards had gone white and grown all the way down to their bellies. It had never once entered my mind that I would get to that point. I never pictured myself seated on a shaykh's square cushion uttering fatwas in the feeble voice of the elderly, a voice I would hardly even be strong enough by then to bring out of my throat.

Take your grandfather Sayyid Murtada. What people remember him most for are the fatwas he gave at the end of his life. As Abu Atif came back at me with this, he repeated those words my grandfather had used when he pronounced that a wife could cancel the effect of a triple and irrevocable statement of divorce uttered by her husband if she exposed herself to the waves of the sea instead of to sex with another man before remarrying her husband. I was very young when I heard this—it was even before I went to Najaf—but even then I thought it amounted to no more than a bit of clever mental footwork which didn't require a lot of learning, or even a little learning, to practice. I took people's readiness to believe such things—and indeed to hold them up as great feats—as simply a sign of how gullible they were and how little they understood. Once I was in Najaf, my classmate Sayyid Mudar and I would ridicule my grandfather's fatwas by spinning out what we thought were their logical conclusions. If that was really correct, we would say, then why had women given up swimming in the sea? We even ridiculed my grandfather himself, saying that he—at the age he was then—certainly must have known what a woman would feel when a strong wave slammed into her, there, where a man's member would normally slam into her.

We're here, Abu Atif, I say as I park my car in the space next to the mosque wall. Let's wait for them inside. They'll be here as soon as the children tell them we are here.

I was always remembering my friend Sayyid Mudar, because I always felt such a need to talk to him about the things I couldn't divulge to anyone else. To laugh with him about matters I couldn't react to when I was with other people in any other way than by toying with my beard and looking like someone deep in thought, as though I had just been asked my opinion on a particular issue and was expected to respond with a decree on how the matter should be handled. I wanted to talk with him about the songs we used to sing together in the evening, always being on our guard that nobody walking along on the road outside could hear us. I longed to sing them again with him, even so many years later, and even if it had to be in very faint voices that we would be careful to keep so low that my wife wouldn't hear us if we were sitting in my reception room at home. To tell him what I felt about her—my brother's wife—and even to take him there so that I could say to him, Here she is, Sayyid Mudar. What do you think?

Abu Atif, who had become the only person I ever talked to, wanted me to be the person I was supposed to be when I came to Shqifiyeh in the first place. I tried many times to hint at some of the things I was thinking. I wanted to test whether he was capable of hearing me out, when what he would hear would not be anything like what he expected. But the only response I got from him was that little glance that seemed to suggest he hadn't heard, or that he got what I was saying but was too embarrassed to let me go on if this really was what he had heard. And now here he was insisting I stay in Shqifiyeh and not abandon it to these people, when he didn't have a clue about who they were or whether they were really from the place they said they were from.

They're late, Abu Atif . . . we've been here half an hour and not a single one of them has shown up.

They don't want us here with them, he said. He was quiet for a moment and then added, The best thing for us to do is to go back to our own home town.

Come on, let's take a walk. How can they know we are here if we don't show ourselves?

Once we were out on the street we saw them, in an alleyway made even narrower by the two facing houses that seemed to crowd in on the lane. There were four men. They weren't walking together, although they all seemed to have the same sense of purpose. We stopped to allow them to reach us, and to go back with them to the mosque. They picked up their pace when they saw us standing still and apparently waiting for them. When the first one reached us he bent his head to kiss my hand. I hastened to pull my hand back as it was correct to do. I did the same with the next two men. We all stood together waiting for the last of the four, who came up panting, leaning heavily on his cane. When he came close and I put out my hand to greet him, he began staring into my face as though he were trying to remember something. He didn't stop staring at me, and he didn't let go of my hand, until one of the others said I was tired and must sit down to rest.

One rotund man, who looked younger than the others, pressed us to come to his home. But we preferred to go back to the mosque in which—as he said—there wasn't even any water to drink. They pressed close around me as we retraced our steps to the mosque, leaving Abu Atif to walk on his own behind us. He began talking to them anyway, asking them whether the houses here were all occupied. To come up with an answer, they began discussing the matter among themselves. Walking in their midst, I turned my head back to communicate to Abu Atif that we were wasting our time: these folks were not going to be any help at all to us.

We're late, said Abu Atif when we arrived back at the spot where I had parked the car.

I echoed him and turned to take a step toward the car, not caring that we were not giving any excuses or apologies before we abandoned the men. They looked bewildered by our rapid turn toward the car and our hasty goodbyes.

These are the folks you'd be living with, said Abu Atif after rolling down his window.

They're the old people, they're not the ones—

The ones who aren't quite as old aren't any different. They're all like that. Maybe it's the water they drink. There wasn't any indication in his voice that Abu Atif was being sarcastic or trying to make a joke, and I turned to look at him as though I needed to know whether he really meant what he was saying about their water.

That's the way they are. I've been here twice asking about a house for you. Both times, the people who went around with me were knocking on doors and asking whoever answered if they knew of an empty house. Just like that, as if this village of theirs is too big for their minds to get around.

It's the water they drink. He said it again and this time he turned toward me to give his words emphasis, as though he wanted to warn me that I would become like them after living here among them for a while.

258

*

My sickness, which I knew intuitively was on its way back to me, still had not quite arrived. Likely it had already decided which part of my body it would alight on this time, but it had not yet struck. I was still at the worrying stage. My fear was causing major sweating spells and often I found my hands suddenly getting so weak that I could barely keep my glass of tea from slipping out of my grip. I would have to be very quick to set it down on the tray in front of me. These are the warning signs, I would say to myself, wiping my lips, moist from the tea, on the back of my hand and standing up, not because I planned to do something but just to stand up; and then to walk a few steps in the confined space, hoping the movement of my feet would help me to forget the furor in my mind.

But to really distract myself from these thoughts I needed to exert myself a little harder. Where are the boys? I would ask my wife. She would respond by saying, for instance, that they hadn't come back to the house since noon. But she didn't stop doing whatever she was doing. There would be no pause as she went about folding the pile of clean laundry she had amassed in front of her. Then I might resort to her again a few minutes later, asking whether they had eaten before they went out. If she told me that they had, I would go back to my seat. I would start thinking about how I hadn't asked her where the girl was. But I wouldn't go back again to ask. If I were to go to her a third time, it would look like I was goading her into asking me whether I was feeling poorly. That's what I wished she would do. That's what I wanted. I wished she would say a word or two to reassure me, even though I knew that her words, whatever they were, would mean nothing. And then, what would I say to her? Would I say it? I'm afraid. But if I did say that, all she would do—and without taking her eyes off whatever piece of clothing she had just picked up—would be to ask another question. What are you afraid of?

And then, I need something real, something she can see or touch. Like saying I am feeling a swelling right here in this part of my body; or that I have seen some blood in my urine. But at this point, still at the stage of fear and anxiety, talking to others is of no use. For instance, it's easy enough for Abu Atif to reassure me that nothing is wrong. He says, Go to the doctor. As if he wants to shut me up. Because what can I say to him after he says to me, Go to the doctor. There's nothing I can say except, All right, yes . . . best thing is for me to go to the doctor.

After all that went through my mind, I came back to find her standing between the beds in the boys' room. Don't you know where they are? I asked.

Who?

The children. The boys, the girl.

Only that quizzical frown that I could detect even in the room's low light. I was on the point of leaving the room when her voice came to me. You're asking about the children a lot.

I want to take them out. Out somewhere in the car.

Where to?

Her question was meant to remind me that they were no longer so young that merely going for a drive was enough of an outing to satisfy them. All I could do in response was to stay where I was, filling and blocking the doorway for a moment or two before walking away, while she let those last two words of hers echo pleasantly through her head again.

I'm going to the mosque, I said, having already opened the front door. But as soon as I was going down the steps I knew I would just sit there among those people feeling uneasy and restless and worried, and I wouldn't even have the energy to return their greetings as I ought. It would be better to take a stroll, exchanging quick short greetings with whomever I happened to encounter on the way. And then I would pick up my pace, so that at least I would look as though I had a destination in mind—the home of someone who needed and wanted my advice.

Those words I said. They were one of those mistakes we make in a moment of haste. I hadn't given it enough thought. I hadn't considered every angle as I ought to have done, before saying what I said in front of them all, there in the mosque. And I hadn't informed Abu Atif. I knew he would think I was neglecting him again. He would see it as a slight. But really, those words just came out of my mouth without any thought to what I was saying, as if they were one of those clichés we say to make people feel good, or the kind of excuse we make when we are ten minutes late for an appointment we've made with somebody.

Those books I have, the ones that belonged to my father, I am going to bring them here.

That's what I said, shifting my gaze to one side of the mosque as if I were proposing that they be put there, against the bare wall where there was nothing else. Without looking directly at any of them—at these men who had now heard me say these words—I could imagine their eyes widening, smiles suddenly on their faces. And then the saliva would dribble out. They would look like people who had won a prize without even entering the drawing. Now they were already thinking about what they must do to ensure that the prize would stay in their hands. They were slow to respond to my declaration. Perhaps they wanted to put some real weight behind the words they would say, which in fact would be nothing more than the usual, God give you his blessings for what you have done, Maulana. And that was what I heard coming from the one who was usually the most silent of them all. He said it lightly, but he accompanied it with that look of confirmation: the gaze that announces an agreement has been concluded.

The idea must have already occurred to me, maybe even more than once, but if it did, I had shrugged it off. There in the mosque it came out of me without any advance warning, with no preparation whatsoever, as if the only reason I said it was to justify my rapid exit a few moments after I had arrived and sat down in my usual corner. After saying what I said, I got to my feet, content with the blessings of God that I had earned. Before taking even one step toward the door, I said, As-salaamu alaykum. With those words—the only response I made to the one man's words of blessing—I was submitting to the pact that had been made and that now I would have to fulfill, after no more than one or perhaps two additional visits to the mosque. Otherwise I would seem—in their presence, and in their view—to have dallied longer than I should in carrying out something I had said I would do.

Outside, as I walked to my house, I was already beginning to ward off the imaginary blows I felt coming down on my head and against my cheeks. I knew that if I tried to excuse myself by making the argument that I had given the books to the mosque, this would not stick for long. Very soon my feelings would return, scolding me for giving the books to these men, of all people, even if I insisted on keeping them as they were now, all together in their cabinet, since I would have to bring that to them as well.

I am going to move the books, my father's books, to the mosque, I said to my wife when she opened the door at the top of the steps for me. I knew that this would not please her but I needed to hear some comment from someone.

She didn't say anything or show any reaction. Nothing more than stopping in her tracks for just a moment, and then that little halfway turn back, but not even enough to put me in her line of vision where I was still standing, just inside the threshold.

Tea . . . I want some tea, I said as I turned toward my usual seat. That was my response to her refusal to answer.

Sitting in my room I began thinking about how there was nothing I could now do other than giving them all of the books. Maybe I could keep back the book in which I had read those passages my father had copied in his own handwriting, to which he had added some little writing of his own. Except for that one, I would give them all of the books, because it would require too much patience and time for me to go through the entire set to put aside any that I might think were important. I had already had a taste of how much this would take out of me. I had felt exhausted, after all, merely at the thought of taking the books from their resting place, one by one, to leaf through them enough to figure out what they contained.

She had not brought me my tea.

I said I wanted tea. Didn't you hear me?

She was still in the kitchen and she gave no sign of hearing me this time either. Annoyed, I got to my feet and went in to her.

Where is my tea? I asked, as though I were just waiting for a word from her—any word—in order to raise my voice.

The can's empty—we don't have any tea left. To show that she was as close to erupting in rage as I was, she yanked the empty tea canister off the shelf and shoved it toward me so that I could see for myself.

Her actions told me this was more than the usual irritation and resentment. Her face was frozen and colorless as she came closer—as though she could force me against my will to take the canister directly from her hand. I showed my unwillingness by balling up my hands and refusing to move. I just stood there blocking the doorway. That was the most I could manage. She looked angrier than I thought I was, and she also looked like she could well carry her anger much further than I was prepared to do. So far that I would not be able to keep up.

Get away! Get away! she began saying, raising her voice and making as if to launch herself through the almost non-existent gap between my body and the door frame. I stepped back, vacating the doorway to let her pass. But she stopped and leaned back against the corridor wall, staring at the tea canister. She lifted her hand, still clutching it. But rather than throwing it down or aiming it at the facing wall, as it seemed she might, she began to cry, a raspy wailing cry.

I had never seen her cry. I had assumed the expression on her face would never change, since she knew only one emotion, the hatred she had for her life. I stood there silently in front of her as she sobbed. The sound grated against my ears. I didn't know what to do. I didn't know how to move quickly enough from my inert state of shock to finding words that would quiet her. I would have found it even more difficult to actually put my hand on her shoulder, or take her hand and lead her into the sitting room and sit her down.

Ahmad is sick, she said as I passed her on my lone walk into the room.

I stopped. I needed a moment to get through all the meanings that the word *sick* could hold.

Sick—how? I asked, going back to her.

Sick . . . we should have taken him to the hospital. She said it as though it was too late for that now.

The schoolteacher whom she had gone back to seeing had worried her, even frightened her. The schoolteacher told her that the pimples breaking out on different parts of his body— eruptions the body used to rid itself of its own filth—were signs of an illness we must get treated. Now, she had said, right now, before it spreads and gets any worse.

I recalled seeing something like this on my own body when I was a boy of his age. First the sores became red and then they suddenly opened. On my son Ahmad's body I saw the same kind of pimples. They had not yet dried up. One broke out on his arm next to another that had gone soft and looked like it was about to disappear, sending the bad odor it had given off back inside his body. There was one sore on the back of his neck and two more at the top of his thigh, one almost level with the lower curve of his stomach. They only hurt when they rubbed against something, he got me to understand, fanning his hand vigorously very close to his skin as if he were trying to cool the heat that these irritated sores brought on.

264

They're pimples, they always show up when a child is entering adolescence.

But I want us to take him to the hospital.

Pimples like this—they're nothing to be scared about.

Yes they are, we have to take him to the hospital.

I didn't want to hear in her words the tone of voice that in itself was an accusation that I was not taking interest in the children as I ought to do. So I told her, as if I were offering room for negotiation, that it would be better to take him to the doctor first.

That's what we should do. The doctor knows more than we do, I said. And the doctor knows more than the school-teacher does.

I am going to take him to the hospital myself, she announced, her resentment and the mulishness it caused beginning to mount again. I bowed my head, showing I was giving in to her, that we would do what she wanted. But her stubbornness didn't flag.

I will take him to the hospital. The schoolteacher—she will come with me.

I was convinced that what was erupting all over his skin was only caused by the chaos of his adolescent body—even though ever since he had been little I had watched him closely, worried that he would contract some illness that would be resistant to treatment. Not even the evident strength of his body could deflect me from my worry. The thickness his muscles had acquired so quickly in recent months, growing harder and bigger, was surely a sign that my son Ahmad was in robust good health. I saw it most in his legs and in his shoulders, which looked too massive now for me to grab as I once had, pressing my fingers down on his muscles. Yet I felt as afraid for him as I ever had. My fear was like a wave rising inside of me that I couldn't repress, welling up whenever I saw him coming toward me, and when he was standing in front of me, and even when he was turning his back to me, about to head off somewhere else.

Likely my fear stemmed from those early days when we first noticed that he was slow to say his first words, and then when he remained mute, neither his eyes nor his hands responding to sounds his mother made right into his face. I don't know where it came from, that feeling I never could shake off, that anyone born with a defect would not have a long life. Perhaps it came from some story I heard as a child, or from an item in the news, or from the suspicion that an imperfection in one's physical features is a warning from God, a sign of an early death. It wasn't Jawdat's fate that had made me think this way. We who knew him never thought he was going to die. If we had, wouldn't the other boys have been more sympathetic to him? Surely they would have brought him into their midst instead of throwing stones to keep him away. And he had created the kind of settled life that didn't foretell an early death. He even bought a second sewing machine to assemble alongside the first one, having established a little business for stitching palm fibers into bath scrubs.

I was the only boy among them who spoke to Jawdat, and I took myself away from their company to be with him. It almost seemed now as if, unconsciously, I had been preparing myself for what would happen to me in the future with my son—indeed, with both of my sons, although I had singled out the first one as the focus of my anxiety and fear.

We will take him to the hospital tomorrow, I said to her, standing outside the closed door to the room where she had shut herself in. She must be worrying, I thought, that she ought to have informed me as soon as the pimples began to appear on his body; and then, when one sore dried up but another was breaking out nearby, she should have informed me. Me, about whom she was always saying she could not understand what it was that could keep me so preoccupied that I seemed oblivious to my sons and my daughter.

*

266

It seemed she knew exactly how to spread her contagious fear to me. When she got him outside, she made him stand on the lintel in front of the steps while she went back inside to get something she'd forgotten. I went over to him and began stroking his cheeks, thinking that maybe he was as frightened as she was. Going down the steps he surrendered to her hold, meekly keeping the arc of his shoulders within her arm. Only when the schoolteacher's voice came to her from below, calling out to her to hurry, did she loosen her grip. When I heard the door below clang shut, I turned to go inside, to watch their progress through the window in my reception room. I realized that my son Ayman had been standing just behind me, leaving a gap between himself and the stair railing. He gave me a wan little smile but he kept looking at me as though he needed to know my reaction to the expression on his face. I smiled back and took hold of his upper arm and we went inside together. But as soon as I pulled the door shut behind me, the full force of my wife's accusations hit me as I saw Ayman turn immediately toward the kitchen and bedrooms, leaving me to go alone into the room where I always sat.

But instead, I followed him. Hiba had just woken up. The minute she swung her feet off the bed she seemed to sense that something around her had changed.

Good morning, my lovely Hiba! I said to her, taking a step or two toward her. When I stood in front of her she lifted her face to me and asked me where her mother was. I took her hand and steered her out of the room to where her brother was standing in the next room, his gaze shifting from side to side. I announced that we were going to eat now, making my usual sign, bringing my hands to my mouth. But Hiba repeated her question. Where was her mother and where was her brother? I told her that her mother had taken him to the doctor to get a shot, and then I walked with her and her brother into the kitchen to see what I could feed them.

As I ushered them in there, Ayman sensed that I was embarking on a task for which I wasn't very well prepared. He hurried ahead of me, took the bread out of the breadbox and opened the fridge to peer at what was inside. He turned to me, inviting me to look with him at the bowls sitting on its shelves. I came forward and bent my head down to have a look. He touched the eggs and nodded as a way of asking me if I meant for us to fry some of them. I wanted to prolong this collaboration, so I began taking out eggs, one at a time, asking him with each one I set down on the counter whether I needed to take out more. He knew I was trying hard to keep him entertained and to reassure him as well. He went along with my artificial little game, putting one egg into my open palms and then another, so that I would eventually be holding such a heap of eggs that we would have to return some of them, one by one, to their shelf.

His inexperienced hands making elaborate movements that weren't required by the task, Ayman began to make our breakfast, pushing me away every time I came closer, wanting to help him. When he had it ready, he put everything on the big tray and picked it up to take it into the next room. I redirected him to the reception room, inviting him and his sister to eat with me. Hiba had stopped asking where her mother was, but she was not saying anything and she was not smiling. She didn't laugh when I said that a bite going into her mouth was like a train going into the tunnel. Maybe that would have only been funny to a child younger than her. She didn't eat much. Ayman was wolfing down the last bites of food, wanting to spring up as soon as we were finished to carry the tray back into the kitchen. So I tried to finish eating quickly too, wanting to allow him to finish up the work he had done to feed us.

He didn't come back to me in my room. He needed a second invitation. When I got up to go and find him I saw that he had begun to get dressed. I asked if he wanted to go out and he shook his head slowly to signal that he wasn't sure, that he hadn't decided what he would do. I didn't ask him to come and sit with me. I knew he would just fidget, and that his sister wouldn't stay long with me either. Soon she would go off to whatever kept her entertained, in there near her bed.

He didn't leave the house, and he didn't do anything on his own that made any sound I could detect. As I sat there in my usual spot, I mused that he probably wouldn't go out because he was so used to being with his brother in everything he did. If he were to put himself to the test—if he went out by himself on this occasion to do things they were accustomed to doing together—he would be taking a risk. He wouldn't know what to do or how to act on his own among the boys he usually sat with in the mosque, or walked with outside the village, he and his brother passing food between them, their portion of the provisions that everyone was meant to have a share in.

I wasn't doing anything either. I put off for another time the task of standing in front of the bookcase long enough to see whether there were any books I needed to keep with me here in the house. I was even too lethargic to get up and go into the kitchen to make myself tea, although I was accustomed to having it at this hour. I didn't exert myself at all, only getting up from my seat once to go over to the window, after which I sat down again. It would be a long day, I thought. I must do something as a way of beginning to get through it. I remembered what my wife had said about the children and outings—that they were no longer so young that a mere ride in the car could entertain them. But Hiba still liked it, I found myself protesting silently. I got up to go and ask them whether they would like to go on a little drive. Standing at the end of the corridor, where I would be visible to both children, I saw that Ayman was standing on his prayer rug. He had dropped his hands to his sides and his lips were forming words, which came out of his throat as a babble, audible though unintelligible. I stayed where I was, expecting to see him first lower himself to the floor, and then after a moment to rise from the position of prayer. Then it dawned on me that I ought to listen more closely to that rumble of chanting that he was making, partly by bringing his lips together hard. Maybe I would be able to make out something akin to a real word. Or at least he might emit the easily distinguished, easily heard, sounds of the two first letters of the Bismallah, In the Name of God: B–S–. . . . To pronounce them you had only to work your lips. After all, surely the utmost he could have learned in the mosque would be a particular, repeatable lip movement, and some kind of semblance of how to begin the prescribed prayers.

Ayman is praying, said Hiba from where she was sitting, in the meager light of the room. She didn't move and she seemed completely wrapped up in what her hands were doing. She didn't look at me as she added—in a tone of voice that suggested she was talking to herself—that Ahmad prayed, too.

Do you pray?

No, she said as she engrossed herself again in her play.

Because you're little?

Yes, because I'm little.

I didn't go out of the house that day, and Abu Atif didn't come to visit me. Ayman stayed inside too, moving between the bedrooms and the kitchen. He was anxious about his brother: to me, his constant pacing back and forth through these small restricted spaces was evidence enough of how impatient he felt, and how he couldn't do anything but wait. Hiba knew how to entertain herself, absorbed in the doll in her hands and the bits of fabric she dressed it in.

She was late getting home, my wife. I was becoming worried, even scared. Every so often I went to find Ayman, to check on whether he was keeping himself contentedly occupied with something. Returning to my room, I was very aware that, just like my son's, my movements were dictated entirely by the anxiety I was feeling. It was already dark outside when

I heard the car. As soon as Ayman noticed me signing him, telling him the car had arrived, he hurried outside—they were still down in the street—to await their appearance at the top of the steps. I saw my wife reaching to take Ahmad's hand as though she felt she needed to help him up the steps. He let her do it but even at the bottom step he wriggled out of her grasp. He came up first so that she could not take his hand again, and he stayed far enough ahead of her that she couldn't press her hand into his back to show her excessive concern. Once they were at the top of the steps she waited for the two boys to move slightly away from us, as though otherwise they would easily hear her say that they had taken a blood sample and swabs from the pimples, and that they had carried out additional examinations, which had really tired him out. Walking inside ahead of me, she added that they had asked her whether she would prefer him to stay there in the hospital until the results were clear.

So, you mean, they didn't say anything about his condition, what it looked like, even before knowing the test results? Didn't they give it any consideration?

They said we have to wait two days. We won't know anything until then.

In the morning Ahmad's body was already showing what we were expecting. My wife came at a run and said in an urgent whisper that I must follow her. He was still asleep, lying on his back, and his legs, extending beyond the end of the bed, had kicked off the covers. Coming near I could see the red spots spreading everywhere. When I lifted the cover to reveal the rest of his body I saw spots everywhere, like so many pinpricks that it was impossible to count them. Without being conscious of what I was doing, I hurriedly woke him up, tugging at his upper arm and then putting my hands against his cheeks and moving his face to the right and to the left. His eyes opened suddenly and wide; he stared me in the face.

I didn't know how to ask him whether he was in pain. His mother, standing behind me as though she was waiting to see how much I could do, couldn't do anything either, beyond putting her hand out to touch the red spots covering his leg. She told me I ought to put my hand on his forehead to see if he had a fever. But he didn't want any of this, lying there subject to our invasive hands and our peering faces. He got out of bed. We stepped back to allow him to walk. That way we could see how he was on his feet.

His movements around the house seemed normal. The first thing he did was to go into the kitchen to get something to drink. He hoisted the pitcher to see if the water still in it was enough to satisfy his thirst, and then he raised it higher and tipped it, so that the water poured directly into his mouth. When he turned and saw us—his mother and me—standing in the doorway, he flashed a smile at us that vanished quickly, as his smiles usually did. He was glancing around to see what he should do next.

Perhaps sometime during the night he had become aware—before we did—of what was breaking out all over his skin. Waking up, getting up, and even though he saw us bent anxiously over him, it didn't occur to him to scrutinize whatever it was he saw us staring at. Lifting the water pitcher high, what he saw stippling his hands did not give him pause. When he went back into the bedroom to check on whether his brother was still asleep, I couldn't help feeling awed at how, despite his condition, he could move around and behave as though nothing had changed in him.

In whatever direction he turned, with every step he took, his mother hovered close behind him. Every so often she gave me a look, as though she were interrogating me about what was the matter with him. Behind his back, she began wagging her index finger at me, apparently trying to get me to understand that now—right now!—we must take him back to the hospital.

*

The fear of illness. My lurking fears, and my expectations. I knew it would strike, but it had stricken him rather than me. When that sick fear had come back to me this time, it had been a premonition of what would happen to him, not to me. As we were on our way to the hospital I was somehow very sure that this was not a question of the two of us being hit at the same moment. I didn't feel that certainty out of any sense that destiny was incapable of doing such a thing. Nor was it a matter of thinking in a certain way about God's mercy. It just didn't fit with what I was able to recall about the way people lived and how and when they fell ill. Once again—and now Ahmad was sitting beside me in the car—I started wondering, though perhaps more aggressively, what it was, in the lives we have and the places we inhabit, that made illness part of us. The day after I learned of my own illness, when I was back at home, I began staring at the wall and muttering to myself that it must have been the damp in the walls of our house that had made me ill. At other moments I would tell myself that the reason I was singled out for this illness was that I had given in to becoming what I didn't want to be; I was sick because I had obeyed my father. Or, I would tell myself that it had happened because of the tension, the heartsick gloom or at least the dullness of my life with the woman I had married. Or maybe it was the food she had cooked, which I and then my son had put into our bodies.

She was sitting in the back seat, directly behind her son as if to keep him as close to her as possible, in reach of her embrace should something happen to him while we were on the road. Every five minutes she leaned forward and stuck her head as close as she could to his, to ask him if he wanted her to do anything for him. Every time I glanced into the rearview mirror at her face, looking as though it had been carved from a single piece of dried leather, I found myself thinking that it was she who had given birth to him deaf and dumb, and now

273

she was making him ill. And then, she was frightening him even more, in his condition, by looming over him every few minutes and forcing him to twist around to her just to figure out that she was asking him if he wanted her to do anything. She scared him, I could see that. Now he was putting his hand out to me, asking me to stop the car. What does he want? she asked. Then she turned to him to ask him—in words—what he wanted. He balled up his fingers, making certain I saw him, to get me to understand I needed to stop and wait. He got out of the car and went into the field at the side of the road. He was looking for a place where he could conceal himself enough from passing cars to do his business.

You should have gotten out with him, she said to me, opening her door as though on the point of getting out herself.

From my seat I could follow where he walked and where he turned to go behind a heap of stones and soil, then stood to let out the rush of urine. He was as strong as he should be at his age but he was sick, too. His body was a haven now for the germs and other organisms that cling to invalids in droves. Now he was shaking off the final drops, zipping up his trousers, and taking a step. His movements were two or three seconds behind my imagining of them. He appeared from behind the little rise where he had taken shelter.

When he reached us I raised my hand as a signal, asking him whether it was all right if I drove on. He nodded and settled into his seat, staring at the road ahead.

He had to get out and do his business because he's scared, I said in a half whisper as though it were for her ears only. She didn't say anything in response but she knew I was accusing her of frightening him. Instead of responding she lifted herself slightly off the seat and shifted position so that her face was close to his; she didn't turn around again until she had stroked his face all over, top to bottom, as though she were giving him some kind of a blessing. He began blinking: these movements of hers unsettled him. He turned to me. Perhaps he wanted to see whether her movements were bothering me as well.

It wasn't just one doctor we faced there. A lot of them crowded around his bed and they all began to talk to each other as they turned repeatedly to a particular part of his body—now here, now there—that they had already studied. I was waiting for an appropriate moment to speak up. I wanted to ask them what it was that he had. But they were still all talking to each other as they began to drift away from his bedside.

Don't let them go away like this, she said to me, thinking they wouldn't understand her speech. One doctor in this crowd had been slower than the others to leave the room. He wanted to know something about my son Ahmad that had nothing to do with his illness. He asked us whether Ahmad had studied anything. He meant, had he spent any time at the schools where children like him went? His mother was quick to inform him that there was nothing like that in our region. There was no such organization, no school where someone like him could learn. He seemed already to know what we were going to say. He didn't even let her finish her words. He seemed satisfied simply by the fact that she appeared eager to talk. He told us that very recently a tiny apparatus had been invented that transmitted voice vibrations from the ear into the brain. With such a tool, children who were born unable to hear and so unable to speak could begin developing their ability to do both. His presentation didn't convince me that this was something I must do if Ahmad came through his illness. Nor did it strike me as something I must do for Ayman. This doctor appeared to be the most junior among his colleagues and I didn't find his advice about something we should do later on, after Ahmad left the hospital, very reassuring. My wife seemed to feel exactly as I did. She was waiting for him to finish his speech and leave. She didn't seem to even want to ask him what he thought of Ahmad's condition.

I'll stay here, she said, announcing how we were to divide up our roles. I didn't respond by saying I knew more than she did about hospitals. I accepted her decision. But I did say that first we had to find out what the doctors had to say.

We waited for more than an hour in that cramped room. Ahmad was quiet and subdued, not resisting lying there, only his eyes moving, but—not wanting to meet the gaze of either of his parents—he shifted them back and forth among the little room's few features: the low ceiling made of cork squares, the metal railing along his bed that they had raised so he wouldn't fall out, the white sheet that he gripped tightly as if he needed to judge exactly how soft it was. We just stood over him, and waited. When it finally seemed that they were about to do something for him, this didn't come from any of the doctors who had been talking at his bedside earlier. They charged a young man with a goatee to inform us that they would soon be taking him into a larger room. He paused clearly to allow us to ask something. But it was obvious to us that we were not going to learn anything from him, after my first question about how long my son would stay in the hospital. We don't know at the moment, he replied. We have to wait and see. To officially end the pause he had allowed for our questions, he called for the nurse, who was waiting just outside. He came in pulling behind him the bed that would transport Ahmad to his room.

I left her there to follow the nurse's rapid walk down the long corridor with Ahmad's bed in tow. Being in that tiny room—and on my feet the whole time—had tired me out and left me feeling restless. As soon as I could see the bright outdoors I felt better and I had a sudden desire for a carefree, aimless outing. A line from a song had even slipped out from somewhere in my head, but I cut it short even before I could figure out which song it came from.

Once I had reached the point where the traffic thinned, I began thinking that it was really unnecessary to rebuke myself just because the strains of a particular song were suddenly fill-ing my head. It wouldn't make his illness any worse, and it wouldn't make my fear for him any less real. What harm was there in letting that song, or whatever fragments of it I had memorized, circle inside my head, one stanza after another? Indeed, what damage would it do if a few lines slithered out through my lips, half sung and half spoken? Why do you blame me . . . Why do you blame me . . . Whyyy do you blame me . . . If you could see those eyes . . . How lovely they are . . . Sleepless nights . . . .

Singing like this, my wrist resting on the edge of the rolled-down window, could have looked like a defiant challenge to anyone who came along. My voice was rising, moving beyond the confines of that tune I had remembered. When I stopped, unable to remember any more of the lyrics, and returned to the beginning, I seemed to be insisting on the measure of my freedom not to rebuke or punish myself.

Why do you blame me . . . . Now I launched into it as though I were shouting the words into someone's face. I repeated that one phrase again and again and again, exhaust-ing myself with the effort and pushing my obstinate repetitions as far as I could. I went on repeating it until it was whirling around in my head of its own accord, leaving my mind free to work without heeding the rhythms of it.

I am not one of those people who demand of God whether He put them on this earth in order to torment them. That's what I said out loud, saying it to my brother's wife now that I had turned my car into the lane leading to her house, as if I were here without exercising any will of my own. This time, once I reached it I was not hesitant in the least. I didn't linger outside waiting for her to appear and invite me to come in. When she peered out of the gap made by the half open door, she found me already in front of her, standing there as though I had come to give her some news. She realized this as soon as she saw me. She didn't give me that playful smile that would say to me, Oh, it's you? I went inside the moment she stepped back from the doorway, murmuring, Come in, welcome. She followed me inside and stood facing me, waiting for me to begin saying whatever it was I had to say.

Ahmad . . .

She kept looking at me, letting me know that she was not going to speak before I finished telling her whatever it was I had come to tell her. When it became evident that what I had to tell her was bigger and more serious than an ordinary every-day malady, she put her arm around my waist and guided me further in, sitting me down on the sofa.

Coffee? she asked, but maintaining her cautious attitude, alert to what I might say about Ahmad.

He's with his mother. In the hospital.

Wait—I'll make coffee, she said, as though whatever I was going to say next about my son ought not to be said as hastily as this.

I'm not staying long. Ayman and Hiba are alone in the house.

We won't be long, she said as she hurried into the kitchen. From in there, she called out, How long has he been in the hospital?

I wanted at all costs to avoid appearing like I was on the brink of breaking down in sobs. I didn't want to give the impression either that my feelings of bitterness and anger weren't serious. But, I told myself, I must not look like I'm about to start crying.

I am not one of those people who ask God whether He put them on this earth in order to torment them, I said, as a way of announcing my protest at what Ahmad was going through, while at the same time disavowing any hint of blasphemy. But needing to give myself leave to explain the anger I felt, I lifted my eyes to the ceiling and said, I am not one of those people who would say wonderingly, But the boy prayed to God, in spite of being afflicted with deafness.

She remained silent. It wouldn't seem appropriate for her to attempt to calm me down or mollify me—the man of religion, me of all people—by responding with a platitude of the kind that remind us to fear God and seek His ever-present mercy. It wouldn't be seemly for anyone to do that, and anyway, it wasn't the kind of thing she would say. It would just make her look like one of those village women.

Instead she began asking me what symptoms he had shown that led us to take him to the hospital. Whether his temperature was high, for instance, or if he had vomited, or was complaining of so much pain that we had to rush him there. She was choosing her words to reassure me; she wanted to imply that whatever he had, the doctors would take care of it. You'll see, tomorrow it will be fine, she began saying. It's just a passing touch of something, it will go away. Tomorrow—you'll see, it will be fine.

I should have stopped her repeating these words of consolation; just as I should have stopped myself from looking as though I needed them as I tried to manage my anxiety. They really should have been stopped, those comforting words and the sympathetic manner that returned her to being our kin. A relative of the family and my brother's wife, back when my brother was still alive. What she wanted was to be who she had been when we were together in the car coming back from that little outing that had been a fiasco. To be sitting next to me, seething and elaborately inaccessible, while I cadged furtive glances at her bare hands with their glossy bright red nail polish.

I'll go now, I said, starting to get up. But before I could leave I needed some kind of gesture that would restore the image of her that I found so alluring. All I needed was a small sign, something that would not be out of place in the circumstances that the news of my son's illness had created, but would bring that other face of hers back into focus.

Stay for a little while more, sit down. It won't make a difference if you are a quarter of an hour later getting home.

To help her give me what I wanted, I said to her, No, I really have to go. I put my hand over hers, just for a second or two, to return us just slightly to what had been between us, while at the same time keeping myself in the state I was in.

It was as though I had made a pact with them but then had reneged. I could see this in the hard looks I caught them giving me, stares they retreated from as soon as they could see that I had noticed. They acted as if they were waiting expectantly, at the very least, for me to fix a time when I would deliver the books. As if they were waiting for me to apologize for my slowness to act by explaining, for example, that I was delaying it until I had rearranged the furnishings in my house; or that I was delaying it until I was not quite so busy. Or they were waiting for me to inform them that my son's illness was taking all my time and energy—my son whose absence they had not even asked about. They hadn't inquired why his brother was not there in the mosque, either.

I knew I had no need of those books. I knew I would not spend any time taking one of them from the shelf to look at it, and then replacing it to pull out another one. But I recognized how it terrified me to remove them from my home. I must have felt that I would be breaking an oath made to my father, or falling short in fulfilling the one request he had made of me. The books, he had said to me, in that moment when he woke up. He knew that it was a rare moment of alertness and he must seize upon it. Or perhaps he had been saving up his dwindling energies just for this: before lapsing back into his semiconscious state, he was determined to bequeath to me what he had inherited. He wanted them to remain with me, in my home, a trust he was passing on to me from his father and his grandfather and his grandfather's father, all the way back to the first in our line who had decided to pick up a feather quill and write those words, those earliest books. In the way that my brother's face would appear to me, sometimes looking merely sarcastic and other times rebuking me, I knew that my father's face would come to me, too. You gave them the books? he would ask me. He wouldn't just ask, he would turn it into an exclamation as he brought his forehead almost close enough to mine that they were touching—that brow that was so shrunken now that I could almost cover it completely with the palm of one hand.

I will not answer him, I thought. I will not say to him: You have died, as I had said to my brother. I will not say to him: You yourself have never opened that bookcase, never once! Ever since I was a little boy—never.

Yet I still felt appalled at the idea of taking these books to them. But I will do it, I thought. I will not read them, I responded to my father. My children won't read them either. Perhaps—I said to my father—the books could be of use to them, there in the mosque. Maybe they'll push the boys who are my sons' ages to begin reading them, or to learn how to begin reading them.

These are not for the mosque—these are ours, he answers me back, and now he is using that tone of voice he had in his prime. That resounding voice that is almost a shout, that voice that tells the man he is confronting that he is about to lift his walking stick and will shortly bring it down hard on his head.

What do you think, Abu Atif, should I give them the books or not?

But you promised them.

I could make them forget.

They won't forget. You will go on seeing those looks on their faces that you say take you by surprise. They're giving you those looks deliberately. They want you to catch them looking at you like that.

But I don't need the books, Abu Atif, and my sons, too, you know . . . .

*

281

My son Ahmad was sitting up in bed, wearing a hospital gown, exactly the kind I had worn not so long ago. The red spots that had erupted across his body had disappeared. I put my hand out to touch his bare leg as if I wanted to see for myself whether any traces of them could still be felt. They're gone, I said to his mother, smiling. She answered that he was very tired of being in bed, but wouldn't leave it.

Why not, Ahmad? I murmured as I moved out of the way the metal frame where the sacs of medication hung. Come on, get up, let's walk. He didn't push my hands away but he gave a little shake of his head to tell me he wasn't going to get up.

He's embarrassed about walking around like this, in a hospital gown, she said, her eyes on the parts of his body that the gown left visible.

Using grimaces and hand gestures I got him to understand that I too had had to walk like this, pulling medications along with me. I went around to the other side of the bed to close the snaps on his gown so that his back was entirely covered.

He won't do it. He isn't getting out of bed.

We'll walk here in the room, I said to him, pointing to the floor and tracing a path with my finger to show what I meant. Only here, inside these four walls. He looked at the door, trying to tell me to close it.

This is one of the things he has learned at the mosque, she said, as she watched him cover up as much as he could of his legs, even if no one but us would see him.

I tried again, telling him that I myself had walked around in a hospital gown like this. He smiled. He must have been imagining me walking through the corridors in such a ridiculous piece of clothing, walking among the female nurses and passing rooms whose doors were all wide open.

He didn't walk. He didn't go anywhere except to the bathroom. Even going there, he twisted around several times to see if this garment was revealing anything that it shouldn't. He went in and closed the bathroom door.

The spots will come back. They removed them with medication. They could return.

As she spoke, she sounded reconciled, even contented. She said it as if she were giving me good news; telling me that this illness was less dangerous than we had thought.

You mean, he doesn't really have that illness?

Not unless the doctors were lying to me.

And the pimples, those swellings all over his body?

I don't know, they might come back.

What did they say about them?

They said they will know something from the samples they took but the results aren't back yet.

When the bathroom door opened and Ahmad appeared, his face looked very white—the color had drained out. He was stooping and his hands were gripping the medication frame hard. He's about to faint—quick, get hold of him, she said, rushing toward him and opening her arms to clamp them around his middle, pinning his arms. I told her to move away, once I had my arms around his body, leaving his arms free. I told her to call for the doctor while I got him back to the bed. He was too heavy for me to lift. He had put himself in my hands, but his eyes were wide open and he was looking around. The nurse came at a run and took Ahmad's weight from me. It's just a dizzy spell, he said to us reassuringly, before adding that we should not have left him alone in the toilet, because if he had fallen while in there, he could have hurt himself.

So he is still sick? I asked, watching the nurse pull the sheet up to cover Ahmad entirely.

He should not have been left alone in the toilet. We are here. If you press this button we will come.

We know—we know that, my wife snapped at him.

I intended to ask the nurse how long Ahmad would have to stay in the hospital, but her angry voice drove him out of the room. So I went over to Ahmad instead, to see if he still looked dizzy. He spun his hand to say that his head was still spinning around. And then he slid his hand from his chest up to his throat. He was telling me that he was about to throw up.

But nothing came out. Just those sounds that exhausted him, bringing tears into his eyes and causing him to break out in sweat. I was standing behind his mother, who had put the sickness bag to his mouth. I began saying, every time he gathered his forces trying to expel what was in his stomach, Yes—get it out, come on, bring it up, out of there. I didn't realize I was raising my voice. I didn't realize I was trying to drown out the sound coming from his empty hollow throat.

As we were removing the books from the cabinet, I said to Abu Atif, I am going to stop wearing this jubba and this turban. He laughed; or rather, being Abu Atif, he showed that he was barely suppressing a laugh. What kind of work are you going to do, then? he asked. A schoolteacher?

I shouldn't have accepted what he decreed for me.

Who?

My father.

Abu Atif wasn't pulling the books out in stacks. In fact, he seemed to be looking at them, reading the words on the binding, and then opening the book to see what the script looked like, or how yellowed the pages were or whether they were worn by use.

If we go on like this we'll still be working on it two days from now, I said, and added as a joke that we must hurry because they were all waiting for us.

Look at how they stitched this book. It's like they pounded it with nails.

To push him to go faster, I took the book from him and slid it onto the top of the stack.

But we have to see what's in them! Back in those days they used to hide money between the pages of books. Imagine, if we found some old money—those really old bills that were nearly as big as a prayer rug, he said, moving his hands apart to show me how large those ancient bills really were.

He was entertaining himself. In fact, he was making a game out of it, and he was enjoying every moment. I no longer felt annoyed at his liking for jokes. It didn't embarrass me, for instance, when he asked me whether I would go to work as a schoolteacher.

Let's work faster, Abu Atif. Or—maybe it's better—let's just leave everything where it is. I'll take care of it tomorrow.

But they're all waiting at the mosque. They're expecting the books to arrive so they can start reading them right now, he said, his voice heavy with mockery.

Ahmad would not die, but he would not be cured. In the car, he seemed happy to be leaving the hospital. He turned to me now and then to give me a smile, and then fell back into whatever it was that had been absorbing him. He twisted his head around to where his mother sat in the back seat as if to make certain she was still there. The doctor had told her that the attack he had had would happen again, and every time it did, we must bring him as quickly as we could to the hospital. When she asked whether his illness would be painful, he didn't give her a direct answer. All he did was to tip his head to the right and then to the left, indicating that anything was possible. The illness is in his liver, she told me. And when it seemed to her that this illness had gotten us to listen to each other, she said we must learn how to behave with him and what to do for him, not just for his illness, but for everything—the way he was in the house, and his relationship with his brother and his sister.

It seemed as though this new situation had allowed her to reorganize her entire life. Her idiocy riled me when I saw her face in the rearview mirror, flushed with that haze of confidence. She was sitting up straight, her neck and face stretched forward, leaving a space between her back and the seat, as if she was trying to race with the car, to make it move faster, to hurry our arrival so that we could begin our new life, marked out by her new program for it.

Did they tell you we have to be quick about getting him back to the hospital?

They said not to delay like we did this time.

Did they tell you what would happen if we did take our time?

I didn't say this in order to correct her on anything she had said, nor to shake her sense of reassurance and optimism. But I did want to show that I thought her outlook was ridiculously simplistic, and perhaps to reverse her mood, which I found exasperating. I wanted to make her feel the bitterness she ought to be feeling.

Leave him alone, he knows how to get out of the car by himself.

Her arms were extended toward him. He had turned halfway in his seat and he didn't know what more to do. I had stopped the car very close to the door so that anyone who might be in the square would not see him getting out, and also to keep him from having to walk any distance. She dropped her arms to her sides but she maintained her watchful position, ready to grab for him if he fell or seemed dizzy.

Go on in, I said to her, with a little push so that I could stand where she was standing, able to shut the car door once he had gotten out.

When they were both inside the iron door I climbed back in to repark the car where I usually put it. I felt energetic, as if my body could do anything, despite the long way we had come, and I wanted things to move quickly. In a moment I was with them at the bottom step. Ayman had come down and his sister had followed him. She was uttering some words, as though talking to herself. There was nothing I could do or say except go ahead of them and take Hiba's hand. I asked her playfully if she'd cooked a meal for herself and her brother.

They weren't far behind, in any case. I let them enter the house before me since there was nothing particular I could do that would satisfy this sudden burst of energy. She would handle everything once we were inside anyway, I knew. I would go into my sitting room and I would try to subdue these energetic feelings, which nothing I did could use up.

It was likely that I would soon hear her voice, calling out or complaining, no longer showing the submissiveness she had given in to on the way from the hospital. Hearing her call out or wail, I would know more or less what they were doing in there. Maybe she was trying to change Ahmad into his nightclothes? Was she trying to get him into bed for the night, or would he insist on sitting up because he wasn't ready to sleep? From in here I would likely know which it was, from the words or the sounds I would hear. From time to time, I would get up and actually go in there to check whether I had heard what I thought I had heard, to see if I had been right. To check on him by seeing him with my own eyes. Then I would return to where I always sat, my head full of the thought that after a day or two of observing Ahmad, I would be able to know what his life was going to be like and what it would be like for us, living with him.

A second time, I told Abu Atif that I meant to take off my jubba and turban. This time he seemed to be listening more carefully. He didn't smile in that way that told me he thought I was saying this without even believing, myself, that it might actually happen. Maybe he thought Ahmad's illness had made it harder for me to say things without thinking about what they meant, to say something just because the idea of it had come into my head. And he saw too that he must check his tendency to tease me, and joke with me, and receive what I said with a look of mischievous doubt. At this age? he asked. He waited a few seconds before raising his eyes to look squarely at me. But how will you live? he asked. I didn't answer as he expected, perhaps because I did not want to elaborate on everything I was thinking about. All I said was that I would arrange my affairs and live as other people did.

Are we going to get on with taking the books to those men?

He got up. He waited for me to get up so that we could both walk the few steps over to the books. We had removed some of them from the cabinet, leaving them in piles stacked up on the floor. He stood behind me so that I could take out the rest of the books that sat on the shelves and hand them to him to be set down wherever there was space on the floor among the piles that were already there. He said he didn't understand how a man of religion could stop being a man of religion. What will people who know you say? And then—aren't you afraid?

What should I be afraid of?

Of having known religion and then leaving it?

Somehow I didn't want to make it easier for him by telling him that I was abandoning the jubba and the turban but I wasn't abandoning religion.

Do you think my sins will be doubled, Abu Atif? And that God will make me pay more than He does others?

Say: Are those who know equal to those who do not? he quoted, with a little smile that hinted he knew he was trespassing on my territory by reciting the Holy Word.

I smiled back, and handed him another pile of books. He tried to stack them atop the pile in his hands that already nearly reached his chin.

Well, anyway, I will try it. I'll see what life is like when I'm not wearing these things. I'll try it, Abu Atif.

He laughed, straightening up from the pile of books he had set down. He made a tentative, quizzical little gesture as his way of asking whether I really thought I would ever go back to being a man of religion once I had stepped away.

We'll tell them to come and get the books, I said. They were all out now, in stacks across the floor.

You mean, you are going to give them away, just like that, and they won't pay anything for them—since you aren't planning, it seems, to start going to the mosque again.

Perhaps . . . but should we give them the bookcase as well?

Or get rid of it. If you leave it here the worms in that wood will creep into every piece of furniture in the house.

It was only a couple of days before Ahmad was out of bed. He wanted to get up the morning after his return from the hospital but his mother kept him there, making certain that his brother and sister were nearby most of the time to entertain him. On the second morning he woke up before any of the rest of us were awake. He woke us up moving around the house, and he couldn't stand being the only one awake. When he made it very clear to us that he wanted to wash, my wife, clean clothes in her arms, asked me pointedly whether it would be better if I went into the bathroom with him. But she abandoned that idea as soon as she saw my reaction.

He came out of the bathroom with his hair already combed and his dirty clothes in his hands to give them to his mother. He had combed his own hair, she told me. She was trying to convey something that she didn't know how to explain in any other way. I couldn't tell whether she thought this was a good sign and was happy about it, or whether she was sympathizing with him and feeling a bit morose. His brother was standing nearby, waiting for him to finish, ready to be with him. Their mother said they must eat: Ahmad has to eat, he cannot take the medication without eating, she said. But she hadn't prepared anything. Trying not to show my annoyance, I remarked that it would have been a good idea for her to get some food ready for them while Ahmad was still in the bathroom. I walked into the kitchen and opened the fridge. Looking inside, I couldn't decide what to take out. She wasn't far behind and she shoved me away from the open refrigerator door. She began peering at each shelf in turn, exactly as I had been doing.

They were with me in the reception room, all three of them, when she was suddenly there with three rounds of bread wrapped around filling. I had no idea what she had stuffed into them. All this, they'll eat all this? I asked her. She didn't answer. They came forward, a bit intimidated by the bursting loaves that their stomachs would not be able to hold. This is a lot for Ahmad . . . he won't be able to handle it, I said. Her response was that the medicine would burn his stomach if it reached the lining.

When I realized that the two boys intended going to the mosque, I teased Ahmad by pointing to his combed hair, asking what this had to do with the mosque. He didn't laugh but he did go along with my question by raising his eyes, making a show of wanting to see his own hair. When it occurred to me all of a sudden to ask them to inform the men there that the books were ready and could be taken, and that they must send someone to move them, I realized with a start that I was directing my words at Ayman, even though he was the younger brother. That bothered me. It got me to look at them, the two of them together, and to communicate with both of them, telling them to go ahead of me, that I would come along soon afterward and would tell the men all of this myself.

The doctor said he has to take the medicine every day, she said, the bottle of medication still in her hand.

He didn't tell you how long he should keep taking it?

I don't know, he didn't say anything about that.

I took the bottle from her and began reading the label. I was still turning it around in my hands when she handed me the other medication, a container of tiny pills. I glanced at the pills and shoved them back over to her.

These too—you don't know how long?

You should have asked. You know hospitals better than I do.

Have you forgotten about Abbaniyeh?

I had fetched Abu Atif from his home. I wanted him with me at the mosque.

I've stopped thinking about Abbaniyeh. I got tired of it before even going to live there.

So you'll stay here with us?

I don't know.

I sensed that he was turning to me with something to say. But whatever it was, he kept it back.

Don't you think I have a right to do what I want or don't want to do? I asked him.

You have children, don't you think about how they are going to live?

Do you think I would abandon them? Do you really think I would try to run away?

I was vexed with the mosque the minute I stepped through its door. The boys sat, legs crossed, crowded around one corner of the interior, listening to an older boy who sat in their midst. The three men who seemed always to be there looked piously attentive to all that was going on around them but there was nothing in their hands to truly occupy them. When they saw me, standing just inside the doorway with Abu Atif, they hurriedly got to their feet and scurried over toward us. The precious ones were here, said the man who greeted me first and shook my hand. He was referring to my sons. But they left, he added, because Ahmad got tired. They performed their prayers, he said.

I didn't want to stay, not among them. I left it to Abu Atif to tell them about the books. All three men beamed when they heard the news. It wasn't just because they wanted the books. I knew that. By giving those books to them, I was putting the final seal on my submission to them. I was handing over the mosque.

Now? Do you want us to move them right now?

I nodded. That was all. I turned to Abu Atif. He would let them know that we were waiting for them at my house.

They did not take long. Coming through the iron door they announced their arrival noisily by calling out for permission to come in. As soon as they were at the upper doorway they put their hands silently to their chests and kept their eyes so low that they couldn't even see their way into the reception room. Itfaddalu, come in, Abu Atif began repeating, and as soon as they were well inside he pointed the books out to them.

Should we take them all?

Take them all.

One of them picked up a stack and handed it to his companion, and then lifted another to give to the other man with them. He followed the two of them out, clasping a stack. He asked me whether he should close the door. He made me a sign that they would come back as soon as they had taken the books over there.

They can take the cabinet as well, I said to Abu Atif, walking off toward the bedrooms to see how Ahmad was.

Chapter Eight

WAS I PREPARING MYSELF TO begin a new life? Or simply trying to conclude the life I had been living? The next step—likely a final step—was the moment when I must take off my turban and my jubba. The moment when I would have to step outside the door to my home wearing the clothes that ordinary people wear. Letting go of the books didn't leave any worrisome impact on me. I felt no regret, no feelings of loss. All that remained was my vague memory of those men of old whose names had circulated in my family's home, men to whose memory perhaps—I didn't know—I should add my father's name. Our forefather Sayyid Ismail, our forefather Sayyid Abd al-Husayn, the scholar whose grave-shrine people went on visiting until it was in ruins and the dome collapsed onto his tomb. And our forefather Sayyid Ali who had astonished the assembled shaykhs of Istanbul when they summoned him to make his case before them. These men's names had been a repeated refrain in our home for as long as I could remember. Although I heard about them day after day and year upon year, they had always remained faceless. In their days no cameras existed, not like the one my grandfather stood in front of one day, posing his two sons at his sides. All those men had were words. Words that were handed down from them, words in my head that I had tried to turn into their facial features. Words I made into faces. Or sometimes I imagined them as shadows without faces, beings who had never even possessed faces. Words I would intone over and over, and lines they wrote out with their feather quills onto ancient, already yellowed pages that would then be sewn by someone else to other pages, to become books. Letting go of those books didn't leave any niggling aftereffects. I felt no regrets and no sense of loss. I didn't belittle myself or berate myself for letting them go. I didn't ask myself or anyone else, Who am I to lose my grip on what those men wrote down and committed to heart, generation after generation? Maybe I didn't know the value of what I was bequeathed. Maybe I really had come to have no sense that there existed a powerful relationship between myself and them. Or maybe I was simply getting ready to begin a new life; or I was on the brink of feeling that the life I had lived was sufficient and I was ready to bring it to an end. To take off my jubba and my turban, just like that, a simple action, without any knowledge about, or thought to, how I would be once I had done it, or what I would do next. But what I had come to realize in these moments was that I must not hesitate or put it off. If I did, I would simply remain mired in the no-place where I was; I would remain exactly as I had always been, inhabiting this room of mine, doing nothing except waiting for the sun's rays to creep forward on the tiles beneath me until I inched my feet away as I sat there, inert. I knew I must not hesitate about any of the things I needed to accomplish to make certain that my abandonment of who I was now became final and complete, so that I could truly tell myself that I would not return to that self ever again.

I will not go to her home, I would tell myself; and then I would find that in spite of myself I was in the car, moving along but slowing down, held back, and then suddenly accelerating to a speed that was urgent, the car responding to the bouts of hesitation in my head, which moved me forward and pushed me back. Sometimes I stopped, having gone not even a quarter of the distance to her house. Other times, I gave my indecision more time, swerving onto the side of the road and stopping the car, weighing up my yearning to go the rest of the way to her home against my determination to return to my house, and struggling endlessly with it. I would give myself reasons why going on should prevail against going back, and then I would come back at myself with arguments for returning over going forward, as if I were tossing pieces of wood on the fire, some kindling to stoke the first proposition, and then some to revive the second one. I even colluded with myself against myself. Among the arguments I came up with were ones that, if I accepted them, would make it impossible for me *not* to stay away from her. I told myself—in language that sounded as though I were arguing a case for the prosecution—I would not put my mouth there in the place where my brother's mouth once was. Indeed, I added language that made it seem like he was still alive. I would say *his lips* instead of *his mouth*, or I would even substitute *his spittle*. I did it to force myself to imagine his wet lips there, and thus my lips too, there where his had once been, on that pale body.

As I summon that body, alive and real in my imagination, I hurriedly avert my gaze, and I suppress that image, because otherwise I might cling to it and never let go. Perhaps I am just clinging to it, pulled magnetically by the images that come into my mind, in a state of raw desire and anticipation. I watch myself: I am moving my face and eyes closer as though she is now here in front of me, in my grasp, close to my lips. I watch myself: I am about to lick what I have licked before, that expanse of skin at the bottom of her neck, her upper chest, all of it bare, there for me to see, so that I have to quickly toss a bigger length of kindling, which will be quick to light, onto the hungry blaze of my efforts to step away.

To move back even further, to abandon it all, I start to erase her as if I can simply wipe my hand across my brain and she will be gone. In her place I set my brother, crouching in that photograph Bilal brought out from the darkness of the cabinet that housed it. I see my brother, his eyes now turned to me, staring at me from behind the plate of glass that imprisons him as it presses hard against him. I can only see his eyes, not his face. That look whose meaning is never clear, sometimes angry and other times jesting, an expression that shifts rapidly from anger to playfulness or from playfulness to anger, that gaze I do not understand and that does not fit easily into my memory of who he is, or who he was. Sometimes I tell myself he is just trying to confuse me and keep me in a state of unease. But I will never know whether he truly did not care what I was doing with his wife here in his house. I will never know whether he was cursing me for it. But you died, I say to him, glancing at the mirrors before I begin to turn the car around. You are dead, I tell him.

I am going to stop wearing my cloak and my turban, Abu Atif, and I won't go on holding prayer beads in my hand, I said to him, putting my hand into my pocket to take out my string of prayer beads.

Take it. It's yours.

He hesitated to take the beads. Maybe he was worried about this being the beginning of my abandonment, the beginning of my act of removing the clothes I had always worn. From behind the prayer beads dangling in front of him, he said, These are your father's prayer beads, God's mercy be upon him.

It doesn't matter. They're prayer beads like any other string of prayer beads. And anyway, I have his entire house to preserve my memory of him.

His house, closed and locked upon his furniture and belongings, and upon the smell of him too, that odor that didn't come with him when I brought him to my house. His fragrance remained there, and I knew I would smell it as soon as I crossed the concrete path at the front of the house. That smell still clung to the place and filled it, and it always would, despite the age of the place and the dust that had seeped in through the cracks and openings.

Take it, Abu Atif, and put your trust in God, I said, giving it a shake in front of him to end his hesitation.

He took it. He raised it, swinging it back and forth in front of his eyes, and brought it to his nose to breathe in the odor he thought was still there—the legacy of my father, not of me.

The furthest point I would reach on the route to her home was that open space above the house that was lined with trees, the place where I stopped my car once and waited for her to return home. I couldn't go any further than that rise. And all I was capable of doing while I sat there in the car was to keep myself from descending to where she was, from going to her, though I knew that if I started that descent I would turn around and retrace every bit of distance that my car had gone. I would stay there, staring at her front door and hoping it would open. Hoping she would come out to see whether anyone had arrived. That was what I was watching for, as I ranged my eyes across the house and onto the lane that led to it. I would think about those strong-looking legs and high-heeled feet, so captivating as they moved across the room; and her hands, the fingernails painted bright red; and her practiced fingers, her chest, the longing in her bosom, which surely could not be satisfied by me alone. That powerful body, the muscles and nerves of it a plenitude beyond what a mother exerts to raise her son, to invite his classmates to come and laugh together and eat cake on his birthday. From where I had stopped, several times I almost started on the way down, putting myself in the place of the other man whose arrival I was watching for, observing myself coming along that road, walking. Because I had the sensation of being very near to her, I even saw myself turning on the engine to begin my descent. But it only lasted a few seconds before I turned it off.

I talked with Abu Atif because I didn't know anyone else. It pleased him that I accepted his teasing and also his advice.

He didn't mind if I didn't act according to what he said; it was enough if I gave him an amiable, flattering smile or nodded my head as though I were telling him that I had heard and understood.

He thought I was doing no more than making an empty threat to abandon my turban. According to his way of thinking, that was something no one would ever actually go as far as doing. Tomorrow, things will change, he would say to me. He believed I was threatening to do it out of a need to reject what God had brought upon me and my children. I adapted my words to suit what he believed. I answered him by asking, How will things change, Abu Atif? I left it to him to understand that I was talking about my son Ahmad's illness, and his deafness, and his brother Ayman's deafness. I reminded him of it, two or three days later, there in front of my house, as we—my wife and I—brought Ahmad out to the car when his body was covered again in swellings and sores. I just inclined my head slightly to show him what we were dealing with, as I went around to the other side of the car to open the door of the front passenger seat. He—Abu Atif—thought I was saying again to him, How will things change? That was what he was thinking, as I raised my hand to say goodbye before the car moved away.

This time—the second time—Ahmad stayed only two days in the hospital. He didn't need to be there even that long. Now the doctors knew what they had to do, without carrying out any examinations or tests. So, we'll have to come to the hospital every two weeks, she said after counting the days between his first stay and this one. I didn't know whether she felt as comfortable, happy even, as she had seemed before.

We were still at the hospital when she told me the doctor had said that beginning with the next visit, we would not be paying any of the costs of his treatment. The Ministry will cover it, she said, suppressing a smile.